# KILL ME AGAIN

## PAUL BISHOP

AVON BOOKS ◆ NEW YORK

KILL ME AGAIN is an original publication of Avon Books. This work has never before appeared in book form. This work is a novel. Any similarity to actual persons or events is purely coincidental.

AVON BOOKS
A division of
The Hearst Corporation
1350 Avenue of the Americas
New York, New York 10019

Copyright © 1994 by Paul Bishop
Published by arrangement with the author
Library of Congress Catalog Card Number: 93-90657
ISBN: 0-380-76890-9

First Avon Books Printing: May 1994

AVON TRADEMARK REG. U.S. PAT. OFF. AND IN OTHER COUNTRIES, MARCA REGISTRADA, HECHO EN U.S.A.

Printed in the U.S.A.

RA 10 9 8 7 6 5 4 3 2 1

Sunlight streamed through a large open window highlighting the pale white body of the victim as it angled across the four-poster bed. The head and right arm were off the mattress, pointing floorward. The acute angle of the head exposed the ragged wound across the side of the victim's neck. The hand at the end of the long, graceful right arm touched the floor in a pool of congealing blood.

The impact of the white-on-white-on-white was heightened by the dramatic slash of dark red that had flown in an arc, like an angry brush stroke, from one side of the bed across the white wall and the off-white window sheers to speckle out across the flat-white ceiling.

A trail left behind by the soul as it fled the body.

# KILL ME AGAIN

This one is for Kevin and Mari Staker.
Friends, inspirations,
and
patrons of the arts.

# ACKNOWLEDGMENTS

Many thanks are due to Deputy District Attorneys Scott Gordon and Mary Hanlon for invaluable legal pointers, legal research, heated mock court sessions, and unflagging enthusiasm for this project. Eating at the King George has been enriched by our lunchtime sessions.

During my career as a police detective, I have had a number of female detective partners. There are three in particular who, over the years, have provided inspiration for this story: Sandra Hendricks, Karol Chouinard, and Jae Thomas. This book is also very much for them.

**1**

**F**ey Croaker looked up from the arrest report that had been occupying her attention and saw Lieutenant Michael Cahill crossing the squad room toward her. As she watched his approach, she felt a familiar chill of anticipation wash over her. Goose bumps thrilled up her neck. Her Irish mother always told her that the feeling came from someone walking over your grave. If that was true, Fey hoped they were walking softly.

"The first stiff of the new year?" she asked when Cahill was close enough.

The detective lieutenant shook his head in genuine amazement. "Damn it, Fey. How do you do that? How do you always know when I'm coming to tell you we've got a cold one? It's spooky."

"It's instinct."

"I don't care if it's ESP. It's still spooky."

Fey took off her reading glasses and let them drop by their cord onto her chest. "Where's the body?"

"2008 Mirrorwood." Cahill held out the pink phone memo with the scribbled information.

Fey took the note and glanced at it quickly. Without her glasses on, she had to hold it at arm's length. "Isn't that the new town home complex? . . . What's it called? Oak Vista Estates? The one only dope dealers and Ferrari salesmen can afford. Up off of San Vincente and Barrington."

"Yeah. And it's a sure bet the homeowners' association isn't going to be real pleased about the situation. The people who live in the complex are paying through the nose for private security and all the other amenities."

Fey looked at Cahill. "Come off it, Mike. Those people

put more money up their nose in a day than they pay in homeowners' fees. That kind of stuff is just pin money to them."

"Anyone ever tell you you're a cynic?"

"Yeah. It's why I'm good at my job." Fey stood up from behind her desk. She checked her watch. Eight-thirty A.M. A hell of a way to start the day. "Who found the body?" she asked.

"The maid. She thinks it's the owner . . ." Cahill grappled with his memory and then pointed to the memo he'd given Fey. "I wrote the name down."

Fey gave the pink slip of paper another long-distance glance. "Miranda Goodwinter?" she read with a question in her voice.

"Sounds right," Cahill said. "Anyway, the body is female, white, fortysomething. Naked. The maid didn't take too close a look. Too much blood."

"So no positive ID?"

"Nothing beyond the maid's guess, which is probably going to turn out to be good."

"I don't recognize the name. Any political or big-time money overtones yet?"

Cahill snorted. "Hey, you know how it works. This is West L.A. Unless the stiff is a homeless, there's always political or big-time money overtones. Do you think the Oak Vista Estates homeowners' board are going to stand by quietly while we go about our business? Hell, no. They're going to be screaming bloody murder to both the chief's and the mayor's office. If we don't solve this one in a hurry, our butts are going to be in the middle of the skillet."

The West Los Angeles Division was the jewel in the crown of the Los Angeles Police Department—the gem of all eighteen geographic divisions. Many of L.A.'s richest areas, including Brentwood, Bel-Air, Cheviot Hills, and Pacific Palisades, fell within its jurisdiction.

Beverly Hills had their own Japanese-technology-worshiping police department bordering the West L.A. division to the east. The city of Santa Monica had a similar setup on the division's west wide, although they favored a more liberal mode. And the northern border along Mulholland Drive possessed some of the most expensive and isolated estates in the city, if not the world.

West L.A. was the rich filling in a money sandwich.

When Fey had first promoted in to West L.A. as a detective two with sixteen years on the job, Cahill had taken her aside to explain the divisional facts of life. Things were handled differently in West L.A., Cahill told her, because the rich never went up the chain of command. Instead, they started at the top and let the crap roll downhill. The rich were different and expected to be treated differently.

This different treatment didn't mean the rich never went to jail. But it did mean officers better be damn sure of what they had before slapping the cuffs on some movie star's brat. It also made things very tough for an officer who stopped someone for drunk driving only to find out that the lawbreaker was on his way home from a thousand-dollar-a-plate fund-raiser for the mayor.

Neither did the difference mean that the rich automatically had all their crimes solved and recovered all their property. But it did mean that a detective better be prepared to jump a little higher when a councilman's wife said there was a trespasser on her grounds while her husband was out of town on a junket. This was true even if there was no trespasser, and the only reason the wife had called was because she was lonely and horny and wanted some attention from the stud of a uniformed officer who she knew would respond to her 911 call.

Fey played the game with the rich very well. She was known for her "bedside manner" and for her ability to soothe even the most ruffled of feathers. She was also known to solve a lot of crimes and put a lot of suspects behind bars. In an enclosed world where reputation counts for almost everything, Fey was a rising star. The respect, however, was still grudging because she was still undeniably a woman in a man's world. A bitch in the locker room. A nigger in the woodpile. Different generation, but the same prejudice.

After four years in West L.A., her abilities led to her promotion to detective three. Two years later, she was given the homicide unit to supervise. It was the top detective spot in the division, and Fey was the first woman to ever head the unit. She was very pleased at first to have overcome that barrier. Then she found out that orders had come down from on high to put a woman in the spot—not because a woman, or specifically Fey, deserved the spot, but because a token had to be presented for public relations purposes.

Fey's initial reaction to this news had been anger. She almost stalked into Cahill's office to throw her badge and gun on the desk and resign. Cooler thoughts prevailed, though, and on reflection she decided that it didn't matter what the motivations were that placed her in the position. She—Fey Croaker—was still in the position, and it was up to her to prove that she could do the job, not because she was a woman, but because she was a damn good detective.

Fey had worked homicide earlier in her career as a detective one, and later as a detective two, and she had learned quickly that the supposed differences between the rich and poor were only superficial. When you worked homicide, dead was dead. Murder had no respect for wealth.

Now Fey sighed and massaged the bridge of her nose with the thumb and index finger of her left hand. Her nails were long, but the bloodred polish on them was chipped.

She felt a deep sigh dissipate in her chest. You always wanted the first body in January to be easy, a self-solver. It set the tone for the rest of the year. This one felt rough.

She shoved together the paperwork she had been shuffling and stood up. "Have the coroner and the SID lab boys been notified?"

Cahill nodded his head. "The uniforms radioed for them as soon as they saw the stiff."

"How about an ambulance crew?"

"On the scene now."

"Good. Okay. Who are the blue-suiters on the scene?"

"8-A-64. Reeves and Watts."

Fey visibly cringed. "Why did it have to be Reeves? He wouldn't know a suspect if one came up and jumped in the backseat of his police car. He probably hasn't gotten any further in the investigation than trying to put the make on the maid. Watts is okay, but he's still very wet behind the ears."

"What can I tell you?" Cahill asked. "If working homicide was easy, we'd let someone from the mayor's staff investigate."

"Heaven forbid," Fey said, and rolled her eyes before becoming serious again. "Do me a favor?" she requested. "Send the uniforms a message over the MDT to make sure they've got the crime scene taped off, and that they are staying outside the residence. The last thing we need is the crime scene contaminated by Reeves doing his kleptomaniac act or Watts flicking cigarette ash over all the evidence."

"Anything else?"

Fey took a breath before continuing. "Yeah. Make sure they've got an incident log started and that they're keeping the maid isolated from any other witnesses."

"Will do," said Cahill.

"Oh, and make sure they keep the ambulance crew there until we arrive. I'm going to want to interview them and find out what they touched or moved."

Cahill said, "Check." He had a lot of faith in Fey. She was very methodical in her investigations and didn't miss a trick.

Fey picked up the unit's sign-in sheet and stared at it. "I'll take Hatcher with me," she said, making a notation on the sheet.

"Why don't you take Colby?"

Fey gave Cahill a sharp look. It was very unlike the lieutenant to question who she assigned to a case.

Cahill caught Fey's glance and held up a hand in mock defense before she could retort verbally. "Colby asked specifically to be assigned to this one," he said in a conciliatory tone. "And he knows the lay of the land up there."

Fey grimaced. "What does that mean?" She didn't like Colby. Supervising him was bad enough, but she loathed the thought of actually partnering him on a case. "Just because he dresses like a wannabe movie star with the taste of a two-dollar whore doesn't mean he knows the rich any better than the rest of us."

"Come on, Fey," Cahill said. "Give the guy a break. He's a good detective. He just needs a little experience."

"Not to hear him tell it," she said.

As if on cue, Alan Colby came up the back stairs and

cut a swath across the squad room. Tall and athletic, he walked past the random clumps of desks that were scattered around the room, and flashed a grin at Cahill and Fey.

"Was somebody talking about me?" he asked, as if picking up leftover vibrations of conversation. "My ears were burning."

"Grab your stuff," Fey told him as she reached down to take a shoulder-holstered Smith & Wesson .38 out of her desk drawer. "As if you didn't know, we've got a stiff waiting for us up in Brentwood."

"Hot dog!" Colby said.

"I'm glad you find death something to be happy about," Fey said nastily.

"Chill out, Frog Lady. I'm just turned on by a challenge."

Fey halted in the process of slipping on her shoulder rig. "I won't tell you again, Colby. Don't—I repeat, don't—call me Frog Lady."

"You got to love that pose, don't you, Lieutenant?" Colby said, referring to the fact that Fey's position, half in and half out of the shoulder rig, pushed her arms back and thrust her bosom forward as if it were an item offered for display.

"It's impressive," Cahill said.

Fey just shook her head and shrugged the shoulder holster the rest of the way into place. "Why is it that men never grow out of adolescence? Thank God women aren't fixated on various parts of the male anatomy. If we were, then both sexes would be useless."

The lieutenant's secretary giggled when she overheard the comeback. Fey grinned at her. "It's like trying to keep a room full of five-year-olds busy," she said. The secretary laughed again.

"Come on, Colby," Fey told him. "You're slowing me down."

**2**

**D**espite Fey's disparaging words, Alan Colby would have looked good on the big screen. He had high cheekbones, full lips, and a shaggy mane of crow black hair that he was constantly being told to cut. His eyes were clear with an unusual bright green tint to the irises and a slight Oriental cast to the lids.

His lean build testified to long hours of workouts. Often competing in triathlons, Colby was ranked as one of the top thirty triathletes in the nation. On two occasions he had won gold medals in the police olympics, and on another he had placed fourth in the Ironman competition in Hawaii. Working out was something of an obsession with him.

His clothes were straight from the pages of *GQ*: Italian suits and shoes, Oriental silk ties, and French cuffed shirts with expensive cuff links. He wore them all well on his tall whipcord body and could have made a living as a model without even trying. Fey had more than her share of battles with weight, and Colby's flaunting of his slimness only added to her dislike of the man.

Colby's smile was right off the silver screen as well. He could melt them in the aisles when he let loose with his trademark grin. Right now he was flashing his ivories at the maid who had discovered the body. It was making the interview difficult, and driving Fey mad.

"Knock it off, Colby," Fey told him quietly. "Her bank balance isn't big enough to interest you."

"Meow," said Colby. He turned his grin in Fey's direction. "I love it when you show your jealous side."

"Why don't you go play in traffic?"

In all her years on the job, Fey had seen a lot of detectives come and go. Colby might be the current flavor of the month, but Fey kept telling herself that he, too, would pass. He'd recently been assigned to homicide as a reward for breaking a huge car theft ring while assigned to the divisional auto theft unit. Apparently he was still riding high on the notoriety.

As the homicide supervisor, Fey had objected to being forced to take on a detective she wasn't comfortable around. In her mind, Colby's flashy clothes, flashy jewelry, flashy car, and flashy style added up to bent copper. She couldn't prove it, but her instincts were rarely wrong.

There was a problem, however. The homicide unit was on a cold streak. They were suffering from four "unsolveds" in a row, and Cahill had insisted on an injection of new blood. As a result, Colby had simply flashed his Cheshire cat grin and picked canary feathers out from between his teeth. Nobody came out and said the cold streak came about because a woman was in charge of the unit, but the sentiment was clearly apparent.

Fey was convinced that somewhere, somehow, Colby had something on someone. She didn't want to admit to her own working-class snobbery by putting Colby's success down to talent and hard work.

There was another thing that Fey didn't want to admit to herself. Down where her primal sexual instincts lived, Colby's good looks tripped her switches. She disliked him, but physically he turned her on. She couldn't help her response, and that pissed her off to no end.

For his part, Colby knew he did things specifically to irritate Fey. He hadn't been interested in the maid, but he knew it would upset Fey if it appeared as if he were. There was something about Fey that brought out the worst in him. If he looked at it objectively, she was probably a pretty good detective, but he still didn't think she deserved to be running the Homicide unit.

The reasoning behind his feelings was something that he didn't want to examine too closely. As in other unresolved relationships in his past, analysis might reveal personal faults to which he didn't want to admit. In the short run it was easier to simply accept the feelings and leave the reasoning locked up in a mental closet somewhere. That way you never showed any weaknessses, never gave anyone the edge.

When Fey and Colby had arrived at the security gates of the Oak Vista Estates, they found themselves doing battle with an overeager security guard who was worried that the events of the evening would put his job in jeopardy. He insisted on checking their ID, and then radioed to another security guard, who was inside the complex with Reeves and Watts, to make sure Fey and Colby were authorized.

By the time the security gates were swung open to allow the detectives' beat-up sedan to pass through, Fey was fuming. "Wuss butt," she said, referring to the security guard. "He'll probably let the press straight in as long as they promise to take his picture."

On the other side of the vehicle, Colby was strangely quiet during this tirade. Fey looked over to see him staring out the passenger window at the opulence of the surrounding community.

"There's no way, Colby," she said, snidely.

Colby brought his attention around to her. "I don't follow you."

"There's no way you'll ever be able to afford one of these units on a cop's salary."

Colby shrugged. "Why not? You live in a house on a couple of acres somewhere to accommodate your horses and all the flies they attract, don't you? That must have cost you a pretty penny in the California real estate market."

"I was lucky," Fey said. "I bought that property before the real estate boom." She felt angry because Colby had immediately put her back on the defensive.

"So maybe I'll follow your example. I'll get married and divorced several times, take all my exes to the cleaners, and then I'll be able to move right in here. They'll probably be glad to have me. Having a real cop on the grounds would give the homeowners a sense of security. And after all, I don't need room for animals, and I don't gather flies."

Fey bit back. "Don't flatter yourself. You're no real cop."

The complex the two detectives were driving through looked like something out of *Architectural and Landscaping*

*Monthly*. The exteriors of the two- and three-story town homes were done in mock Tudor style and built over matching two-car garages. White stucco was crisscrossed with black oak beaming, and highlighted with old-fashioned red brick or silver-gray quarry stones. There were perhaps 150 units, each attached to another unit by one common wall. Not one of them cost under $550,000.

The grounds surrounding the units were green and rambling with babbling brooks, low split-oak fencing, and other lush touches that cost a fortune in upkeep. An army of grounds keepers were kept busy tending the roses, trimming the mature oak trees, and mowing the extensive greenbelts. And all that was before they began tending to the private nine-hole golf course that ran across the back length of the complex.

Fey saw an ambulance and the black-and-white unit parked in front of 2008 Mirrorwood. Reeves was standing outside of the vehicle with the driver's door open. Next to him was one of the complex's uniformed security guards.

Through the squad car's rear window Fey could see Rusty Watts sitting on the passenger side talking to a woman in the vehicle's backseat. Fey assumed she was the maid.

On the lawn in front of the house were several citizens standing in a group. Three men and two women all dressed in casual clothes or sweatsuits. Any one of the outfits would have cost Fey two weeks' salary. One of the women walked up to the open door of the town home, grabbed hold of the doorframe, and leaned in to peek inside.

There wasn't a glint of yellow crime scene tape to be seen anywhere. Fey could feel herself getting pissed off. Not the best frame of mind to start an investigation in which the first six hours were the most critical. She parked behind the ambulance, and both she and Colby climbed out.

"Get those people off the lawn, and get that woman away from the door," she told Colby. Turning on her heel, she started walking toward the squad car without looking back to see if he was following her orders.

Reeves straightened up and smiled when he saw her approaching. Each arm of his blue uniform shirt sported a pair of chevrons identifying him as a training officer. "Howdy," he said, in a put-on cowboy accent.

"What the hell are you doing letting those people walk all over the crime scene?" Fey demanded, opening up with both barrels.

Reeves's smile turned to a look of confusion. He swiveled his eyes toward where Colby was herding the citizens off the lawn like a collie with too many sheep to tend. "There's nobody in the crime scene. That's upstairs in the bedroom."

"How long have you been on this job, Reeves?" Fey didn't wait for an answer and just plowed straight on. "Didn't Cahill send you a message to tape off the scene?"

"Yeah, but we didn't need to. We just closed the door to the bedroom. That was enough to keep everybody out."

"How the hell did you ever become a training officer?" Fey did not have much tolerance for incompetence. "This whole damn complex is a crime scene. Now, get off your dead ass, dig some crime scene tape out of your trunk, and get this area protected. And if I find out you've smudged any prints by closing the door to the bedroom, I'm going to initiate a 181 so fast, you'll be doing freeway therapy before the ink is dry on the paperwork."

"Freeway therapy" was the term for the unofficial department discipline of transferring an offending officer to the farthest division from his home. Reeves looked aggrieved and pained, as if he were a child being disciplined by an overbearing parent for no reason, and turned to slowly do Fey's bidding.

Fey knew Reeves would now start spreading the word about what a bitch she was, but that didn't bother her. She'd lived with it all her career.

If a male detective had chewed Reeves out, Reeves would have been seen to be at fault, and the male detective would have been admired as a kick-ass, no-nonsense copper doing his job.

However, because she was a woman, other male officers would rally to Reeves's defense, and Fey's outburst would be put down to PMS or some equally moronic placebo. It wouldn't matter that Fey was right, or that Reeves was nothing more than a lazy drone who never did more than he had to in order to get by. All that would matter was gender stereotypes. Reeves was a macho, fun-loving guy, and Fey was a frigid bitch who complained about every little thing.

Fey leaned into the interior of the police car. She smiled at the woman who was smoking in the backseat, and then looked at Watts. He was also smoking a Marlboro cigarette. "Do you have a crime scene log started?" she asked him.

"You bet." Watts held up a sheet of continuation paper attached to a clipboard. In a neat, precise hand, he had printed down everything that had happened, along with time notations, since he and his partner had discovered the body.

Fey looked at the list and handed it back. "Good," she said. "I can even read the thing." She smiled. "Log in the arrival of my partner and I, and keep the list going until I tell you differently."

"Okay," Watts said. He was still a rookie and eager to both please and learn. Fey had seen him around the station and felt he had potential. Reaching over, Fey took the cigarette out from between Watts's fingers and took a long drag. "Filthy habit," she said.

"I know."

She took another hit and handed the cigarette back. "You didn't light one of these up in the residence, did you?"

Watts shook his head. "Who do you think I am—Reeves?"

Fey laughed for the first time since Cahill had handed her the squeal. She felt some of the tension flow out of her.

"No," she said. "I wouldn't think that of my worst enemy."

Colby materialized behind Fey's shoulder and started flashing his ivories at the maid in the backseat of the police car. She was a young and slender Latin woman with curly black hair and a scared look in her eyes.

"Did you get the names of the looky-loos?" Fey asked Colby when she became aware of his presence.

Colby displayed a handful of field interview cards. "They didn't take kindly to being questioned, but I charmed them all."

Fey rolled her eyes. "How about the ambulance crew?"

"It's Kyle Digby's crew."

"Thank goodness for small blessings. Digby's done enough of these to know what he's doing."

"Digby said he walked a straight line to the body to check for vitals. Said it was a foregone conclusion. Victim's carotid was severed. Blood spurted everywhere. Digby declared the victim dead on the F-660 form."

"Okay, keep it to attach to the death report. Any of the other crew go inside?"

"Digby said just him. He knows how you like to keep the scene as virgin as possible. Kind of like your reputation."

Fey didn't rise to the bait.

Turning back to Watts, she said, "Get on the radio and whistle up another patrol unit to help secure the location. I want to go inside and have a look before the coroner and SID show up." She looked again at the woman in the backseat. "I take it this is the maid?"

Watts nodded as he picked up the radio mike. "Yeah. Lucia Cortez." He handed Fey an FI card with the Latin woman's basic information filled out neatly in the assigned boxes.

Fey pulled back from the front seat of the police car and opened the rear door to slide in next to the maid. Colby took her place on the front seat.

"Hello, Lucia. I'm Detective Croaker, and this is my partner, Detective Colby. Do you speak English?"

"Yes." The maid bit the word off as if she were scared to let further sounds burst from her mouth.

Fey could tell the woman was extremely nervous. Her eyes kept bouncing around the interior of the squad car, making her seem like a frightened animal looking for an escape route.

Fey noticed Colby turn up the intensity of his smile when he noticed how lush the maid's body appeared to be under her tight black-and-white uniform.

"Knock it off, Colby."

"Yes, ma'am," he replied sarcastically, and turned up the wattage another notch.

Fey tried to ignore him and returned her attention to the

maid. "Lucia, I'm sure that all of this was a terrible shock, but I need to ask you a few questions, okay?"

"Okay," the maid said, cutting off the word again with a firm clamping of her mouth. She'd finished the cigarette she'd been smoking and seemed at a loss of how to dispose of the butt. Fey took it from her and handed it to Colby, who put it in the ashtray.

"How long have you been in this country, Lucia?" Fey asked. The immediate fear that flashed into the woman's eyes confirmed Fey's instincts. "It's okay," she told the woman, placing a reassuring hand on the maid's arm. "We don't care if you are here legally or not. You aren't in any trouble, and we aren't interested in deporting you."

"You no send me back?"

"No," Fey said. "When we are all done here today, I'll have somebody drive you back to wherever you're living."

"But I have other houses to clean today. I get fired if I don't turn up."

"That's okay," Fey said. "Tell me who you are working for and I'll have somebody talk to them and make sure they understand. All right?"

The woman nodded. "Okay."

"Now," Fey said. "What time did you get here today?"

"Eight o'clock. My boyfriend drop me off outside." With the mention of a boyfriend, her eyes flicked again to make contact with Colby's.

"How did you get into the house?"

"I have a key. I let myself in by the front door. I called out to Mrs. Goodwinter, but she no answer."

"Mrs. Goodwinter? That's the name of the woman you work for, the woman who lives here?"

"Yes."

"Is there a Mr. Goodwinter?"

"I no know. Mrs. Goodwinter, she live alone."

"How long have you worked for Mrs. Goodwinter?"

"This is only second week. She only just move in. I come on Tuesday and Thursday for four hours, and then I go and clean for Mr. and Mrs. Barstow down the street."

"How did Mrs. Goodwinter come to hire you?"

The maid shrugged. "I see her moving in about two

weeks ago, and I come over and ask her if she need anybody to do her cleaning. She tell me to start the next Tuesday." She looked at Colby again and self-consciously ran a hand through her hair. She recrossed her legs, and there was a whisper of black nylon.

Fey glared at Colby. She returned to questioning Lucia. "What did you do after you entered the residence?"

"I thought Mrs. Goodwinter might still be asleep, so I went upstairs to check."

"You didn't start cleaning?"

"No. I didn't want to make no noise and wake up Mrs. Goodwinter and get her mad at me."

"Okay. You went upstairs to the bedroom. Then what happened?"

Lucia began to cry. "The door. It was a little open. I pushed it the rest of the way open, and then I saw her on the bed." The maid put her hands up to her face and began to cry harder.

Fey put her arm around the woman. "It's all right," she said.

When Lucia calmed down a little, Fey asked her, "Did you go any further into the room?"

"No. I was too scared. I run down the stairs and outside."

"You didn't call the police?"

"No."

Fey looked over at Watts.

"The radio call came out as an 'unknown trouble—woman screaming.' There was no PR or call-back number," Watts explained.

Fey spoke to Colby. "Use the mobile phone and call communications right away. I want the 911 tape with the call on it and the printout with the address of the original call."

Colby grunted and slid out of the car.

"Are you sure that the person you saw on the bed was Mrs. Goodwinter?"

"Yes . . . No . . . I think so."

Fey patted the woman's arm again. "That's all for now, Lucia. I'm gong to want to talk to you again later. Is that okay?"

"*Sí* . . . Yes. Okay."

Fey climbed out of the backseat and walked around the car to the passenger side. She signaled to Watts, who climbed out to talk to her.

"Take care of her," Fey said. "I don't want anyone else talking to her, and I don't want her to leave the scene. She might split on us and we'll never find her again, so don't let her out of your sight."

Watts looked confused. "You think maybe she did it?"

"No I don't," said Fey. "But I'm not going to take a chance on being wrong."

**F**ey stood on the threshold of the victim's residence. Colby stood behind her slipping plastic bootees over his Italian loafers. Carefully Fey took a pair of latex gloves out of her pocket and pulled them on as if she were a surgeon preparing for an operation. A small satchel was slung over her right shoulder.

Taking a deep breath, she cleared her mind of all exterior input. This was the moment of an investigation in which Fey felt almost down to the core of her being. The split-second high before plunging into the deep end of a dank and seemingly bottomless pool.

Time was ticking.

It took six hours from the time a detective first received a murder call-out until the best chance of solving the case disappeared in a heartbeat. Twenty-four hours later the case began to slow down. After forty-eight hours the main leads were cleared off the desk and you began to start looking for anything you might have missed. At seventy-two hours the bell rang and the time on all your options ran out.

Beyond seventy-two hours, solving the case became a long shot. A crapshoot. A needle-in-the-haystack proposition.

Seventy-two hours and time was ticking.

Fey checked her watch and made a mental note of the time. Colby would be following along behind her, making a hard copy of the same thing on his clipboard. He would already have notes of the time they had received the original call, how that call had been made, and who had made it. As they continued, he would be noting down the outside and inside temperatures and the weather conditions. All of these things could turn out to be no help at all, or they could turn out to be crucial at a trial held months or years later. Notes were far better in court than memories that had become blurred, or had blended in with every crime scene a detective had ever worked.

Fey stepped under the crime scene tape. Reeves had gone out of his way to string it everywhere in sight, as if he'd been a dog marking out his territory.

It was time to go to work.

The inside of the town house was opulent and beautiful. It was as if pages of an interior decorating magazine had been clipped out and given life. Large burnished squares of Italian tile with rough gray grout slid underfoot, leading the way into the spacious open floor plan currently in vogue.

Exposed beams crossed the high ceilings to tie in with the Tudor exterior. Across the back of the house, large windows and French doors spilled light through gauzy eggshell draperies. The tiled floor was decorated with expensive throw rugs ranging in styles from Aubusson to Oriental to Persian. Couches and chairs with lots of cushions were seemingly scattered at random, but were actually placed at aesthetically strategic spots. The biege textured walls sported rounded corners as if the house were designed to be lived in by someone who had to be kept away from sharp edges.

Fey memorized it all with a glance before walking in a careful line directly from the front door to the curved stairway. With her hands down by her side, she walked slowly, looking ahead to where her next foot would fall, making sure no piece of vital evidence would be disturbed by her passage.

Behind her, she could feel Colby correctly dogging her footsteps like a child following his father through the snow.

At the top of the stairs, Fey stopped again to take in the surroundings. She was conscious of the weight of the gun hanging snugly in its holster under her arm. She tested the air as if she were an animal sensing for danger. There was almost no possibility that the suspect was still on the scene, but it was always a possibility that had to be considered. When Fey had first been assigned as a detective trainee years earlier, she had come across a murder suspect hiding on the shelf of a walk-in closet twelve hours after he'd done the dirty deed. The incident had been like lightning striking—a once-in-a-career instance—but the chance still had to be considered.

The magazine-perfect decorating theme was continued on the town home's upper level. Fey thought it was beautiful, expensive, and charming, but impersonal. There seemed to be no mark anywhere of the owner's individual personality other than to say she didn't have one—the fact that there is no pattern being a pattern in itself.

All the doors to the rooms leading off the landing were open except for one. Fey realized that the closed door, having been shut by Reeves, hid the crime scene. She walked to the door and looked at the door handle. Any chance of prints on the doorknob had probably been screwed up by Reeves, but she didn't want to compound the error. Taking a Swiss army knife from the satchel, she selected the longest blade and shimmed the door with all the adroitness of a professional burglar.

The door swung open and Fey felt the electric charge of anticipation, fear, and discovery zip through her. The room was picture-perfect—a murder captured on canvas by an old master—another leaf from the decorator's handbook. This time it was an illustration of the use of white. Every shade from stark to eggshell to lace was represented by either the carpet, the chairs, the bed, the lampshades, the comforter, the walls, or the ornate plastered mantel across the white fireplace bricks.

Sunlight streamed through a large open window, highlighting the pale white body of the victim as it angled across the four-poster bed. The head and right arm were off the mattress, pointing floorward. The acute angle of the head exposed the ragged wound across the side of the victim's neck. The hand at the end of the long, graceful right arm touched the floor in a pool of congealing blood.

The impact of the white-on-white-on-white was heightened by the dramatic slash of dark red that had flown in an arc, like an angry brushstroke, from one side of the bed across the white wall and the off-white window sheers to speckle out across the flat white ceiling.

A trail left behind by the soul as it fled the body.

Fey felt Colby behind her, not touching her but still pushing her to enter the room.

"What's the matter?" he asked, when she still didn't move. "Not scared of dead bodies, are you?"

"I've seen more naked dead ones than you've seen naked live ones."

"You picking out your lovers from the morgue again?"

Fey grunted but still did not budge. "Just hold your water and try to learn something."

"So what's to learn?"

"There is something alive in this room, and it isn't the body on the bed."

Colby stiffened. "A suspect?" His voice was disbelieving.

Fey shook her head. "No. I don't think it's human."

"What the hell are you talking about? Ghosts or something?" The tone in Colby's voice had turned from disbelief to ridicule.

"Just wait. Give me the clipboard."

Colby handed the board over Fey's shoulder. She took it from him without taking her eyes off the scene in front of her. Using the pencil attached to the board by a length of twine, she began to sketch the crime scene on a clean sheet of paper. She worked fast with sure strokes, creating almost a piece of art—a still life of death—as opposed to the more typical drafting floor plan, which she would leave to Colby. When she was done, she handed the board back to her partner.

"Well," he said.

"Well, what?"

"What about this nonhuman presence?"

"It's not ready to come out yet." Fey smiled to herself. She knew she was getting to Colby.

"You're weird," Colby said, and forcibly pushed his way into the room. "What do you think you are, some kind of witch or something?"

"At least you're pronouncing it with a *W* instead of a *B* for a change."

"Ain't that much difference," Colby said.

"Just follow me and take your notes." Fey started to move toward the body. Her eyes scanned the floor and she was careful to touch nothing. When she reached the body, she began talking softly and slowly, giving time for Colby to write it all down.

"Victim is female, white, red hair. Approximately five feet four inches, one hundred twenty pounds. No obvious scars or tattoos visible at this time. Lots of freckles. Emerald green fingernail and matching toenail polish. The body is naked and there are no obvious signs of bruising or other contusions or abrasions. There are no apparent foreign objects protruding from the body. The mouth is open slightly and is smeared with red lipstick. The smear appears to have occurred before death, possibly through a kissing motion, as opposed to a smear consciously applied by the suspect."

Fey moved around the bed to get another view. She noted a pale green nightgown on the floor and pointed it out to Colby. He flipped the pages on the clipboard and made a note of the position on his crime scene drawing.

Fey continued her dialogue. "The victim's legs are slightly spread open and there appears to be a white discharge seeping out of the vaginal area. Again, no there are no apparent foreign objects, and there are no visible signs of a struggle."

Returning to the side of the bed where she'd started her examination, Fey crouched down and examined what she could see of the body's sides. "Postmortem lividity appears normal for the position of the body," she said. Lividity is the bruising that occurs in a dead body when the blood settles. If a body has been moved, the lividity would not be consistent with the body's new position. She reached out and touched a pale white arm. "Rigor is present."

Next she turned her attention to the wound. "The victim has an aproximately two-inch gash on the right side of her neck that appears to have severed the carotid artery." The autopsy would come later and give the official cause of death, but Fey's observations would start the ball rolling. "The wound appears to have been made by a sharp object other than a knife because of the tearing of the skin. Possibly an ice-pick-type weapon." Fey looked up at Colby. "Are you getting all this?"

"I'm just a happy little stenographer. Do you want me to sit on your lap?"

"Shuuuush . . ." Fey held up a hand.

"What?"

"Shut up!" Fey's voice was quiet but insistent.

Silence.

Colby shuffled his feet, and Fey shot him a dirty look.

A cry sounded faintly. Like a baby with a pillow over its face.

"What the hell," Colby said.

The noise sounded again.

"Where is it coming from?"

Fey was very still as she crouched beside the bed. The dust ruffle at her feet moved slightly.

"I think we've found ourselves a witness," she said as a sleek white cat suddenly jumped into her lap.

"Shit," Colby said in disgust. "You and your inhuman presence. How did you know about the cat?"

"Experience."

"My ass."

"If you say so."

"Come on."

"I used my eyes, Colby." She was pleased she'd got his goat. "I saw the cat hairs on the tiled floor downstairs. They were the only things not left behind by the decorator in this entire place."

"Okay, but how did you know it was in the room?"

"Because I know cats."

The animal was really yowling now, as if it were trying

to tell Fey everything it had seen. Fey wrapped her arms around it and stood up. She thrust the bundle of fur at Colby. "Take him down to the car and secure him."

Colby fumbled with his clipboard as the cat squirmed around. He'd been so shocked when Fey handed the cat to him that he'd accepted it automatically.

"Leave a window slightly cracked so he can get air, but don't leave it down enough so he can get out. Then see if the photographer has arrived and send him up."

"I'm not an errand boy, Frog Lady." Colby was indignant. Pressing the squirming cat and clipboard to him with one hand, he tried in vain to brush cat hair off his suit jacket with the other. Frustrated, he raised his voice. "And I ain't no fucking cat sitter."

Fey turned slowly to look at him. "Consider yourself lucky." She smiled evilly. "This is probably the closest you're going to get to a pussy until this investigation is over."

"**W**ho the hell shoved a burr under your partner's saddle?" Eddie Mack asked as he came in through the bedroom door. Camera gear sprouted from his body like fruit on a tree. "He looked like he wanted to strangle that cat."

Fey laughed. "Adversity is good for him. It helps build character." She turned from her study of the body to greet the new arrival. "How are you, Eddie? Busy shift?"

"I'm doing okay, but I've been busier than a set of jumper cables at a Mexican wedding. I've just come from a triple over in Newton, and before that, there was a drive-by in Seventy-seventh."

"Welcome to L.A., where we treat you like a 'King,' "

Fey said sarcastically. The sentiment had become a catch phrase for the continuing explosion of violence in the city.

Eddie swiveled the strobe on one of the cameras slung around his neck. He was a short man made ugly by thick black hairs blossoming out of his nostrils, and a tennis-ball-sized lump on his neck. He was stuffed into a mishmash of clothing that even a thrift store would reject, but his equipment was state-of-the-art and in pristine condition. He'd bought all the equipment himself, knowing that the city would never lay out for it. "You want the usual shots with an order for an extra set?" He'd worked with Fey before and knew what she expected.

"That's fine," Fey said. "And make 'em sharp, Eddie. I want to crack this one fast."

"Hey! When have I ever given you anything but my best work?" Eddie sounded wounded.

"Never, Eddie."

"Damn right."

"How about sticking around and shooting anything the print people come up with?" Fey asked. Taking photos of prints before they were lifted made sure that you still had a usable piece of evidence if the print disintegrated during the lifting process.

"Sure. No problem." Eddie looked up from fiddling with his equipment. "Oh, I get it," he said, realizing why Fey was being so careful. "This must be your first stiff of the new year."

"It sure as hell won't be the last."

Eddie guffawed and then glued his eyes to the view-finder. Without waiting any longer, he started triggering film. "Hell of a set of gazzongas for an old broad," he said as he viewed the body from behind the defense of his lens.

In the bursts from the strobe, Fey looked at the dead woman with the big gazzongas. It made her sad. Even in death, the woman was not safe from the vicious bite of sexual innuendo.

*Who were you?* Fey silently asked the body. *Who were you?*

Backing away to the door, deep in thought, she almost collided with the coroner, Harry Carter.

"Oops! Excuse me," she said as she stepped aside.

"Looks like you're getting a little too wrapped up in your work as usual," Carter said.

Fey smiled at him. "Just trying to solve this one without any clues. Cart-before-the-horse time."

"Coming up with answers before you know what the questions are, huh? If anybody can do it, you will." Carter was an older man and enjoyed the role of father figure. He also liked Fey and was one of her big supporters.

"What's the head coroner doing here anyway?" Fey asked him. "I thought you'd become too much of a big shot to come out in the field anymore. I expected Simms or Wiley."

"Simms is out with the flu, and Wiley got himself caught stealing gold fillings. Big investigation going on."

"No shit?" Fey said, slightly shocked.

Carter rolled his eyes. "Yeah. Down at the coroner's office we're no different than police officers. We're our own worst enemies. The political-damage-control types have been trying to keep it out of the papers, but the story is going to leak eventually."

"Good grief. So as a result you get to come out and play with the common folk."

"Let me tell you, it makes a nice change. It beats the pressures of doing celebrity autopsies all to hell."

"Yeah, but you won't get a book out of this one," she told him. Carter had made a big splash with a nonfiction book recounting the stories behind the deaths of numerous celebrities on whom he'd conducted autopsies.

Carter shrugged. "Who needs to write another book? The publishers have got some hack to grind out a new series of mysteries featuring a coroner as the main character—some kind of high-priced Quincy. They're going to publish them under my name. I talk to the hack a couple of times on the phone and then sit back and rake in the hefty advances and royalties. When the books come out, I make the book-signing rounds as if I wrote every word, assure everyone that the next installment is well under way, and then leave the public and the talk-show hosts thinking I'm some kind of Renaissance man. I don't even have to read the damn things."

"Sounds sweet."

Carter shrugged expressively, and a smile split through his beard. "It's a living." He hefted his black bag. "You better let me get to work."

Fey smiled back and let him slip by into the crime scene. Two men from SID, the department's Scientific Investigation Division, followed through behind him. One would be a latent-print expert, and the other would be a specialist in biological stains. Fey didn't recognize the stain specialist, who was lugging around a huge Woods lamp, but she did know the print man. He nodded a greeting.

"Hey, Steve. How are you?" Fey asked in response.

"Can't complain. Nobody would listen anyway even if I did."

"Let Eddie Mack follow you around and pop a few flashes before you lift anything. Okay?"

"Sure. You want anything else special?"

Fey smiled engagingly. "I know it's a big place, but can you give me a top-to-bottom on this one?"

"You got it."

Fey smiled again, said, "Thanks," and left them to it.

She retraced her steps down to the front door.

"Hey, Frog Lady," Colby called to her from the living room. "Looky, looky what I found." He held up a woman's handbag.

Fey shook her head. She shouldn't have let Colby off the leash. He was like a two-year-old who kept getting into all the lower kitchen cupboards. There was a hell of a lot more they should have done before starting to root through handbags and wallets. Still, she kept her temper in check. The damage was done. Getting pissed would only make things worse.

She walked over to stand next to the formal dining table, where Colby was laying out his finds.

He handed Fey a California driver's license.

"Miranda Goodwinter. Like the maid said," he told her.

Fey took the small card and looked at the flash-flattened picture. There was no doubt it was the woman upstairs on the bed. The harsh photo had brought out all of the age lines that had been relaxed by the death repose.

"Did you find an address book?" she asked, flipping the license back onto the table.

Colby riffled through the pile of items that had come out of the handbag: wallet, makeup, short-handled brush, hair clip, assorted papers, matches, cigarettes, checkbook, keys. "Not yet. There's some other ID in the same name, though," he said, handing Fey a stack of plastic and cardboard rectangles that had recently resided in the wallet.

"Any photos of friends, relatives, ugly babies?" Fey asked as she shuffled through the stack.

"Not in the purse. And I didn't see any on the walls or furniture as we came through. It's something I always check for."

Fey raised her eyebrows.

Colby cut loose his maddening grin. "Ease up, Frog Lady," he said. "You might not like me, but that doesn't mean I'm a bad detective. If you'd loosen up a bit, you might find that I'm not too bad at other things either." His implication was made clear as his grin turned to a leer.

"Come back and see me when you reach puberty, Colby," Fey told him.

Colby laughed, unoffended. "Everyone tells me you're a tight-ass."

"That's right. I'm tight as a duck's ass, Colby, and that's water-tight. You'd do well not to forget it."

"Ooooh. Yes, ma'am."

Fey shook her head at Colby's sarcastic tone. It was another one of the many things that irritated her about him. One second he could display the professional sense that all top detectives develop, and the next moment he acted as if he'd never outgrown the phase of male development where sex was a dirty joke and women were something to snigger about while smoking cigarettes behind the school gym.

The combination of traits did not sit well with Fey. She liked people to either be one way or the other; it made them easier to deal with. With someone like Colby, she didn't know which way to jump—she could rely on him in some areas, but had to keep her defenses up in others. It was a situation that led to stress, so rather than attempt to walk a tightrope between the characteristics, Fey simply distrusted

Colby in all areas—making it very hard for her to be objective about him.

Fey looked down at the cards in her hand again and shuffled through them for a second time. "Did you notice anything strange about this ID?" she asked.

"It's all current issue," Colby replied, switching back to his professional mode. "From the driver's license through the credit cards, the auto club card, and the library card. All of it is fresh."

"Good answer," Fey said, in the manner of a popular television game-show host. "You get to move on to the bonus round."

"It's as if this babe was brand-new," Colby continued. "If it weren't for her stretch marks and wrinkles, you'd have to think that she'd just popped out of the womb."

"Interesting analogy, but it's not far off," Fey agreed. "New condo. New ID." She surveyed the room around them. "All the furniture looks new."

Colby agreed. "Even the television has that piece of plastic film still stuck up in the corner of the screen."

Fey walked over to the coat closet and pulled it open. Inside the closet there were several expensive coats hanging on the rack. Fey checked the sleeves. Two of them still had the manufacturer's tags attached. "Fresh from the boutique," she said.

Picking up a checkbook from the pile on the table, Colby checked the balance. "She opened this account with ten thousand dollars, probably all in brand-new bills." He looked further. "She's only used two checks from the pad. They're the ones where you have to fill in the name and address part until the printed ones arrive."

"Does she have a car?"

"The uniforms ran a DMV on the new Beemer in the driveway. It's registered in the name of our victim. That is, if it is her name. I'd say she was running from something, but she didn't run far or fast enough. She got caught."

Fey's silent words echoed in her head gain. *Who were you?*

"She's run before," she said. "The ID and the rest of this setup is too sophisticated for a first-timer. Go upstairs and tell

Carter to get us a second set of prints off the corpse and then
put them through FIN." The Fingerprint Identification Net-
work would kick out a match if the victim had ever been
printed anywhere for any reason such as military, criminal,
professional licensing, and so forth. "Also tell him we need
a dental chart. Maybe we'll get a line on her that way."

"You suck eggs this way, Grandma," Colby said. His
grin was as vibrant as ever. He moved reluctantly toward the
stairs.

*One day, pal,* Fey thought, *your dentist is going to be
handling you as a trauma case.*

**F**ey was waiting outside when Colby and Harry
Carter finally came down from upstairs. Reeves had at least
done the job of stringing the crime scene tape properly the
second time around. After he'd roped off as much of the
house and grounds as he could, he had set up a second buffer
of tape a little farther out. The public and the press would be
kept behind this second buffer, but other police officers and
brass could enter the VIP area. That way the crime scene was
still protected, and yet the other officers on the scene didn't
have to mix with the general public. It also provided an area
for the police brass to preen themselves and to be seen impor-
tantly doing nothing.

Fey had checked in with Mike Cahill, who was standing
in the VIP area along with the two other detectives assigned
to Fey's homicide unit—Vance Hatcher and Monk Lawson.

Hatcher was tall and blond with a potbelly that belonged
on a stove. He favored old-fashioned polyester leisure suits,
loud ties, and penny loafers. One of his shoes had a tarnished

penny stuck in the slot. The other one didn't. Despite appearances, he had the highest clearance rate on the team.

Standing next to Hatcher, Monk Lawson looked as if he came from another planet. Shiny black skin, muscles still compact from his days as a top collegiate sprinter, hair sheared close to his skull with a stylish razor slash running through it. He wore a purple shirt with a peach tie under a lavender suit. For some reason, though, he and Hatcher got along well.

"How did the Schaffer case go?" Fey asked him as she stepped into the VIP area. She could see a lot of the neighborhood residents gathered behind the second buffer of tape. Among them she also recognized the faces of several reporters from the local television stations. Bad news didn't travel anywhere near as fast as news that could be sensationalized.

Lawson shrugged. "Pretty much a piece of cake. Our witnesses were nailing him all the way down the line. His lawyer called a time-out, took his client aside, and came to us on bended knee for a deal."

The homicide unit was also responsible for investigating ADW cases—assault with a deadly weapon. Reginald Schaffer had taken a baseball bat to his neighbor's head when the neighbor let her poodle crap on his perfectly manicured lawn. Damn near killed the woman. Did kill the dog.

"Did we cut the deal?"

Lawson smirked. "We figured, why should we? Juries don't like people who are cruel to animals. If he'd have just hit the broad, he might have had a better chance. But when Schaffer smacked that dog out of the ballpark, he signed his fate. We turned down the deal, and Schaffer copped out anyway."

"Sounds like he didn't have much of a choice."

"Rock and a hard place."

"Good job," Fey told him. Lawson simply nodded.

Fey turned to Hatcher. "How about you?"

"I got the Taylor spousal abuse filed, but the district attorney referred it over to the city attorney's office. We only got a misdemeanor count filed."

"Shit! His wife took twelve stitches under her eye from where he punched her . . ."

"I know, I know." Hatcher held up his hands placatingly. "What can I say? The DA felt it was provoked."

"Yeah, right." Fey shook her head in disgust. "She tries to stop her husband from spending the rent money on booze, and that gives him the right to pop her one? She should have known better than to provoke him, I guess. She should have at least waited until he came home drunk before making him punch her out."

"Come on, I didn't reject the filing," Hatcher said, still on the defensive. "I argued the case, but you know the DA's mentality in these situations."

"I know it, all right," Fey said. "It's the same mentality that figures every woman who wears a short dress is asking to be raped."

"How come you never wear short dresses?" Colby asked as he walked up with the coroner on his tail.

"I don't want to distract you from what little work you do," Fey retorted quickly. Monk Lawson laughed. Like Fey, he didn't care for Colby a whole lot. Monk's mother and four older sisters had always raised him to respect women. Colby's sharp tongue might score a lot of points with some of the other guys, but Lawson always looked on him with disdain.

Lawson got on well with Fey. He found her to be a fair and sympathetic supervisor. She could be tough when she had to be, but she didn't throw her weight around needlessly. Lawson also respected her because it didn't seem to matter to her one way or the other that he was black. As long as he did his job properly, she didn't send any extra flack his way.

Colby, on the other hand, had a chip on his shoulder the size of a redwood. Lawson knew it pissed Colby off to work for a woman. Somehow Colby had it in his head that it belittled him. Colby had never been directly disrespectful toward Lawson over the issue of race, but Lawson believed that sexism and racism had much in common. If Colby was overtly sexist, he was most likely racist as well—only he hid it better.

"What have you got for me, Harry?" Fey asked the dapper coroner, who was now standing next to Colby.

"I'll have more later, naturally, but right now I can tell you that your stiff has been dead for about eight to ten hours.

From the type of wound, I'd say you're looking for a weapon with a sharp point, but not a knife."

"Ice pick?" Fey asked.

Harry shook his head. "Nah. I'd say something like a screwdriver. Flat-head, not Phillips."

"What else?"

The coroner shrugged and consulted a small notebook. "The weapon was used in a slashing motion. Right to left—making your suspect most likely right-handed. Carotid artery was flayed open. Victim bled to death in about ten seconds. The suspect probably caught some blood splatter. The victim shows evidence of recent sexual activity. I may be able to tell you later how recent, and if it was forced. Other than that, the big news is she definitely isn't among the living anymore; and it's time for me to go to lunch. I have a date."

"Thanks, Harry," Fey told the coroner. Will you be handling the autopsy?"

Harry checked another page in his notebook. "I've got two others lined up for this afternoon." He thought for a moment, looked at his watch. "If you want to be there, how about tomorrow morning around ten? If not, I'll have the results typed up for you and sent over by late tomorrow afternoon."

"I'll be there," Fey said.

Harry bobbed his head in acknowledgment.

Two coroner's assistants brought the body out of the townhome's front door wrapped in a black body bag. Press cameras began to whir, and the gathering of citizens behind the second barrier began to surge forward imperceptibly. Everyone wanted to see something even when there was nothing to see. It was the same phenomenon that caused mile-long traffic jams for fender benders that were already off to the side of the road.

"What's your next step?" Cahill asked Fey.

She thought about it for a moment or two. "If you want to give the press a statement, Colby and I will go back inside and do the crime scene search."

"What about the maid?"

Fey nodded toward Lawson. "Do you have time to take a formal statement for us?"

"No problem," he replied. "I've got a couple of luke-warm leads on the Bradshaw caper to run down, but that can wait until this afternoon."

"Great. When you're done with the maid, you can send her home, but make sure we have some way of contacting her again if we have a need."

Lawson turned on his heels with military precision and moved off in the direction of Reeves and Watts's squad car.

"Do you want me to help with the search?" Hatcher inquired.

"I think we can handle it," Fey told him. "I don't want too many cooks in on this one. Can you head back to the station and get today's paperwork handled? Make sure we don't have any surprise bodies in custody." Hatcher was a detective two and therefore the unit's second-in-command. He was in charge when Fey took a day off or was on vacation.

"Okay," he said. "Do you want me to split the new cases between Monk and myself?" Aside from murders, suicides, other suspicious deaths, and ADWs, the homicide unit also investigated spousal batteries where someone was in custody, kidnappings, and various other felonies.

"Yeah. Leave Colby and me clear to work this one for a while. When we get done here, we'll all gather back at the station for a powwow." Fey looked at her watch. "Say three o'clock?"

"Sounds fair. I'll tell Monk."

Just because all of the unit's detectives were tied up investigating a fresh murder didn't mean that the rest of the unit's work load screeched to a halt. There were still citizens out there who didn't give a damn about how busy the detectives were, and continued to keep hitting each other with blunt instruments, shooting at each other, chasing each other around with knives, kidnapping each other, and basically raising hell in general. Murder took precedence, but life and crime rolled on.

Back inside the town home, Fey and Colby prepared for a major systematic search of the premises. They split up the rooms on the second floor, with Fey taking the crime scene bedroom, the master bathroom, and one of the spare bedrooms. Colby took the two other bedrooms and the guest bathroom. When they were done, they would switch rooms and check each other's work.

She felt like a voyeur as she pawed through the dead woman's bedroom drawers. Searches were the worst kind of privacy invasion—looking for dirty little secrets in the nooks and crannies of another person's life. Fey always felt there was something perverse about the process, as if she were a sneak thief rummaging around for a pair of dirty panties to abscond with.

She also had a bad feeling about the whole case scenario in general. It was too antiseptic. Almost staged. A place for everything, and everything in its place. Either the victim was incredibly anal-retentive, or she'd had the money just to go out and order everything brand-new that she'd needed to fill up the drawers and walk-ins. A life assembled by the numbers—"I'll take four of those, two of those, and three of the others. Oh, and give me a couple of those red ones over there."

The dresses in the closet were a uniform size eight, with shoes to match each outfit. None of the shoes showed any signs of wear. The clothing was expensive, mainly in blacks, reds, and maroons. There were a half dozen white blouses, an even dozen pairs of slacks, a couple of casual summer dresses, three business suits, and two formal gowns. The clothing was top quality, even down to the two sets of designer sweats.

In another drawer there was enough lingerie to stock a small Victoria's Secret. It ran the gamut from skin-flick kinky to modest weekday-labeled panties. It boasted of an active sex life, but like the clothing in the closet, the lingerie appeared brand-new.

The only thing in the bedroom that seemed to have any history was the jewelry in a large fabric-covered chest. There were a couple of unique pieces that Fey thought they might be able to trace if they had trouble getting a line on the victim.

Again, there were no address books or Christmas card lists. No compilation of tax returns or monthly bills—not even a payment book for the new BMW. Fey had a feeling the car had been bought for cash. There were no photo albums, no memento knickknacks, no used ticket stubs, no cherished stuffed animals. No detritus of a life lived.

From all appearances Miranda Goodwinter's life was as limited as that of a blow-up doll sitting on the shelf of an adult bookstore. Somebody had used her as a depository for sexual lust and then deflated her and cast her aside. There didn't seem to be anything else. She'd been alive, and now she was dead.

And dead was nothing more than simply dead.

*Who were you?* Fey asked silently again as she looked at the rumpled sheets where the body had so recently reposed.

She stripped the sheets from the bed, turned the mattress over, checked under the bed and in the nightstand. No clues, and no murder weapon.

In the master bathroom she found fresh, name-brand makeup, an unopened box of sanitary napkins, toothpaste, a single toothbrush, and various hairbrushes and assorted other products. There were no prescription drugs, no illegal drugs, and still no clues.

"Anything?" Colby asked, sticking his head in the door.

"No," Fey replied. "How about you?"

"Sterile, baby, sterile. This place has been picked whole-sale out of a catalog. The victim, whoever she was, didn't seem to bring anything with her from any sort of past life. It's like she didn't exist before she moved in here."

"Let's do the downstairs."

Splitting up the rooms again, Colby drew the living room, the den, and the attached garage. Fey took the family room, the kitchen, and the laundry room.

In the kitchen there were three glasses in the sink and a bowl of chips and dip on the counter. The dip was rapidly molding. Fingerprint powder had been splashed over everything in sight.

The refrigerator yielded milk, a couple of grapefruits, three bottles of good champagne, and a half dozen cartons of yogurt in various flavors. Not exactly the cook-at-home type, Fey thought.

The cupboards were mostly empty except for a brand-new set of pots and pans. There was a new set of glasses and an everyday set of china and silverware.

Under the sink was a trash basket. Fey spilled it out on the floor. The only thing of any real interest was two empty champagne bottles of the same brand as in the refrigerator.

A little bit of luck popped up out of a kitchen drawer that was filled with the receipts for all the furniture and decorating. Fey set those aside with the empty champagne bottles to deal with later. Who knows? she thought. They might be all they had to work from in trying to reconstruct the victim's background.

There was nothing on the notepad beside the phone. Fey ran the lead of a pencil sideways over the top sheet, but there was no residue from anything previously written on the page above.

With a deep sigh, she turned her attention to the laundry room. There was a new washer and dryer in matching pastel colors. Next to them on the floor was the first sign of normal life that Fey had encountered—a large plastic basket with dirty laundry plopped into it.

Fey opened the front-loading door of the dryer. A big fluffy white towel spilled out. Fey pushed it back in and shut the door again. She checked the washing machine tub. Empty. Methodically she checked the contents of the washing powders and soaps on the shelf above the appliances. Nothing.

Looking at the laundry basket, Fey bent down and picked through the soiled accumulation of underwear and towels.

Almost automatically she again noted that the underwear was expensive. It should have been hand-washed, not just dropped in with the towels to be run through the normal cycle. Maybe the victim was planning on separating the items later.

Fey looked at the towels again. She took off a latex glove and felt them with her bare hand. She brought a bundle of the towels up to her nose and inhaled. The commercial term "springtime fresh" ran through her mind. The towels were clean.

Feeling her pulse increase, she turned back to the dryer and opened the door again. The white towel spilled forward again. Fey grabbed it and pulled it clear.

She crouched down to look into the drum.

"Oh, shit," she said under her breath.

"**W**hat do you have there?" Colby asked loudly. Fey's concentration had been so centered that she hadn't heard him approach.

"For hell's sake, Colby!" His voice had startled her. "What are you trying to do? Give me a heart attack?"

Colby grinned. "Just keeping you on your toes."

"You're getting awfully close to stepping on them, and when you do, I'm going to cut you off at the knees."

"Oooh," Colby said in a high voice. "I love it when you talk dirty."

Fey ignored him and turned back to the dryer. Colby bent down beside her to look in as well.

" 'Oh, shit' is right," he said. With the latex gloves still on his hands, he reached into the drum and began to pull out banded stacks of fifty- and hundred-dollar bills. There seemed to be a never-ending supply.

As the stacks grew in front of the dryer, Colby turned to Fey. "What do you say, Frog Lady?" he asked. "Fifty-fifty?"

Fey couldn't quite believe he was serious. She'd felt the young, flashy detective was bent, but this was a bit too obvious.

Colby suddenly upped his offer. "Okay, you're the boss. How about sixty-forty?"

When he still didn't get any response from Fey, Colby reached back into the dryer and pulled out another handful of banded bills. "I'll tell you what. There's still a lot of money in here. How about I promise to keep my mouth shut for a seventy-thirty split? I can't be fairer than that. I've got bills to pay, you know, and an image to keep up." He reached back into the dryer again and pulled out two banded bundles that didn't contain money.

Fey's face had turned seriously red during Colby's monologue. When he turned to face her with the two new bundles in his hands, she was about to boil over.

He grinned. "A joke, Frog Lady. Just a joke," he said. Believe it or not, I've got more money than I'll ever need."

"I've told you before, stop calling me Frog Lady, damn it. You're really beginning to piss me off. And maybe you do have more money than you need, but I doubt you have more than you want."

It was Colby's turn for a reddish flush. "You may think you're a hell of a detective, Frog Lady." Colby emphasized the derogatory nickname, knowing there was nothing Fey could really do about it as long as he didn't use it in public. "But you know nothing about me. One of these days you'll climb down off your high horse long enough to see things as they really are."

"What are you talking about?"

"That's what I'm trying to tell you. You wouldn't know what I'm talking about because you've got it made. Because you're female, you get to live in a coddled little world on this job. Nobody wants to upset you in case you beef them, or pull a Franchon Blake and sue the city because you got passed over for a promotion. You just flash your legs or your tits, and up the promotion ladder you go."

Fey laughed. She couldn't help herself as the guffaws and giggles flooded out of her. The absurdity of Colby's thought process almost doubled her over with hilarity. "Yeah, right, Colby," she finally managed to gasp out as she leaned back against the washing machine. She wiped a tear of amusement from her eye. "Damn. You ought to be onstage at the Comedy Club. You crack me up."

Colby stood silent, a grim look on his face.

"You are one jealous and confused little boy." Fey actually reached out and put a hand on Colby's shoulder. "I'm sure the two women lieutenants who were my original detective oral board were real impressed when I flashed my tits at them." Fey erupted into another fit of laughter.

"Come on," Colby said. "You can't deny that the only reason you got the detective three spot in this homicide unit is because you're a woman. Everybody knows that pressure came down from the chief's office to give the spot to a female."

"That may or may not be true," Fey said, finally calming down enough to catch her breath. "But it's no different than any of the other favoritism-type promotions that go on in this or any other department. There are guys who get promoted because they go to the same church as someone else. There are people who get promoted because they've got themselves a rabbi who has been molding them in their own image for years. Others promote because somebody somewhere says we have to have a certain number of blacks, Hispanics, or Asians at certain levels. And every once in a while, someone will get promoted because they deserve the damn promotion in the first place.

"That's the real world, Colby. It's not a redneck, lily white, male-bonding, white-hoods-and-keep-the-niggers-and-women-in-their-place world anymore. And I'm sure you think that's a damn shame, but it's time you grew up. After all, you pulled a heck of a lot of your own strings to get yourself assigned to this unit and even to this case. So all this sour grapes and crying-in-your-beer stuff is nothing more than the pot calling the kettle black. As far as you're concerned, it's only favoritism when somebody other than you gets the spot."

"That's not what I mean, and you know it."

"I don't know it, because that's what it sounds like you mean."

"But—"

Fey dropped her hand from Colby's arm. "I don't have time for any more buts today, partner. Lets just get on with what we're doing. Time's ticking."

Colby didn't quite know how to respond.

Fey shook her head, a wry smile racing across her mouth. "Come on, let's call a truce, okay?" She pointed at the last bundles Colby had pulled out of the dryer. "Now, what are you trying to strangle in those poor reverse-discriminated white hands of yours?"

"Some truce," Colby said, and stared down at his hands as if he'd forgotten they were attached to the end of his arms.

After a second or two, he turned and dropped the bundles on top of the washing machine. He popped the rubber band on the larger bundle and sorted through its contents. "Interesting," he said in a subdued voice, as if making an effort to get over the emotion of his outburst.

Fey picked up the other bundle and unwound the rubber band around it. She flipped quickly through the contents. "This is another complete set of ID in the name of May Wellington. Victim's photo on the driver's license."

"Same here," Colby said, still shuffling through the other bundle. "Only the name on this set is Madeline Fletcher." He looked up at Fey. "What kind of scam was this woman running?"

Fey again flashed back to her silently repeated question. This time she voiced it out loud. "I wonder who she really was."

Colby waggled his eyebrows. "I guess we're going to have to make like detectives and find out, aren't we?"

Fey waggled her own eyebrows, as if the two of them were engaged in a Groucho Marx impersonation contest. "And let's hope that when we find out her true identity, we'll also find out who killed her."

"You must be dreaming, Frog Lady. Life is never that simple."

The cat yowled incessantly all the way back to the police station.

"We should stick the damn thing on the roof and use it for a siren," Colby complained, holding his hands to his ears.

"Have a little compassion, partner. The poor animal is terribly upset," Fey told him. "How would you feel if you saw someone you cared about murdered right in front of your eyes?"

"You can't compare how an animal feels about something to how a human feels about something," Colby grumbled. "Anyway, cats don't care about anybody. The stupid animal is only upset because it lost its meal ticket."

"You are really Mr. Sensitive. I bet you even volunteer to work off-duty security jobs protecting animal research labs."

"Screw you."

"Snappy comeback."

The cat turned up the noise a notch. Colby twisted around and flailed his left arm at the animal, who was crouched on the backseat of the vehicle. The cat lashed out and clawed Colby's hand deep enough to draw blood.

"Shit," Colby screeched. He stuck his lacerated hand in his mouth and, in a lightning motion, whipped his 9-mm Beretta out of its hip holster.

The cat was faster than Colby, however, sensing what was coming and diving for cover under the front seat.

Fey was even faster than both of them, and as Colby turned back to the front of the car, planning to stick his gun under the seat and blast the cat to hell, his nose collided with the barrel of Fey's wheel gun.

"Whoa! What the hell are you doing?"

Colby reached out as if to knock the gun away, but Fey simply shoved it forward against his forehead. He froze.

Fey was still driving with her left hand, switching her gaze between Colby and the road ahead. "If you try to hurt that cat, I'll plaster your brains across the landscape. And if you don't think I'm serious, do me the great pleasure of testing me."

The cat had gone silent.

"No problem," Colby said, finally. His face was blanched of all color, his eyes wide and shocked.

"Now, calm down and put your gun in its holster," she told him.

Moving very slowly, Colby put the 9-mm away and secured the holster's safety snap closed across the top.

Fey reluctantly lowered her revolver and then reached across her chest to shove it back into its shoulder rig. She put both hands back on the wheel before stopping for the traffic light at Santa Monica Boulevard and Butler. When traffic cleared, she turned right on Butler to cover the last five hundred yards to the police station.

Pulling into the small POLICE ONLY parking lot beside the station, she found a slot and braked to a halt.

Colby was sitting straight ahead, staring out the windshield.

"You're a fucking madwoman," he said, without looking over at Fey. His voice and tone were matter-of-fact, almost as if he were in shock.

Killing the ignition, Fey leaned her head back against the headrest. She sighed deeply. "Colby, I don't know if you are a good cop or a bad cop. I've got a feeling you could be a hell of a detective, but it's going to take a major attitude adjustment on your part."

She expected some kind of response to this, but Colby kept his mouth firmly shut.

"Ever since you were assigned to this unit, you've had a King Kong–sized chip on your shoulder," Fey told him, her head still back, her voice low. "I don't know what you have against women—maybe your mother took you off the tit too soon—but if you don't stop trying to bust my chops, you're going to find out that I can play hardball with the best of them."

Still no response from Colby. He held himself as if he were a sullen child enduring a lecture—the less response, the sooner the ordeal would be over.

Fey took a deep breath and let it out before continuing. "If you don't like working for a woman, I'll happily get Cahill to sign a transfer for you. But let's get one thing straight: You're going to go before I do. You may be some kind of a hotshot, but I've earned my stripes—whether you think so or not—and that entitles me to the same respect you would show a man in my position."

Colby still didn't look over at her. "Are you through?" he asked.

Fey sighed again. "Yeah, I'm through."

Without saying anything further, Colby opened the car door and got out. He slammed the door closed and walked away.

"Okay," Fey said aloud to herself. "I tried." She reached over to get her purse from the backseat. As she did so, the white cat emerged from under the front seat and hopped up next to the purse.

He let out a pathetic yowl.

Fey petted him. "I'm sorry, boy," she said. "Are you hungry?"

The cat yowled.

Fey knew it was stupid to think the cat was answering her, but she couldn't shake the feeling that the cat was trying to communicate in its own fashion. Her fingers scratched the top of the cat's head and received a purring noise in response.

"I'll have to figure out what to do with you later," she told the animal. "But right now I've got to go back to playing detective."

The day had turned cool and overcast, so Fey didn't feel bad about leaving the cat in the car. She did, however, take the time to bring back some water using an old, inverted hubcap as a bowl. She put the water on the passenger-side floorboards, and left the animal to its own devices until she had a chance to come up with a better solution.

Inside the station, she headed for the upstairs squad room. On the way she nodded to a few of the uniformed faces with whom she was friendly, and checked the homicide unit's box in records for new crime reports. It was empty.

Taking up almost the entire second floor, the squad bay was a beehive of late afternoon activity. Fey had come up the back stairwell that led directly into the work area. There was also a front stairwell for citizens that emptied out into a small lobby area decorated with silk trees and a large, framed flag from the 1984 Olympics. There were also several bulletin boards filled with pertinent information for citizens, including an 800 number for complaints if someone didn't get exactly what he or she wanted.

When Fey had first seen the 800 number posted, she'd finally admitted to herself that police work was never going to be the same again. Too much had happened as a reaction to the Rodney King arrest to ever let the department again become the world leader in policing that it had once been. Fey loved the job, but like many of her contemporaries, she was now looking forward to her retirement, when she could get out of the city and never look back. She'd be glad to leave it to the politicians, liberals, and hidden-agenda loudmouths to fight over as if they were hyenas stealing from a lion's kill.

The incident involving Rodney King, a black man whose violent arrest had been captured by an amateur cameraman on videotape, had literally shocked the world. The video had been shown on television over and over again, ad infinitum, until there didn't seem to be a single place in the world where it wasn't a source of dinner conversation. All cops in L.A., good or bad, suddenly found themselves trying to explain to aggressively inquisitive friends and relatives an incident that had no reasonable explanation that straights would understand.

Cops understood it, though. They might have been appalled and sickened by it, but they understood it. And while the politicians and the police brass fought one another for scraps, the working cops held their heads up and continued to do their job. Rodney King or no Rodney King, there were still crimes to solve and criminals to put in jail. The straights still needed protecting from one another.

Life and crime went on, and there sure as hell wasn't anyone else willing to jump in and do the job—*Be a cop! What are you, crazy or something? Them suckers get shot at! Shit, not me, man.*

The unprecedented media coverage of the trial of the officers who'd arrested King, the politically motivated destruction of L.A.'s police chief, and the findings of the Christopher Commission assigned to investigate the LAPD in the wake of the King incident had resulted in hundreds of knee-jerk measures like the 800 number hot line for complaints against the police.

Fey had read the Christopher Commission report cover

to cover. In her mind it made the Warren Commission report on the John Kennedy assassination look like gospel.

Behind the detectives' lobby there was a long hallway hiding several interrogation rooms, a cot room, a small cubbyhole for the division's computer nerds, and a softly decorated, nonthreatening room for interviewing rape or child abuse victims.

The other side of the lobby led into the squad bay. One end of the bay was walled off to form a good-sized room for the fraud and forgery investigators. There was another small office, with windows looking out into the bay, for the detective lieutenant in charge of the squad, Mike Cahill. The rest of the room was taken up with clusters of desks assigned to different divisional investigative units—juvenile, sex crimes, robbery, burglary, auto theft, and homicide.

Phones rang, files were filed, cases were assigned and investigated, suspects and victims were interviewed, jokes were told, coffee was poured, administrative details were handled, audits were audited, photo lineups were composed, and every once in a while a crime was solved—if you were lucky. One thing cops rarely had to worry about was job security.

Over at the homicide unit's desks, Vance Hatcher had his feet up talking on the telephone, and Monk Lawson was talking to two patrol officers. Monk raised a hand in greeting when he spotted Fey.

Dumping her purse beside her desk, she slipped out of her shoulder rig and slid it into a side drawer.

Hatcher hung up the phone. "You look fried," he said to Fey.

She dry-washed her face with one hand. "I'm okay," she told him.

"Where's Colby?" he asked.

"Off somewhere sulking," Fey said. "Actually, I hope he's gone to see if he can hurry along the FIN run on the victim's prints."

"We'll be lucky to see those before the end of the week."

"We'll see," Fey said. "Colby claims he's got a contact down at the FIN unit that can expedite things."

"Probably some little groupie who can't wait for him to get into her pants."

"Probably," Fey said. "Though only God knows why."

Hatch laughed. "He might not be your cup of tea, but I've seen him pull a few rabbits out of his hat before. If he says he has a contact, it's probably true."

"Let's hope so, for our sake."

"How's the new case look?"

"It's going to be a rough year," she told him. "It always is when the first murder is this complicated."

"You never know," Hatch said. "We might get a break."

"Unlikely. You haven't heard the half of this one yet. It's right out of the 'Twilight Zone.'" Fey plopped down into her chair. She picked up a file from her in box and checked through it. "The sixty-day follow-up on that transient John Doe is due," she said to Hatch. "Did you or Monk come up with anything further in the last couple of days?"

Hatch grunted. "It's still a loser. You know what it's like in this division. We've got the very, very rich and the very, very poor, and never the twain shall meet. Both groups ignore each other, and both are closed communities to working-stiff coppers." He shrugged. "The poor bastard who was murdered in the drainage ditch probably tried to put up a fight when some other wino tried to roll him for his short dog. The prick who did it has probably frozen to death by now while sleeping rough in the sheriff's area. We'd never hear about it, and even if we did, there'd be no way to put it together."

"Okay," Fey said. "Write it up as best you can. Let's at least keep the paperwork on schedule." She pulled out another file. "What about the Bradshaw caper?"

"That's Monk's baby," Hatcher said.

Hearing his name, Monk Lawson closed out his conversation with the two police officers and came over to join the confab.

"I think we've got enough on Bradshaw's brother-in-law, Lance White, to go to the DA," he said in response to Fey's question.

Fey could tell from Monk's manner that he was holding something back. Maybe something good for a change. The unit needed a break. "That isn't what you said last time we talked about the case," she said. "What's happened since?"

"Well, Lance hasn't surfaced since the killing. The victim's wife, Shirleen, finally broke down and told me today that she'd told good old Lance all about the times Bradshaw used to beat her, and Lance had threatened to do something if it ever happened again."

"And did something happen again?"

Monk's even white teeth appeared between his lips. "Sho' 'nuf, missy."

Fey hated it when Monk went into his simpering plantation slave act. It didn't seem to embarrass Monk, but it embarrassed her. She couldn't imagine herself feeling comfortable mocking being a woman by slipping into Shirley Temple cuteness, even for a laugh. But she realized that was her hang-up. Monk seemed to have no problem mocking the fact that he was black—he'd risen above being bothered by stereotypes. On the other hand, she thought, perhaps his self-parody was simply a deep-rooted defense.

"Well?" she encouraged, waiting for the black detective to be more forthcoming.

"On the night of the murder," Monk started, "Bradshaw split Shirleen's lip open for supposedly making a pass at some guy in a bar. Shirleen says that she and Bradshaw were both drunk when it happened, but she got pissed because blood from her lip dropped down over a new blouse she was wearing. She split with a full mad-on and went to cry on Lance's shoulder."

"I take it Lance got himself all worked up?" Fey interjected.

"Apparently," Monk agreed. "In any case, he grabbed a genuine Louisville Slugger and headed out of the house. Shirleen says that she thought he was just going to go over and put the fear of God into Bradshaw, but Lance came back about forty-five minutes later looking like the devil was after him. He threw a bunch of clothes into a suitcase, wouldn't tell her what happened, and that's the last anyone has heard or seen of him."

"Do you believe her?"

"Shit, it took me long enough to get the story out of her. Yeah, I believe her."

"No. I don't mean about what happened that night. I'm talking about whether anyone has seen or heard from Lance."

"Oh." Monk seemed to think about it for a couple of seconds. "I'm working on that. Give me a little time and I think I can get her to tell me where he's hiding. If not, we'll set up a surveillance, and I think she'll lead us to him."

"You've got motive and opportunity," Fey said, "but I still don't see it as enough for the DA."

"Ahh," Monk said, with a twinkle in his eye. "I saved the best for last. I found the murder weapon."

Fey raised her eyebrows.

Hatch took his feet off the desk and leaned forward. "You didn't tell me," he said to his partner.

Monk obviously enjoyed being the center of attention. "I have to keep one or two surprises up my sleeve."

"Okay, I give up," Fey said. "Where did you find it?"

"The murder happened on a Wednesday night, but the body wasn't called in until late Thursday afternoon, right?"

"We'll stipulate to that," Hatch said. "So what?"

"So I was looking at the crime scene photos and there were several empty trash cans sitting curbside. I checked the trash pickup schedule for that area and found out that the refuse trucks go through there about ten A.M. on Thursdays."

Hatch caught on immediately. "Between the time of the murder and the time it was called in."

Monk was almost dancing with the excitement of his discovery. "It gets even better," he said. "I contacted the refuse company and talked to the guys who pick up on Bradshaw's route. It turns out that the driver has a ten-year-old kid who's really into playing baseball. When he saw a perfectly good bat sticking out of Bradshaw's trash can, he pulled it out and kept it. He was saving it to wrap up for the kid's birthday next week."

"I don't believe it," Fey said, although it was obvious she did. "That was a hell of a piece of police work."

"The trash truck driver was real upset about having to give the bat up. He's got a whole brood of little trash pickers, and money is tight. The bat was probably going to be the only gift the ten-year-old got for his birthday. I was so damn happy to find the murder weapon, I went out and bought a bat and a glove and gave it to the guy to give to his kid. It made me feel good, but I hated to see the guy cry."

"Really?" Hatch asked.

"Yeah. It was amazing. Big old muscular guy. Big fat tear running down his cheek. The man loves his kids."

"That was a hell of a nice thing for you to do," Hatch said, impressed.

"Hey, I was just trying to do what was right."

"If you two are done with the male bonding crap," Fey interrupted, "perhaps you can tell us some more about the damn bat. You and your partner can go out and hug trees and beat war drums on your own time."

Monk picked up an SID report from his desk. "I took the bat straight down to the lab. They bitched and complained about how busy they were, but they finally came across. Even though the trash driver had cleaned it up, they were still able to find traces of blood in the wood. They match the victim's blood type."

"And how do we tie the bat to the suspect?"

"Shirleen's statement that she saw Lance take it with him when he left to go have a chat with Bradshaw."

Fey's face took on a wary expression, as if she wasn't quite satisfied with the answer. "It might fly," she said, eventually. "At least it might be enough to get the case filed. When are you going to take it over and present it to the DA?"

"Will tomorrow be okay?"

"Yeah. Keep me posted. And don't let the DA continue the case for further investigation. We want either a filing or an outright reject so we can clear the stats on this thing."

"You got it," Monk said.

"You done real good, son," Hatch told Monk.

"Absolutely," Fey agreed quickly. She wished she'd been the first to offer the compliment, but she found giving praise very hard. She had trouble with the feeling that if she praised someone for something, it gave him a license to take advantage of her in the future when a situation arose where she had to take the disciplinarian roll. There were a hell of a lot of mixed signals for women in supervisory positions over men. If you tried to be one of the boys, you were considered easy. If you took a more reserved roll, you were an ice queen. Finding a middle ground was something Fey was still striving for—if a middle ground actually existed at all.

"What about this new caper?" Hatch asked as Fey threw the files she'd been checking back into her in box. "It sounds as if it's going to be a problem."

"What do you make of these?" Fey asked. She reached into her purse and pulled out the victim's three sets of ID. The money from the dryer was in a box in the trunk of the police car. They would have to count it later and book it into evidence, but Fey didn't want to do that in a squad room full of well-intentioned but nosy detectives who weren't involved in the case.

Working his way through the cards and papers Fey had given him, Hatch passed each piece on to Monk as he finished with it. The faces of the two men were creased with concentration, and Fey marveled, as always, at how good detectives managed to compartmentalize their thought processes.

All thoughts of the Bradshaw case, or the John Doe transient, or the day's earlier court appearances and other activities, had been swept away in favor of total attention to the issue on hand. It was all very existential—each case existing strictly within its own absurd universe, unaffected and unrecognizing of anything outside of that universe—total attention to the here and now.

The ability to compartmentalize, to not be overwhelmed by the demand for attention on too many fronts, was essential to the emotional makeup of a good detective. It was, however, a trait that played hell on interpersonal relationships. Spouses and offspring often felt closed out, unable to break into the other universes that a cop kept to himself, and therefore felt ignored or unimportant. This often led to divorce or alienation. Perhaps, Fey thought, they could now lodge their complaints with the 800 number instead.

"This is unreal," Monk said as he set aside another piece of the victim's identity collection. "Miranda Goodwinter; May Wellington; Madeline Fletcher. Who the hell was this woman?"

"My question exactly," Fey told him.

Hatch had left his desk and walked over to the small cubbyhole the detectives used as a coffee room. He came back now carrying a small tray with three personalized mugs filled with steamy black liquid perched atop it.

As he handed out the cups of "cop fuel," Fey remembered the old joke about the citizen who runs up to the front desk of a police station.

"Come quick," he says to the desk officer. "There's a dead cop lying naked in an alley across the street."

Being sharp enough to think he can see through the citizen's story, the desk officer asks him, "If the body is naked, how do you know it's a cop?"

"Because he's got an erection and coffee pouring out his ears."

It was an old joke, Fey knew, because there were too many women on the force these days to make the punch line judgment valid.

"If we don't break this one fast," Hatch said, sitting down and taking a sip of his scalding brew, "Monk and I will keep on with the old stuff, and catch anything new that comes in, so you can stay on it."

"Thanks," Fey said. "But if we don't break this one fast, the lieutenant will have our heads served up on a platter with apples stuffed in our mouths."

"Won't he be happy with the Bradshaw result?" Monk asked.

"He'll be happy, all right, but it will only keep him off our backs for a short while. We had eight unsolveds out of twenty-two bodies in the division last year. That isn't a great batting average. Up until this break with Bradshaw, we've been riding a four-body losing streak, and the powers that be are getting very antsy. You both know as well as I do that my butt is on the line here."

"The unsolveds aren't your fault, boss," Hatch said, concerned. "The last four have all been nowhere cases. We've worked them to death, and with the exception now of the Bradshaw case, the clues closet is empty. Nobody could have done any more with them."

"Do you think that excuse is going to fly at the next supervisors' meeting? They're going to chew over the Bradshaw thing and then demand to know why we haven't been able to work the same kind of magic on the other cases. They won't care that baseball bats in trash cans only come along every millennium."

Hatch shrugged and turned his attention back to the pieces of identification on the table in front of him. He was actually surprised he'd been promoted as high as D-2. He knew he was a good detective, but he'd never been good at playing the promotional politics game. He also knew he wouldn't want the added responsibilities that Fey carried as a D-3.

He didn't have ambitions beyond the pride he took in doing his job to the best of his ability. He had no desire to promote, or do anything else, until he retired in another couple of years. Then he and Lorraine were going to grab his pension and take off for their retirement cabin outside of Seattle. Nothing but fishing and sipping. No dirtbags, no politicians, no "stinkers," "floaters," or babies with their heads bashed in. After a while, maybe even his nightmares would go away.

"This stuff is really good," Hatch said as he worked his way back through the papers Fey and Colby had recovered from the victim's residence. "Driver's licenses, Social Security cards, credit cards, even library cards."

"You get tired of one life and you step right into another as if you were a snake shedding its skin," said Monk. "The ultimate goal of conspicuous consumption."

"And then there's these," Fey said. Dipping back into her purse, she came out with a folder filled with other documents that Colby had found at the bottom of the dryer drum. "Birth certificates, school transcripts, passports . . ." She took the items out of the folder and spread them across her desk. "And down in the car, we still have a nice round million in cash."

Fey still wasn't sure quite what it was that tipped her off to take a second look in the dryer. Maybe it had been instinct, or perhaps experience. After twenty-two years on the job, there didn't seem to be much difference between the two.

Hatch let out a low whistle when Fey mentioned the money.

"A million in cash?" Monk asked in disbelief. "In cash?"

"Yeah."

"I haven't seen that much in cash since I was working dope," Hatch said.

"I've never seen that much in cash," Monk said. "Can I go down and get it? I just want to run my fingers through it. Smell it. Take it home and stuff it in my pillow to dream on."

"Down, boy," said Fey. "You'd never be able to get it out of the car. I've got an attack cat watching it."

Hatch laughed. "I heard about the cat. Man, was Colby pissed off at you!"

"What else is new?"

"What are you going to do with the vicious beast?"

Fey shrugged. "Barring coming across the next of kin or some relative—which in the light of all these different identities doesn't seem likely—I guess he will have to go to the pound."

"Balls!" said Hatch. "I know you better than that. You might come across like a hard-ass on the job, but I know you won't let that cat be put down by the humane society."

Fey smiled, almost shyly. "You're probably right. Constable and Thieftaker probably won't mind a cat around the stable."

"Not unless they're friends with the mice," said Hatch.

Monk was frowning. "Who or what are Constable and Thieftaker?"

"My horses," Fey said, and pointed to a photograph under her desk blotter of two well-groomed quarter horses.

Hatch picked up one of the passports from Fey's desk. He flipped through the pages before setting it down again and picking up another. "Maybe we should send this stuff over to Questioned Documents. See if they can tell us what is forged and what isn't."

"You have something in mind to do with the results?" Monk asked him. Like Colby, he was a D-1. Unlike Colby, he was always ready to learn something new.

Fey answered for Hatch. "Forgers are like painters. They

all have a distinctive style. Little flairs or special touches that indicate their work. Sometimes it's an ego thing, and sometimes it's not a conscious effort, but you can still spot the technique."

Hatch opened up one of the passports and showed Monk a page full of visa stamps. "A few years back there was a guy named Justin Otekan. He was an Englishman who was reputed to be one of the best art forgers in the business.

"Rumor has it that even museums would sometimes hire him to paint replicas of priceless paintings from their collections. If they wanted to take the original down for security purposes, or restoration, but didn't want to advertise the fact that the painting was being moved, they would hang Otekan's copy in its place. Nobody ever caught on."

"And your point?" asked Monk.

"Otekan was also known to produce perfect American passport forgeries for pin money. The only problem with the damn things was that every one of them had the same three visa stamps—Great Britain, France, and Switzerland. If you came across a passport with just those three visas, chances were it was an Otekan forgery."

"So you're saying that if we can find out which of these items of identification are actually forged, we might be able to get a line on the forger, who might then be able to give us a clue to the true identity of our victim."

"No flies on you," Hatch said.

There was a commotion on the back stairs, and the three detectives turned to see Colby swagger into the squad bay. He looked smug and pleased with himself.

Fey, Hatch, and Monk looked at him with anticipation as he stopped next to them. Mike Cahill had also seen Colby enter, and sensing something was up, he appeared as if by magic in the midst of the homicide unit personnel.

"I've got good news and bad news," Colby said, shaking a fistful of fax paper in his left hand. "The good news is I was able to get the FIN run taken care of, and there's a successful hit." He pulled out a specific fax sheet and scrutinized it.

"Can we do this without the drama?" Fey asked him, knowing he was purposely drawing out the suspense.

"Ah, here it is," Colby said, ignoring Fey's comment. It was as if nothing she had said to him in the parking lot had registered. "Eleven years ago our victim was fingerprinted after being arrested for shoplifting in San Francisco. Her name at that time was Miriam Cordell."

"So what's the bad news?" Fey asked, figuring Colby would get to the point faster if she played his straight man.

Colby's grin widened to take in his whole audience as they hung on his every word. "The bad news is that ten years ago, good old Miriam got herself murdered."

"**H**ow the hell could she have been murdered ten years ago in San Francisco and end up dead again on our doorstep this morning?" Fey kept her voice calm. The last thing she needed was Colby trying to make a farce out of this case. "Either the FIN people made a mistake, or we've got the first recorded case of two different people with the same set of fingerprints."

"The FIN people didn't make any mistakes," Colby told her. His voice held a tinge of anger. "I called them direct after finding out about the murder situation. Instead of running the prints through the computer a second time, they hand-searched the records and pulled the hard copy of Miriam Cordell's prints from the shoplifting arrest. Then they used the hard copy to do a comparison with the prints we faxed them off of our stiff. There's no question they belong to the same person."

"Bullshit!"

"Hey! Don't climb all over me, Frog Lady. I'm only the messenger. You're the big-deal detective."

"Cool it, Colby," Mike Cahill said evenly. He could

see the confrontation coming and wanted to immediately defuse it.

"What about the fax we sent them?" Monk asked. "Maybe it wasn't clear enough. Maybe the prints are close, but not exact, and comparing off a bad fax copy makes them look alike."

Colby shook his head. "No way. They said the first fax copy of the prints was clear, but I sent them another copy anyway. Same result. Miriam Cordell and Miranda Goodwinter were the same person."

"The first name, Miriam, is consistent," Hatch put in. "Miriam; Miranda; May; Madeline. All *M*s. Can't be a coincidence."

Fey shrugged, reluctant to buy in to the idea just yet. "Okay, I'll buy the prints," she told Colby. "But how did you come up with the stuff on the murder? I know that didn't come from the FIN people."

"I called SFPD direct after FIN told me the Miriam Cordell prints came from a shoplifting arrest in the Bay area. I wanted to see if they had anything else on that name."

"And?"

"And their records unit ran the name every which way and came up with the 187 report listing her as a homicide victim."

"What were the circumstances?"

"I don't know yet. The records unit could only tell me what was in the computer listing. The suspect on the murder report was listed as Isaac Cordell. Their computer also showed two other connected reports—an arrest and an arson report."

"Pretty smart work," Cahill told Colby.

"Thanks, Lieutenant."

"Wait a minute," Fey said. "None of this explains how our victim managed to pull a resurrection act only to get herself murdered again ten years later."

Colby turned to her. "I'm working on it. The detective who investigated the case retired a couple of years back. SFPD is going to contact him and get him to give us a call."

"What about the original reports?"

"They're on microfiche in the bowels of San Francisco

PD's Records and Identification Division. The supervisor I talked to there said he'd get them pulled up and Express Mail them to us overnight."

"Seems like you touched all the bases," Fey said, grudgingly. "I guess there isn't much more we can do with that angle until we get the reports or hear back from the detective who handled the case."

"What do you want us to do while we wait?" Monk asked.

"Are you and Hatch clear?"

Monk looked over at Hatch who nodded and said, "The new reports were light today. There's nothing that can't sit on the back burner for a while."

"Great," said Fey. "I want you guys to go back out to the scene and canvas the neighborhood. Door-knock every unit if you have to until we find ourselves some kind of witness. Keep a list of any units where there's no answer. We'll go back and pick those up later. Colby and I will book our evidence into property and meet you out there when we're done. Okay?"

"Sounds like a plan," Hatch said. "Who's going to start the murder book on this case?"

"I'll run it," Colby said, in reference to the job of keeping all the reports and related memos together for later reference.

"No, I'll start the book," Fey told him. "I want you to start cranking out the crime report and start chasing SID to give us anything that they came up with at the scene."

Colby looked as if he was going to protest, but he seemed to think better of it and shut his mouth with a snap.

Monk saw the action and smiled to himself as he and Hatch grabbed their jackets and headed for the door. In Monk's estimation, Fey Croaker had her work cut out trying to supervise Colby, but he also thought she was easily equal to the job.

The fact that Fey was a woman never bothered Monk, just like the fact that he was black never bothered him. He always figured that there were some things in life that were put there to challenge you. You couldn't change these things, so it didn't make a lot of sense to waste energy worrying about them. Anyway, even if he had the choice, he wouldn't change being black. And after watching her do her job, he doubted that Fey would give up being a woman despite any added challenges.

According to Monk's bottom line, the only thing that really mattered was being good at your job. He'd worked for Fey long enough to see that she was damn good at doing hers.

"Can I leave you two kiddies alone for five minutes without your pulling each other's hair out?" Mike Cahill asked, once Monk and Hatcher had gone.

"Why would you even ask that question, boss?" Colby said quickly, before Fey could get in a reply. "Fey and I have no problems. Do we?" He turned a vicious smile in her direction that no one else could see.

Internally Fey could feel her emotions flip-flopping. She didn't really understand what was behind her ambivalence toward Colby. Sometimes she could keep herself in check and treat him with nonchalance and superiority. Other times, when her guard was down, his damn inherent sexiness touched something inside her. And still other times, she felt violent and aggressive toward him.

This time her emotions settled into the latter area.

"We both have big problems," Fey told him, a cold fury at his goading escalating inside her. "My problem is trying to figure out who slashed Ms. Risen Again's throat. Yours is trying to find a psychiatrist who won't get scared off after one session."

9

**B**y the time Fey arrived home that night, she was almost dead on her feet. There was a note under her front mat from her neighbor who took care of her horses when she couldn't be there. Thieftaker had a loose shoe, and Constable appeared to be off his feed. Fey groaned and took the note inside where she dumped it on the living room table along with the day's mail. She shucked her purse and her jacket and then returned to her car to get the white cat.

Fey had expected the cat to be skittish after a day filled with extraordinary circumstances. However, after she had transferred the cat from the plain detective sedan to her own car, the animal had simply curled up on the passenger seat and gone to sleep.

Once on the floor in Fey's house, the cat began to whine and wrap itself around Fey's legs.

"I know what you want," she said to the animal, bending down to scratch its head. "You must be starved."

The cat followed her into the kitchen and kept up a constant racket of excited, if unintelligible, conversation as Fey opened a can of tuna.

All the way home, Fey had tried to decide what to call the cat. There had been no collar and tag with the animal's name on it, nor had there been anything in the victim's house to indicate the cat's moniker. Hell, there hadn't been anything in the house to indicate the victim's true moniker. It was the weirdest case of identity Fey had ever come across.

After much deliberation, Fey had decided on Brentwood—after the area where the victim had lived—as having the equal amounts of class and irony that make for the best cat names. She tried it out now as she flaked the tuna onto a saucer.

"Here you go, Brentwood," she said as she set the food on the kitchen floor. "Good Brentwood." She stroked the cat's long back as it dived nose-first into the tuna.

The cat was totally oblivious to his new name, and Fey realized she could have called him Attila the Hun and he wouldn't have cared as long as she fed him.

Watching Brentwood eat, she pulled open a kitchen drawer and took out a sealed packet of cigarettes. Fumbling with the packet in indecision, she eventually put it back where it came from and closed the drawer again. She had quit the habit two years earlier, but the urge was still strong upon her, and never more so than when under the stress of a fresh homicide.

The rest of the day at work had been a bitch. The mountains of paperwork had been waded through, the press had been dealt with, and a large amount of shoe leather had been wasted canvasing the town home complex for witnesses without success. There remained a short list of units where nobody had been home. Two of those units were close enough to the victim's residence to perhaps be of some use, but Fey didn't hold out much hope.

The facts surrounding the victim's multiple identities and the money found in the dryer had been kept back from the press. The last thing any detective needed on a case like this was a media circus. When they had more of a handle on the situation, she would give the news out to a couple of reporters who could be trusted to get at least half of the information right when it went into print.

She put a bowl of water down next to the saucer of tuna and left Brentwood to his own devices. Kicking off her shoes, Fey bent to pick them up and carried them into the bedroom. She picked up her jacket along the way to hang in the closet.

The house was a long, low ranch-style design set back against the foothills of the San Fernando Valley. There was an attached three-car garage and a half-circle drive. The exterior was a pleasing blend of red-tiled roof, adobe-colored plastering, and bleached split-rail fencing. The front yard consisted of low-maintenance flower beds filled with cacti and yucca trees, and a long strip of Kentucky bluegrass was kept in shape by a local youth looking to pick up spending change.

Fey had bought the property after her first divorce. She had married young and wrong, looking for a way to get out of one abusive situation only to find herself in another. Her first husband had inherited a successful contracting business from his father, and after two years of putting up with his fists, Fey had never felt guilty about taking him to the cleaners—as Colby had called it earlier in the day.

Once, when she'd been feeling extremely cynical, she had told a therapist that she had earned the money the old-fashioned way—with her body. The therapist had been a male and hadn't understood the joke. She never went back to see him again. The cost of earning that money with bruises and broken bones was far too high for her to waste time with someone who had no concept of that price.

The house itself had been built after marriage number two. Fey had been on the job for two years when she found herself swept off her feet by Johnny Killerman, a dashing motor cop as macho and sensitive as his name implied. There was something about the black boots, the Harley, the macho mustache, and the last-of-the-cowboys image that still to this day sent a tingle up her spine.

There had been no physical abuse this time around, but Johnny was interested in only three things—motorcycles, guns, and sex. Romance, travel, education, reading, or any kind of police work that didn't involve speeding around on two wheels was a waste of time as far as Johnny was concerned, and he couldn't understand why anyone else would be interested in those types of things.

Johnny also had a lot of trouble with the concept of keeping his dick in his pants when he wasn't at home. Fey got real tired of hearing other women talk about how good Johnny was in the sack. She also wondered about how low some of these women's standards were. From her own experience she knew Johnny to be all acrobatics and no passion, and after five years of playing mother to a man who refused to grow up, Fey packed her bags and took a walk.

She let Johnny buy her out of the house they had bought, and used the money to start construction on her current residence. Bit by bit she had scrimped and saved to complete the structure. Finally, five years later, she was able to move in.

During that time, Fey was still battling with her own emotional demons and drifted into a series of casual affairs. She drank hard, she played hard, and she kicked ass on the streets. She was one of the guys, or at least she thought she was until she realized the guys had a double standard—what was good for the gander was not good for the goose as far as the gander was concerned. A guy's reputation was enhanced by drinking and whoring, but a gal's reputation was ruined by the exact same behavior. It took Fey a long time to live down the stigma.

It was toward the end of that time that marriage number three came and went. Yank Conners was a hard-living hockey goalie with the Los Angeles Blades—a second-division farm club that was a proving ground for the first-division L.A. Kings.

The funny thing was that for all his fierceness on the ice, Yank was a fairly sensitive person when it came to relationships. He sent flowers, wrote bad poetry, made love gently, and could listen with as much intensity as he could talk.

Life looked good for a change, but then fate intervened as it so often does. The Chicago Blackhawks bought up Yank's contract and offered him a starting position with their first-division club. Yank wanted Fey to come with him to Chicago, where fame and fortune awaited. Fey wanted Yank to stay in L.A., where she had her own important career as a cop.

She could still remember the night, as if it were yesterday, when they held each other and cried into the small hours of the morning. Marriage or career? Which one was more important? Neither one could determine if they had made the right decision.

Yank had gone to Chicago, and the marriage had lasted long distance for another year before it died with a whimper instead of a bang. Yank went on to appear before sold-out houses for every game, and Fey moved into her dream house to lick her wounds. She knew now that love was possible—that she was capable of a good relationship—but she also knew that love demanded a very high price in compromise.

Yank's career had been cut short by injury, but he had found an even better niche for himself on the Blackhawks' coaching staff. He'd remarried and now had three little prospective goalies to provide for.

He and Fey had stayed in touch over the years and even saw each other whenever the Blackhawks came to town. Their relationship was one of love's strange tangents—incomprehensible to anybody but those involved. They also figured that their ongoing relationship was none of anybody else's business, including wives and current lovers.

The house had become Fey's castle. Gradually she had decorated the interior in country fashion with straw dolls, gingham kitchen curtains, wood and fabric couches, Rockwell plates, hues of rose and blue, and horse-related geegaws.

The house had become her sanctuary, the fulfillment of her childhood dreams. It was a place where she could be close to her horses, and it was a place where she could be totally independent. She often thought of it as the Land of Fey, an extension of her inner self. Lock the doors, run up the flag, and defend the walls against all intruders.

Like the rest of her house, the bedroom was neat and tidy. There were two phones with attached answering machines in the room—one on the dresser and the other on the nightstand. The answering machine on the dresser showed two messages waiting. The machine on the nightstand registered another.

Fey checked her watch. Eleven P.M. She still had time. She ignored the machine on the dresser and pressed the replay button on the machine by the bed.

"You have one message," advised the electronic voice before the machine rewound.

Fey waited.

*Beep.* "Hi, honey. I heard you hooked into a real whodunit." Fey smiled as she instantly recognized the voice of Jake Travers. "I know you'll probably be out late working, but if you get in before midnight, give me a call."

Travers was an experienced deputy district attorney. He and Fey had become close friends over the course of winning several big cases together. After losing a big one, they had also become lovers.

"If you don't get back in time," the message continued, "I'll touch base with you in the morning. The Hansen case is coming up for trial next week, and we need to make sure all the wits are ready. Talk to you soon. Love you."

The machine voice took over again. "That was your last message."

Love, Fey thought, reflecting on the message. Did she love Jake? Probably. But she loved her freedom more. Twice he'd asked her to marry him, but she had demurred. She'd been down that path enough to become intimate with its pitfalls. She was too set in her ways now, too comfortable with her life-style. She could be a friend or a lover now, but not a spouse. She loved Jake, but he would never be hanging his suits in her closet.

She knew it was still before midnight, but she had things to do. Rather than calling Jake back, she slipped out of her work clothes and pulled on a pair of jeans, an old sweatshirt, and a pair of beat-up jodhpur boots. Leaving the bedroom, she made her way to the bar in the living room. She filled a glass with ice, took a bottle of 7 Up out of the small refrigerator, filled the glass to two-thirds, and then topped it up with vodka from a bottle in the even smaller freezer section of the refrigerator.

She took the glass with her to the sliding glass door that led out to the back of the property, turned on the exterior lights, and headed out to see to her horses.

The rear yard ran back for a full acre before sloping sharply upward to meet the scrub that marked the beginning of the foothills. There was a large, partially covered patio attached to the house that extended out to surround a lap pool and a Jacuzzi. Behind the pool was a five-foot brick wall with a wooden gate at one end.

Fey let herself through the gate and into the dirt corral area. The corral was surrounded by an iron-railed fence and contained a structure of horse boxes at one end. Her two horses nickered as they became aware of her presence. Trotting over to the iron-railed fence, they stuck their necks over for their noses to be nuzzled. Fey talked softly to both animals as she slid between the rails and entered the corral itself. Patting Thieftaker, a dark bay gelding, she checked the loose shoe on his left hind hoof. She swore softly. The farrier would have to pay a visit before the horse could be ridden again.

Constable was a black gelding with a gleaming coat and regal bearing. He stood two full hands higher than Thieftaker and was a recent addition to the family. Fey patted him and checked him over to see if there was any noticeable reason for him being off his feed. His right front leg felt slightly warm. If it was still warm in the morning, Fey knew she would have to have the vet out as well. With the cost of caring for two horses, Fey was glad she didn't have kids to raise.

Kids, however, were one thing she didn't have to worry about. Her father had taken care of that problem.

After checking the feed and water bins in the horse boxes, Fey left the horses and returned to the house. She checked her watch again. Eleven forty-five. She knew she'd better hurry.

Throwing off her clothes, she turned on the radio in her bathroom to catch the sports scores. From the shower she could hear the announcer rambling on about basketball scores and college sports. Finally he got around to putting out the information that the Kings had lost their hockey game to the Chicago Blackhawks by a score of five to two.

Fey smiled as she dried herself, put on perfume, and slid into a soft nightgown. She would call Jake in the morning. A five-to-two win meant that Yank would be in a very good mood when he arrived. She went to check the champagne and fresh strawberries and cream that she'd put in the kitchen refrigerator that morning.

Life for the victim was over, but Fey had learned long ago that life for the living went on.

The following morning Fey allowed herself an extra fifteen minutes sleep. Making love with Yank always left her feeling stress-free, relaxed, and deliciously naughty. The infrequency and the secretive nature of their liaisons added spice to the encounters. They were both friends and lovers, and their relationship had survived the long term because it did not suffer from the demands and everyday stresses that normal romantic, dating, or spousal ties engendered.

Fey stretched her legs across the bed and felt an unfamiliar lump down by her feet. She opened one eye to peer down at Brentwood. The cat was perched at the bottom of the bed with his feet all tucked in underneath him. His eyes were wide open watching Fey—seeming to will her awake.

"Good morning, Brentwood," she said.

The cat yowled back.

There was a dent in the pillow next to Fey's where Yank had slept. He'd told her the night before that he would have to leave early since the team was catching a morning flight to Vancouver for another road game, this time against the Canucks.

She vaguely remembered his weight shifting off the bed while it was still dark outside. A little later, she had felt the brush of his lips against her cheek. With her eyes closed she had whispered an endearment and drifted deeply back into the land of nod.

Once out of bed, she wrapped herself in a white terry cloth robe and struck out for the kitchen. She put a pot of coffee on for herself, and put a saucer of milk down for Brentwood, who was more interested in attacking her fuzzy bunny slippers. She wrote a sticky-note reminder to pick up cat food and stuck it to her purse.

Once she had a cup of coffee inside her, she put on her ranch clothes and spent an hour taking care of the horses. Constable's leg was cool and he happily munched into his morning feed. Thieftaker, however, had not fixed his own shoe, and Fey left a note for her neighbor, Peter Dent, to call the farrier to come out and take care of the problem.

Peter was a magazine writer with three horses of his own. Like Fey, he lived alone. Fortunately, he was also more than willing to take care of Fey's animals if she had to be gone or was working overtime. It was a good arrangement that Fey always likened to a single parent's problems with child care. Domestic horses, like children, did not take care of themselves.

After showering and washing her black shoulder-length hair, Fey dried off and then stopped to examine her body critically in the mirror. At five foot nine, she was a big woman with a big bone structure. The hours of horseback riding she put in kept everything firm and toned, but there was no denying she was twenty to thirty pounds above what she would like to weigh. Jake affectionately referred to her alternately as "Rubenesque" or "zaftig." Fey figured either term was better than "chubby."

She knew her large breasts were a feature that attracted a lot of men. When she was younger, that had been important, but lately she had been giving thoughts to breast reduction surgery due to developing back problems. She'd discussed it with her doctor, but still found the idea took a little time to accept.

Still looking in the mirror, she realized with pleasure that her legs were still good and that the sharp bone structure of her face was also wearing well. Her complexion was smooth with few of the wrinkles that on a man would have been deemed character lines, and her hair held the same gleaming shine of health as Constable's coat.

Her hands, however, gave her age away. She was constantly rubbing lotion into them and regularly had her nails done, but working with her horses and spending hours in the sun had taken their toll.

Finally she shrugged at herself in the mirror. She still looked and felt pretty good for an old broad. She might envy the youth and energy of some of the rookie females on the job, but she knew all of the heartbreaks each and every one had ahead of them, and there was no way she wanted to trade places. She was proud to be a survivor.

Back in her bedroom she continued to ignore the flashing light that told her she had two messages waiting on the dresser answering machine. While she dressed, she picked up the portable phone from the nightstand and called Jake. He came on the line after the first ring.

"Hello."

"Hi, kiddo," Fey said. Thoughts of making love to Yank zipped briefly through her mind, trying to push every guilt button they could find, but she firmly shoved them aside.

"Hey! How are you?" Jake was always upbeat in the morning. "What's this I hear about you bringing bodies back from the dead to be murdered again? Don't you have enough work?"

"Apparently not," Fey said. "I'm beginning to think the

victim was part cat, and this was just another of her nine lives. She's got more identities than a successful check kiter." A night's sleep had not presented Fey with any new angles from which to approach the case. It appeared to still be a matter of plodding police work.

"Do you have any suspects?"

"Hell, Jake, I'm not kidding when I tell you we're not sure yet who the victim really was. I'm hoping the files San Francisco is sending down will provide some answers."

"Life is never dull."

"Not in this town."

"How about the Hansen case? Is our victim going to be available?" Jake asked, changing the subject.

"Yeah. I've got her stashed in a women's shelter. She's safe and getting counseling. She'll be ready when we need her." The case Jake was referring to was the third time Ned Hansen had been arrested for spousal battery. Twice before, the victim, his wife, had backed out of testifying. This time around, though, Fey felt they stood a chance.

"Good," Jake paused. "How about letting me take you out to dinner tonight?"

"That would be great," Fey said, "but it depends on which way this case takes off today. I'll call you."

"You got it. I miss you."

"Me, too," Fey said, and hung up.

Jake Travers was a good man, she thought as Brentwood made his presence known by rubbing himself around her ankles. She bent down to absentmindedly stroke the white bundle of fur. There weren't many good men around anymore, it seemed, who weren't married, weren't gay, and could put together sentences containing several words of more than two syllables. She considered herself lucky.

As she made the bed, she touched the pillow that still held the impression of Yank's head.

She considered herself very lucky.

**11**

When Fey entered the squad bay that morning, Hatch and Monk were already busy at the homicide unit's desks. Hatch was sitting in Fey's chair with a short stack of reports in front of him. He was wearing a white nylon long-sleeved shirt that even an FBI agent wouldn't be caught dead in. The shirt was stuffed haphazardly into black Sansabelt pants over scuffed black slip-ons. One of the shoes had the tassels missing. His tie was a wide orange and black abstract of the kind five-year-olds buy for Father's Day.

"What does it look like?" Fey asked him, referring to the stack of new crime reports.

"We got a couple of ADWs that need some follow-up. In one of them, the victim took fifty-eight stitches to seal up the gash in his head."

Fey gave a theatrical flinch. "Damn, what did he get hit with?"

"A jack handle. The fight took place in the parking lot of the Armory. The suspect didn't like the way the victim talked to one of the waitresses."

"Typical," Fey said. "What about the other one?"

Hatch pointed with his chin toward his partner. "Monk's talking to the victim right now. From the sounds of the conversation, it's going to be a sign-off."

"The victim doesn't want to prosecute?"

"Nah. It's a roommate squabble. Two alternate life-style types. One threw a glass at the other. The victim was mad last night, but they kissed and made up over the telephone when the suspect called the victim from jail. The victim was on the phone to Monk as soon as we walked through the door—he wants to get his buddy sprung."

"That's fine by me," Fey said, shaking her head. "Get the victim down here to sign the report off, and then get Monk to run it by the city attorney's office for a reject."

Hatch nodded at Fey's retreating back as she headed for the coffee room. When she came back with a steaming mug in her hand, Hatch had moved over to his own desk. Fey sat down.

"Anything else?"

"Nothing of importance. All the other reports are twos or threes." Reports fell into three classifications. Those with clues or named suspects were category ones, and had to be investigated and handled within fifteen days. Category twos were reports where there were no solid leads—a partial license plate or the description of an unknown suspect—and the detective only needed to contact the victim within thirty days to make sure there was no further information. Reports where there was no information of any kind to point toward a suspect were classed as category threes and were simply filed and forgotten.

Fey would never dream of saying anything to Hatch about the way he dressed. He was a good detective and an excellent right-hand man. He kept the unit's paperwork flowing and was a fountain of experience and information. Having him in the unit made Fey's job a lot easier. If Hatch wanted to dress like a reject from a thrift store, Fey had no problem cutting him the necessary slack.

"Where's Colby?" she asked.

"Down in the jail doing the paperwork on the glass-throwing ADW suspect."

Just then Monk hung up the phone. Hatch and Fey looked over at him expectantly. "The victim's coming down to sign off."

Hatch told him to run the sign-off past the CA for a formal reject.

"Why?" Monk asked.

"You know that all domestic violence cases need to get formal rejects," Fey told him.

"Domestic violence cases, sure. But this is two guys living together."

"Are they roommates or lovers?"

"Lovers apparently."

"Then it's still domestic violence and needs a formal reject. This is the age of nondiscrimination."

Monk rolled his eyes, but didn't argue.

"Oh," he said, snapping his fingers. "Cahill wants to see you as soon as you come in."

This time it was Fey's turn to roll her eyes. "Stand by, ladies. Here comes the pressure."

She took another gulp of her coffee and headed toward the lieutenant's office.

Cahill's door was open and Fey stepped through, rapping twice on the doorjamb as she entered. At one end of the large office there was a round conference table with several chairs, and at the other end Cahill sat behind a large desk. Mementos of the Marine Corps decorated the walls along with a blowup of Cahill and three police academy classmates. The office seemed larger than it was due to the wall of miniblinded windows that looked out into the squad bay.

"You wanted to see me?" Fey asked.

Cahill looked up from his desk.

"Good morning," he said. Fey felt a chill run through her as she could immediately tell Cahill was not his normal self. "Nice of you to grace us with your presence."

Fey looked at her watch. It was only eight-fifteen. She didn't usually start work till eight-thirty. She sat down in the chair in front of Cahill's desk. "What are you going on about, Mike?" she asked. "I was here until ten o'clock last night."

"Colby spent the night here. Caught a couple of hours sleep in the cot room and got back on the job."

"Bully for him," Fey said. She could just see Colby making a big production out of that major sacrifice.

"Look, Fey. We need to wrap this case up fast. I don't like the turns this thing is taking. It's close to getting out of hand. We need a couple of good clearances to get our stats up. We can't afford to have another unsolved on our plates."

"Who said this case was going to be an unsolved? We've been on it less than twenty-four hours—"

"Let me put it another way," Cahill interrupted. "You, personally, can't afford to have another unsolved."

"Mike, what's going on here?" Fey was perplexed by

Cahill's change in attitude. "Where is this bullshit coming from? First you act like you're behind me all the way, and now you're making veiled threats about pulling the rug out from under me."

Cahill put his head down wearily. "There's a backlash coming down from the brass," he said quietly. "The chief is playing 'smile and grovel' again with the mayor and the police commission. They're screaming about crime in the city as usual, and our stats are making the big chief come down on our bureau little chief, and the shit rolls downhill from there. They don't want to know why we have four unsolveds in a row, they simply want cases cleared."

"Wonderful. What do they want me to do? Find a way to make them all suicides?"

"If you can."

"Mike!"

Cahill put up his hand to stop any further outburst. "I know you're doing the best job you can, Fey. I truly believe you're the right cop to head up our homicide unit. However, this department has become more political than ever. None of us have the protection we used to have, and I for one don't want to go back to patrol as a morning watch lieutenant. Neither one of us can afford to have another unsolved on our hands."

"We may have a break on the Bradshaw case—"

"I know all about it. Colby filled me in—"

*I bet he did,* Fey fumed to herself.

"—but it isn't going to be enough if we get stuck with another whodunit."

"Okay. You're the boss," Fey said wearily. All the stress that Yank had helped her relieve the night before was suddenly right back on her shoulders. "We'll work this thing until we break it." She stood up to walk out.

"Oh, one more thing, Fey," Cahill stopped her.

"Yes?"

"Colby seems to be doing a hell of a job on this case. He's really into it. I think you need to back off him a bit. Give him some room. He might surprise you and catch a killer for us."

"Pardon me, Mike," Fey said evenly, "but I don't have time for any more of this shit."

Cahill looked like he'd been slapped.

"Now, if you'll excuse me," Fey said in the same even tone, "I've got crime to fight." She turned on her heels and walked out of the office.

The look on Fey's face when she blew past her desk, grabbing her purse as she went, almost made Vance Hatcher dive for cover. Neither he nor Monk said a word as Fey stormed by them, nor did they look up from their desks until she was out of the squad bay.

"Damn," said Monk. "That is one pissed-off lady."

"Thank God Colby wasn't up here," Hatch said. "One word out of him would have set her off like an A-bomb."

Monk looked over at the rear exit from the squad bay through which Fey had disappeared. "That much repressed rage certainly makes you understand why they used to name hurricanes strictly after women."

"Amen, partner. Amen."

Leaving the squad room, Fey walked down a short corridor with bathrooms on one side and the vice unit's office on the other. At the end of the corridor was a heavy door which gave access to a small roof area that extended over the slightly larger first floor. The station's generators were gathered together in the center of the area and surrounded by a ridiculously small running track.

Fey pulled the door open with a vengeance, stepped through, and slammed it behind her. On the roof, the generators were working noisily. So angry that she was having trouble getting her breath, Fey fumbled in her purse and pulled out a battered packet of cigarettes along with a chewed-up pack of matches. This time she didn't hesitate. Old habits die hard, and all reformed smokers have their hidden, just for emergencies, stash. She tore the cellophane wrapper off the cigarette pack as if the secret of life were contained in the interior.

Her hands shook as she had to use three matches before she could get the tip of the cigarette glowing. She inhaled and felt the nicotine rush flash through her system with orgasmic pleasure. She took a second drag—the smoke caught in her throat and she began to cough. She tried to control it, but she eventually doubled over with the hacking.

The purse, which was slung over her left shoulder, slipped off and dropped to the rooftop. Still hacking, she threw the lighted cigarette away from her as if she were casting out a demon. The pack was still clutched in her left hand, but it was now squeezed into an unusable mash of squished tobacco.

When she finally recovered her breath, she switched the pack into her right hand and wound up like a pitcher on the mound to throw the hated thing over the low wall at the roof edge. Letting it fly, she watched the pack fall about a foot short. Fey's chin dropped down onto her chest. Throwing was another thing they never taught girls to do.

After a few seconds, she walked over, picked up the pack, and calmly dropped it over the wall. She hoped somebody important would be walking past beneath her. She looked over. No such luck.

Trying to take a deep breath again, she spread her arms apart and placed her palms flat on the top of the low wall.

"Shit," she said quietly as she looked across the street at the police garage and then farther to the courthouses contained in the next block.

I'm forty-three years old, she thought, and I still let things get to me as if I were a twelve-year-old who'd been told she couldn't shave her legs yet. When am I going to grow up?

Come on, girl, get a grip. You know how the game is

played. You can't take your ball and go home. There are crimes to solve.

"Shit," she said again out loud. Taking a couple more deep, calming breaths, she mentally shook herself and turned to go back inside.

From the far side of the homicide unit's desks, Hatcher was the first to see Fey walk back into the squad bay.

"Stand by," he said to Monk. "Here comes trouble."

"Is she still mad?"

"Hard to tell. She hasn't sprouted horns or a tail, though, if that's what you mean."

Fey tossed her purse onto her desktop with a crash. It landed next to several Express Mail envelopes. Monk and Hatch looked up at her.

She shrugged. "Okay, so I lost it. Sue me."

"Not a chance," said Hatch. "It happens to all of us."

"Yeah, but you have an excuse," Fey said.

"I do?"

"Yeah. You're a male."

Monk laughed, and the tension was broken.

Fey smiled at the two detectives. "Let me get another cup of caffeine," she said, "and then we'll get down to business."

In the coffee room she filled her cup with the cinnamon coffee some brave soul had brewed up, and looked at a group of candid photos pinned to the bulletin board. All of them had been taken at a promotion party for one of the other detectives about a week before. Various rude comic captions or balloons had been added to some of the pictures. There was one of Mike Cahill caught looking down the scooped neckline of the cocktail waitress bending over his table. The caption read: "Dr. Mike checks for plastic surgery scars on his latest patient."

Another photo showed a drunken Vance Hatcher with his arm around the newly promoted male detective. The comic balloon that pointed to Hatch read: "Now that you're a real detective, we'd like to invite you to join the Tee-Hee Club. Meetings are twice weekly in the locker room."

There was also a group photo of Fey and three other female detectives all squishing together around a table to get into the picture. The anonymous caption read simply: "The Crack Squad."

Fey shook her head when she read the caption, but she didn't make any move to take it down. There would be those who found it funny, and if the caption were taken down, something worse was bound to be put in its place.

There was a photo of Colby sitting at a table all by himself. The camera had captured a fleeting look of confused vulnerability on his face. Fey took out a black felt pen and added the words: "So much time. So few friends."

Turnabout was fair play.

Colby was back at his desk next to Monk's when Fey returned to the unit. He had his head down finishing off a 5.10 form and preparing to fill out a felony package for the wife beater who had been booked overnight.

"Did the victim turn up yet?" she asked.

"Monk is having her sign off the report now. I'll run the paperwork by the CA when he's finished, and we'll have this case out of our hair."

"Until the next time he hits her."

Colby shrugged. "Or she slips a knife between his ribs."

Grunting her agreement, Fey sat down at her desk and pulled over the stack of Express Mail envelopes. She took her glasses out of her purse and slipped them into place, fitting their chain around the back of her neck.

"Okay. Here we go," she said as she saw what was in the first envelope. "These are the reports from San Francisco on the Miriam Cordell case."

Colby stood up and waked behind Fey to look over her shoulder.

"Easy, boy," Fey said, but without rancor. "I know you're anxious, but my butt is riding on this caper. I'll pass these over to you as I finish reading them."

For a second, Colby seemed to be looking for a challenge in Fey's words. Not finding any, he kept his mouth shut and returned to his desk. Before sitting down again, he carefully adjusted the fabric of his dark okra-colored slacks so the knees wouldn't bag. Fey watched the ritual, but bit back the sharp-tongued comment that popped into her mouth. As much as she hated to admit it, she needed Colby working with her on this case, not against her.

Settling her glasses in place, Fey dug into the SFPD reports. Contained within the dry jargon and unusual abbreviations, which made up the mass of most police and court narratives, was the story of a terrific piece of police work that resulted in bringing about the successful conclusion of a tough, fifty-fifty, win-or-lose court case.

By all appearances Isaac Cordell had been a successful businessman who enjoyed the fruits of his labors to the fullest. At thirty years old, he owned a string of furniture stores with his partner, Adam Roarke; had a home along the shore of wealthy Sausalito—just over the Golden Gate Bridge from San Francisco; drove a new Cadillac and docked a thirty-eight-foot Bayliner with twin diesels in the local marina.

He also had a beautiful wife—Miriam Cordell née Curtis.

Apparently, however, all wasn't bliss and roses for the lucky couple. A year after they were married, Miriam—newly anointed to the rich-and-bored—was arrested for shoplifting. Two years after they were married, Isaac—his business floundering—wrapped his wife in an anchor chain and threw her off their boat in a bid for the million-dollar insurance policy he'd taken out in her name.

The arson report attached to the case dealt with the burning down of one of Cordell's furniture stores prior to the murder. It had apparently been a clear-cut arson job. The insurance company's refusal to pay off placed Cordell in the position of having to pursue other more desperate measures to raise capital—like murdering his wife.

The detectives on the case had done a hell of a job putting the case together, but their evidence was still mostly circumstantial since the body was never recovered from the bottom of San Francisco Bay. Nevertheless, Isaac Cordell was quickly found guilty and shipped off to prison for the murder of his wife. The case set a number of legal precedents, but these soon became nothing more than discussion points or trick questions to be used by lazy law school professors.

Case closed.

Fey was starting to read through the reports again when

the homicide unit's direct phone line rang. She scooped it up a split second before Colby could get to it.

"West Los Angeles Homicide, Croaker. Can I help you?"

The voice that came back over the wire was sure and tinged with a soft Scottish burr.

"Hello. This is Card MacGregor. I'm a retired detective from SFPD. I have a message here to call a Detective Colby. Seems like he doesn't have enough work down there, so he's had to go and dig up one of my old bodies."

"Thanks for calling back, MacGregor. This is Fey Croaker. I head the divisional homicide unit down here. Colby works for me." Out of the corner of her eye, Fey caught Colby looking at her with thinly veiled animosity as she imparted this information. "Hold on for a second," she said to MacGregor. "Let me get him on the line as well."

She covered the phone's mouthpiece with one hand and gestured at Colby with the other. "Pick up the phone," she told him. "It's Card MacGregor, the detective who handled the Cordell case in San Francisco." Fey figured that having Colby listen in would be easier than trying to repeat everything later.

Colby's fist swallowed the receiver on his extension, and he punched himself into the line with the forefinger of his other hand.

"Okay, I'm on board," Colby said.

"Hello," MacGregor said again in response to the new voice.

"We understand that you retired a couple of years ago," Fey said.

"From the department," MacGregor told her. "But I was still too young to quit working altogether, so I found myself a cush job doing free-lance stuff for the insurance companies."

"How's the pay?"

"It keeps the wolf from the door," MacGregor told her. "Now, what's all this nonsense about one of my old homicide victims being found dead again?"

"Do you remember a case from ten years ago involving a man by the name of Isaac Cordell?" Fey asked him.

"Sure," MacGregor said. "It caused quite a stir at the time because it was the first time anyone in this jurisdiction had been convicted of murder without the body being recovered."

"Well, it seems that the reason your body was never recovered was because there never was a body to be recovered in the first place."

"Come again . . ."

"If fingerprints are to be believed," Fey explained, "your victim—Miriam Cordell—survived her ordeal at sea only to be murdered again, ten years later, down here in our neck of the woods. This time under the name Miranda Goodwinter."

A rusty chuckle rumbled down the phone lines. "I'll be damned," MacGregor said. "I've had nightmares about that case ever since it went down. We put it all together, but it never did set easy with me. I knew there was something not quite right about the whole setup."

"I've just finished skimming the official reports," Fey said. "Can you add the color commentary?"

"It was a strange case from the beginning," MacGregor said. "The harbor police had original jurisdiction over the case because the murder occurred within the bay, but—if you'll excuse the pun—they found themselves out of their depth pretty quick and asked us to take over."

"I take it you didn't have a problem with that request?"

"Not really. The harbor police do a hell of a job keeping the weekend boaters in line, chasing speeders, and investigating illegal dumping, but murder is pretty much out of their league. There was some discussion over whether the Marin County Sheriff's Office or SFPD was going to handle the case—since Cordell's boat was berthed out of a marina in Sausalito—but the crime took place on the city side of the bay, so we got stuck with it."

"Handling a floating crime scene must have been a new experience for you," Fey said.

"It definitely had its challenges," MacGregor agreed, in the happy voice of a grandfather about to tell a bedtime story to the wee ones. "The boat was a beauty called *The Missy* after the owner's mother—not his wife or a lover—his mother, if you can believe it."

"The owner was Isaac Cordell?"

"Yeah. A strange bird he was too. Cordell was the kind of guy who knew how to spend money, but had no idea how to make it."

"I thought he owned a chain of furniture stores?" Colby said, with a question in his voice.

"His old man, Sam Cordell, was the one who started the stores and made them successful," MacGregor told him. It was clear he didn't like being interrupted, and Fey shot Colby a glance that had *shut up* written all over it.

"Isaac had no business sense," MacGregor continued. "He took over the stores when he was twenty-five going on sixteen. There were three Cordell's Furniture stores in the Bay area, and within two years he was on the brink of bankruptcy. Had to take on a partner—I think his name was Roarke—to keep everything afloat."

"Did the infusion of cash help?" Fey prompted.

"For a while. I guess Roarke helped to run things, but Isaac was still the majority shareholder. Problems started up again, though, about a year later when Isaac decided to get himself hitched to an older woman."

"How much older?"

"Ah, there was really nothing in it. Isaac was then twenty-eight, and Miriam was thirty-three. Five years is nothing in my book, but when we were investigating the case, there were a lot of people who were casting aspersions on her for being a cradle robber."

"Why?"

Fey could almost see MacGregor's shrug over the phone line.

"I'm not sure, never having met the woman," the retired detective said eventually. "But I think it was down to the fact that she was viewed as a mercenary—a gold digger. Isaac was apparently considered one of the most eligible bachelors in the area. He didn't appear to be gay, he had money in the bank, and a lot of mothers would have liked to see their daughters settle him down. By all accounts, however, Isaac was tied very tightly to his mother's apron strings. She was a demanding old bitch, who was probably the main reason behind Sam Cordell jumping into an early grave."

"That's the Missy who Cordell named his boat after?"

"One and the same. Missy had less money sense than Isaac, and had no interest in running the business. Trying to keep her happy was probably why Isaac had so many business problems when he first took over from his father.

"Missy, however, only stuck around long enough to suck all the profits out of the business before she up and stroked out. And low and behold there Miriam was, seemingly out of nowhere, to sweep Isaac off his feet and give him another female anchor on which to cling. There was a short courtship, a civil ceremony, and then she settled in to spend any of the money Missy had left behind. There were a lot of noses put out of joint."

"You sure remember a hell of a lot about all this stuff," Colby said.

"I should," MacGregor told him. "It was probably the most high-profile case of my mediocre career. I researched the whole setup to make sure I wasn't missing anything that could come back and haunt me later. I never figured on the victim still being alive, though."

"I take it Isaac had to start borrowing against the business to keep his new wife in bubbles and Brie?" Fey asked, hoping to get MacGregor rolling again.

"A familiar story, huh?"

"I've run across it once or twice," Fey said. "Did Roarke—the business partner—know about the new money problems?"

"He claimed he didn't, but it's hard to tell. About a year and a half after the marriage, the Cordell's Furniture store down in the Tenderloin district burned down. It had been well insured, but the insurance company was screaming bloody murder about paying up."

"There was an arson report in the package that was sent down to us on the case. I take it that the report pertains to the burning down of the furniture store?"

"Yeah. It was arson, all right, but the problem was proving that Cordell or his partner had anything to do with it. They both denied the charges vehemently, but the motive was obvious. They needed the insurance money to keep the other two stores running. Both men, however, had an alibi for the night in question, and even though the arson squad squeezed a few of the local firebugs, none of them coughed."

"A dead end."

"For the arson squad. But we were able to get the case introduced into court as evidence to show a pattern of monetary desperation on Isaac's part."

"How did you slip that one by his lawyer?"

"It wasn't hard. By the time the case got to court, Cordell was so broke, he had to use a public defender. It was the PD's first murder case, and she didn't know whether she was coming or going. I wouldn't want to try it now, though. From what I hear, the woman has turned into a real barracuda."

"Good for her. What about the murder itself?"

"Isaac's story is that he and Miriam had taken *The Missy* out for a chug across the bay—"

"How the hell could Cordell afford to run a motor cruiser if his business was going down the tubes?" Colby jumped into the conversation again.

"The man was trying to keep up appearances to the very end. It was one of the things that didn't set well with me about the case. I think the guy truly loved his wife like he loved his mother—was wound around her little finger. My gut instinct was that murdering her was the furthest thing from his mind. He was trying too hard to hang on to her. The boat was due to be repossessed, his Cadillac was leased, and everything he had was mortgaged to the hilt—the house, the businesses, everything—all to keep Miriam in the style to which she'd quickly become accustomed."

"The court didn't buy that scenario, though?"

"No. My partner and the district attorney viewed the situation as all the more reason for him to want to get rid of her. And after all the other evidence was in, I had to agree with them."

"Without the body, though, it must have been a tough case to prove," Fey said, trying to imagine herself confronted with the same set of circumstances.

"Not as tough as you might expect. The circumstantial evidence was pretty damning."

"Are you talking about the million-dollar insurance policy Cordell had taken out on his wife?" Fey asked, referring to the information she'd picked up from the reports.

"That was a big part of it," MacGregor said. "The policy had been taken out a year earlier, and the premiums were up-to-date. Cordell, however, denied any knowledge of the policy. We looked into it, but everything looked in order. Miriam had been subjected to a full medical in order to qualify for the policy, and all the paperwork and premium checks had been signed by Cordell. Cordell even denied knowing anything about the account that the checks to pay the premiums were drawn on, but again his signature was all over the paperwork."

"Forgeries," Fey said.

"We certainly didn't think so at the time," MacGregor said. "But if you say the victim was still alive until yesterday, I'd have to agree with you."

"What kinds of other evidence did you have?" Colby asked.

MacGregor seemed to take a moment to gather his thoughts. "The biggest thing was probably the SOS Miriam put out over the international distress channel. She and Cordell were out on the bay when Miriam put out an interrupted message that gave the name of their boat and the fact that her husband was trying to kill her. The coast guard and half the boats in the bay converged on the scene to find Cordell in the middle of a tizzy-fit, claiming that his wife had fallen overboard."

"I take it nobody bought the story," Fey said.

"Not after the distress message. Things got even blacker for Cordell when the harbor police did an inventory search of the boat, before impounding it. There was no anchor or anchor chain on board. They also conducted an extensive search for the body, even dragging several areas of the bay, but obviously they had no success." MacGregor paused for a few seconds and there was the sound of a cigarette being lighted. Fey felt the urge surge through her body anew.

There was a long exhale and MacGregor picked up his tale again. "When the case was turned over to us and we found out about the insurance policy, the arson, the business problems, and the extent of Cordell's financial straits, we had motive coming out our ass. Then Roarke came forward and really nailed Cordell's hide to the wall."

"Roarke was the business partner, right?" Colby asked, trying to keep everything straight.

"Yeah." MacGregor confirmed. "On the day after we get the case, Roarke strolls into the office as bold as can be and tells us that Cordell had told him he was planning to do away with Miriam to get the insurance money and save the business. Roarke had told him he was crazy, never dreaming Cordell would follow through."

"I imagine Cordell denied that also," Fey said.

"Wouldn't you?" MacGregor asked rhetorically.

"It didn't appear to do him any good in the long run."

"No. The jury didn't buy the denial, and the rest of the evidence was solid. He bought himself a life sentence, and we moved on to the next case with everyone telling us what a great job we did."

"Seems cut and dried," Colby said.

"Yeah, but you haven't heard the best part."

"What's that?" Fey and Colby asked in unison.

"Well, Cordell couldn't get the insurance money, of course, because he'd been done for the murder."

"Okay—so?"

"Well, there was a second beneficiary on the policy who walked away with a cool million."

"Let me guess," Fey said, her mind jumping ahead to the various possibilities. "The business partner—Roarke—right?"

"Are you sure you're not psychic?"

"Where's Roarke now?" Fey asked.

"Your guess is as good as mine. He certainly didn't put the money into the business. He sold off the furniture stores piecemeal to pay off the creditors and then he got the hell out of Dodge."

"What about Cordell?" Fey asked. "He's going to be damned surprised to find out the woman he's spent the last ten years in jail for murdering was alive until yesterday."

"I doubt he'll be surprised," MacGregor replied. "He said all along he didn't murder her."

"Where's he doing time?"

There was a pause before MacGregor replied again. "Don't you know yet?" he asked eventually.

"Know what?"

"It made all the papers up here. Some hotshot lawyer started championing his case about a year ago—did a lot of rabble-rousing, getting people all shook up. Finally managed to get the parole board to review the case."

"And?" The anticipation in Fey's voice was clear.

"And about six weeks ago Cordell was paroled," MacGregor said, with the satisfaction of a consummate story-teller bringing his tale to a close. "He's on the street. And if I were him—knowing I hadn't killed my wife—I'd be pissed off and looking for the bitch."

**13**

"This thing is getting more complicated by the minute," Lieutenant Cahill said with a shake of his head. Fey had just finished explaining to him the details of the San Francisco murder case that she'd picked up from Card MacGregor. "It's the damnedest thing I've ever come across. What's your take on what really happened up in Frisco? Collusion between the wife and the business partner with a sort of twist on Double Indemnity?"

"Probably," Fey said. She was sitting in one of the chairs surrounding the circular conference table in Cahill's office. Colby was sitting two chairs away, and Cahill was ensconced behind his desk. "Looking at it in retrospect, you can see how all of the circumstantial evidence that sent Cordell off to the big house could have been manufactured once you accept the fact that his wife didn't die."

Fey had spent another twenty minutes on the phone getting Card MacGregor to fill in more of the details surrounding the murder of Miriam Cordell, the trial and conviction of Isaac Cordell, and the possible connections to Adam Roarke—Isaac's business partner.

At some point in the conversation, Colby had punched into another line and started furiously dialing other numbers to follow up on the information MacGregor was giving them. His first call was to the state parole board. After being shuffled around from extension to extension and listening to seven minutes and fifty-six seconds worth of Muzak, he obtained the information that Isaac Cordell had been paroled to the Los Angeles office under the auspices of a parole agent by the name of Patty Kline.

Another number brought him the information that Kline was out of her office, but Colby forced the issue and convinced the parole office switchboard to contact Kline through her pager. Between computers, cellular phones, pagers, and all the other electronic wonders of modern life, Colby often wondered how police work was ever accomplished in an earlier age. However, when he stopped to think about things, he realized that the bad guys made as much, if not more, use of modern technology as the police. It was move and countermove. Every time the bad guys came up with a new scam, the good guys had to find a way to outmaneuver it. Electronic gizmos only made the scams more complex. They didn't change the face of crime—it was still nothing more than an attempt to get something for nothing, no matter what the cost to someone else. It was the job of the police to turn "nothing" into a very high price. Cops and robbers. Robbers and cops. It was all a balancing game played on a very high wire—except the scales were tipping. The current score was ROBBERS and cops, and if the game didn't turn around soon, civilization would fall off the high wire and be surprised as hell to find out there wasn't any safety net below.

Kline surprised Colby by returning his call within five minutes, which indicated that she must be new on the job—most old-timers would have ignored the page, or at least waited till the second or third call. On the phone, though, Patty Kline was efficient and no-nonsense. She immediately grasped the significance of what Colby was telling her and swung into action.

She told him she was already on the way into her office. She would fax Colby the file photos of Cordell as soon as she could get her hands on them, and then she'd head over to the station to help with further follow-up. Colby thanked her. He also thanked the Lord for small blessings in the shape of people who still cared about what they did.

Cahill sat at his desk thinking. Colby had filled him in on the facts surrounding Cordell's parole and current residence in a halfway house in the southeast end of the division known as The Hood.

"Shit," said Cahill after a minute. "There's a hell of a lot of loose ends. We know anything about this lawyer who swung Cordell's parole?"

Fey shrugged. "Not yet. MacGregor said her name is Janice Ryder and put her somewhere in her early thirties. Said she'd made a name for herself in the San Francisco public defender's office before switching hats to the district attorney's office and finally to private practice. MacGregor has been on both sides with her and said he liked it a lot better when they were both on the same team."

"When did she hook into Cordell's case?"

"According to MacGregor again, it was about a year ago—right after she went into private practice. She must have been doing it *pro bono* because Cordell didn't have anything left after fighting his case the first time around. She finally won the parole judgment about six weeks ago—"

"—And the next thing you know, the wife he supposedly murdered turns up dead under another name not five miles away from the parole halfway house where Cordell is living."

"Stinks, doesn't it?"

"Like a wet hound dog." Cahill gave away some of his good-ol'-boy origins. "What about the business partner?"

"We don't have a line on Roarke yet. However, if he's still around and found out about Cordell being paroled, he could have panicked and done the victim in for real this time to protect himself."

"It looks like the broad herself— What name was she using?"

"Goodwinter."

"Yeah, whatever. Anyway, if it's like you said, and

Goodwinter only slipped into this new identity a few weeks ago, she could have also known Cordell was out and changed identities to make sure he couldn't find her."

"Then why didn't she clear out of town?" Colby asked.

Cahill shrugged. "Who knows? Maybe she just knew he was paroled and had no idea he'd been relocated to L.A."

Fey stood up and began gathering together the papers in front of her. "Well, we aren't going to solve this thing sitting here guessing. Like Mike said, there are too many loose ends. So we better get our butts in gear and start running them to earth. Is the parole agent here yet?"

Colby nodded. "She came in about ten minutes ago. She's ready to go over and do an unannounced parole check on Cordell and search his pad. We're invited along."

"I love it," said Fey. "No warrant necessary when a suspect is on the yo-yo string of parole."

"It's one of the few breaks we've still got in this game," agreed Cahill.

There was a knock at the door to Cahill's office and Monk Lawson stuck his head around the door. His grin was wide and white. "Bingo," he said, and stepped completely into the room.

He held up the six-pack photo lineup he and Colby had put together when they had received the faxed photo of Isaac Cordell. Cordell's picture was nestled in the number two position, surrounded by five look-alikes. It was a bleak photo, but of surprisingly good quality for having come off the fax machine.

When Fey had first seen the head-and-shoulders shot, she realized that mama's boy Isaac had picked up some habits in the pen that Missy probably wouldn't have approved. He had been a big man to begin with, and now he was prison-big—pumped up by empty hours of pushing iron and doses of smuggled steroids. The frame of the six-pack covered up the "white power" prison tattoo on Cordell's massive chest that indicated the choice he had made to survive in a world not of his own choosing.

"I tracked down the other guards that work the shack in front of the victim's condo complex as well as roving security," Monk said. "Unfortunately none of them were able to identify Cordell."

"That's too bad," Fey said. "It would have been nice to come up with someone who could place Cordell at the scene."

"We have," Monk reported with a smile.

Fey looked confused. "But you said—"

"I said the guards couldn't identify him, but I found someone else who could." Monk smiled again. "I did a door-to-door again through the complex and found a neighbor—an old lady who watches the street like a hawk. She picked Cordell out of the lineup without any trouble, and she can place him at the scene on the night of the murder."

"Damn good work," Fey said, beating Cahill to the punch this time.

The three detectives looked at their boss.

"Pull him in," Cahill said, after a beat. "Take the full team . . . and wear your vests."

**14**

When Etta Cinque opened the door of her two-story boardinghouse, she immediately knew it was "the man" standing on the doorstep.

"Whaa choo wan?" she asked Colby, breathing whiskey fumes into his face.

Colby hadn't been prepared for the vision of womanhood who now stood before him. He figured Etta had to tip the scales at close to 350 pounds, and at just over five foot in height, she was almost as wide as she was tall.

The landlady's skin was a deep, shiny black with dark purple highlights that clashed horribly with her bright orange housecoat. She wore an ill-fitting wig above day-old makeup, and she hadn't taken a bath in over a week because she hated fighting her own weight getting in and out of her showerless tub.

Etta ran the boardinghouse as a halfway home for ex-cons trying to readjust to society. The state paid her a monthly fee, and her boarders were also required to come up with bucks of their own to make up the rest of the rent. The situation kept Etta well stocked with microwave dinners, chocolate, and whiskey, but that didn't mean she always felt like cooperating with representatives of the hand that fed her.

"I ax you whaa choo wan, white boy. Whaa the man wan here?"

"We want to speak to Isaac Cordell," Colby told her, reading all the trouble signs that were flowing out of Etta's hostile presence. "We understand he rents a room here."

"You can unnerstan whaaever you wan, but you ain't comin' in here witout no warrant."

"I'm afraid you've been watching too much TV, lady," Colby said coldly. "We don't need a warrant. We have Mr. Cordell's parole officer with us. She can search Mr. Cordell's room at any time—"

"Colby!" Fey yelled from behind him.

Her shout was unnecessary. As soon as Colby saw Etta start to close the door, he slammed his shoulder into it. The speed of his reaction caught Etta off guard, and when the door smashed into her, she staggered backward like a wayward bowling ball hunting out the gutter.

"Which room?" Colby demanded as he blasted across the threshold.

Patty Kline answered in a shout from behind Fey. "Second floor. Third door on the left." As Cordell's parole officer, she'd been on the premises on two prior occasions.

Fey followed Colby into the residence and was right behind him as they pounded up the rickety stairs that led to the second floor. The house was dank and dark, smelling of greasy food and human sweat with an overlaying odor of cat piss.

Hatch and Monk had remained outside the house—Monk in front, and Hatch to the rear. It was a standard setup. They knew they had to cover all the exits because ex-cons were ever unpredictable. Even if they weren't wanted for anything, they would run on the slightest provocation. It was a survival instinct gained through osmosis while in the pen.

Once on the hallway landing, Colby moved quickly to one side of Cordell's door. His right hand held his 9-mm in the low-ready position. With his left hand he tried the door handle.

Locked.

Fey eased past Colby and took a covering position on the other side of the door. Her .38 was out of its shoulder holster and nestled in her left hand. Before leaving the station, she'd changed into jeans, a sweatshirt, tennis shoes, and a police raid jacket for the job. A wide leather belt around her waist supported handcuffs, speedy loaders, a can of tear gas, and her rover.

Knocking sharply on the door with the knuckles of her right hand, she called out, "Cordell! Police officers! Open the door!"

There was a loud scuffing noise from the other side of the door. Without waiting for anything further, Colby placed himself in front of the door, raised his knee, and kicked out. His Italian loafer slammed into the door just above the lock. The force of the kick tore the sole half off the soft leather shoe while splintering the doorframe as the dead bolt burst loose. The door sprung in two inches before coming to an abrupt halt as it banged against a hidden obstacle.

"He's got it blocked with a dresser or something!" Colby yelled. He hit the door with his shoulder, but it only gave another inch. "Shit!" he said as a splinter of wood tore a hole in his jacket.

The sound of breaking glass came from inside the room.

"Don't be an idiot, Cordell!" Colby called out to the man inside the room. "Give it up!"

Fey keyed the transmit button on her rover. "Hatch! He's coming your way."

Colby hit the door again, but it still wouldn't give. Turning, he started back down the stairs again and ran smack-dab into the awesome bulk of Etta Cinque. This time she was ready for him, and Colby bounced off her as if he'd been hit by the entire L.A. Raiders' front line.

"Get out of the way!" Colby yelled. He waved his gun at her, but it had no effect.

"Yoo don be comin' inoo my house, Mr. Man, an thin yoo can kick stuff aron an' get away wit it. Mr. Cordell's a decent man, an yoo got no cause to be messin' wit—"

Colby sunk his fist into the fat woman's stomach. The whiskey fumes almost blew him off his feet as air belched out of Etta's mouth.

Etta whooped for oxygen, but didn't move.

Colby hit her again, but she just smiled viciously before smacking him backward with a swipe of a fleshy arm. Colby went ass over teakettle and crumpled on the stairs.

Fey had seen the start of the confrontation, but had left Colby to it. There wasn't room enough on the stairway for all three of them, and meanwhile Cordell was getting away.

Turning back to the hallway, she ran to the door next to Cordell's. This one was unlocked, and she entered it on the run with her gun up and ready.

The stale smell of sweat and marijuana in the room was like an almost overpowering physical force. On a camp bed across one wall a thin body was flopped out oblivious to the commotion swirling through the boardinghouse. Fey spared the body a quick glance and then moved directly across to the window that looked out across a back alley. It was painted shut.

The rover that she had slid back into its belt holder crackled with Hatch's voice. "He got by me. The bastard is running southbound in the alley. I got cut by falling glass, and he got by me. I need an ambulance."

Fey swore loudly. The body on the bed didn't move. Incongruously Fey wondered if they didn't have another dead body on their hands. Pulling the rover from her belt again, she keyed the mike. "Monk!" she yelled. "Get a broadcast out and get to the back of the house to cover Hatch. Do it now!" She didn't wait for a reply. Instead she threw a disgusting pile of clothing off a metal folding chair standing in a corner of the room. Grabbing the back of the cleared chair with both hands, she swung it hard into the glass of the window, sending crystal shards on all directions. It was only after she'd completed the action that she realized she was probably raining more glass down on top of Hatch. "Son of a bitch!" she yelled at herself.

After quickly clearing as much glass as possible from the window frame, she tossed the chair aside with a crash and internally gathered her nerve. If Cordell could survive the jump, so could she—even if the big four-O had come and gone. Without stopping to think further, Fey put one foot on the windowsill and launched herself into the air.

The ten-foot drop came to a jarring halt that sent spasms through her knees that she knew she would feel for weeks. Following her momentum, Fey rolled forward onto her right shoulder and came up into a limping run. Her .38 was in her hand and fire was in her heart.

A quick glance to her side revealed Hatch on the ground under Cordell's window. He was holding a bloody arm, and there was also a long gash down the side of his face dripping blood everywhere.

"It looks worse than it is," Hatch said, in response to her unasked question. He could tell Fey didn't believe him, and changed tacks. "I'll survive," he said grimly. "Just get the bastard!" With a bloody finger, he pointed in the direction Cordell had taken. "Be careful. He's a big mutha."

"Fuck careful!" Fey said, and moved away.

After a hundred yards her breath began to rasp through her throat, and her legs were beginning to feel like jelly. She usually rode her horses three times during the week and both weekend days. The activity kept her firmed up and fit, but it did nothing to get her in the kind of physical shape demanded by this kind of pursuit.

The alleyway behind the boardinghouse was a rabbit warren of carports, apartment back entrances, and cross-alleys. A dog barked hysterically somewhere to Fey's left, and she cut between two buildings in the direction of the noise.

Trash and rotting garbage were strewn everywhere. Above her, the buildings seemed to fold in on themselves as if they were being bowed and ravaged by some kind of internal cancer. The daylight diminished and the world rapidly became a strange gray color. Several black children looked at her in wonder as she ran past. Their mothers, sensing danger from the white man's world, yelled at the children to "Get your butts inside!"

A cat screeched and flew out of nowhere to skitter across her path and disappear. Fey almost capped off a round at the damn thing as her heart leapt into her throat.

As she ran on, adrenaline pumped unchecked through her body, sharpening her brain, slowing down the world around her, and putting her into the zone—a natural danger high that is more addictive than any drug. The only sound she could hear was the pounding of her own biological pulses. Breath wheezed and staggered in and out of her lungs as if she were an ancient crone with a four-pack-a-day habit. Her gun was up and ready, and her eyes almost filled her face as her peripheral vision worked to the maximum.

She caught movement to her left.

A garbage can crashing down toward her.

Turning and throwing up her gun hand, she deflected the blow slightly. The impact, however, still drove her to her knees and numbed her arm. Her gun exploded out of her grasp like a startled hawk taking flight.

She rolled instinctively to her right, but she wasn't quick enough to escape the kick that smashed into her ribs. She grunted and kept rolling, eventually coming to her knees with her arms held out defensively in front of her.

"Shit, you're a woman. They sent a fucking woman after me."

Shaking her head, Fey focused on the speaker and saw that Isaac Cordell was even bigger than what she had anticipated from his mug photos. His naked chest rippled with smuggled steroid and jail-built muscles above a pair of jeans that rested easily on slim hips before running down to his bare feet. A wide belt was looped through the jeans, with a large buckle cinched at the center.

Cordell had stopped his advance, which gave Fey time to stagger to her feet.

"They sent a mother-fucking woman after me," Cordell said again.

Fey ignored his outrage. "Give it up, Cordell," she said shakily. "Just turn around and put your hands behind your back."

Cordell actually laughed. "No fucking way I'm letting a woman take me in." He suddenly lashed out with an apelike arm that connected solidly with the side of Fey's head.

Her body dropped to the ground like a stone, and her head felt like it had been turned around on her neck. What happened to the mama's boy Card MacGregor had told her about? This guy was a maniac.

Sluggishly she tried to scramble after her gun, yelling out abuse at Cordell that was lost in the drone from the police helicopter doing a low pass overhead searching for Fey. She felt herself punched in the back and dropped flat on her stomach again. Cordell started to work her over with his feet. If he had been wearing boots or shoes, he probably would have killed her.

Forgetting the gun, Fey went into survival mode. If she could just hold on, help would be there quickly.

Quickly, however, might not be quick enough to save her life.

Fey rolled away from the kicks and kept rolling until she slammed into the wall of a surrounding building. Calling on every nuance of strength she had left, she pushed herself upright and turned to face Cordell with the building wall behind her.

"Come on, mother-fucker," she said, tasting blood at the back of her throat.

"Feisty little bitch, ain't you?" Cordell said, an evil smile turning up the corners of his mouth. He was advancing toward her—a hulking mass of brawn on the move. His short, red brush cut capped a melon face full of malice and prison carbohydrates. The body of an ape that God had decided to turn into a man at the last moment.

Fey noticed two things simultaneously. The first was the fact that the police helicopter had moved away. It was still circling, but it had moved away from the air space directly above.

Cordell had noticed as well.

"Stupid muther-fucks don't know where you are, do they?" he said. His voice was calm, tinged with amusement.

Fey felt for the rover on her belt, but when she pulled it out she saw that the battery pack on the bottom had twisted off during one of her violent meetings with the ground. The thing was useless. Less than useless actually, because she couldn't even think of a way to use it as a weapon.

She thought of trying to bluff—key the mike and request help as though the rover still worked. The idea, though, was abandoned while only half-formed because it was clear from Cordell's expression and laughter that he knew the score.

The second factor that Fey had picked up on was the fact that Cordell was no longer running away. His demeanor had changed from flight to fight. Somehow her being a woman had triggered a violent response in Cordell that she knew she was going to live to regret.

"I thought all you cops ran in packs," Cordell said, still not advancing toward her. Fey was breathing heavily and didn't bother to respond. She watched Cordell cock his head sideways to look at her as if he were a curious cocker spaniel. "Yet here you are, all on your little lonesome. A gift to me."

Fey knew she'd been stupid to run after Cordell alone, but she'd thought Colby would soon be on her trail. Etta must have proved more of an obstacle than anticipated.

"Fuck off," Fey said. She tried to move along the wall, but stopped as Cordell moved to shadow her.

The big man's face had clouded over. "You better watch your mouth, bitch. I'm not going to take that kind of shit off of you or anybody. You bastards railroaded me, and I'm going to make it my life's work to fuck up as many of you as I can. If you're lucky, I may let you live."

Fey kept trying to think of ways to stall. If she could keep Cordell talking, surely help would get there soon. She listened for the police helicopter, but it seemed farther away than ever.

"If you don't give it up, Cordell, you're just going to make things that much worse for yourself."

"Things can't get any worse than what I've been through," Cordell said. He took a step toward Fey. "Boo!" he said, flinging his arms out at her without making contact. She flinched backward. Cordell laughed. "I'm through listening to women. Women have fucked me over my whole life—my mother, my wife, my fucking parole agent, all of 'em. Now it's time I fucked 'em back."

"What about your lawyer? The one who got you paroled?"

"Fuck her too!" Cordell yelled.

He charged at Fey. She tried to sidestep, but her legs and feet wouldn't coordinate. Cordell slammed his shoulder into her and drove her back into the wall of the building. Consciousness started to fade as Fey slipped down to her knees. From far away she heard Cordell talking to her. "Yeah, baby, that's a nice pose. Just like the love canal boys in prison. I'm going to fuck that pretty mouth of yours and then I'm going to turn you around, break you open like a shotgun, and fuck you in the ass—just like they did to me in prison—only there was seven of them there for my initiation."

Fey felt a huge hand take the top of her head in a solid grip. She heard the sound of a zipper being pulled down and opened her eyes to see the length of Cordell's erect penis in front of her face. It bobbed up and down slightly as Cordell flexed his sphincter muscle.

She looked up, suddenly feeling she was ten years old again. Through the fog in her brain she saw her father's face transposed over Cordell's features.

She heard her father's voice as clear as it had been all those years ago. "You're a bad, filthy little girl. You're making Daddy have to punish you again. You'll suck my dick and like it. And if you tell anyone, I'll cut your little brother's dick off. You wouldn't want that to happen, would you?" The harsh voice would gradually soften slightly. "Come on. Show Daddy that you're his favorite little girl."

The male stench of Cordell's unwashed crotch swept into Fey's nostrils as he pushed his penis into her face. She felt sick to her stomach.

"You're going to suck it and like it, bitch." The words were her father's, but the voice this time was Cordell's.

Rage overflowed from somewhere deep in the primeval recesses of Fey's soul. Anger exploded through her veins as if it had burst through a dam.

Fear. Frustration. Confusion. Pain.

Hatred.

Fey remembered the vow she'd said every time her father had violated her: *never again, never again.*

She'd been too small and helpless to keep that vow when she was ten. But the years had made her stronger. She had survived, and eventually her determination to never again allow herself to be abused, debased, or shamed became an unbreakable vow.

*Never again. Never again.* The words filled her being as Cordell pushed his penis toward her face again.

"Open your fucking mouth, bitch, or I'll kill you right now!"

With a power born of sheer determination, Fey stiffened the thumb of her left hand, took a deep breath, and drove its sharpened nail deep into the base of Cordell's scrotum. The big man's scream matched the decibel count of Fey's own explosion of sound as she brought forth a scream from the center of her childhood pain.

As Cordell doubled over, Fey smashed the palm of her other hand into the center of his face. His nose splattered flat and blood spewed in a long arc across the ground. The attacker had suddenly become the attacked, and Cordell had no idea which way to turn to get away from the Jekyll and Hyde of the helpless rabbit that had instantly turned into a wildcat.

Coming to her feet, Fey viciously kicked out into the side of Cordell's left knee. The power of the kick tore ligaments and buckled the knee like a tree snapped by a hurricane. Giving no respite, Fey slammed a palm into Cordell's shoulder and spun him around. Knowing that her next action would be considered deadly force, she hesitated for a split second before wrapping her right elbow under Cordell's chin and then locking up the carotid choke hold by placing her left arm behind Cordell's neck. As she squeezed her arms together, the carotid arteries on either side of Cordell's neck were shut down, effectively stopping the flow of blood to his brain. Within seconds, the big man was flopping around like a dying fish. His bowels evacuated as his eyes rolled up in his head and consciousness fled.

When she was sure Cordell was out, Fey released the hold, rolled her prisoner over on his stomach, pulled the handcuffs from the back of her belt, and used them to secure his hands in the small of his back. When she finished, her strength deserted her and she slumped down onto her knees beside Cordell.

Where the hell was Colby? she wondered. Where the hell was anybody in a blue uniform?

She swore a bitter blue streak, but inside her soul a little ten-year-old girl was smiling.

Her vow remained unbroken. *Never again. Never again.*

**15**

Colby came running full pelt around the corner of the building nearest to Fey. His gun was in his hand and his face was pale except for an ugly, red welt over one eye. His usually immaculate hair was mussed and his sartorial elegance was a thing of the past. As he ran, the sole of one Italian loafer flapped up and down like something borrowed from a circus clown.

He slowed as soon as he saw Fey. Finally stopping next to her, he bent over at the waist and put his hands on his knees to catch his breath.

"You look like hell," he said after a second. His voice was as casual as he could muster under the circumstances.

"And you're a day late and a dollar short," Fey rejoined. "And you don't exactly have a whole lot of room to be talking about appearances." Fey's tone held the same casual note as Colby's, but for once there wasn't an underlying malice in their exchange.

Colby took a closer focus on Fey and saw the extent of her condition. "Are you okay?" he asked.

Fey tried to stand up and grunted before staying slumped down on top of Cordell. "I don't know," she said. "There's more of me that hurts than doesn't."

Colby pulled the rover off his belt and spoke rapidly into

it. Almost immediately the sound of the police helicopter increased as it finally pinpointed Fey's position with the help of Colby's directions and moved overhead. Colby continued talking into the rover until a black-and-white unit arrived on the scene, followed rapidly by an ambulance. The uniformed officers took custody of Cordell—throwing him none too easily in the back of the patrol car—and the ambulance attendants took custody of Fey.

A detective car pulled up containing Monk Lawson and Patty Kline. They both exited the vehicle and walked over to where Fey was being attended to by a paramedic.

"How is Hatch?" Fey asked.

"He's fine," Monk said. "They took him to the hospital for stitches, but the ambulance crew seemed to think he'd be okay."

"Great— Ouch! Watch it," Fey said to the paramedic who was poking her in the ribs. "Who trained you? Quasimodo?"

"Yeah, but I could never get used to wearing a hump," the paramedic replied as he continued to probe.

"Just what I need," Fey said, "a comedian."

The paramedic finished taking her vital signs and pulled the sethoscope out of his ears. "We're going to put you on the stretcher now and take you to the hospital," he told her as he waved his partner over.

"Like hell you are," Fey said. "I hate hospitals."

"Don't be stupid. You may have internal injuries, and I'm pretty sure a couple of your ribs are cracked or broken."

Fey grunted. "Just tape me up, damn it. I'll survive. I'm not going to the hospital."

"Fey—" Colby started in to change her mind. He was sorry Fey had been hurt, if only because someone might question why he hadn't been around to back her up, but he figured she deserved what she got. She was the one who took off by herself, trying to do a man's job. And if she was made to stay in the hospital, it would certainly get her out of his hair.

"Shut up, Colby," Fey cut him off. "I don't need a wet nurse. I caught the mother-fucker, and it's my responsibility to clean him." Fey could already hear the gears turning in

Colby's mind. If she was in the hospital, he'd quickly find a way to make everyone think he'd made the arrest.

"Come on, partner," Colby said, consciously not using his favorite Frog Lady tag. "You're taking this macho thing too far. Nobody is going to look down on you for going to the hospital."

"Would you go?" Fey asked him. She was having trouble keeping the pain and anger out of her voice.

Colby opened his mouth and then closed it. He didn't have a comeback to that question. Fey was staring at him, and he finally answered her with a shrug.

"Case closed," Fey said. She turned back to the paramedic. "Tape me up and I promise if things get too rough, I'll check myself into the hospital."

The paramedic surprised Fey by sticking a needle in her arm.

"Ouch!" she said again, and a few seconds later she was out like a light.

"Look at that," the paramedic said calmly. "Guess we'll have to take her in and get her checked out."

Colby shook his head. "She is going to be pissed at you when she wakes up."

"At least she'll wake up," the paramedic said. "This lady is in a lot of pain. She needs X rays, and I want a doctor to make sure she isn't in any danger. You cops all think you're immortal."

"Haven't you heard?" said Colby. "Being immortal is a prerequisite to get on the department." Actually, the way he felt, Colby wished he were the one lying on the stretcher.

The following morning Fey was already in the office when Monk and Hatch arrived. Even with her ribs taped up, she felt as sore as hell. A dark bruise ran down one side of her face, emphasized by a purple shiner.

"What the hell are you doing here?' Hatch asked. "You look like you've been dragged through a hedge backwards."

"Don't give me a bad time," Fey said. "You look just as bad as me, and you're here." Fey felt like wincing when she looked at Hatch. There was a white plaster running down the side of his face, hiding the stitches underneath, and his sleeve was rolled up to expose the thirty-two stitches along his arm. "How many stitches did they put in your cheek?" she asked.

"Eighteen," Hatch said. The plaster made his mouth move awkwardly when he talked.

"Are you going to need plastic surgery?"

"Nah. Lorraine says she thinks scars are sexy. She's always wanted to be married to a pirate." Lorraine was Hatch's third wife. Ten years younger than him and a sexual dynamo who left him wrung out but happy almost every night. Nobody had thought the union would last, but the honeymoon had been going on for three years now with no cracks in sight.

"Did you get Cordell booked and squared away last night?" Fey asked, turning toward Monk.

"Yeah. Colby and I took care of it," Monk said. "Colby booked him, and I did the reports."

Fey nodded. "Did Colby interrogate him?" The thought pissed Fey off a little because she had wanted the first shot at talking to Cordell.

"We left him to sweat for a while in an interview room, but the second Colby went in to talk to him, Cordell started yelling for a lawyer. Refused to waive his rights before they were even read to him."

Fey thought for a second. "Did he ask why he was being arrested?"

"I don't think so."

"That's interesting," Fey said. "The DA might be able to make something out of it." She was a firm believer that the things suspects didn't say were almost as important as the ones they did.

"I don't think we'll need to worry about getting a statement from Cordell, though," Monk said with a grin.

Fey raised her eyebrows. "Why not?"

Monk stretched out the suspense by not answering. He looked at Hatch with a huge black-and-white minstrel smile.

"Come on, damn it, give," Fey demanded. "I'm not up to playing games."

"We recovered the murder weapon in Cordell's room," Monk told her.

"No shit?" Fey said.

"No shit. We went back to his pad with Kline, the parole agent, and did a search under her authority. Colby was poking around in the closet and recovered a tool chest. Inside was a flat-head screwdriver that was caked with blood and skin."

"No way," said Fey in disbelief. "You're yanking my chain."

"I'm not," said Monk with a laugh. "It's no lie."

"How could anybody be so stupid?"

"Nobody said you had to be a rocket scientist to commit murder," Hatch said. "He obviously didn't kill the woman the first time, so maybe catching up with her was just a coincidence and he killed her in a fit of rage without planning it out."

"I don't like coincidence," Fey replied thoughtfully. "I guess it could have happened that way, but I don't like the feel of it."

"If criminals didn't fuck up, we wouldn't catch them."

"Yeah, I know. But keeping the murder weapon in your room?"

Hatch and Monk both shrugged.

"Has the lab returned anything positive on the screwdriver yet?"

"You must be kidding," Hatch said. "Even with the rush we put on the damn thing, the earliest we'll hear anything is this afternoon."

"Fingers crossed then, and let's hope it's good news when it comes through."

There was a clattering on the back stairwell and Colby breezed into the squad room.

"Hey, Frog Lady," he said in surprise when he spotted Fey. "I see you talked them into letting you out."

"Not quite," Fey said. "They took my clothes away, but I mugged a nurse for her uniform and discharged myself."

Colby laughed. "How you feeling?"

"Like a dog trying to poop in the rain—miserable. But I'll get by. How about you?"

Colby nodded. "About the same," he said. "That fat bitch could sure throw a punch, and my clothing bill will add up to about the same as your hospital bill."

"My heart bleeds," Fey told him.

"It's nice to see things back to normal," Monk said to Hatch.

Lieutenant Cahill stuck his head into the squad room from the outer lobby. "If the bunch of you are done comparing war wounds, you have a customer at the front counter, Fey."

"Okay," Fey said. She stood up slowly from her chair, trying not to wince, and started forward. She didn't know what to expect, but she knew that something this early in the morning couldn't be good news.

Standing at the counter in the squad room lobby was a petite blonde—all legs and California good looks. Her fine golden wheat-colored hair was pulled back from her face and secured in a ponytail that dropped to her waist. Her high cheekbones were sharp enough to cut glass, and her perfect nose was complemented by piercing blue eyes. The entire package was poured into a hand-tailored skirt and jacket ensemble completed by a scoop-necked silk blouse and a glitter of diamonds at ears, neck, and wrist. Fey took one look and wanted to bury herself under a rock.

Men would die for this one.

She figured Colby's hormones would do themselves an injury as soon as he took his first look.

Fey knew the woman spelled big trouble. The bitch hadn't even opened her mouth, and yet Fey felt she was entering a battle of wits unarmed.

"Detective Croaker?" the woman asked, before Fey had a chance to introduce herself. "I'm Janice Ryder—Isaac Cordell's lawyer."

Oh shit, Fey thought, here we go!

**16**

**F**ey poured herself a cup of coffee and tried rapidly to gather her thoughts.

Colby sauntered into the coffee room where she was standing and refilled his own cup. "Who's the good-looking spinner?" he asked, having seen Fey walk Janice Ryder down the hall to one of the interrogation rooms.

"Cordell's lawyer."

"Hell," said Colby. "If I could get her to handle my case, it might be worth getting arrested."

"Colby, she would chew you up and spit out the pit before you managed to get to first base."

Colby laughed. "Fortunately, Cordell didn't damage your sarcastic streak."

"I think that's the only thing he didn't damage."

After their initial contact at the squad room front counter, Fey had led Janice Ryder into one of the station's interrogation rooms and abandoned her there. Fey needed time. She was bound and determined to get the upper hand in the confrontation, knowing that first blood had already gone to Ryder. She would deal with Cordell's lawyer when she was good and ready, and not before.

"I take it you booked Cordell on the open murder charge?" she asked Colby.

"Absolutely. We added on charges of resisting arrest and battery on a police officer, and then took the entire package over to Judge Taylor, who gave us a 'no bail' deviation. Kline also slapped a parole hold on the bastard, so he's not going anywhere."

"I'm not so sure," Fey said. "I have a funny feeling his lawyer has something up her sleeve."

"It's what's up her leg that I'm interested in."

Fey shook her head in disgust. "Don't you ever give it a rest?"

When Colby and the other officers had arrived on the scene of Cordell's arrest, Fey had not told them about the sexual attack that Cordell had made on her. She had justified this omission in her mind by convincing herself that they had enough charges to play with without complicating the case further. However, the truth of the issue was that she couldn't face the inevitable comments that would have been made at her expense. Colby would have had a field day, and past experience had proven to her that the other males she worked with would have gone jokingly along. Nobody would have meant to be malicious—except maybe Colby—but she would have always felt somehow tainted in their eyes. She had kept hidden for years the abuses that her father had heaped upon her, and even though she had been victorious over Cordell, she was not about to allow his actions to destroy so much of the acceptance she had worked to achieve.

When she had choked Cordell into unconsciousness, his penis had shrunk down and slipped back into his pants. If anyone had noticed that his pants were unbuttoned and unzipped, they hadn't said anything—probably figuring it was a result of his hurried exit from the boardinghouse, or that they'd somehow come undone in the altercation.

In some ways the situation created a strange bond between Cordell and Fey. If he kept his mouth shut, so would she. And her silence at the time made it almost impossible to start throwing around charges at a later date. Anyway, what charges could she bring? Forced oral copulation? The intention had been there, but the act had never been completed. Assault with intent to commit forced oral copulation? Maybe, but it was still her word against his and would be damned hard to prove without any corroborating evidence, of which there was none. Attempted rape? The facts wouldn't support the charge. Lewd conduct or indecent exposure? Again maybe, but who gave a damn about misdemeanors? All in all, Fey still felt she was better off keeping her mouth shut. A conspiracy of silence that had plagued women since Adam was chasing Eve around the garden.

Fey drank her full-strength brew slowly, leaning back against the wall of the small coffee room. She didn't feel up to confronting the ice queen who was waiting for her in the interrogation room, but it had to be done.

"Do me a favor," she said to Colby. "Go up front and set a tape running for the big interrogation room. I want a record of what goes on in this conversation."

Colby nodded his agreement and went to do Fey's bidding. For once he went without argument. Fey wondered why for a moment, and then realized she'd given Colby the perfect opportunity to sit around in the recording room and listen to everything that went on. She'd not only have to be careful about letting Janice Ryder gain the upper hand, but she'd also have to be sure not to give Colby something to sink his teeth into. Heaven knows she was sick of having to constantly cover her own ass.

She poured a second cup of coffee into a Styrofoam container, threw in a dash of powdered creamer and a package of Sweet & Low. She just knew Cordell's bitch of a lawyer would never let real sugar cross her lips.

When Fey opened the door and entered the interrogation room with her peace offering in hand, Janice Ryder was pacing around the small space in a snit.

"Are you through with your little game? Have my heels cooled enough for you, Officer Croaker?"

Fey looked at her and smiled. She set the cup of coffee she had brought for Ryder on one side of the table and took a seat on the other. "My demotion from detective to officer in your eyes is duly noted," Fey told the other woman in a calm tone of voice. "It's a good tactic, but like my keeping you waiting, it's basically a waste of time. Can we cut the crap and get to the nitty gritty here? What is it exactly that you want?"

Janice Ryder sat down in the hard, straight-backed chair on the other side of the table from Fey. The interrogation room was very stark with piss yellow walls and gang graffiti scratched into the back of the wooden door and the top of the table and chairs that were the room's sole pieces of furniture.

For a few seconds, Janice Ryder didn't answer Fey. She looked around and focused on the room's only decoration—a cross-stitched sampler that was jury-rigged to one of the acoustic metal walls. The homily on the sampler read: "No man has a good enough memory to be a successful liar." Fey followed Janice's gaze and smiled. She thought the saying was appropriate for the setting, but her favorite was a carved wooden sign over the interrogation room in an Air Force MP station. That sign had read: "You came in here with information and a pretty face. You can't leave with both."

"Well?" Fey said eventually.

Janice Ryder turned to look at her. It was as if she had been having an out-of-body experience and had only just returned to reclaim her physical form. Fey wondered where the other woman's mind had been and felt a shiver run down her spine.

"Is this conversation being recorded?" Ryder asked.

"Absolutely," Fey told her.

"Why?"

"For my protection. I have a feeling that this is going to be a high-profile case, and I want a record of everything that transpires in the event there are questions about it later."

"Are you always this careful?"

"Always," Fey said. "Look, you were the one who came in here all hot and bothered. I've got work to do, and thanks to your client, I feel like hell. Now, what can I do for you?"

Ryder picked up her coffee and took a sip. She made an unladylike face and quickly set the cup down.

"After a while you develop a taste for it," Fey said, watching Ryder's reaction to the coffee. She realized Ryder was using delaying tactics as an irritant, and decided not to be drawn.

"What I want," Ryder said eventually, "is my client's immediate release from police custody with all charges dropped."

Fey couldn't help but laugh. "And I want to be the queen of Sheba," she said. "You must think I'm a few fries short of a Happy Meal."

"I'm serious."

"If you are, you must have earned your law degree on some other planet. There is no way your client is walking away from this one. The case is open and closed. All wrapped up with a Christmas ribbon. Dead bang."

"The problem with dead-bang cases is that they're often only dead in the water."

"What's your point?"

"My point, Detective Croaker, is that a man can't be tried for the same crime twice. You are accusing my client of murdering a woman who was once his wife—a woman whose murder he was convicted of ten years ago. My client's years in prison have paid off his debt to society for that crime. You can't convict him again for murdering the same woman—that's called double jeopardy, and on this planet, Detective, double jeopardy is against the law."

**F**ey looked shocked. "You're out of your mind! Double jeopardy—that's the most ridiculous thing I've ever heard."

"Consider the facts." Janice Ryder confidently overrode Fey's protests. "Isaac Cordell has already been tried and convicted and served his time for the murder of Miranda Goodwinter, aka Miriam Cordell. Even if he did murder her this time—and I'm certainly not indicating that he did—it would be double jeopardy to attempt to convict him again. Any way you slice it, you can't murder someone twice."

"Wait just a minute. How the hell do you know about the connection between Miranda Goodwinter and Miriam Cordell? That information hasn't been made public."

"Guess again, Detective." Janice Ryder slid her slim calfskin briefcase onto the tabletop and flipped open the catches. From inside she removed a copy of the front page of that morning's *Los Angeles Tribune*. She dropped the newsprint on the table and swiveled it toward Fey.

Fey held Janice's eyes for a second and then dropped her gaze down to the newspaper. She scanned the headlines and then, with a sigh, reached out and picked up the pages for a closer look. "Well, shit," she said softly.

The banner headline across the top of the paper dealt with another Middle East crisis, but below that story a secondary headline carried the message: MURDER DONE TWICE— Woman Believed Murdered Ten Years Ago Found Dead Again. There was a grainy black-and-white photo of Miriam Cordell, obviously taken years earlier, next to a photo of Miranda Goodwinter being taken out of her home in a body bag. The caption read simply, "Miranda Goodwinter or Miriam Cordell?" The accompanying article contained little factual information about the current case, but ghoulishly rehashed all the details from the San Francisco case when Cordell was convicted, as well as speculation concerning his current arrest.

Fey felt deflated. How the hell had the paper latched on to the story so quickly? Damn, she thought, we have a leak in the division. And she was convinced she knew exactly who the leak was. It would go a long way toward explaining where all the extra money came from to support his flashy life-style.

Fey sighed again. "Counselor, you obviously think you can come in here and blow me out of the water by dropping all these little bombs in my path. However, your client is still under arrest for murder, and he will stay that way until the court decides differently—"

Ryder jumped into the middle of Fey's narrative. "I'd think twice before you try to take this case to court. Not only is my client innocent, but it's clear that Miriam Cordell was alive until two days ago, which clearly shows that my client should never have been arrested and convicted in the first place. It's also clear that the state's liability over Isaac Cordell's false imprisonment is going to be very high. Any further blunders on the part of the people will only result in the forthcoming civil suit increasing in magnitude."

"Life is hard and then you die," Fey told her. "Isaac

Cordell is as guilty as sin. We have eyewitness testimony placing him at the scene of the crime—"

"We both know that's about as reliable as a tissue in a rainstorm."

Fey held up her hand and plowed on. "And we have the physical evidence of recovering the murder weapon at your client's residence—"

"A nice tidy frame-up," Janice Ryder interrupted again. "Just like ten years ago. You're just looking for a way to wrap this murder up fast and cover up the mistakes the police have made in the past. Isaac Cordell is your best chance to do that in a hurry. Well, it's not going to happen. Cordell was framed once for the murder of his wife, and you're not going to do it again!" Janice Ryder's voice had risen passionately.

Fey leaned back in her chair and waited for Ryder to wind down. "A very pretty speech, Counselor, but it's not going to wash," she said, eventually. "I am in no position to release your client at this time. That is something to be decided by the district attorney or in a court of law—"

"Neither of which have served my client well in the past—"

"Quit trying to bust my chops here," Fey said, her own voice on the rise. She stood up and placed both her hands on the tabletop, supporting her weight as she leaned forward to get in Janice Ryder's face. "Tougher nuts than you have tried it over the years and have come away losers. If the civil liability you're trying to threaten me with is such a big deal, then I'm going to play this situation strictly by the book."

"I want my client released."

"So does every other defense lawyer in this godforsaken city. Grow up, Counselor, and get a grip on reality."

Janice Ryder snapped her briefcase closed with an angry gesture. "When will my client be arraigned?"

"The people have forty-eight hours from the time of arrest. The sooner you let me get back to doing my job, the sooner I'll get around to arraigning Mr. Cordell." Fey stepped over and opened the door to the interrogation room. "Counselor?" she said, with an ushering gesture toward the opening.

Janice Ryder stood up and walked out of the room.

"This is far from over," she said as she passed Fey. "Before this is done, I'm going to have your ass on a platter."

"Take your best shot." In her own mind, Fey finished the sentence with the word "bitch."

"I swear she's a piranha, Jake," Fey said as she sat in the deputy district attorney's small office.

Jake Travers was a tall, slim man who looked more like a hard-bitten saddle tramp than the DA's head filing deputy. His thick black hair came to a widow's peak low on his forehead before sweeping straight back to tickle his collar, and his tanned face had enough wrinkles and crow's-feet to give him character—on a woman they would have been considered ugly. At thirty-eight years old, he was still considered a rising star, and possibly a strong candidate for DA during the next election year. He had divorced four years earlier; his world revolved around his job, golf, and fishing.

Having been friends for many years, and lovers on and off for the previous five, Jake and Fey were happy with their relationship. At this specific point in both their lives, it suited their needs by asking no commitments beyond friendship and bed. They both knew, however, that they couldn't remain static forever. Sooner or later, the relationship would have to evolve or die.

"Sounds like she got your goat," Jake said. His deep voice held a note of amusement. It wasn't often that somebody got the better of Fey Croaker.

"Oh, stuff it," Fey said with resignation. Jake knew her almost too well. "What about all this double jeopardy stuff?"

Jake shrugged and stroked his chin. "Well . . . I don't know . . ."

"What does that mean?"

"That means, she may have a point. I can see a definite constitutional argument. Whether or not it will hold up is another question . . ."

"Does it mean you're considering not filing this case? Come on, Jake. The bastard slit the silly bitch's throat! What difference does it make if he did it ten years ago or two days ago?"

"Don't get your knickers in a twist. All I said is that she

may have a point. We're going to have to find a way to blunt it."

After getting rid of Janice Ryder, Fey had gone back into the squad room with her head spinning. She wanted to believe that Ryder's argument was purely bluster, but there was a gnawing grain of doubt working away in the pit of her stomach. She knew she needed this case wrapped up tight to secure her position as the homicide unit's detective three. If this caper got screwed up and slipped through her fingers, she could very easily find herself shipped off to handle the juvenile unit—the traditional home for female detective supervisors. The shift wouldn't be a demotion in rank, but it would be a hell of a drop in prestige, and there was nothing she would be able to do about it. She could hear the divisional sharks now. "Put her in charge of juvenile. If she fucks up there, nobody will care."

The attitude wasn't fair. There were some damn good people who had dedicated their careers to working juvenile— officers and detectives who in many cases had made a difference in young people's lives. However, the assignment didn't carry with it the promise of big glory cases.

Waiting back at her desk were a stack of phone messages from reporters following up on the story that the *Tribune* had broken in their morning edition. Fey was positive Colby had tipped off the *Trib*'s reporter, but there was nothing she could do about the situation, so she chose to ignore it. She also chose to ignore the press messages and the insistent ringing of the homicide unit's direct phone line.

"What are you saying to these reporters?" she had asked Hatcher and Monk, who were processing the day's paperwork.

"We're referring them all to you," Monk told her. "And it's not making them very happy."

"Tough shit," Fey said, and dropped the messages in the trash can beside her desk. "Keep taking messages and file them with these others," she told them. "When we know more about what's going on, we'll do a press conference. Till then, fuck 'em."

"You got it, boss lady," Hatch said. "That shiner of

yours, though, is going to come across great on the television screen."

"It would certainly get my sympathy vote," Monk said.

"Shut up," she said good-naturedly, sensing nothing behind their gentle ribbing. "You guys think you're a couple of real clowns, don't you?" She took a quick look around the squad room. "And speaking of clowns, where's Colby?"

"Court. He's got the prelim on Mason Dunnet today."

"Right, right," she said, remembering. "That should keep him out of my hair for a while."

The Dunnet case had been a self-solver. Neighbors had reported gunshots coming from inside the Dunnet residence. When patrol officers arrived, they found Dunnet standing over the rapidly cooling body of his wife while literally holding the smoking gun. Dunnet had happily copped out at the time, but now some public defender was attempting to make a federal case out of the situation. The PD was trying to develop a male version of the "burning bed" defense by stating that Dunnet had been forced to kill his wife before she killed him through her administering of ongoing physical and mental abuse.

From her desk, Fey gathered up the package containing all of the reports and information to date pertaining to the murder of Miranda Goodwinter and the arrest of Isaac Cordell. She got her car keys and signed herself out to the district attorney's office in Santa Monica. She had to get off the dime and get the case filed so they could arraign Cordell on the charges. "It's cases like this one," she told the other two homicide detectives as she was leaving, "that convince me God is a man."

"Why's that?" asked Hatch, ever willing to play the straight man.

"Because if God was a woman, she wouldn't have screwed things up this badly."

Fey drove the short distance to the DA's office on autopilot. Her conscious mind was filled with all the possibilities that her interview with Janice Ryder had brought to the surface. There was no telling what a jury or a judge would do with the double jeopardy situation if indeed one did exist.

There was a well-publicized case from a couple of years earlier, Fey remembered, where patrol officers had arrested a burglar inside a residence while the owners were away on vacation. It seemed like a dead-bang case—until it went to court.

In front of the judge it came out that one of the arresting officers had become a little overzealous and put a parking ticket on the defendant's car, which had been parked in front of a fire hydrant for a quick getaway. While out on bail, the defendant had appeared in traffic court, where he pled guilty to the parking infraction and received a fifty-dollar fine. When the burglary charges came to court, the defense attorney argued that his client had already pled guilty to a charge stemming from the case, and had been punished by paying a fine. To try him on further charges would place his client in double jeopardy and would therefore be illegal. The judge agreed, and instead of going up the river for five years, the defendant was immediately released to go back to his chosen profession.

In a court of law, anything was possible, a fact well-known by any copper worth his or her salt. And Fey realized Janice Ryder had been right in at least one area—dead bang didn't mean squat.

Fey also realized that there were a ton of other items that demanded attention before the case would be anywhere near ready to go to court. There were so many unanswered questions pertaining to the first case up in San Francisco, let alone the myriad of unknowns related directly to the victim herself.

Before this point, Fey and the other homicide detectives had been scrambling to beat that magical seventy-two-hour deadline, and in accomplishing that feat, they had incurred a lot of physical and mental wounds that needed licking. But now the fast and loose part of the case was over with. It was time to buckle down to the grunt work of making sure their case held up—and that was going to be a bitch, especially with a firecracker like Janice Ryder trying to thwart their every move.

Now, sitting across from Jake Travers, she felt almost overwhelmed by the magnitude of what was still to be accomplished.

"Look, Jake," Fey said. "I'd be obliged if you would handle this whole thing yourself from the arraignment on down. I don't know what kind of fat Ryder is going to throw into the fire, but I'd sure feel a lot better with you there to handle things."

"I haven't said I'm going to file the damn thing yet."

"Oh, you'll do that, all right," Fey told him.

"And why's that?"

"Because you can't resist a challenge, and because I know you won't be able to resist taking on Janice Ryder."

"You mean personally, or in the courtroom?"

Fey gave Jake a sly smile full of open sexuality. "In the courtroom, of course. If you take this on, I promise you won't have enough energy left to deal with her personally."

Jake Travers looked suitably shocked. "Promises, promises," he said.

Fey knew she was playing dirty pool, but when the playing field of life was tilted against you, you had to go with whatever weapons you had in your arsenal. Sex was constantly used against women, so sometimes it was nice to be able to turn the tables and use it to your advantage.

She also knew she enjoyed sex a lot more when she controlled the reins.

Isaac Cordell's arraignment was to be held in Division 90, which was housed in the court buildings across the street from the West Los Angeles Area police station. Fey had managed to get the complaint filed and typed up in time for afternoon court. This required her to walk Cordell from the station jail, where he had been held overnight, to the sheriff's lockup at the back of the court building. If the "no bail"

status held up during the arraignment, he would be transported from the courthouse to county jail, a facility run by the sheriff's department. There he would remain until his preliminary hearing.

Colby was already back from morning court when Fey returned to the station. She collared him and took him with her to escort Cordell across the street. Going into the station jail to pick the prisoner up, Fey felt her guts begin to churn, and every ache and pain in her body seemed to intensify. She had taken a couple of painkillers, but she was tired, so very, very tired. She knew, however, that she still had to get through the afternoon before she could collapse.

Cordell stood up from his bunk when he saw Fey and Colby approaching the bars of his cell. The jailer unlocked the cell door, and Fey moved to stand in front of it. Her eyes locked with Cordell's, but the big man didn't move or say anything.

"We're here to take you to court," Fey told him. Her mouth was dry and she was barely able to save her voice from cracking. "I want you to turn around so I can put the handcuffs on you." Cordell didn't move. Fey shrugged. "Don't fuck with me, Cordell," she said with exasperation. "I don't need any more macho bullshit. Don't make me come in there and kick your butt again."

Cordell stared at her. "You are one tough dyke, aren't you." It was a statement, not a question, and there was a curious note of respect hidden somewhere behind the words.

"No, I'm just old and tired and I ache everywhere. Now, turn around."

Cordell slowly turned his back to her.

"Put your hands behind your back, palms together as if you're praying."

Cordell complied, and Fey moved into the cell with her handcuffs in her hand. It was one of the toughest things she had ever done. She realized she was scared of this man, and that made her angry. His presence seemed to bring out in her all of the childlike insecurities that she thought she had conquered long ago. She realized, not for the first time, that it was impossible to escape your childhood. Its dark edges and hidden frights were always with you, waiting to ambush you at any given moment.

As she got closer to Cordell, the smell of the man's stale sweat filled her nostrils. She saw the tension ripple across his shoulders, but did not hesitate to firmly grab his left wrist and secure the first cuff around it. Holding on to the second cuff, so Cordell couldn't pull it away from her if he decided to go off, she waited for a second before securing the other wrist. The small wait between the handcuffing of the hands sent a very strong message—it told Cordell that if he wanted to go for it, she was willing to go up against him again. The second passed, and with it Fey achieved psychological dominance.

The short walk across the street to the sheriff's lockup was taken in silence. Fey walked on one side of Cordell, with Colby on the other. The weight of the .38 revolver, which Colby had recovered from the arrest scene, seemed to hang more heavily than normal under Fey's arm. It was as if the inanimate object were attempting to fan the embers of her anger toward what Cordell had tried to do to her. Their hidden secret.

The gun seemed to be somehow whispering in Fey's ear—the words echoing over and over in her head. "Shoot him. Kill him. Make him pay. Put him out of your misery." Fey struggled to shove the thoughts from her mind and was grateful when they reached the back door to the lockup.

A uniformed sheriff's deputy came forward and took custody of Cordell.

"He's for afternoon arraignment," Fey told him as she handed him the prisoner transfer paperwork.

"No problem," the deputy said. He knew Fey slightly and looked pointedly at the bruising on her face. "Looks like you were put through the ringer."

"You should see the other guy," she told him, and pointed with her chin toward Cordell.

"Really?" the deputy said in surprise. He took in Cordell's size with a brief, impressed glance and then hefted his baton from its ring on his belt. "You maybe want us to teach him a few manners?"

"I'd say things are pretty even right now," Fey said. "I don't think that will be necessary."

"Too bad," the deputy said. Fey, the deputy, and even Cordell all knew the exchange was merely a ritual and not a legitimate threat despite the validity of the sentiment.

The deputy removed the cuffs from Cordell's wrists and held them out toward Fey.

"Thanks," she said as she took them. Cordell still had his back to them as she and Colby turned to walk away.

Another deputy used a key to open the lockup door so the two detectives could exit. They nodded to him and stepped through.

"That's one tough bitch," she heard Cordell say as the deputy slammed the lockup door behind them.

Colby turned to look at her. "From tough dyke to tough bitch," he said. "Is that an improvement?"

The arraignment court was in Division 90 on the ground floor of the court building. At one-thirty Fey met Jake Travers at the front doors of the court and entered with him.

Bill Swanson, the regular arraignment DA, was surprised to see Travers. He was also relieved when Travers explained why he was there.

"It's just for the one case," Travers told the younger DA. "I have no idea if this defense lawyer is going to try and pull something out of her bag of tricks, but since I'm handling the damn thing, I wanted to be here on the off chance there are any surprises."

"No problem," Swanson said. He considered himself a climber and wanted no part of any case that might rock his boat. If there were going to be any fireworks, he was more than happy to have Travers there to take the heat.

Looking around the courtroom, Fey could see a handful of people scattered through the visitors' chairs in various states of anxiety. An empty jury box lined the left wall, and the traditionally high judge's bench stood imposingly in front of the counsel table, which was piled high with briefs.

The doors to the courtroom opened briefly and Janice Ryder stepped through. She had changed her outfit since her morning confrontation with Fey, and she looked stunning in a pale blue sheath with a touch of pearls at ears and neck. Her hair was loose and fell attractively over her shoulders in soft curls. Her calfskin briefcase had been switched for a white leather model that matched her pearls.

"Damn," said Jake softly. "Is that the piranha?"

Fey nudged him hard with her elbow. "Shut up and stop drooling."

There was the sound of a buzzer and the bailiff stood up to announce, "Please remain seated. Division 90 is now in session, the Honorable Judge Martin Beckworth presiding."

The level of noise in the room dropped to a low murmur as the judge exited his chambers while still zipping up his robe—an action that revealed a T-shirt and jeans underneath. He took his seat behind the bench and reached for the first docket from the court clerk.

Taking out a pair of cheap reading glasses, Beckworth peered at the notation on the docket. "Call *People v. Isaac Cordell*. Case number SA047951."

Jake and Fey were seated next to Bill Swanson at the counsel table. Travers stood up to speak. "Jake Travers for the people, Your Honor."

Janice Ryder pushed open the wooden swinging gate that acted as the boundary between the gallery and the courtroom's working area. She stepped up to the counsel table and placed her briefcase on top of it. "Janice Ryder for Isaac Cordell, Your Honor," she said, parting with a glowing flash of perfect teeth.

"What the hell have you got me into?" Travers asked Fey sotto voce.

"Where is the defendant?" Beckworth asked.

As if waiting for the perfect cue, there was a knock at the back door of the courtroom and the bailiff opened it to admit Isaac Cordell and an accompanying deputy. The bailiff took custody of Cordell and walked him over to sit next to Janice Ryder. The bailiff removed the cuff from Cordell's left hand and secured it around the right arm of the chair.

Beckworth peered over his reading glasses at Cordell. "Sir, is Isaac Cordell your true name?"

Cordell stood up, trailing his still-cuffed arm behind him. "Yes, Your Honor."

"Thank you. You may be seated," Beckworth told him.

He shifted his gaze to the much prettier Janice Ryder. "Counsel, is your client ready for arraignment?"

Janice stood up. "No, Your Honor. There is a jeopardy issue here. My client has already been tried for these charges, and any further prosecution is barred by my client's Fifth Amendment rights precluding double jeopardy."

Beckworth looked surprised. Arraignments were rarely anything but routine, but this one looked like it was going to immediately get out of his depth. He didn't like to be placed in the middle of a problem situation—that's why he was in the arraignment court. All of a sudden Janice Ryder didn't look so attractive to him. "Mr. Travers?" he asked the DA, looking for clarification.

"Your Honor, I'm not sure exactly what Counsel is driving at here. There does not appear to be any jeopardy question as far as the People are concerned, and since the People have had no formal notice of such a motion, I feel it would be inappropriate to litigate such a motion at this time. This is simply the arraignment, and I believe any question of jeopardy would be better handled at the preliminary hearing."

Janice Ryder came to her feet. "Excuse me, Your Honor, but this is a fundamental right that we're dealing with, and neither the People nor the Court have any jurisdiction to proceed any further with this case since jeopardy prevents any further prosecution."

Beckworth was not a happy camper. This was not something he was willing to go into. He looked over at the high-rise stack of dockets for the afternoon session and considered the eighteen holes of golf he wanted to get in before dark. With all things considered—especially his golf game—his decision was easy: Pass the buck.

"Counsel," he said to Janice Ryder, "as you know, this is a calendar court, and I am not in any position to litigate this issue at present. The more appropriate forum would be in Judge Grant's court before the prelim."

"Your Honor—" Janice Ryder attempted to interrupt, but Beckworth forestalled her by holding up his hand.

"I'm sorry, Counsel, but I have made my decision." He shifted his focus over to the seated Cordell. "Mr. Cordell, you are charged in complaint number SA047951 with one count alleging a violation of Penal Code section 187—murder. Counsel, do you waive further reading of the complaint and charges?"

"Yes, Your Honor," Janice Ryder said through jaws that were visibly tight.

Fey smiled—loving every second of it.

Beckworth was continuing. "I am therefore going to enter a plea of not guilty for your client. I am also noting your motion, and putting it on the record that this arraignment will in no way affect your ability to pursue this matter in Judge Grant's court." Beckworth turned to his clerk, an older woman with an orange flower-print dress, a bun of flyaway gray hair, and steely intelligent eyes. "Becky, what's the matrix day on this case?"

Becky shuffled a stack of papers on her desk to consult her calendar. "Your Honor," she said after a moment, "the ninth day is Wednesday, the eighteenth."

"Fine," Beckworth said, accepting the date and making a notation on the docket in front of him. "This matter is set for prelim on Wednesday, the eighteenth of January, in Judge Grant's court, that being Municipal Court Division Ninety-six." He flipped to a page in the docket and peered at it briefly. "I see that at this time the defendant is being held without bail, and I note that there is also a parole hold. This seems appropriate. Counsel, do you wish to be heard?"

"Your Honor, I believe that if the facts surrounding this case were allowed to come out, it would be clear that there should be no parole hold, nor indeed should there be any charges alleged against my client that would require—"

"Ms. Ryder," Beckworth interrupted. "I have already ruled on this issue, and I am not going to waste any more of the court's time repeating myself. Now, do you have anything pertinent to the question of bail?"

Janice Ryder's cheeks glowed from the rebuke, and she had a tough time getting her next words through her teeth. "No, Your Honor. The defense would only request that an 'own recognizance' report be prepared before prelim."

"Fine. So ordered." Beckworth happily banged his gavel. "Thank you. Next case."

The bailiff rehandcuffed Cordell and turned him back

over to the custody deputy. Janice Ryder picked up her brief-case and stalked out of the courtroom without a backwards glance.

"Whew," Jake said. "That lady is wound up tight enough to explode."

Fey nodded thoughtfully. "Could be because she went out on a limb to fight for his parole up in San Francisco, and now it looks as if Cordell has blown everything she worked for."

"You think she's pissed because Cordell bit the hand that fed him?" Jake and Fey had moved out of the courtroom behind Ryder and watched her through the building's glass wall as she walked quickly through the civic center.

"It could be," Fey replied. "She certainly seems one for causes. But I don't know—I think there's more to it."

"Well, we better find out," Jake said. "Because we don't want her exploding all over us."

"Ain't that the truth," said Fey. "Ain't that the truth."

19

Isaac Cordell sat on a bench in the lockup chained to a Mexican junkie on one side and a black robbery suspect on the other. He tried to calm himself. He had been through this before and survived—thrived actually—and he could survive it again.

His head hurt. The throbbing seemed to come right from the center of his brain. It wasn't a new pain, however. He'd been living with it for almost two years. The prison doctor had told him what it was, but hadn't offered much hope for a cure. Cordell knew what the cause of the pain was, and that made him even angrier. He hadn't deserved to go to prison, but because of the things that had happened to him there, he now had the pain in his brain—a pain that would never go away.

He knew he'd been innocent when they originally convicted him of murder. But that hadn't done him much good. The law didn't give a shit about innocence or guilt, right or wrong, justice or injustice. The only thing the law was good for was to be twisted and turned to the advantage of those who controlled it.

He had hopes the woman who was his lawyer knew how to control the law. She had done it once before—somehow she had convinced the prison board to grant him parole. If she stayed with him, she might be able to do it again.

If she stayed with him.

All the women Isaac Cordell had ever been close to had used him and then abandoned him. It didn't matter that he would have done anything to please them. Love, like the law, was only something that those in control twisted and turned.

He had loved his mother—for all the good it did him. Like his father before him, nothing he ever did was good enough to please her. He'd been tied to her apron strings by an emotional umbilical cord tough enough to resist the sharpest surgeon's scalpel. Despite his physical size, he had never been strong enough to break away from his mother's demanding presence.

Living at home, he had watched in silent agony as his mother drove nail after nail into his father's coffin. She drove him to succeed in business, and the Cordell's Furniture stores were a testament to how much a desperate man can achieve, yet still fall short of expectations. Finally Isaac's father had taken the only way out he felt was left to him—he'd swallowed a .22-caliber bullet on a rainy Saturday afternoon. Even at that, he'd tried to accommodate his wife by committing the suicide in the shower stall with a small-caliber bullet so there wouldn't be much mess to clean up.

Isaac had been repressing his feelings for twenty years when his father ate his gun for dessert. During that time he had come to blame his father for his mother's spoiled disposition. If once his worm of a father had stood up to the woman—put her in her place, smacked her in the mouth—

just once, then maybe life might have been different for all of them.

Trying to take over the running of the family business was a nightmare. Cordell's people skills had been learned from his mother, not his father, and he began to lose employees, customers, and money at an astonishing rate. His mother, however, continued to insist on living in the high style to which she had become accustomed—all the while demanding more and more—and Cordell found himself as trapped as his father had been.

When his mother was run down in the street by a hit-and-run driver, Isaac was struck by both a sense of guilty relief and an overwhelming feeling of abandonment. The torment in his life was gone, but so, too, the rock to which his life had been tethered.

And then Miriam was there to rescue him.

Sweet, divine, loving Miriam. A surrogate mother dressed in the body of a sexual temptress. She swept him off his feet. He wined her and dined her and bought her diamonds and rings. In return she filled the empty void his mother left by giving him direction and driving him to achieve in his incompetent way.

When he had the time to think about it later—and he had a lot of time to think about it all later—he realized that the only difference between Miriam and his mother was that his mother led him around by his nose, and Miriam led him around by his cock. One woman repressed his sexuality while the other exploited it. Both women savaged his emotions for their own gain. And over the years he spent in prison, the love that he'd had for them turned to the white-hot hatred that now drove his every waking hour.

In prison he had not only learned to hate. He had learned to fight, to stomp, and to destroy. He had discovered inside himself what he liked to think of as his feminine side—the same greedy, selfish, controlling traits that had made up his mother's character.

He had also learned how to wait. Prison had given him a lot of practice at waiting. Ten years worth of waiting, until another woman had suddenly appeared to tell him she was going to get him paroled.

Isaac hadn't believed Janice Ryder at first. He'd already applied for parole twice and been turned down. But Ryder had fought for him, spent hours going over and over the circumstances of the case with him until she knew each and every aspect more clearly than he did.

Cordell knew he hadn't murdered his wife. He knew she must have gone over the side of the boat of her own free will—probably hooked up with scuba gear that she'd put on after making her phony distress call. And after Roarke, his supposed business partner, had told the police the lies about Isaac, telling them he planned to murder Miriam for the insurance money, it was very clear to Isaac who must have been waiting in a boat nearby to pick Miriam up.

After those revelations, even more became clear to Isaac concerning the insurance policy he knew nothing about—the insurance policy that damned him and made Roarke a rich man.

Miriam liked rich men.

Janice Ryder, on the other hand, didn't seem to care about money one way or the other. She never asked him for a dime for all the effort she put into getting him paroled. He still had no idea why she had championed him in the first place. He had asked her once, but she had ignored the question and distracted him with further talk of getting him released on parole. He didn't understand it, but he didn't care. All he cared about was getting out.

For all the good it had done.

He'd spent ten years in prison so somebody else could enjoy life on the outside with a million dollars in his pockets. For ten years Isaac had thought and dreamed about that money and the freedom to spend it. He wanted that money and he wanted revenge, but in order to have it, he had to be free. Janice Ryder had somehow managed to get him that freedom, and because of that, he didn't care what her motives were.

Now, however, it looked as if circumstances were following a familiar sequence. Sitting in the lockup, Cordell wondered if Janice Ryder would stay with him, or if she had got whatever it was that she wanted from him and would now abandon him like all the other women he'd ever known.

Past experience had taught him not to rely on her. She was—after all—just another woman.

Chained to the men on either side of him, who in turn were chained to others, and others to the others, he waited with his guts churning half in anger and half in fear.

A deputy, with his gut hanging over his belt and buttons of his shirt straining, walked along the line of prisoners. A name tag sewn to the breast of his grubby shirt identified him as Deputy Booker. His partner was a tall, sleek model who wore one-way, wraparound sunglasses even in the dim overhead lights of the lockup. The partner's name was Taggert, and he followed behind Booker with a clipboard. As Booker checked and read off the name on each prisoner's wristband, Taggert put a tick next to the corresponding name on the roster attached to the clipboard.

When Booker checked Cordell's wristband, he obviously recognized the name. "Hey, Taggert," he said to his partner. "We got us an honest-to-goodness celebrity here."

"Oh yeah? Who is he?" Taggert was less than interested. He thought Booker was a dumb fuck who should be kicked off the job—not necessarily for the betterment of the department, but because then Taggert wouldn't have to put up with him. Taggert was working the jail transportation detail only because it gave him three or four hours a day of on-duty time to work out. However, that benefit was often outweighed by having to deal with the likes of Booker and the idiots who were chained together in front of him.

"This here's Isaac Cordell," Booker announced to everyone within earshot.

"Never heard of him," Taggert said. "What show is he on?"

"He ain't on no show," Booker told him. "He's a criminal celebrity."

"You mean like a mob guy."

"Nah. Even better. I read about this guy in the paper today. He figured out a way to kill his old lady twice. Can you believe it? Fucking whacked her ten years ago, but then the bitch comes back to life and he has to get himself out of jail and whack her again." Booker's big oval face grinned into Cordell's. The challenge was there—unspoken, but almost with a physical life of its own. Booker knew he had the upper hand, knew he could do or say whatever he wanted, and there was nothing Cordell could, or would, do about it. "Fucking broads." Booker projected his fake sympathy toward Cordell. "Can't even trust 'em to stay dead." He laughed and dropped Cordell's wrist to move on to the next man in line.

When the line was checked and approved, Booker led the chained men outside to a waiting sheriff's transportation bus. Getting the men situated on the bus as they fought with the confusion of being attached to one another was like a well-rehearsed scene out of a Keystone Kops flick. Eventually, however, an awkward truce was struck between comfort and security, and Taggert eased himself into the driver's seat.

Booker stood at the front of the bus with his baton held easy in his hand. "Listen up, dip-shits. There ain't no emergency exits on this bus and there ain't no emergency oxygen, barf bags, toilets, beverage service, or in-flight movies. If we crash while driving over water, there ain't no flotation devices under your seats, so you might as well just kiss your asses good-bye." He paused for an appreciation of his humor, but there were no takers. "We'll be driving at approximately fifty-five miles an hour," he continued, flogging a dead horse, "at an altitude of about five feet. Our arrival time at county jail will be about forty-five minutes. So just sit quietly like good little dip-shits, and we'll see if we can't get you all deloused in time for dinner. Don't piss me off or rock the boat, and we'll all get along just fine. On behalf of the pilot and myself, we hope you enjoy your flight and will join us again real soon." He guffawed loudly and sat down behind Taggert, patting him sharply on the shoulder.

Taggert, who had heard it all innumerable times before, shoved the bus into gear and pulled out into traffic. One of these days he'd like to take his baton to Booker and shove it where the sun doesn't shine. Yeah, that was certainly something he'd enjoy.

At the back of the bus, Cordell's bulk was squeezed in next to the Mexican junkie. The Mexican was beginning to need a fix, and was fighting hard for control. Snot ran out of his nose and dripped from the ends of his gunfighter's mustache. He looked over at Cordell with a brand of fearful interest.

"Hey," he said quietly to get Cordell's attention. "Are you really that guy Booker was talking about? I read about it myself in the paper today. I read good, man, you know? I'm teaching my kids, you know?"

Cordell looked over at the pathetic prisoner. "You ain't going to be teaching them much from in here," he said.

"Hey, man. It's not my fault, you know? It's this fucked-up society. A guy like me don't got a chance, you know?"

Cordell swiveled his head forward again. "Yeah. I know."

Encouraged by this response, the junkie pushed on. "Are you really him? You know—the guy who killed his wife again?"

Cordell grunted.

"Hey, man, the paper said you got arrested by the Frog Lady—Detective Croaker, you know? Is that right? She's a real ball-breaker. She arrested me twice last year. I got out of one, but I did a ninety on the other. She's bad news, you know?"

Cordell was silent. He thought about Fey Croaker. He'd been thinking a lot about her. Every time he moved, his testicles felt as if they had been snapped off.

Yeah, he thought about Fey Croaker. He thought about how good his fist had felt smashing into her face. And he thought about how bad it felt when the helpless kitten turned into a lioness. There wasn't much he wouldn't give for a second crack at her.

"Did you know she put her own brother in jail?" The Mexican's question caught Cordell's attention. He turned his head back to look at his seat companion again.

"What do you mean?"

The Mexican looked happy that he was able to provide this big man with information. The protection of having a friend the size of Cordell went a long way in the jail system. "They sent me up to Wayside to do my ninety last time I got arrested—"

"What's Wayside?" Cordell interrupted.

"It's the county's honor ranch. They got medium and maximum sections up there, but almost everybody is in the minimum-security section. You can almost just walk away from the place, but it's not worth it since most people that are sent there only have a small amount of time to do."

"What about Croaker's brother?"

"Who? Oh, yeah. His name is Tommy Croaker, you know?"

"What was he in jail for?"

The junkie smiled. "He got a habit that takes a bigger bite than mine. Ripped his sister off one too many times and she did him like a dog. Sent him up on a county lid for burglary, you know? Can you believe that—her own brother?"

"Is he still there?"

"Should be. I got out after doing forty-five of my ninety. That was a week ago. He still had six months to go, and the Frog Lady had it fixed so he had to do the full stretch."

Cordell's brain started to churn. He'd learned the ins and outs of the jail system the hard way, and he knew with the right moves, he might get himself out to Wayside.

Once there, he knew he could make use of Croaker's brother. Junkies were easy to use. They'd do anything for a little dope.

After that, he'd have to see. He had not been a bad man when he'd gone to prison the first time, but prison had made him bad. He'd made his bones in prison, and the irony of getting away with that first murder in prison amused him since he was in prison for a murder he didn't commit.

Now they were trying to send him back to prison again. But one thing was for certain—this time they weren't going to send him down for a crime he didn't commit. Since they were charging him with murder, he'd have to be damn sure to get free long enough to commit one.

And he knew the perfect victim.

# 20

It was late again when Fey stumbled through the front door to her house and collapsed in a heap on her living room couch. She felt nauseous, and every bone and muscle in her body ached with fatigue.

Things had gone to hell in a hand basket after she'd left Cordell's arraignment. The pressure from the press had been turned on full blast, and she'd had to work with Mike Cahill to prepare a news release and hold a press conference.

During the course of handling the press, another dead-body call had come in to the unit. This one had turned out to be a suicide, but Fey still had to roll out with Colby to deal with it because Monk and Hatch had been tied up with handling a spousal abuse arrest.

Suicides didn't add to the homicide stats, and there were a number of homicide dicks who were aces at turning triple murders into double murder suicides—not only did that kind of action keep your body count down, but it also solved the damn cases in the process. The paperwork was shuffled, the families of the victims were kissed off, and the cases were marked closed. Everybody was happy—including the murderer.

This case had been a straight-out overdose with no real possibility of foul play. It was an easy case to handle, but it was far from pleasant.

Everything had eventually worked out, but it had taken its toll on Fey's time and energy. It was after dark now, and she felt like seven kinds of shit.

She knew she could have easily taken the day off. Hell, she'd had to fight to get released from the hospital. But the thought of leaving the Goodwinter/Cordell case to Colby had galled her. He would have reveled in taking the credit for breaking the unit's unsolved streak, and she would have been left out in the cold. However, the day's events and confrontations had left her wishing she'd stuck her head in the sand and hid from it all.

With a groan, she rolled off the couch and made her way to the bathroom. From the medicine cabinet she took out a bottle of prescription-strength Motrin, shook two of the eight-hundred-milligram caplets into her hand, and swallowed them dry. She then turned on the shower water as hot as she could stand it and soaked her troubles for twenty minutes under the heavy spray.

When she exited the shower, Brentwood was sitting on the bathroom's tiled floor looking at her with disapproval. The cat's tail swished from side to side in obvious irritation.

"Shit," Fey said when she saw the animal. She'd forgotten all about picking up cat food. Wrapping a towel around herself, she dashed out into the kitchen to open another can of tuna. She was surprised, however, to find a new set of cat dishes on the floor filled with water and dry food. The damn cat was pretty self-sufficient, Fey thought, and then realized how tired she must be to even entertain such an idea.

Looking around, she noticed a note from Peter Dent, the neighbor who took care of her horses, attached by a magnet to the door of her refrigerator. Peter's cramped handwriting reassured her that he had taken over the responsibility for the feed and care of Brentwood and that of the horses. He had read about her case in the paper and realized that she would be overworked. Fey sent up a prayer of thanks to the patron saint of good neighbors, and made a mental note to do something nice for Peter as soon as she had a chance.

Brentwood sauntered into the kitchen and over to the new feed bowls. She ignored Fey as if letting her know that she hadn't been fulfilling her responsibilities.

"All right, all right," Fey said to the cat. "I get your point." She knew she should go out and check on the horses, but she trusted Peter and didn't need any further rejection from her animals. She knew the horses wouldn't react the same as Brentwood, but the damn cat had managed to put her off her stride.

Back in the bathroom, Fey dropped her towel and slipped on a terry cloth robe. She was aware she should have shaved her legs in the shower, but she'd been too damn tired. Shuffling into the bedroom, she saw the two messages on the answering machine she'd ignored two nights ago had been joined by two others. The other machine was empty.

Sitting on the corner of her bed, she stared at the first answering machine's flashing light. Four messages. Four hate-filled missives of confusion and despair. She knew they would be from her brother.

She wanted to ignore the messages, or to reach out and wipe them clean—to take the machine and throw it through the window and never have to be a slave to it again—but there was always that tiny shred of hope that her brother would change his tune.

In her heart she knew he never would. It was impossible, though, for her to admit to that fact. She had spent too many years, and spilled too many tears, protecting her brother from the world, and now she had to face the result of constantly solving somebody else's problems without letting him help himself.

When they were children growing up in their abusive home, Fey had been the eldest. She had let her father abuse her over and over again in order to protect Tommy from the same treatment. At school she was always pulling Tommy's fat out of the fire by intervening with both bullies and teachers. Later, when Tommy began to indulge himself in petty crimes, she had found ways to constantly get him off the hook—efforts for which he was never grateful.

Fey had told herself that Tommy was her brother, her blood, her kin, that she should always be there for him. But when he had turned to drugs, there was nothing she could do. She felt like a failed parent. Taking care of Tommy had become an obsession with her, a fixation that had caused trouble in both of her early marriages.

Her mother and father had eventually drunk themselves to death, a state of affairs over which she felt little emotion. But Tommy's drug habit had turned him into a living corpse, and Fey felt the blame lay heavy on her shoulders that she could do nothing about it.

The final straw came, however, when Tommy broke into Fey's house and ransacked it looking for money or jewelry to pawn for his next fix. After all the years of abuse by those she loved, Fey's outrage had known no bounds and she had pulled every string she could to lock him up.

Since then, she had severed all her ties with Tommy but one—the answering machine. He had the number and called often from Wayside Honor Rancho, where he was being held while serving out his time. The calls were of two types: obscene and threatening, or pleading and pathetic. The latter was designed to play on Fey's guilt feelings. Tommy would whine and cry, beg for forgiveness and plead for Fey to give him another chance, or to at least come and visit him. He would swear he would never touch drugs again and would do anything—anything—if Fey would help him get out.

Fey knew better.

The obscene calls were far worse. Tommy's voice, pitched at the same tone as their father's, would spill vitriolic hatred down the phone lines to fill the air with the sounds of sexual obscenities and threats of bodily harm that would have done a serial sex killer proud. Fey had never known her brother to have such a vivid imagination before being put away.

That evening Fey figured she felt low enough that listening to the messages couldn't make her feel any worse. She punched the machine's replay button and left the volume on very low.

The first two messages were pleaders, as Fey referred to them. Nothing unusual. Run of the mill. The third message was filled with Tommy's anger and hate and frustration. Again, nothing unusual.

The fourth call was something else again. As soon as she heard the new voice, Fey jumped to her feet and pushed up the answering machine's volume.

"Hello, Croaker." The voice sent an iced chill up Fey's spine. She felt rooted to the floor. She became suddenly light-headed and almost missed what Isaac Cordell had to say next.

"I just turned your little brother into a squealing little girl. Did you know he likes taking it up the ass?"

Fey had to sit down. Her heart was slamming around in her chest as if it were a terrified animal.

"Tommy was so grateful to me that he gave me your number. Oh, and he also gave me your address. It sounds like a nice part of town. Perhaps I should come over and pay you a visit. Would you like that? I'll be there real soon, but don't feel like you have to wait up. I can let myself in."

There was a short silence and then a click as the phone was hung up.

The tape ran on.

"Nine fifty-five P.M. . . ."

Fey flinched involuntarily as the machine's mechanical voice kicked in.

"That was your last message."

For three long seconds Fey sat motionless on the corner of her bed as if she were a wildcat gathering her strength for a killing charge. When she finally moved into action, it was at top speed without any time wasted on deliberation or worry.

Coming to her feet, she stepped to the side of her bed, bent down, and pulled out an Ithaca shotgun from behind the dust ruffle. Cradling the shotgun in her arms, she crawled across the bedspread and removed a .38 Smith & Wesson Chief with a two-inch barrel from between the mattress and box springs on the other side of her bed.

As a woman living alone, Fey had never taken her safety for granted. She didn't need to check the loads in either weapon—she knew they were hot. Every month she removed the weapons from their hiding places, cleaned them, and replaced the ammunition.

Putting the revolver in the pocket of her robe, she held the shotgun in one hand as she picked up the phone with the other. Having been raised on B movies as a form of escapist entertainment, she half expected to find the phone line dead and the house lights to be cut any second, but the dial tone buzzed reassuringly when she put the phone to her ear.

Fey didn't know how Isaac Cordell had managed to get from county jail to Wayside. That was something to worry about later. Right now there were more important considerations. She punched the phone's quick-dial button programmed with the number of the LAPD's Devonshire station.

A voice picked up on the third ring. "Los Angeles Police Department, Officer Stokes speaking. Can I help you?"

"Stokes, this is Detective Croaker from West Los Angeles Division. This is an emergency. I need to speak to the watch commander right now."

"Yes, sir." The excitement in Stokes's voice betrayed his rookie stature.

Fey had called directly through to the watch commander rather than punching 911 because she knew she would get a faster response. If she dialed 911, chances were she'd get a recording that all the emergency lines were busy.

Another, more mature voice came on the phone line. "Fey? This is Gene Mallet. What's up?"

Fey was relieved. She and Gene Mallet went way back to the days when they had ridden in a patrol car together.

"Gene, I've got a problem over at the house." Fey gave him the address. "Can you get me a patrol car out here code three?"

"On its way, Fey. Will you tell me all about it later?"

"I promise. Just get them here." She hung up and blessed Gene Mallet for simply doing what she'd requested without wasting time asking questions. She knew Mallet would immediately go to the ACC control center in the watch commander's office, locate the closest available unit to her location, and dispatch it immediately. All being well, she figured she would have backup at the house within five to six minutes.

Moving quickly, she threw off her robe and slipped into jeans and a sweatshirt, stepped into tennis shoes, and pulled her hair back into a ponytail. The shotgun was never out of her immediate reach.

When she was ready, she picked up the telephone again and hit another quick-dial button. On the other end of the line the phone rang five times before a sleepy voice answered.

"Hello."

"Jake, wake up. It's Fey."

"Fey? What's the matter?" Jake's voice seemed to come instantly awake.

"Isaac Cordell left a rather nasty message on my phone machine. I don't know how—or really if—but it seems like he's managed to escape, and he claims he's on his way here."

"Oh, shit."

"No kidding."

"You have to get out of there!"

"I've got a unit on its way, and I'm staying armed to the teeth until it gets here. Then I'm going to the station."

"Why don't you come straight to my place?"

"I will later, but not right away. I've got to be where I can find out what's going on. And for all I know, Cordell is sitting outside right now waiting to follow me to some place where I might feel safe putting my guard down."

"Which station are you going to use as a base? Devonshire or West L.A.?"

"West L.A. It's home base, and I can get things jumping from there."

"I'll meet you there in forty minutes."

"Thanks."

As Fey hung up the phone, she could hear the wail of a police siren coming down her street.

There were eventually six police units that pulled up outside of Fey's house. Four of them were black-and-white patrol units, and the other two were unmarked cars used by the division's special problems unit. Fey knew two of the patrol cops and quickly filled them in on what was going on. She was grateful for the quick response, even though the noise and lights woke up most of her neighbors and brought them out into the street to see what was going on.

Within a few minutes two of the patrol units and the two

unmarked units had returned to their duties. The four police officers from the other two units hung around while Fey threw a change of clothes into a suitcase, along with other overnight necessities, and locked up the house.

Fey had been hoping that Peter Dent would have been one of the neighbors who had been roused by the noise, but she hadn't spotted him outside. She tried him on the phone, but was only able to leave a message for him on his machine requesting that he take care of her animals again. She apologized for saddling him with the unexpected work load, and promised she'd make it up to him at a later date.

Before leaving the house she had searched all over for Brentwood, but the cat had disappeared into some cranny or other and was not to be found. Eventually Fey had no choice but to put down fresh water and refill the dry cat food dish that Peter Dent had provided.

Finally she threw her shotgun on the front seat of her car and headed out for West Los Angeles Division. One of the police units followed her as far as the freeway to make sure her tail was clean, and the other pulled back into a secluded spot near her house in case Cordell had the audacity to actually turn up.

The more Fey thought about the situation, the more she realized that the phone call had simply been a terror tactic. She still refused to speculate on the circumstances that led up to the call—she'd find out about those soon enough—but she was almost positive Cordell wouldn't be fool enough to turn up at her house. If that had been what he wanted, he never would have called. By announcing his intentions, he had short-circuited any chance he might have of pulling them off. No, Fey thought, Cordell was either delighting in starting a game of cat and mouse, or he had something else in mind entirely.

The morning watch desk officers were not overly surprised to see Fey. They were used to the homicide detectives showing up at all hours due to the nature of their work. She nodded hello to them when she came in and then turned away to go up the stairs to the detective squad room.

Automatically she turned on the upstairs lights and put on a pot of coffee. She felt safe and at home in the deserted room. For most cops the station becomes an extension of their lives, a place where they often spend more time than they do in their own homes. It became a comfortable haven, a place where cops were surrounded by a large, squabbling, loving cop family with ties that went far beyond mere bloodlines.

With a cup of coffee firmly in her hand, Fey took a deep breath and picked up the telephone. Driving to the station, she had laid out a course of action that went beyond her initial self-protection reflexes. She still had no idea if Cordell was actually on the loose, or if some jailhouse hophead who knew her brother had given him enough information to play out a sick joke.

Before she sounded the alarm, she needed to verify her information. It wouldn't look real good if she had everyone spinning their wheels while Cordell was wrapped up snug in his bunk.

Her call to county jail went straight through and was picked up on the first ring. She asked for Intake and Detention Control and was connected. She identified herself to the deputy on the desk and confirmed that Isaac Cordell, booking number 3194788, was in custody according to the computer.

"Can you do a visual check for me?" Fey asked.

"Why? I'm telling you he's checked in here on the computer." The deputy's voice had taken on a nasal whine. "If he's in the computer, then he's in his cell all locked down nice and tight."

Fey tried to keep her exasperation in check. She knew going in that she would run into this kind of resistance. "Are you trying to tell me that your computer has never made a mistake?"

"Not since I've been working here."

"And exactly how long has that been? Two months? Three?"

"Six."

"Well, excuse me all to hell. Listen, cowboy, I'm sure you think you've seen everything after six months of working custody, but you ain't never seen me when I get pissed off." Fey made her voice rock-hard. "I am a homicide supervisor, and I started on this job when you were still an itch in your daddy's pants. If I have to drive all the way down there to do my own visual check on your prisoner, and I find out he's not where he should be, then your rapidly spreading butt is going to look like a piece of raw meat. Now, are you going to do a visual check for me, or do I start sharpening my incisors?"

"Okay, okay. I'll check for you, but it will take a few minutes. Do you want to call back?"

"Not on your life, cowboy. I'll hold."

The phone line muted in her ear and Fey took a long swallow of coffee. She played with a pencil on her desk, turning it over and over, and then finally began doodling little moons and stars on a piece of scrap paper. Her heart seemed to be pounding harder than normal, and the acid in her stomach was acting like an Atlantic storm. Fatigue and an overdose of caffeine were working their combined demonic magic.

A noise from the stairwell made her jump and reach for the short-barreled .38 stuffed in her waistband.

"Easy," said Jake Travers, identifying the movement and putting his hands up. "I'm one of the good guys—"

Fey held her hand up as the custody deputy came back on the line.

"You still there?" the deputy asked. His voice held a cocky note.

"I'm still here."

"Well, so is Cordell. Sleeping like an innocent child."

"You checked his wristband?"

"Yep."

Fey felt a thrill of relief run through her. She didn't have an explanation for the phone call yet, but that would come later.

"Is everyone down in county jail still as innocent and pure as the driven snow?" she asked, attempting through ritual humor to lighten her relationship with the deputy.

"Everyone except the deputies," he replied easily enough.

"Listen, cowboy, thanks for checking. I really appreciate it, and I'm sorry for getting on my high horse."

"No problem. These skinny little hypes all look alike, so I'm sure mistakes get made once in a while."

Fey's heart rate went ballistic. "Wait a minute. Did you say Cordell is a skinny little hype?"

"Yeah. Mexican guy with a droopy mustache."

Fey hung her head down.

"Ah, shit," she said softly.

Tommy Croaker sat on a hard-back chair in the middle of an interrogation room that was otherwise empty of furniture. Fey stood behind him with her arms crossed, leaning against the white rubberized wall. She was wearing a wine-colored blouse over black slacks and sensible flats. Her shoulder holster was empty since her gun had been placed into a lockbox before she entered Wayside Honor Rancho's security area.

Colby was resplendent as always in a new blazer and pleated wool slacks. Fey thought he was pushing his fashion statement a bit too far when she caught a flash of his bare ankles above another beautiful pair of calfskin moccasins. He had his head down and his arms crossed as he, too, leaned against one of the interrogation room walls. He mentally complimented himself for his good sense in keeping his mouth shut while Fey interrogated her own brother.

The night before, after verifying that Isaac Cordell had indeed escaped from county jail, Fey had put out an all-points bulletin and then contacted Wayside to check on the whereabouts and condition of Tommy.

At first it seemed that Tommy had escaped from Wayside with Cordell, but later an enterprising deputy had found his prostrate form lying in a clump of bushes outside the minimum security barracks. Tommy had been happily doped to the eyeballs.

There was no sign of Cordell.

When the sequence of events was finally established, it became clear that Cordell had somehow managed to exchange wristbands with Manny Sesteros, the Mexican hype who had been his seat mate on the prison bus and who was later found in the bunk assigned to Cordell at county jail. Manny had been on his way back to Wayside to serve another ninety-day stretch after pleading guilty in court earlier that day. He hadn't seen any reason not to screw with the system that had screwed with him for so long.

At county jail, Booker and Taggert had turned their charges over to two other deputies to process. The two new deputies didn't question the wristband switch, not recognizing the name of Isaac Cordell as Booker had done. Through the bureaucratic faith in the infallibility of the wristband system, Manny had been left at county jail, and Cordell was transported off to Wayside in his place.

As an extra bonus, Cordell had one hit of tar heroin hidden behind his upper lip. The small, brown lump was covered with plastic cling-wrap and had been a gift from Manny, who was later found to have a whole string of the little lumps hidden in his mouth.

The final destination of the tar heroin secreted in Cordell's mouth had been the veins of Tommy Croaker, but only after an exchange of what Cordell considered valuable information. In the identity of Manny Sesteros, Cordell had found himself placed in Wayside's minimum-security compound in time to locate Tommy during the after-dinner recreation hour. After that, gaining the information he needed and walking away from minimum security precautions at Wayside had been relatively easy.

A car was reported stolen in the residential area close to Wayside and was later recovered near the Devonshire Division station that served the area where Fey lived. There was little doubt in Fey's mind that it had been used by Cordell until he was able to find a safer mode of transportation.

While all of this information was being discovered, Fey had notified Lieutenant Cahill of Cordell's escape and the phone call she had received. She then woke up Colby and arranged to meet him at Wayside the next day around noon. After that she had allowed Jake Travers to take her home for the night and put her to bed. With the sheets covering her naked form, and Jake's arms wrapped tightly around her, she had fallen into a deep and exhausted sleep.

In the morning, Fey had awakened to the smell of coffee and sizzling bacon. She lay in bed gathering her thoughts, not wanting to disturb the happy bachelor routine that was going on in the kitchen.

As she lay taking in the familiar surroundings and the enticing smells, she realized for the first time how much she liked Jake's bedroom. It was part of a small, two-story house along one of the canals that ran through the Venice beach area. Jake had renovated it along with the residences on either side, which he also owned. Using the middle of the three houses as his residence gave Jake the luxury of being able to choose his neighbors. The residents rented through a realty company and had no idea Jake was their landlord—another plus in Jake's estimation.

Jake's first wife had taken him for a chunk of change, but he still had enough money from family connections and his own financial dealings to live in Beverly Hills or any of the other ritzy areas that put themselves on display around L.A. Jake, however, would not have been at home there. He preferred the Bohemian and the eclectic, and in doing so he fit right in with the beach and water culture that had always been the trademark of the Venice area—gangs and hippies aside.

Jake had done all of the decorating in the house himself, relying on dark tones and rough-textured fabrics to assert his independence from wifely and other female influences. His ornaments, pictures, and knickknacks reflected his interests in maps and architecture, and his books had taken over every other available space. The books filled several wall-to-wall fixtures and spilled out onto other shelves and free-standing bookcases that had been scattered around the residence with random abandon. The titles ran mostly to law books and "Golden Age" detective stories with a scattering of sailing and nonfiction adventure titles.

Shortly after Fey opened her eyes, Jake appeared in the bedroom doorway wearing nothing but a smile and an apron.

He held a glass of orange juice in one hand and the morning paper in the other.

Fey burst out laughing. "I hate to say this," she said through a fit of giggles, "but you look like the homosexual butler from a French film farce." She cracked up again when she saw the hurt look on Jake's face.

"I thought it had a rather macho appeal," he said, with a mock pout. Thick black hair grew rampant across his chest and arms, covering a wiry musculature. His stomach was flat and hard, and Fey had always thought he had a nice butt.

"You thought wrong," she told him.

"Well, you're just a bright ray of sunshine this morning, aren't you?" He put the orange juice down on the bedside table. "Come on, lazybones," he said. "Breakfast in five minutes." He turned his back on her and twitched his butt as he went through the doorway.

Fey threw a pillow at him, still chuckling.

The healing power of sleep had done its job, and Fey sat at the breakfast table wearing Jake's baggiest white work shirt while stuffing her face ravenously with pancakes, bacon, and fluffy scrambled eggs.

"If I'd known I was going to have a pig snuffling through the trough this morning," Jake said as he sipped a cup of coffee and watched her, "I would have stocked the larder higher."

"Shut up," Fey said, scooping a dribble of syrup from her chin. "I'm enjoying myself. It's not often I have a man around who cooks for me. I'm just showing my appreciation by eating everything on my plate."

"And mine," said Jake as Fey snatched a half-eaten rasher of bacon from Jake's plate and popped it in her mouth.

"What's on your agenda?" he asked.

Fey swallowed her last bite of pancake and pushed her plate away. She made a face. "I'm going to meet Colby out at Wayside to speak to Tommy at noon."

"That's going to be a load of chuckles."

"Tell me about it. However, it has to be done. I doubt there is anything he can tell us about Cordell that we don't already know, but I have to cover all the bases."

"And after that?"

Fey shrugged. "I haven't thought that far yet. I have to see if I can come up with some kind of a plan to track Cordell down, because I can't go around looking over my shoulder for the rest of my life. On the other hand, I think I need to go back to square one with this investigation. All the pieces seem to fit together, but the picture is pretty bizarre. I'm not sure if there isn't something missing." She drained her coffee cup and poured a refill. "How about you?" she asked.

Jake raised his eyebrows and sighed. "Well, there's always the day's regular contingent of filings and problems. But I don't have anything coming up in court for a few days, so I think I'll take some time and dig into this double jeopardy question."

"Do you really think Ryder can actually use that as a defense? Especially now that Cordell's an escaped felon."

"I don't think the escape is going to have any bearing on the double jeopardy issue. If Ryder can somehow pull off the double jeopardy defense and the murder charge is dropped, then the escape and the resisting-arrest charges are almost going to become a moot point. I don't think Vanderwald is going to want the press to turn this into a *Les Misérables* situation—and that's just the type of public outcry that I would expect Janice Ryder to pursue."

Fey nodded her reluctant agreement. She knew that Janice Ryder wouldn't let any opportunity to exploit public outcry slip through her fingers. She also knew that Jake's boss, Simon Vanderwald, was a very savvy political animal who had the instincts of a career sailor when it came to judging which way the wind was blowing. Janice Ryder would scare the pants off him like a sudden force-ten gale off the port bow. There would be no support from that direction.

Fey also wondered silently how much she could rely on Jake to push the case. Those in the know considered Jake as having the best chance of ousting Simon Vanderwald during the next election, and they wouldn't want him to jeopardize their own political interests and backing by going too far out on any particular limb.

Fey gave herself a mental shrug and glanced at the digital clock that was part of Jake's microwave. She still had time for what she had in mind.

"Come here," she said to Jake.

He had changed out of his apron and into a short kimono robe. He looked at her in surprise as he recognized her tone of voice. One eyebrow crawled up his forehead in a questioning gesture.

"Come on," she said. "Don't go coy on me."

It was Jake's turn to laugh. "Are you accusing me of being shy?"

"I'm waiting for you to come over here and prove differently."

Jake pushed his chair back, took two steps to Fey's side of the large kitchen table, and pulled her to her feet. He put his arms around her and kissed her gently, very aware of the livid line of bruises on her face. Most of the swelling had disappeared, but the kaleidoscope of colors was still going to be with her for a while.

"Mmmmm . . . nice," Fey said. She kissed him back harder and wrapped one bare leg around him.

"Are you sure about this?" he asked, concerned for her aches and pains.

She pushed a hand between their bodies and inside his kimono. She grasped him with her fingers and kissed him again, excited by the heat of him. "Does that answer your question?"

Jake kissed her, their tongues like two inflamed serpents, and then made to move toward the bedroom.

"Uh-uh," Fey said, stopping him with a shake of her head and a seductive smile. "I want it right here, and right now." She turned from him and quickly pushed the dirty dishes to one side of the table.

"You're joking," Jake said. His voice had thickened and his robe hung open to expose his own excitement.

Fey had perched her naked backside on the edge of the table. Now she leaned back on her arms, Jake's shirt riding high on her hips. She pulled her knees back and spread herself open to him.

There weren't any other answers or questions needed.

* * *

Colby had been waiting for her when Fey arrived at Wayside at twelve-thirty.

"You're late," he said.

"A master of the obvious," Fey replied.

"What were you doing? Trying to catch up on your beauty sleep? If so, it didn't help much."

"Actually, I was fucking my brains out, if it's any of your business," Fey told him nonchalantly. "I'd consider doing it to you, but it's obvious somebody beat me to it a long time ago."

"Humpf," Colby snorted. "You should be so lucky."

Fey shook her head at him. "Not even if you were the last dick on the planet."

"Well, that just proves my theory about you being a pussy licker."

"Eat your heart out, sonny," Fey said, and twitched her hips as she moved off toward the security building.

She had a hard time understanding why Colby was constantly riding her sexually. It was obvious that with his looks and flash, he could pull women who were far younger and better-looking than she was. But she'd met men like him before. It frustrated them when a woman wouldn't let them get into her panties. They believed there had to be a reason for it, and it certainly couldn't be that they were obnoxious assholes. Therefore, the woman in question must be a dyke or have something else wrong with her.

Fey had learned over the years that the only way to handle men like Colby was to never let them see they bothered you. If they could see that they were unsettling you, it gave them a sense of power—if they couldn't fuck your body, they wanted to at least fuck with your mind.

To keep them in line, you had to slap them down, insult them, keep the upper hand, and ride them back. If you kept it up, they would eventually back off to lick their wounded egos—rising to the bait again only when they had the chance to stab you in the back.

There was no way to turn men like that into friends, or to earn their respect. You were either a notch on their bedpost or you were a lesbian. Fey, like many other women, preferred the mislabeling, because sleeping with the assholes certainly didn't accomplish anything.

Once inside Wayside, Fey and Colby took their guns out and placed them in a series of gun lockers along one wall. They then introduced themselves to the watch commander, who showed them to an interrogation room before sending for Tommy.

Another deputy brought the inmate into the room and sat him down in the single chair. He looked like a frightened rabbit, and Fey thought that at any moment his nose would start twitching.

"Hello, Tommy," she said.

"I don't have to say nothing to you," Tommy whined in the agressive manner of a man trying to show that he isn't scared to death.

The eyes of the scrawny inmate still showed the effects of the drug in his system as they darted around the room. Even though he was in his middle thirties, Tommy's body still looked like it was waiting to mature past puberty. It was soft and anemic-looking from years of drug abuse and malnutrition.

"Why did you do it, Tommy?"

"Why did you put me in this hellhole?" Tommy retorted. "I'm your fucking brother and you sent me to jail."

Colby saw where the conversation was going and kept his mouth shut. Before Tommy was brought to the interrogation room, Fey had filled him in on a little of the background between her brother and herself. She didn't tell him much, but it was enough for him to read between the lines and realize that there was far more shared baggage than she was admitting. Being an only child himself, Colby only understood enough about the semantics of what went on between siblings to be glad he didn't have any.

"We've been over that ground a thousand times, Tommy." Fey's voice was unnaturally calm. "I didn't put you in here. You put yourself in here."

"Yeah, sure. Like I was the one who talked to the fucking judge and asked for the maximum sentence."

"Is that why you gave Isaac Cordell my phone number and address? Because you were pissed at me?"

"Fuck no," Tommy said. "I gave it to him because he offered me some dope in exchange for the information."

Fey's head hung down, and Colby realized she was on the verge of tears. He recognized that in some ways it would have been easier on Fey if Tommy had given up the information simply because he was pissed off at his sister. That emotion would have been far easier to deal with and rectify than the real monkey on Tommy's back.

When Fey remained silent, Colby chipped in for the first time. "Tommy, there's a good chance this bastard Cordell is out to hurt or kill your sister. Did he say anything to you, or is there anything you can tell us that might help us catch him?"

"You got any dope on you?" Tommy asked. "No? Then go fuck yourself with a broom handle. Cordell, or whatever his name is, can fucking kill her for all I care."

Colby looked at Fey.

"Let's get out of here," she said, and pushed herself off the wall by her shoulders.

"Wait, sis—I'm sorry," Tommy said, turning in his chair to face Fey as she reached the interrogation room's door. His voice was a whine, the bravado of a few seconds before nonexistent. "I really didn't mean to tell him anything. I mean . . . you know . . . and then he offered me the dope—"

"Shut up, Tommy," Fey said, and pulled the door open. "It's too late."

"No! No! Wait!" Tommy's voice was imploring. "Don't leave me in this place. You've got to get me out. I didn't mean to tell him anything. He made me take the dope—"

Fey turned around to face her brother, making no attempt to hide the tear running down her cheek. "Don't bother to call anymore, Tommy. I'm going to disconnect the number."

"No! You can't!"

Fey walked out of the room, followed by Colby. She twisted the lock on the outside as she heard Tommy fling himself against the door. She wiped her eye. "He's ready to go back," she told the deputy who had waited outside the room. He gave her a strange look, never having seen a detective cry during an interrogation before, and nodded.

When Fey turned to walk away, Colby followed close on her heels. They retrieved their guns and walked out to the parking lot.

One of the things Fey had told Colby about was the answering machine setup that her brother left messages on, so he had understood her reference to disconnecting the number. "Are you really going to shut down your answering machine number?" he asked, thinking about the emotions of the situation.

Fey seemed to think about that for a moment. "Not for a while yet," she told him eventually. "It's the number that Cordell has, and he may use it again. We should get a tap put on the line just in case."

"You think he's really going to come after you? Wouldn't it make more sense for him to just take off for the boonies and hide out?"

Fey had reached her car and turned to face Colby. "You weren't there in that alley when he and I were rolling around in the garbage. He stopped running when he realized it was a woman chasing him. He enjoyed hitting on me. But I was able to stop him, and he won't be able to live with that."

"You have a high opinion of yourself to think he'd bother sticking around specifically to take you out."

"No, I just have a low opinion of men who enjoy hitting on women. I was there. I saw his eyes when he was hitting me, I heard his voice when he called, and I'm telling you he isn't going to run and hide."

Fey unlocked her car and slid into the driving seat. "And I'll tell you something else for free. I'm not going to run and hide either."

**23**

"**A**ny luck?" Mike Cahill stuck his head out of his office when he saw Fey and Colby returning.

Fey, still fighting to get a tight reign on her emotions, just shook her head and moved on to her desk. Behind her, Colby shrugged his shoulders and rolled his eyes in the lieutenant's direction. "Anything new on this end?"

"Nothing specific pertaining to Cordell," Cahill said. "Hatch and Monk went to the roll calls here and in Devonshire with photos and info-bulletins, so patrol is aware he's out there. They also took care of getting a judge to sign the warrant paperwork and placed it in the system."

Colby had stepped into the lieutenant's office as the two men talked.

"How's Fey doing?" Cahill inquired.

"She had a tough time handling the situation with her brother."

Cahill took that with a grain of salt. Anybody would have trouble handling that kind of situation. "How about Cordell? Do you think he's a real threat to her?"

Colby shrugged. "She seems to think so, but I don't buy it. The guy is probably running for the border as we speak. That's if he isn't across it already." Colby sat down in one of the office chairs. "I mean, what does he have to gain by sticking around to mess with Fey? I think she's just running scared."

Cahill chewed that over for a while.

"Just between you and me, Lieutenant," Colby continued, "I think she has more on her plate than she can handle right now. The whole damn unit needs a shake-up, or you're going to see this string of unsolveds continue."

"I think that still remains to be seen," Cahill said. His tone was cool, letting Colby know he was dangerously close to stepping over the line. After all, if Cahill reassigned Fey, it would be a black mark on his own judgment since he had put her in charge of the homicide unit in the first place. "It looks like she wrapped this case up pretty quick, and it certainly wasn't her fault the sheriff's fucked up and Cordell got loose."

"Come on, Lieutenant. This case was a self-solver from the get-go. There was nothing tricky about it. We found a witness who could place Cordell at the crime scene. We found the murder weapon in his room, and he split on us when we went to talk to him. It wasn't like it was great detective work or something."

Cahill shook his head. "I'd watch it if I were you, pal. You're a long way from being able to buck for her job. Your star may be shining, but remember it only takes one ah-shit to wipe out every atta-boy you've ever earned—and right now you're awful close to a big ah-shit."

"Well, shut my mouth and write to tell the president," Colby said in a fake feminine, southern accent as he briefly covered his lips with his palm. "I just don't know what gets into me sometimes, but it do make me twitter on."

Cahill couldn't help but laugh. "Just twitter your ass out of my office and see if you can't make us both look good by recapturing this asshole."

Colby looked suitably put out. "Can't I wait until after he's had a chance to carry out his threats?"

Fey had planned to take Colby with her when she started backtracking the case, but when she saw him come out of Mike Cahill's office, her paranoia sensors kicked in to overdrive. She knew Colby had been twisting the knife into her back with Cahill, and she retaliated by dumping the day's paperwork on him.

"Wrap yourself around that lot," she told him. Colby opened his mouth to complain, but immediately thought the better of it when he saw the look on Fey's face.

"Where are you going?" he asked eventually.

"I've got to go and make my apologies to Harry Carter

for missing the autopsy, and then I'm going to go by SID and see if they came up with anything further for us from the crime scene."

"Why don't you let me do that stuff?" Colby said. His voice sounded a little strained, and Fey shot him an odd look.

"You worried I'm going to fall apart or something?" she asked him. "Or do you think I need protection?" Her voice held a dangerous edge.

Colby felt his face flush and he turned away, hoping Fey wouldn't see. Fey clocked the rising crimson tide, though, and smiled as she grabbed up her purse and briefcase. "Why don't you take care of the stuff you already have on your plate, and let me worry about the stuff on mine?" That should keep him in his place for a while, she hoped.

As she headed toward downtown in her unmarked detective sedan, Fey thought about the idea of protection. She glanced down at the shotgun on the passenger floorboard and wondered if all her precautions were necessary. Surely Cordell wasn't stupid enough to make a run at her while she was on duty. Then again, he may be banking on that kind of attitude to take her by surprise.

And what about when she wasn't on duty? She had told Jake that she wasn't going to be looking over her shoulder for the rest of her life, and she had made the bravado statement to Colby that she wasn't going to run and hide—even though that was exactly what she felt like doing. There had to be some solution to the predicament, and her mind chewed over her options as she drove.

Harry Carter was in his office filling out paperwork when Fey arrived. It was a small, cluttered office that did not match Harry's position as chief coroner; however, Harry was comfortable in it and refused to move. His face came alive and he stood up to greet her when Fey came in.

"I understand you've had a busy time of things," he said, giving her a genuine smile of welcome and shaking hands.

"You could say that, but it wasn't anything I couldn't handle."

Harry reached out and touched her chin gently as he examined the bruises on her face. "Interesting battle scars."

Fey chuckled. "I prefer to think of them as war paint."

Harry took his hand away. "If you were the winner, how bad did the other guy look?"

"His face looks like the south end of a northbound mule, but it naturally has that feature. His testicles, however, are probably still in orbit."

"Ouch." Harry winced. "That was hardly fighting fair, was it?"

" 'Fighting fair'—now, there's an oxymoron if I ever heard one."

Harry smiled again. "Kind of like jumbo shrimp, huh?"

"Or military intelligence."

Harry laughed. "Coffee?" he asked, turning toward an old-fashioned plug-in pot standing on a counter in the back of his office.

"Sure."

Harry poured brown liquid into two glass measuring beakers, added cream from a jug in a little refrigerator to Fey's and two spoonfuls of brown sugar into his own.

"I'm sorry I wasn't able to make it to the autopsy," Fey said when they were settled. In her heart of hearts, she knew that was a lie since she hated the damn things. They were the curse of most homicide investigators' jobs, but they were a necessary evil. Still she'd only come across two people in her career who actually enjoyed going to autopsies, and she wouldn't have trusted either one of them not to have been a serial killer in a previous life.

"You didn't miss much," Harry said, waving off her apology. "I'm afraid I didn't turn up anything startling or case-breaking. All pretty routine, really." He reached out and pulled a file from beneath a stack of papers on his desk. The stack tilted but held. He opened the file and pulled his glasses down from the top of his head to read it. "Ah, let's see . . . female, Caucasian, approximately forty-five to fifty years old, blood A positive. Sixty-six inches tall, one hundred and thirty pounds. She was in damn good shape for her age—good muscle tone—must have worked out like hell." He flipped over a couple of pages. Fey knew Harry Carter well enough to realize he was using the file as a prop. He could have told her everything that was in it without referring to a single page—even if she were to ask him about it several years later. His memory was almost photographic, but for some reason he enjoyed playing the role of the absentminded professor.

"Time of death was approximately two A.M.," Harry continued. "There was semen in the vagina vault, and from the condition of the sperm, I'd say that she'd had intercourse sometime up to three hours before she was killed. There were no physical indications that the intercourse had been forced." Harry checked his notes again. "The victim had eaten a salad for dinner the previous evening. From the looks of her colon, I'd say she subsisted mostly on fruits, vegetables, and grains—probably a total vegetarian. Her liver was in good shape with no signs of alcohol or drug damage. She didn't smoke—had a strong heart and a good set of lungs. All in all, from the way she took care of herself, I'd say she was somebody who was planning to live forever."

"Or at least until she ran into somebody with a sideline in throat slashing."

"Ah, yes. There is that, all right." Harry flipped to yet another page in the file. "As I told you at the scene, the carotid artery was slashed and the victim bled to death in a hurry. I originally told you that the weapon was a screwdriver, but now I'm not so sure. I don't quite know what to tell you to look for, but it will be something like a screwdriver with, perhaps, a little wider blade."

"But we've recovered the murder weapon," Fey told him. "It was a flat-head screwdriver as you originally told us. The lab hasn't confirmed it yet, but there was blood on the tip and on the handle which I'm sure will come back to the victim."

"Hmmmm," said Harry, raising his eyebrows. "I'm surprised. But if you say so, I won't dispute the fact in court. It could have been a screwdriver, but I still favor something slightly different."

This bothered Fey because she had never known Harry to be wrong.

"I'll keep it in mind," she told him. "Things have happened so rapidly since we caught this call that I haven't had a chance to think straight about all the evidence. I don't feel particularly comfortable myself with the way this whole thing has come together. On the surface it looks like everything has been handed to us on a plate, but I believe that somehow there has to be more to it."

"Like who the victim really was?"

"Exactly," Fey said. "Who was she before she was Miriam Cordell, and who was she between being Miriam Cordell and Miranda Goodwinter?"

"Good point. It sounds like you have to catch your breath and start over from the beginning."

Fey sighed. "That's about the shape of it."

Harry closed the file and threw it back on his desk. "What are you going to do about this Cordell character, now that he's escaped?"

Fey swigged the last swallow of coffee out of her beaker. "One thing at a time, Harry. One thing at a time."

Fey had called ahead from the coroner's office and arranged to meet Annie Thaw at a small sandwich shop across the street from Parker Center. The afternoon was winding down, but Annie had put off eating lunch until Fey arrived. The sandwich shop was located at one end of a small shopping mall, and the two women sat eating sandwiches and chips at a tiny outdoor table.

"How's your life?" Fey asked Annie as they both munched away.

"In case you haven't figured it out for yourself," Annie said sourly, "those fairy tales our mothers reared us on were a bunch of bullshit."

"Ah, I take it you haven't got to the happily ever after part?"

"Give me a break," Annie said. "When was the last time you came across a Prince Charming? Men are slime."

Annie and Fey had been friends for many years. Annie had started working in the Scientific Investigation Division's laboratories on the fourth floor of Parker Center, the police headquarters building, at the same time that Fey had entered the police academy. Over the years the two women had become friends, and Fey had found Annie's scientific expertise to be invaluable. She could, however, live without Annie's bleak view of the world.

"I take it Danny is not keeping up with his alimony and child support?"

"When has he ever been up-to-date with that stuff?"

Danny Thaw was Annie's ex-husband and the father of her two sons. He wasn't nearly as bad as Annie liked to make out, but he could still be a bastard when he wanted to be. On the other hand, Fey realized that life with Annie would be no bed of roses.

"What about the results of the crime scene work on the Goodwinter case?" Fey asked, wanting to cut to the chase.

"Another prime example of why men should be nuked off the face of the earth," Annie replied. "Women would never do something like that to another woman."

Fey knew it was ridiculous to argue with Annie when she was in this kind of mood—feminism was one thing, man-hating another. She also knew that women did do awful things to other women. She'd seen the evidence—shootings, stabbings, bludgeonings, poisonings, arsons. If anything, women were more vicious than their male counterparts when it came to murder and physical child abuse.

Sex crimes, however, were another matter entirely, but this case did not appear to be following that track. There were no indications of any deviant sex acts or any forms of torture. The style of the murder was more consistent with an act of anger, and just because the victim had engaged in intercourse before being murdered did not mean she'd had sex with the murderer. Nor did it mean that she didn't. As usual, sex did nothing more than complicate matters.

"Okay, Annie, I hear you. Men are slime," Fey said, agreeing only to get the ball moving. "Now, what do you have for me?"

Annie took a bite of her sandwich and chewed before talking through her food and spraying crumbs everywhere. "Not much, I'm afraid."

Why did people keep saying that to her? Fey wondered. She needed something more than "Not much." She needed something solid to get her teeth into.

"Come on, Annie. You can do better than that for me."

"Not this time. There were no prints in the room that matched those of your suspect—what's his name?"

"Cordell."

"Yeah, Cordell. Anyway, you're shit out of luck when it comes to prints where he's concerned."

"What about on the murder weapon?"

"Zippo, baby. It was clean. No prints."

"Shit."

"Exactly."

"What about the blood on the murder weapon?"

"There you score some points. The blood is A positive, same as the victim's. The first level of DNA testing indicates that the blood could belong to your girl, but you're going to have to wait another couple of weeks for the long-term testing to be completed. I wouldn't sweat it, though. I don't think there's any doubt."

"Well, that's something anyway." Fey pushed her plate away and fought the urge for a cigarette. "Anything else?"

Annie was silent.

"Annie?"

"You're not going to like it."

Fey rolled her eyes. "What else is new?"

"Okay. Of the prints that were recovered from the scene, most of them belonged to the victim, but there were two other prints that are still unidentified."

"Not Cordell's?"

"No way. Not even close. As best as I can tell, we have prints from a thumb and an index finger. Both of the prints have nicks and scars in them—as if they come from someone who does a lot of hard work with their hands—"

"Construction?"

Annie shrugged. "Something like that type of work. The thumbprint came off of the bedroom door handle. The index finger print was only a partial caught in a smear of blood on the sheet—"

Fey gave an excited start. "That would mean it occurred after the killing blow was delivered."

"I agree, but that causes you a number of problems, doesn't it?"

Fey stopped to think. "Shit," she said. "That means somebody else was there after Cordell."

Annie gave her friend a condescending look. "Get your head screwed on straight, Fey. The print may be a lot more significant."

"Don't say it."

Annie did anyway. "It may also mean that Cordell isn't your murderer."

Fey's heart was pounding in her chest. "Again," she said quietly.

**T**hings were going from bad to worse.

Fey was sitting in the comfortable living room of Mrs. Kathleen Bridges, having another piece of evidence against Isaac Cordell blown right out the window.

After finishing her late lunch with Annie, Fey knew she had to go back to the foundations of the investigation and rebuild the case from scratch. She had felt sure that there would be fingerprint or trace evidence that would tie Cordell to the crime scene. His connection to the victim was logical—motive abounding—but far more would be needed for successful prosecution in court. Getting twelve straights in a jury to agree on anything beyond a reasonable doubt was tricky at the best of times, but when the charge was murder, you practically had to hit them over the head repeatedly with the evidence to win a conviction.

Reviewing in her mind the evidence against Cordell, Fey looked at what had first brought about the certainty that he was their suspect. The first evidence had been the motive provided by Card MacGregor in San Francisco, and that had been corroborated by the photo identification of the witness who lived in the townhouse across from the crime scene. Monk Lawson had come back with the positive identification, and everyone had gone off the deep end, convinced that Cordell was the man and everything would fall into place once he was in custody.

Wrong.

Nothing had fallen into place. In fact, everything had gone to hell in short order.

Eyewitness identifications were notoriously unreliable, and driving back from Parker Center, Fey had determined to pay her own visit to Mrs. Kathleen Bridges, who had so conveniently dumped Cordell in the shit. And even though she had prepared herself for the worst, Fey hadn't been prepared for the surprises provided by Kathleen Bridges.

A stern-looking woman answered the door to Fey's knock and managed to appear both confused and intrigued when Fey identified herself.

"Are you Kathleen Bridges?" Fey asked, slipping her badge back in her purse.

"Why, yes I am," the woman answered. Her voice held a suppressed south Texas drawl. "Is this about the murder across the street?"

Through the partially open door, Fey could see that the woman was in her early sixties with blue-gray hair and the wrinkled face of a lifetime smoker. She was dressed in expensive designer sweats, and it was obvious from the condition of her nails and her hairdo that she had money with which to pamper herself. A single strand of pearls hung over the crew neck of her black velvet sweat top.

"Yes," said Fey. "I'm sorry to bother you again, but I wondered if I could talk to you for a few minutes."

The woman looked confused but opened the door to admit her guest. The inside of the townhome was tastefully furnished, but it was clear that most of the pictures on the walls and the antiques used as decorating highlights had been with the woman for a long time. It was definitely a home, a place where this woman was comfortable with her memories. Fey instinctively knew the woman was a widow, and when she stopped to admire a particularly riveting painting, her judgment was confirmed.

"That is Musashi," the woman said, referring to the Japanese samurai depicted in stunning detail on the canvas. "My late husband was fascinated by the samurai and their code of Bushido. Musashi is perhaps the most famous of the Japanese swordsmen. My husband found that painting while on a business trip in Hawaii. Personally, I find it a little terrifying, but now that Edgar is gone, I don't have the heart to take it down."

"Musashi wrote the *Book of Five Rings,* didn't he?" Fey asked. She was good friends with a retired policeman who was heavily into samurai philosophy and had given her the book once as a gift.

"Why, yes," said the woman. "Are you familiar with the work?"

"Slightly."

"Please, sit down," the woman said, ushering Fey to a nondescript couch.

"I want to talk to you about the identification you made yesterday—" Fey herself couldn't believe it was only the day before, so much had happened since "—of a man you saw going into the townhouse across the street on the night of the murder."

The woman looked confused again. "I don't understand," she said. "What identification?"

Fey paused. "You are Mrs. Kathleen Bridges?"

"Yes."

"And you did talk to a detective yesterday who showed you some photographs." Fey held up the photo lineup Monk had used for the identification.

"No, I didn't," the woman said.

It was Fey's turn to look confused. The woman seemed to have all her marbles—she wasn't that old—but you could never tell. "I'm sorry, Mrs. Bridges, but I was led to believe that a Detective Monk came here yesterday and talked with you."

The woman shook her head in amusement. "I'm sure I would have remembered something like that. The murder is the talk of the neighborhood, and a tidbit like that would have made a good piece of gossip."

Fey didn't quite know what to do or say next. She was

floundering for words when she was saved by a sharp voice from the second level of the residence.

"Kathy! Kathy! Who's here?"

Kathleen Bridges shifted her gaze to an open hallway that ran across the second floor of the townhouse. "It's a detective, Mother Bridges." The woman's eyes came back to meet Fey's and then roll in exasperation. "My mother-in-law," she said softly to Fey in explanation.

There was a series of noises from the second floor, and Kathleen Bridges jumped to her feet. "It's all right, Mother Bridges," she said, moving toward the stairway. "You don't have to come downstairs." She turned her head back toward Fey. "She's a dear, but it takes so long to get her up the stairs to her room."

Fey wondered why they didn't let the woman have a bedroom on the ground floor, and as if reading her thoughts, Kathleen Bridges gave her an answer. "We tried giving her a room downstairs, but she was always underfoot. Before he died, Edgar and I could never get a minute to ourselves. Even now he's gone, it's best to keep her out of the way."

"Hello," said the older woman as her daughter-in-law failed to stop her determined descent. "How nice it is to have visitors."

The woman was slight and stooped and at least fifteen to twenty years older than her daughter-in-law, but her eyes still sparkled and gave her the appearance of a retired fairy godmother. She took small steps over to Fey in a pair of fuzzy mules and a cotton housecoat. She held out a liver-spotted hand, and Fey shook it, feeling the frail bones beneath the parchment-dry skin.

"You're a police detective?" she asked Fey.

Fey smiled. "Yes, I am."

"How exciting for a woman to be doing your job." The eyes twinkled. "In my day, we had police matrons. They took care of the children and the woman prisoners. And now look—"

Kathleen Bridges put her hands gently on the woman's shoulders and guided her to a seat. The woman went willingly enough and sat down while still staring at Fey.

"I'm sorry," Kathleen Bridges said.

"That's quite all right," Fey told her. "It was a pleasure to meet your mother."

"My mother-in-law," Kathleen Bridges said.

Fey held up the photo lineup. "Are you sure you've never seen these photos before?"

"Yes, I'm positive," Kathleen Bridges said.

Fey shook her head.

"I've seen them," Mother Bridges said from her chair.

Fey looked at her sharply.

"Now, Mother Bridges, don't be ridiculous." Kathleen Bridges moved to her mother-in-law's side and patted her on the shoulder.

"But I'm telling you, I've seen them. It was just like on TV."

"What are you talking about?" Kathleen Bridges's voice was rapidly filling with impatience.

Fey leaned forward in her chair. "What is your mother-in-law's first name, Mrs. Bridges?"

The woman stopped her patting movements in midaction. "Why, it's Kathleen, the same as mine . . . Oh, my . . . I never thought . . . I just always call her Mother Bridges. Edgar and I used to laugh about it when we first got married. It was such a coincidence that my name would become the same as his mother's." She shifted her look from Fey to her mother-in-law.

"Do you ever leave your mother-in-law at home alone?"

"Sometimes. She's okay for two or three hours by herself if she doesn't have to make any meals. She's not really a problem that way."

"Did you leave her alone yesterday?"

The woman thought. "I had to run some errands in the morning. I was only gone for maybe an hour and a half. She doesn't answer the door when I'm gone, so I'm sure she didn't talk to anyone."

Fey stood up and walked over to crouch in front of the seated older woman. "Is it okay if I call you Mother Bridges?" she asked.

"Of course, my dear."

"Did you answer the door while your daughter-in-law was out yesterday?"

"I did," the old woman said smugly.

"Mother," Kathleen Bridges said, with another heavy dose of exasperation.

"Oh, do stop fussing," the older woman said to her daughter-in-law. "I was bored, and he looked like such a nice man."

"Was he a black man? A detective?" Fey asked.

"Yes, he was. Very polite and very nicely dressed."

"Did he ask you some questions about seeing somebody enter the house across the street on the night the woman who lives there was murdered?"

"Yes. And I told him what I saw from my bedroom upstairs. It was so exciting talking to a real detective. It was just like on TV."

"And did the detective show you a set of photographs?"

"Yes."

"Are these the photographs?" Fey asked, handing Mother Bridges the photo lineup.

Mother Bridges took the lineup and squinted at it. "Yes, these are the same photos. I picked out this one," she said, pointing to the picture of Cordell. "Your detective was very excited, and I was glad I was able to pick out the right one because I didn't want to disappoint him. He was so nice."

"Is this your signature?" Fey pointed to the name scrawled under the picture.

"Yes, it is."

Thank goodness for that, Fey thought. Mother Bridges seemed pretty sharp, and her identification of Cordell would probably hold up. Her sparkling eyes alone would convince a jury.

"Mother Bridges," her daughter-in-law broke in. "How could you possibly have seen anyone across the street? You know you can hardly see across the room these days even with your glasses." Kathleen Bridges turned her head to speak to Fey. "Her eyesight is so bad, she can't read anymore. I have to bring her books on tape from the library. We also have to put drops in her eyes to keep them clear since her cataract operation. The drops make her vision blurry."

Fey looked closely at the old woman's eyes and saw that

what she had taken to be a sparkle was actually light reflecting off the medicine drops.

"Mother Bridges." Fey took the old woman's hand. "This is very important. Can you honestly identify the man you saw going into the house across the street?"

The old woman looked stubborn for a moment and then shrugged. "Your detective was such a nice young man. I didn't want to disappoint him. I didn't even see anyone going into the house across the street. I just wanted to keep him here for company. He was so nice."

I bet he was, thought Fey. Monk believed he'd found himself a witness who could break his case. What detective wouldn't be nice under those circumstances?

"When he showed me the pictures," Mother Bridges continued, "I didn't want to upset him, so I picked one. I didn't like the looks of this character," she said, pointing again to Cordell's picture. "Your detective was so pleased. He said he'd come back again, but now I guess he won't." Mother Bridges sounded very disappointed. "Am I going to be in trouble?" Her lower lip trembled.

With an effort, Fey patted the old woman's hand and struggled to reassure her. "Thank you for being so honest with me, Mother Bridges." She forced a smile. "And you're certainly not in any trouble."

But I am, thought Fey. And so is this case.

"I'm sorry, boss. I had no idea."

Fey waved her hand in Monk Lawson's direction and sighed. "I'm trying not to be too pissed off, but I expected better out of a veteran detective. Hell, I would have expected better out of Colby."

Fey and Monk were alone in Mike Cahill's office, sitting across from each other at the round conference table. Monk had lowered his eyes to the table, and Fey knew that if the skin on his face had been white instead of black, it would have been red with embarrassment. She felt bad, but she also knew Monk had the chewing out due, and she'd tried to handle it as low key as possible. He'd been the detective who had shown the original lineup to Mother Bridges, and everyone had taken him at his word that the identification was righteous.

"Look," she said, in a softer voice. "I know you thought you had this thing nailed down. The old lady could have fooled a lot of people, and sometimes we get so caught up in what we want to hear that we don't hear what is really being said. You've been around long enough, though, to know you have to go the extra mile to make sure identifications like this don't fall apart on you."

"I know, I know," said Monk. "But I still can't believe it." He shook his head in amazement. "She was so damn convincing."

Fey had to give a soft chuckle because, even though she would never admit to it, Mother Bridges had sucked her in also.

"It was those damn twinkling eyes," Monk said. The chagrin in his voice was so real that Fey couldn't hold it in any longer. She burst out laughing.

Monk's eyes flashed up, but he realized quickly that Fey's laughter did not hold any malice, and he let his own deep chuckle leak out.

The two detectives seemed to get a grip on themselves, and then looked at each other and started giggling all over again until they both had tears in their eyes. The laughter was cathartic, releasing not only the stress of the situation for both detectives, but also the pent-up anticipation that Fey had been carrying around since hearing Cordell's phone message.

When they finally settled down, Fey wiped her eyes with a tissue and tried to get things back on track. "I guess there is no sense crying, or in this case laughing, over spilt milk. Our case is shot to hell, so we're going to have to find a way to patch it up and nail this bastard down."

"You still figure Cordell is the best suspect?"

"At the moment. It's kind of hard to get out from under the fact that the murder weapon was recovered from his crib."

"What about if he was really being framed again, as he said?"

"What do you have in mind?"

Monk shrugged his shoulders. He didn't want to look foolish again.

"Come on, out with it," Fey encouraged.

"Well, I was thinking about this lawyer of his. I mean, what's her stake in all this? The guy was bankrupt when he went into prison, and he sure as hell didn't get rich while he was on the inside, so why is this Ryder broad weighing in on his behalf?"

"You mean you don't believe in altruism?"

"No. And I don't believe she's doing this out of some kind of quest to right a judicial wrong."

"Maybe she's got a movie deal clicking?"

"That might not be as far out as it sounds in this day and age, but somehow I don't think so."

"Me either," said Fey. "And I think you might be on to something that's at least worth considering."

"There's some other points that are bothering me also."

"Like what?"

"Like how did Cordell get paroled in San Francisco and then end up in L. A. within a couple of miles of where the woman he supposedly murdered is living high on the hog? Coincidence? I don't think so."

"Okay, I'll bite on that also. Why don't you do some checking and see if you can find anything that pans out?"

"You got it."

"Along those same lines," Fey said, "we're also going to have to start backtracking the victim. This change-of-identity stuff is a bunch of bullshit. I want to know who she really is, what her story is, and who else might have wanted her dead."

"Sounds good."

Through the window of Mike Cahill's office, Fey saw Hatch holding up a phone and pointing from the receiver to Fey. "Looks as if I'm being paged," Fey said, and stood up to leave the room.

"Boss," Monk said, stopping Fey at the door. "I'm sorry I let you down."

Fey smiled. "I know you are, and that's what makes you such a valuable friend. Some of the others out there—" she jerked a finger toward the squad room "—would have been sorry for screwing up, but they wouldn't have given a damn about how it affected me. Thanks for caring." The two detectives nodded at each other, and Fey walked out to handle the next crisis.

"What do you have?" she asked as she approached Hatch.

"I know you said to screen all of the press calls, but this is a little different. This guy has called three times to talk to you. He insists on talking directly to you—won't tell anyone else what he wants. He also said he's getting ready to go home for the day."

"Is he a flake?"

Hatch shrugged. Fey sometimes wondered if it was a habit he'd picked up from Monk or the other way around.

"For some reason, I don't think so," Hatch said. "He's a straight, all right, but he sounds very professional and squared away."

Fey walked over to her desk. "What line?"

"Eighty-four-ten."

She pulled a clip earring off her left ear and picked up the phone. "Detective Croaker," she said into the mouthpiece.

"Hello," said an assured male voice. "My name is Longley—Myron Longley. I am the manager of the Wilshire Boulevard branch of the Beverly Hills Savings Bank."

"What can I do for you, Mr. Longley?"

There was a slight hesitation, and then Longley asked, "I take it you are the detective in charge of the Miranda Goodwinter murder investigation?"

"I am."

Seemingly reassured by this response, Longley continued. "My concern is that I saw the picture of Miriam Cordell in the paper yesterday, and the photo of the police taking that poor woman's body out of the house after she'd been murdered. And then there was all the conjecture about whether

Miriam Cordell and Miranda Goodwinter were the same person . . ." Longley's voice trailed off.

"Yes," said Fey. She was beginning to think this guy was a flake anyway, even if he was the manager of a bank.

"Well, I might be wrong, but I think I recognized the photo of Miriam Cordell as one of the bank's customers who recently closed out her accounts by withdrawing a very large amount of cash. The problem is that I knew the customer as a Mrs. Monica Blake . . ." Longley's voice trailed off again.

Bingo, thought Fey. "Don't move, Mr. Longley. I'll be right there."

Fey checked her watch as she and Colby approached the front doors of the Wilshire Boulevard branch of the Beverly Hills Savings Bank. It was almost six o'clock, and Fey realized the bank had been closed to customers for almost two hours.

The front door was locked, but Fey tapped on it and displayed her badge to a uniformed guard on the other side of the glass. The guard nodded at Fey, held up his index finger in a "just a moment" gesture, and walked away. He returned in a few seconds being trailed by a dapper-looking man in a well-cut black suit who was brandishing a key.

The man was short with slicked-back hair that was almost as shiny as the patent leather brogans covering his feet at the other end. Through myopic lenses held in fashionable black frames, the man thoroughly scrutinized Fey's badge and identification before unlocking the door.

"Mr. Longley?" Fey asked as soon as verbal communication was possible.

"Yes. Please come in." The man stood out of the way to hustle the two detectives inside and then looked both ways out the door before closing and locking it securely. His actions were of a fastidious man who was expecting bank robbers to be moving in on his domain at any second.

There were still several tellers in the bank who were going through the procedures of closing out their drawers. Longley gave a set of keys to a nicely dressed woman whom Fey took to be the assistant manager, and told her to take care of the vault and deal with the tellers. She nodded solemnly, as if this were a great responsibility she was being entrusted with, and moved off to do the manager's bidding.

At a large black desk in the back of the building, Longley ushered Fey and Colby into chairs set on a Chinese carpet in front of the desk, and took his rightful position behind the desk. He smoothed his pants carefully over his backside before planting himself down. He fiddled around adjusting the precise position of his desk blotter, and Fey could see Longley was having trouble parting with his bank's secrets.

"We appreciate you contacting us, Mr. Longley," she said to broach the awkwardness. "It isn't often that we have a financial institution offer us information without the dint of court orders and other time-consuming obstacles."

Longley smiled, an action that immediately transformed his face from the typical banker's poker visage to that of a naughty little boy. "I'm sure that is true, Detective Croaker. Banks like to treat their customers' confidences as if they were as sacrosanct as those told in the confessional. In reality, however, there is very little other than a manager's feelings of petty power to stop banks from cooperating with the police."

"A refreshing point of view," Fey said, still not quite sure what Longley was driving toward.

The bank manager smiled again. "I have to admit that my attitude is the result of having both a brother and a son involved in law enforcement."

"Ah," said Colby. "The picture becomes clearer."

"Quite," said Longley, with a nod of his head in Colby's direction. "But there are other factors as well."

"And they are?" Fey asked.

Longley turned his attention toward her. "Whenever a customer withdraws a large sum of money from their account—and by large, I'm talking in excess of half a million dollars—or closes out an account containing a similarly large amount of cash, a manager takes that as a personal affront and wants to know the reasons why. Firstly, because it hurts the assets of the branch, and secondly, because one of the hazards of the trade is that managers come to look on the bank's money as theirs, and we begrudge giving it up."

Fey laughed. "How did you ever wangle your way into a manager's position with those kinds of insights?"

"My uncle owns the bank," Longley said. The corners of his mouth turned up slightly. "Nepotism is a wondrous thing, don't you agree?"

Fey and Colby both realized the question was rhetorical and waited for Longley to go on.

"Under normal circumstances, perhaps I wouldn't have thought to call you, as I'm still not sure that my Monica Blake is the same woman as the one in the photo. They look very much alike, however, and I have been unable to contact Mrs. Blake since she withdrew her funds. It seems she has disappeared." Longley checked his watch.

Fey shifted in her chair. Longley might be willing to cooperate, but it was obviously going to be on his own time schedule. "I take it there were some other circumstances surrounding this case that made you call?" she asked.

"Yes. Two circumstances, in point of fact." Longley looked up as the uniformed guard from the front door approached the desk and signaled to him. Longley raised his hand in acknowledgment, and then returned his attention to Fey as he stood up. "Please excuse me for a moment, but one of the circumstances has turned up to meet you." He walked away from his desk, fishing again for the front door key from the depths of his trouser pocket.

Fey looked at Colby and made a perplexed face. Colby shrugged and mirrored her expression. Their silent consensus of opinion seemed to be to go with the flow of events and see what happened.

Longley returned in less than a minute with another man in tow. The second man was tall and thin with a gaunt face ravaged with the pockmarks that spoke of traumatic teenage acne. Dark, hooded eyes gave him the appearance of a half-asleep bird of prey. He wore a good-quality but ill-fitting gray suit, a starched white shirt with an expensive blue tie, and black wing tips.

Colby figured there were probably initials monogrammed somewhere on either the cuffs or pocket of the starched shirt, and he had no problem categorizing the guy as some kind of federal agent. Even without saying a word, the walking stick figure practically screamed his occupation.

Longley brought over another chair. "This is Mr. Kyle Craven," he said, by way of introduction. "He's an IRS investigator."

Both Fey and Colby felt fear move in their bowels. If there was any law enforcement agency in the country—nay, the world—that had more power and fewer checks and balances than the investigative arm of the Internal Revenue Service, neither one of them could think of it. Without much effort, an IRS investigator could even scare the hell out of agents from the government's ultrasecret National Security Agency.

IRS agents were God unto themselves, and if you didn't want to find yourself at the wrong end of an audit, you meekly did whatever they asked and got the hell out from under as quickly as you could.

Craven's slow smile would have done credit to a corpse. He could smell the fear in the air and found it invigorating—a Hannibal Lector of the CPA set. "Hello," he said in a deep voice. "I'm from the government, and I'm here to help you." He sat down without offering his hand.

The man thinks he's a comedian, Fey thought as she cringed inwardly. Colby had gone visibly pale at the disclaimer. And even Longley seemed affected by Craven's presence as he scuttled back around to the minimal protection offered by the far side of his desk.

Craven produced his rictus grin again, still enjoying the effect he knew he was having—the effect he would always have on anyone who had any inkling of the power possessed by the IRS, an unconstitutional organization condoned by the government as a necessary evil. "No, I mean I really am here to help you," the stick figure said, even though he knew no one would believe him. "No pressures, no hassles. If indeed Monica Blake, Miriam Cordell, and Miranda Goodwinter are the same person, I might be able to shed some light on your case since I've been tracking the woman and her financial dealings for almost twelve years now."

"One of the circumstances I was explaining to you," interjected Longley.

"Can we please start from the beginning?" Fey asked. "I'm getting out of my depth here."

Longley nodded and sat forward, leaning his arms on his desk. "I'm sorry. I know all of this must be a bit confusing."

"It might be tough to believe, but most cops do have IQs higher than Nerf balls," Colby said, resorting to his natural sarcasm when confronted by an awkward situation. "So if you think you could spell the situation out quickly in words of three syllables or less, we can get on with things." A look from Craven almost froze Colby in midsentence, but he did manage to get the words out, and Fey was proud of the effort.

"I do apologize," said Longley. "I'm a bit at odds and ends with this situation myself. From what Mr. Craven has been telling me, I can hardly believe it myself—"

"Please, Mr. Longley," said Fey forcefully.

"Ah, yes. Sorry." Longley took a pause to compose himself. "Whenever a customer extracts a large amount of cash, there are forms that have to be filled out for the IRS and various other entities. It was through the forms that were filled out on the part of Monica Blake that Mr. Craven came to contact me."

"How long ago was this?" Fey asked.

"About five weeks."

Fey nodded at that. Cordell had been paroled six weeks ago, and it looked as if Monica Blake, aka Cordell, aka Goodwinter, put on her running shoes as soon as she found out. "What was so strange about Monica Blake's withdrawal that it came to your personal attention?" she asked Longley.

"You mean besides the amount?"

"Yes. But for the record, how much did she withdraw?"

Longley cleared his throat and pulled a sheet of paper out from under his blotter and consulted it. "A little over three million dollars."

"Holy cow!" Colby said, with a low whistle.

"Ditto," said Fey, slightly stunned by the amount. She remembered the new checkbook—for an account at another bank—that they had uncovered at the crime scene. There had been a freshly deposited two hundred dollars added to the one thousand dollars that had been used to open the account. She also remembered the million dollars in cash she had discovered in the dryer.

Either amount was a long way short of three million.

"The problem was," Longley continued, "that Mrs. Blake's account with this bank was minimal by our standards. Rarely did she have a balance in excess of five thousand dollars."

"So how did she expect to withdraw three million dollars then?" Colby asked.

"On the day before she came in to the bank, we received a three-million-dollar wire transfer to deposit in her account."

"From where?"

"A bank in the Cayman Islands."

"Hello, offshore banking," Fey said.

"Exactly," Craven chipped in, and then went silent again.

Colby and Fey glanced at him and then returned their attention to Longley.

"Yes. As Mr. Craven says, 'exactly.' When a bank receives a deposit of that size, or any deposit of over even ten thousand dollars, they are required to fill out a form notifying the IRS. There are large fines and penalties for noncompliance."

"Did the transfer surprise you?" Fey asked.

"Only mildly. It wasn't until Mrs. Blake came to the branch office the following day requesting to close out her account by removing a little over a million dollars in cash, and asking that the remaining two million be transferred to a brokerage house to purchase bearer bonds."

"Bearer bonds?"

"Yes. Basically a monetary draft payable to anybody that has the bonds in their possession. As good as cash, only in far higher denominations for easier transport."

Fey and Colby exchanged glances. There had been a million dollars in cash in Miranda Goodwinter's dryer, but no bearer bonds had been uncovered. Neither had the bonds surfaced at Cordell's crib. And if he'd been stupid enough to bring the murder weapon back to his room, why not the bearer bonds as well if he had taken them?

Fey shifted in her chair to get a better look at Craven. "And how do you figure in to this scenario?" she asked.

"Quite simply through the fact that I've been chasing this woman, as I said, for over twelve years. I've tracked her forward through six different personalities—seven if you count Miranda Goodwinter—and backward through at least four identities. Much to the irritation of my professional pride, I have never been able to establish her true identity, and now there is the further frustration that somebody else caught up to her before I did."

"How can you be so sure that this woman you've been tracking is the same person as Miranda Goodwinter?" Fey asked.

"Have you not established on your own that Miranda Goodwinter and Miriam Cordell were the same person?"

"Yes."

"Well, I know that Miriam Cordell was but one of the identities assumed by the woman who has led me a merry chase for more years than I care to remember."

"But how have you managed to tie all of these women together?"

"Money and murder, Detective Croaker. One makes the world go round and the other stops it."

**26**

"**N**obody likes the IRS," Craven said, stating the obvious in his oddly modulated style of speech. "But that's because everybody cheats on their taxes. Even people who don't think they're cheating on their taxes are always fudging a little bit here and a little bit there. It's the American way."

"Are you expecting sympathy?" Fey asked, showing surprise. "The role of a poor, little, misunderstood Internal Revenue Service investigator doesn't suit you."

Craven actually laughed. Threw back his head, opened his mouth, and guffawed. Fey instantly realized she liked Craven better when he was being serious, as he appeared even more menacing when he was amused.

Craven got a grip on himself eventually and wiped his eyes with the tip of an index finger. "Detective Croaker," he said. "I make no bones about the fact that I enjoy my job."

"No shit," said Colby softly, but everybody ignored him.

"However," Craven continued, "that doesn't make the necessity of doing my job any less."

"And what exactly is your job?"

Craven seemed to think about that for a moment before replying. "My job," he said eventually, "is tracking down those individuals who seek to avoid paying any taxes at all, and in doing so show contempt for all the other citizens who are still doing their share despite their petty attempts at cheating."

"What about the organized tax protest groups?" Colby asked.

Craven winced. "Please, spare me. Fanatics are not my bailiwick—misguided scum that they are. No, my quest is the individual, the criminal with no political agenda, the man or woman who holds up their middle finger to society as they rob us blind."

Fey wanted to cut to the chase. Craven was having too much fun orating from atop his high horse. "And how does this apply to Miranda Goodwinter?"

Craven's features darkened. "A pariah with no conscience and an insatiable greed for money."

Craven went on to describe how he had tracked Miranda Goodwinter for years, always an identity behind her, able to use her paper trail to establish each new identity only after she had shed it like a snake skin and moved on. And in each shed identity, she left behind a chaos of murder and financial gain.

"Are you saying Miranda Goodwinter was some kind of black widow killer?" Fey asked as the scenario became clear.

"Exactly," Craven said. "Twenty-two years ago, as

Marsha Wallace, she picked up a tidy sum of fifty thousand dollars when her first husband fell down a flight of stairs and broke his neck. She also inherited his minor estate and disappeared without a trace.

"Next we switch to twenty years ago when, as Madeline Fletcher, she picked up a hundred thousand dollars when her new husband was killed in a drunk driving accident. This time she plundered the estate before leaving behind a penniless thirteen-year-old stepdaughter to be raised by impoverished grandparents."

"Sweet lady," Fey commented as Craven plowed on.

"Fifteen years ago, as Mavis Curtis, she cops a cool five hundred thousand when yet another husband has a sailing accident and drowns. The poor bastard couldn't swim and didn't sail before she came into his life and insisted on buying the boat." Craven paused briefly for breath.

"Then there's the Miriam Cordell identity, which you're already familiar with. She picked up her first million-dollar payoff in that scam, although it ran a little differently than her usual MO." Craven reached into a slim valise he had brought with him and withdrew several computer printouts. He reviewed them quickly and then continued with his narrative. "As far as I can tell, our lady went underground for a while after the Cordell affair. The whole thing was probably far too public for her—threatened to tip over her whole apple cart. However, I almost bought off on the whole scam myself. It looked like she'd finally bitten off more than she could chew and was sleeping with the fishes.

"I wouldn't have thought much about it except for the fact that six years later, I all but tripped over another case involving another *M*-name woman—May Wellington this time—and it looked like the chase was on again."

"You knew she was alive and you didn't do anything to clear Isaac Cordell?" Fey asked.

"I only believed she was alive, Detective Croaker. I couldn't prove anything at the time. And anyway, Isaac Cordell's father had ripped off the government for more than his share of tax revenue, and having the son behind bars for the sins, or debts, of the father without him knowing it had a rather nice ironic appeal." The death's-head grin came and went with startling speed.

Shit, Fey thought, save me from the self-righteous.

Craven looked at his printout again. "After May Wellington there was Mona Ford, and after Mona there was Maxine Trent. And with each identity, Lady M was leaving behind a trail of high-priced husbands six foot under, each one of them providing for her in advance should they bite the big one unexpectedly. The whole cycle appears to have become an obsession with her. As they say, men kill most often for sex. Women, on the other hand, kill most often for money."

Fey shook her head in wonderment. "And that brings you all the way up to Monica Blake and Miranda Goodwinter?"

Craven nodded. "With some slight variations on the theme. Something appears to have spooked Monica Blake into running, because there doesn't seem to be any dead husband or lover left behind."

"And Miranda Goodwinter hadn't had a chance to establish herself yet," Colby added, seeing the trend.

Fey looked bothered. "I don't understand how the Miriam Cordell scam fits into the pattern. It was hardly the same method of operation that she'd used previously."

"That bothered me as well," Craven said, "until I really considered the situation. On the surface, Isaac Cordell would have looked like the perfect candidate for our lady to get her claws into. My theory is that Lady M—I really can't think of her by any other name since I've never been able to establish her true identity—bumped off Cordell's mother and put herself in a position to fill the gap in Cordell's life. Once hooked into the picture, she realized too late that there was no money left in the estate—not even enough for Cordell to get a good-size life insurance policy."

Fey's mind was racing. "So you think this woman—whoever she is—took out a policy on herself . . ." She trailed off.

Craven picked up the thread. "Using a chunk of the money she had accumulated from her other scams—"

Fey came back on the ball. "And somehow worked it

out with Cordell's business partner to fake her own death and pick up the million dollars secondhand after Cordell was sent to jail on the manufactured evidence!"

"Go to the head of the class," Craven said.

"Damn," said Fey, still trying to absorb all the implications. "And what about Roarke, the business partner?" she asked.

"Disappeared from the scene, never to file a tax return again," Craven told her.

"How did you come by all this information?" Colby interrupted to ask.

The gaze that Craven turned on Colby was that of a teacher to a student who had just urinated on his shoe. "Tax returns and numbers are my life, Detective Colby. I use numbers and forms and obscure rules and regulations to tie people up in little knots too tight to wriggle out of and get away. I scan thousands of computer printouts a day in my quest to make sure dear Uncle Sam gets his fair share out of your pocket." He waved his hand around the bank's interior. "Institutions like this one thrive on cash transaction forms and other pieces of paper that send red flags flying. I track drug dealers and money launderers and organized crime racketeers until I am blue in the face and the thrill is lost. But every once in a while I come across someone like Lady M who puts the meaning back into the chase. When that happens, I pay attention, and slowly but surely a case is built—" he held up a hand and squeezed his fist together "—until I have my quarry where I want them!" Craven's voice had hopped an octave, and he suddenly seemed to realize his mask of civility was slipping. With an effort he comported himself back to a more stable state.

"It looks as if this one got away from you," Fey said.

"Perhaps in this life," came the stoic reply.

**B**y the time Fey and Colby arrived, the promotion party at Two-Step Tilly's was in full swing. Tilly's was a country/western club located on the border between Pacific Division and West L.A., and was often frequented by coppers from both areas. It wasn't the traditional cop bar run by a retired blue-suit with an all-gun-toting clientele, but more of an eighties urban cowboy version that provided a safe haven from time to time for cops to let their hair down.

The party was in honor of Paul Trotweiler, a young P-3 detective trainee who had recently been promoted to full detective. The promotion was sending him from West L.A. to Southwest Division, hardly a desirable move except for the change of stature. Given a year or two, he could probably make his way back out of the ghetto to a more preferred area, which would leave a hole in the ghetto for another sucker chasing promotion. Unless he was very lucky, getting back to West L.A. could take a lot longer—the waiting list was currently three years long.

Still, in the spirit of euphoria that new promotions bring before the reality of location sets in, Paul had coughed up six hundred bucks to Two-Step Tilly's bartender. The beer and liquor would therefore flow down the throats of the other West L.A. detectives and selected guests until the tab ran out. Most everyone would leave at that point, but there would be a hard-core group who would then start digging into their own pockets for some serious drinking.

Sponsoring your own promotion party was a tradition that ranked with bringing in several dozen doughnuts on your first day in a new division. You weren't forced to do it, but if you didn't, there were a lot of ways that life could be made

socially tough for you. And anyway, you owed a debt for all
the free drinks you had sucked down at other promotion parties, and all the fat pills supplied by others that you had
swallowed over early morning coffee.

Fey waved at the raucous group of about thirty detectives who had sequestered one corner of the bar next to the
dance floor. Colby moved away and headed for the men's
room. Fey headed for the bar.

On the way to the party, they had talked over the information overload Craven had plugged into their heads. It was
all very interesting, but they were both undecided as to how
it would help them nail Miranda Goodwinter's killer. The information certainly provided motive, but they already had
that in abundance where Cordell was concerned. Craven's information served to define that motive, but did it shed any
further light on the case? Coupled with the fact that everything else in the case against Cordell was falling apart, did
the sordid history of Miranda Goodwinter give a lead to any
other suspects? The answers were all still evasive.

Fey's head spun with all the possible implications. She
knew she would have to give her subconscious time to work
over all the input before she would be able to have it make
any sense. In the meantime, getting mildly drunk had a definite appeal.

Vance Hatcher made room for a chair between himself
and Monk, and Fey sat down with relief. She raised her glass
to Jake Travers, who was at another table. He winked back at
her. Several people knew about their relationship, but they
still played it fairly cool in public.

"Any word on Cordell?" Mike Cahill asked from across
the table.

Fey shook her head. She'd managed to put the threat of
Cordell being on the loose out of her mind while Craven had
been dumping his information all over her. Now, with
Cahill's reminder ringing in her ears, she decided that perhaps
she would get more than just mildly drunk.

"Any joy from the bank manager?" Hatch asked.

"I don't know yet," Fey told him. She felt suddenly exhausted. "And it's all too much to go into tonight." She finished off the second half of her beer and waved to a waitress

carrying a full tray. "Let me cut the dust with a couple more of these, and let's talk about something besides the damn case for a change."

"Here, here," said Monk, taking a fresh beer for himself from the waitress's tray.

Somebody cranked up the jukebox, and the voice of Clint Black came booming out of the speakers spread around the room. A number of couples headed for the dance floor, including several pairings from the gathered detectives. Slacks, ties, and shoulder holsters had been traded in before leaving work for boots, jeans, and hidden backup guns.

Fey took in the scene as the chatter around her rose to compete with the music. Mike Cahill's thigh was being massaged under the table by one of the station's record clerks. If his wife were to find out, Fey knew she'd skin them both alive. At another table one of West L.A.'s robbery detectives had a lip-lock going with a female detective who had recently transferred to another division. Fey figured their spouses wouldn't be too happy with the scene either.

Colby had come back from the bathroom and had pulled yet another chair into the group. He quickly knocked back a couple of beers to catch up and then started on a third.

All in all, the contingent for the promotion party was made up of perhaps thirty detectives, a dozen or so faces from uniformed patrol, four off-duty record clerks, a couple of well-liked DAs, several of the younger station volunteers looking for husbands—not caring if they currently belonged to somebody else—several of the older volunteers simply enjoying the outing, and another half dozen cop groupies.

The groupies all had their reasons for hanging out with the cops, and all paid the price of inclusion in some form or another. A couple were hard-core "cop fuckers," the traditional bimbos whose day wasn't made unless they'd had some hunk between the sheets or on the backseat of a patrol car. Most, however, were good-hearted straights who enjoyed flirting with a world outside their own staid existence. These straights gained access to the fringes of the group by providing their outside-world services to the area cops at cost or graits—free meals at restaurants; computer equipment or service to cops who didn't know a RAM from a byte; private vehicle mechanic work—all valuable barter for cops stretching paychecks to cover alimony-hungry spouses and L.A.-area mortgages.

En masse, the gathering from West L.A. was large enough to pretty much take over the bar. Tilly's regulars tolerated these incursions into their turf because the management liked having the cops come in occasionally to keep everyone on their toes. For their part, the cops could let their defenses down slightly due to the factor of safety in numbers. They were the biggest fish in a small pond, and if anybody outside the group wanted to challenge them, there was instant backup to settle the situation favorably. Gang mentality as applied by the "good guys."

Jake came over and whirled Fey out onto the dance floor. With five beers under her belt and no food to speak of since breakfast, she was feeling a slight buzz and was glad for the movement. They joined the circle of dancers and broke into a fairly smooth Texas two-step.

"You doing okay?" Jake asked.

"Ask me again after another couple of beers."

After one turn around the dance floor, Jake felt a tap on his shoulder and turned to see Colby standing behind him. Colby's eyes were bright with too much alcohol consumed too fast.

"Do you mind?" Colby asked. The challenge was clear in his voice.

Jake stepped back with a shrug to Fey and let Colby cut in. He knew Fey could easily fend for herself.

"I thought I'd managed to get rid of you for the day," Fey said as Colby guided her away. "What's the matter? Are all the groupies on to you already?"

"Come on, Frog Lady, lighten up. This was the easiest way I could think of to get my arms around you."

"Get off it, Colby. I'm a fat old broad."

"You're not that fat and you're not that old."

Fey sneered. "Thanks for the compliment, but the only reason you think you want to have me is because I won't let you. The unattainable is always desirable."

"Are you saying you're unattainable?" Colby ran a hand lightly across Fey's breasts.

"Certainly where you're concerned." Fey twirled out of her partner's grasp, gave him a mocking tilt of her head, and walked off the dance floor. Taking another beer off the bar, she sat down again, this time next to Jake.

"Looks as if you've developed a fan club," Jake said, his eyes teasing her.

"Shit. The guy is a walking hormone with an asshole. He thinks he can stab me in the back with one hand while frigging me off with the other."

Jake laughed.

"No, I'm serious," Fey said. "It's typically warped male logic. He knows I'm his boss, but because I'm a woman, he figures that if he can find a way to get into my shorts, that will somehow give him control over me."

"One good lay and you'll be jelly at his feet." Jake was still laughing.

"I told you," Fey said, throwing a pretzel at Jake. "Typically warped male logic."

"It worked for me," Jake teased.

"Fuck you, counselor. You can jerk off tonight." Fey sat back in her chair and crossed her arms over her breasts.

"Hey, let's not go overboard here."

Fey shook her head in resignation. "I should know better than to try and turn one male against another in this day and age. It's that bonding shit, right? Something to do with Monday night football and beer commercials?"

"Right," Jake agreed. "Also lots of tree hugging and chanting. Rediscovering our essential maleness that has been squelched by years of sensitivity training."

"Good-bye, Alan Alda. Welcome back, Grog the Caveman."

"Exactly."

"Well, shit, Grog. Why don't you scrape your knuckles over to the bar and get me another drink before dragging me by the hair back to your cave."

"You got it. Beer?"

"No. It's time to switch to the real stuff."

Fey watched as Jake moved off, carrying their empty glasses in his hands. The lightweights in the West L.A. group had thinned out. The top station brass had already split before

Fey and Colby arrived. They had paid their respects, wallowed through one drink, and then left the troops to enjoy themselves. It was the politically correct thing to do. Also, if the party got out of hand, they wouldn't be hit by any of the shit coming off the fan.

There was still a sizable contingent of coppers present, however, and even though Paul Trotweiler's money was long gone, the liquor was still flowing smoothly. There were several larger groups of males and females mixed together around the tables with no sexual overtones beyond shouted one-liners and innuendoes that set everyone giggling as if they were all naughty schoolchildren.

The single male-and-female matchups had moved off to darkened corners or to the intimacy of the dance floor. These couplings were noted and gossiped about, but the sanctity of the open secret would not extend beyond the group to outsiders or spouses of either gender. What went on within the police family stayed within the family. The unspoken agreement for infidelity was that only a member of the thin blue line could truly understand another—a belief that led to a conspiracy of blue silence and acceptance, a bonding that went beyond mere marriage vows, church commitments, or blood relations. If you were a cop, you were in. If you weren't a cop, you were out. Volunteers, attached civilians, and groupies could only penetrate so far. The rules were the rules. In or out. Cut and dried. Simple.

Good cop or bad cop, you took the mark of the badge with you to the grave. You weren't one of God's children, or one of God's sheep. The mark of the badge made you a wolf. God's wolves.

It was either that, or cops were just genetically unfaithful.

Colby sauntered over and leaned on the table next to Fey's chair. He looked at Jake's retreating back.

"What is it with you and the counselor? Trying to fuck your way into another promotion?" His voice was loud enough to be overheard by several of the other coppers at the table. Monk went to stand up and intervene before trouble broke out, but Fey shot him a look that froze him in his tracks.

Several of the female officers sitting at the table were watching Fey intently as if some secret communication had passed silently and invisibly between them.

Fey smiled at Colby. "You know, you really are pretty good-looking," Fey told him. "Perhaps you're right." She stood up next to Colby and swayed her body into his.

She kissed him full on the mouth as the cops gathered around the table hooted and hollered.

Colby was literally caught off balance. Leaning back against the table with Fey's substantial weight pressed against him did not leave him any way to maneuver. Through the alcohol haze that had emboldened his initial move, he realized he might have bitten off more than he could chew. He tried to brazen his way out.

"Why don't we blow this pop stand, Frog Lady?" he asked, his voice husky. Despite himself, he could feel an erection building as Fey straddled his thigh and rubbed her mons against him.

"Oh, you smooth talker," she said. She kissed him again, all tongue and spit, grinding her body into him, pressing her hardening nipples into his chest. She'd learned very early how to turn a man on, and about the power it could give her over him. The group at the table roared their approval. They knew Fey had Colby on the hook.

When Fey broke the kiss, she continued to press herself against Colby. She kept one hand wrapped behind his neck, controlling his movements as she would those of a strong stallion she was riding.

"You're heating up, partner," she said in a sultry bedroom voice full of lust and teasing. Fey waggled her free hand behind her back. One of the other women at the table, sensing what Fey had in mind, placed a freshly opened bottle of beer in the hand.

Fey kissed Colby again, her mouth wide and open on his, her tongue flying between his lips to entwine with his. She brought the hand with the bottle around and rubbed it over the obvious bulge in Colby's groin.

"My, my," she said admiringly, staying close to him again as she broke the kiss. She took her hand from behind

Colby's neck and grabbed the waist of his loose-cut slacks and pulled it forward.

Colby struggled slightly, thinking Fey was going to reach her other hand down to grope him, but he was obstructed by the table behind him and Fey's weight in front of him.

"Come on, Fey," he said, his voice thick. "Not here."

"Why not?" Fey asked. "I can't think of a better place—" Still using her body to hide her actions from Colby's sight, she placed the open mouth of the beer bottle inside his pants and let the liquid pour out ". . . to cool your jets," she finished.

"What?" Colby said, sounding confused, and then the icy cold wet of the beer hit his skin. "Shit!" he said and tried to push Fey away.

She buried her face in his shoulder and leaned into him, bending him across the table. Colby struggled and pushed himself away until his back was flat on the table. Beer glasses, chips, salsa, and ash trays were scattered everywhere. The other detectives and their companions stood up, jumping clear of the debris and laughing at the spectacle.

Leaving the beer bottle to empty down his pants, Fey backed off and stood laughing with her hands on her hips. Colby cursed her and struggled to pull the bottle out. He eventually removed it by standing up and shaking it down one leg of his pants like a slap-stick comedian. The groin and one leg of his pants were soaked with the beer. Everyone fell into convulsions of laughter.

"You fucking bitch," he said to Fey, looking down at himself. "You'll pay for this."

"I wouldn't pay you for anything," Fey said, still laughing. "Especially, not a beer flavored erection."

The crowd of detectives hooted at the slashing remark.

Colby grabbed a napkin from the floor and began rubbing ineffectually at the stains.

"Shit," he said again as he gave up. He looked around at the faces staring at him, sensing their delight at his discomfort. It pissed him off. For his whole life he'd never been able to keep friends on his side. He could never understand what he did that turned people against him.

In school he'd always been a top athlete, but he could never find a way to get a team behind him. Somebody else was always voted the captain, even when they weren't as talented as Colby. He could never understand why being the best wasn't good enough.

And now, as a detective, his arrest and conviction record was one of the highest on the department, yet nobody seemed to give a damn. They refused to give him credit, ready to jump at any chance to see him flounder. The bastards were just jealous. Well, fuck 'em.

"Go ahead and laugh, you assholes," he said as he began to storm out of the bar.

"Cute butt," one of the other female detectives called out loudly. It tripped everyone's laughter button again, and even in the dimmed lighting it was possible to see the flush of red flare up the back of Colby's neck. He turned around and gave everyone the finger.

Fey watched him go. Her initial pleasure at showing him up was slowly being replaced by a feeling that she had been out of line—carried the joke too far. She'd fought fire with fire perhaps, but shouldn't she have been above that? Why had she let him make her so mad? She tried to close her mind to the thoughts.

Jake returned to the table.

"Did I miss something?" he asked casually, bringing the group laughter back again.

The party at Tilly's finally wound down around eleven P.M. A few stragglers hung on until midnight, but Jake and Fey split arm in arm around ten-thirty. The thought of going home and facing the threat of Cordell lying in wait did not appeal to Fey at all. Despite her tough talk from earlier in the day, Fey was not yet prepared to walk the tightrope of acting as bait to lure Cordell out of the woodwork. There were still a couple of things that she hadn't had time to set up before she could debut that act. Until then, another night in Jake's bed sounded as if it was a good idea.

Or it had sounded at first as if it was a good idea.

Heavy-headed with exhaustion and alcohol consumption, she had barely managed to get her clothes off before falling face-first into Jake's pillows. Several hours later, she was sleeping the sleep of the dead when something brought her back to the surface of awareness.

A man stood beside the bed looking down at her, his dark outline nothing more than a darker black against the dark of the room's interior. Not fully conscious yet, she still somehow registered the fact that the man was naked and aroused.

She flinched with fear when he reached out to touch her. Memories exploded from deep inside her psyche.

"Get away from me!" she screamed, drawing her legs to her chest and flailing out ineffectually with her arms.

"Easy, girl, easy. It's just me." Jake reached out to grab her wrists as they whirled about.

"Get away from me, you fucker! I won't let you! I won't let you!"

"Fey. Fey. It's me, Jake. Calm down." Jake's words fell on deaf ears.

Fey was well aware now on the surface that it was Jake in the room with her. The thought that it might have been Cordell had only briefly flitted through her mind, and then disappeared under an avalanche of suppressed emotions sprung from her Pandora's box by a combination of alcohol and déjà vu. The image of her father standing beside her bed, naked and aroused.

When she was thirteen, she had awoken to the same scene. Her father standing over her in the dark, as he had so many times before. Only this time there was something different. The male smell of him was the same. The heat emanating from his groin, where it pressed into her side, was the same. But there was something different in his attitude. The anger was there as always, but this time it had become almost another living entity in the room with them.

"You fucking slut!" Her father's angry whisper had reached her ears with the force of a shock wave.

Fey sat up in bed, the blankets falling away from newly forming breasts hidden behind a teddy-bear-motif nightshirt. "Daddy? What?"

He smacked her across the mouth. "You keep your fucking voice down, you evil little slut. If you wake your mother up, I'll have to beat her too." He hit her again. This time on the side of the head with his closed fist. Her father had been a policeman, too, only in a time when corruption had run rampant, and he knew how to hit and cripple without leaving a mark.

"Daddy!" The thirteen-year-old Fey kept her plea to a vocal level of a whimper.

"I know what you did with that Higgins kid from down the street."

"No, Daddy. I didn't do anything!"

"Keep your voice down, you filthy little tramp!" Garth Croaker cuffed his daughter roughly across her right ear. Fey's head rocked on her shoulders, and she fell back across the bed.

Her father climbed onto the bed and pinned Fey down with his knees. "You let him fuck you, didn't you?"

"No, Daddy, no! He only kissed me."

The flat of Garth's hand flashed out, smacking, left, right. "Liar!"

"No!"

Again the slapping hand, left, right. "Lying, filthy, little bitch. You'll just have to be taught a lesson not to do filthy things with every little boy who comes along."

And the lesson consisted of all the filthy things Fey had never done with anyone—except when forced to do them with her father.

And then, as usual, there was even more anger after he had spent himself.

Only this time it was worse. Much worse.

The sledgehammer that was Garth Croaker's fist

smashed time and again into the heart of Fey's wide-spread legs and across the soft flesh of her abdomen.

Again. And again. And again.

A never-ending nightmare that would never stop, not even when the physical act was finished.

The doctor had been a friend of the family. A tame medic. A known abortionist whom Garth Croaker had kept out of jail on more than one occasion because there was always a use for a doctor who could keep his mouth shut.

He fixed the bleeding. Saved the life of the poor thirteen-year-old girl on his operating table.

Good old Doc Martin.

He saved the girl, but he couldn't save everything. Fey would never be able to conceive a child of her own. Still, her life was saved. Wasn't that enough of a miracle?

Good old Doc Martin.

One of dear old Dad's drinking buddies.

Six months after saving Fey's life, he forced himself on her while her father held her down.

Now, in the present, in Jake's bedroom with the man she loved standing beside her, Fey trembled with the fear of old scars torn open. Images flashed through the alcohol that still fogged her mind and scared her half to death. The nightmare that never ended.

"Fey? Fey? What is it?" Jake's voice seemed to reach her from far away.

She flinched when she felt a hand touch her arm, and drew herself up into a protected ball. She felt the damp of tears on her cheek, and the ever-suppressed scream stuck in her throat—because you'd better not wake Mommy. But Mommy was dead, and so was Daddy. He can't hurt you anymore.

Want to bet?

Jake didn't know what was happening, but he had the good sense not to push things. He had been returning from the bathroom when he had paused beside the bed to watch Fey sleeping. It was a private pleasure that always pleased him. When she had started to rouse, the thought of making love to her had suddenly aroused him. And then she had screamed.

He stood back when he saw the effect of his touch and made soothing noises. Calling Fey back from whatever hellish landscape her mind was dwelling in.

He turned on a low bedside lamp and watched as Fey returned to normal. Color seeped back into her face. Her trembling slowed. The visible beating of her heart beneath her naked breast subsided. Her eyes focused.

And then she reached out for him. Crushing him to her. Fiercely wrapping her legs tightly around him, as if trying to meld her body with his.

Back in control of the lovemaking, she found the now soft length of him with her hands and stroked him back to erection. With a fevered cry she opened herself and swallowed him into her, tight but determined.

And she rocked. And she cried. And he held her, without asking for explanation, until they slept.

**J**anice Ryder did not do mornings well, and as a result she was not a happy camper when the phone beside her bed roused her from a deep sleep.

"Whatzit?" she inquired in a sleep-drenched voice.

"Ms. Ryder, this is Cabo, the night manager. I'm sorry to disturb you so early, but an important package has just been delivered for you."

"Package?"

"*Sí.* A large envelope. It is marked urgent."

"Who delivered it?"

"I don't know. I had to go into the manager's office to answer the phone, and when I came out I found the envelope on the reception counter."

"I'm not expecting any packages or envelopes."

"But it is marked urgent."

Janice Ryder looked at her clock and sighed. Six-thirty A.M. "All right, bring it up." She didn't wait for Cabo's reply before hanging up. She rolled over in the bed and closed her eyes again, but after a few seconds, she groaned and threw the covers from her before sitting up slowly. She needed coffee. Strong coffee to kick-start her heart.

Sitting on the edge of the bed in naked splendor, she stretched by pulling each knee individually to her chest, wiggling her foot, and then straightening her leg out again. She flexed her torso and rolled her head around on her neck several times. Eventually she stood up and wrapped a light robe around her just as there was a knock on her front door.

She had chosen the exclusive Century City Towers Hotel because of the anonymity and security it offered her, and for the easy access it gave her to the surrounding Los Angeles area. She had reserved the room for three months, but hoped to be checked out far sooner if everything went according to her plan. The problem was that Isaac Cordell didn't seem to appreciate what she was doing for him, and by escaping, had pretty much screwed up her original plan three ways to hell.

Still, plans were made to be changed, and one of the things Janice Ryder did best was think on her feet.

As long as it wasn't in the morning.

She opened the front door on the security chain and peered out. Cabo, a smooth-looking gigolo type, was standing outside with a perky look on his face. He handed her the large manila envelope and stood waiting.

Janice wondered if he expected her to ask him in and screw his brains out or something. If he was, he was in for a big disappointment. She didn't like the smooth and oily types. Then she realized he was expecting a tip.

"Just a second," she said. Leaving the door open on the chain, she walked over to the living room coffee table and rummaged through her briefcase until she found two rumpled dollar bills. She took them back to the door and shoved them out through the opening.

"Thanks," she said as Cabo whisked the bills out of her hand and did a quick disappearing act with them.

"Is there anything else you need, Ms. Ryder?" he said, innuendo dripping off his every word.

"Sure as hell not at this time of the morning," Janice told him, and slammed the door.

How I hate people who are bright-eyed and bushy-tailed in the morning, she thought. She walked back toward the bedroom while looking more closely at the envelope she'd accepted from Cabo.

On first inspection, it was nothing impressive—an over-size manila envelope with her name printed in the middle in black marker, and the word "urgent" printed below it in red marker. She turned the envelope over. It was blank on the back, but the locking flap had been clasped down and then taped.

Janice threw the envelope on the bed and picked up the phone from the night table. She never ate after three in the afternoon, so breakfast was her big meal of the day. When room service came on the line, she ordered fruit; a mushroom, tomato, and bacon omelet; wheat toast; yogurt; and coffee. Lots of coffee.

After hanging up, she looked at the envelope again. She had no idea who it was from, but the whole scenario spelled out the conclusion that the contents of the envelope were going to be dynamite. She wasn't ready yet to handle dynamite. Ryder's rule number one: Coffee first, then dynamite.

She reached for the envelope and then pulled back again empty-handed. Best to stick by the rules, she decided.

For as long as she could remember, Janice Ryder had been a driven personality. She knew people often referred to her as an ice queen, a coldhearted bitch, a calculating, frigid, anal-retentive cunt, and many other nonflattering terms that the less-driven reserve for those who are more determined.

For her part, Janice agreed with most of the tags except for *frigid* and *cunt*. The latter was just a word that she hated. It simply held no meaning beyond a demeaning and sexist slur. And as far as frigid went, that was nothing more than a handy label for her husband to throw at her when she refused to engage in the sexual games with groups of three or more that seemed to be the only way he could get turned on. The term hadn't gotten him far, however, in the divorce settlement that left her easily able to afford staying for three months at the Century City Towers.

She made no bones about being driven. She had some specific goals to attain in this life, and she'd have plenty of time later to kick back and take things easy. Until then, going with the flow was not in Janice's personal dictionary.

It had taken her until she was thirty-one years old before she found and was capable of taking on the case of Isaac Cordell—a man whose original innocence she'd believed in absolutely and positively from the start.

Her peers had told her she was a fool to take the case, that there was nothing in it but a certain loss and a smear to her professional reputation. But Janice had five years of hard slog behind her in the public defender's office and the district attorney's office, where she'd performed brilliantly, but had chafed at doing what others told her. Now, in accordance with her personal plan, she was in private practice, and she didn't give a damn what her peers and her detractors thought.

The Cordell case had been perfect for her purposes. She couldn't have set up the situation any better if she'd planned the whole thing from the start. And she'd achieved a brilliant opening victory in her first move when she'd won parole for her client.

The toughest thing about the whole scenario, however, had not been the legal wrangling—that had been fairly straightforward. No, the biggest problem that she had to overcome so far had been gaining the confidence of her client. Ten years in jail had not been kind to the man. Oh, physically he was a fine specimen of almost monster proportions, but survival behind jail walls had twisted his emotional and mental makeup into a perverted and evil spiral. And after all the time she'd spent with Cordell preparing his case and securing his release, Janice had no doubt what she was releasing on the outside world—a psychotic killer, but still the perfect weapon for her purposes. And the cold, calculating, frigid, anal-retentive cunt bitch didn't care. She'd deal with the consequences after her goal had been finally achieved.

Room service knocked on the door and wheeled in a cart full of goodies. Janice signed the check and added a generous tip. Anybody who brought her coffee deserved a generous tip.

She immediately raided the coffeepot. Double strength as requested, black, no sugar, piping hot. Swallow it down without it touching lips or tongue. Wait for it to hit bottom, and boom, bring on that caffeine rush.

Two cups down. Fruit and yogurt devoured. Omelet and one slice of toast half-eaten. Third cup of coffee in hand. Heart in gear. Eyes open. Time to expose the contents of the envelope.

One long red fingernail slipped under the flap and slit open the top of the envelope. She slid the contents out into her hand. One typed sheet of paper. Double-spaced, half-full. Her eyes rapidly scanned the words. She'd been right, it was dynamite. Absolute dynamite.

She turned the photograph over. It showed two women embracing in a nightclub. Janice stared at the photo dumb-founded.

She'd been wrong.

This wasn't just dynamite.

This was a nuclear explosion.

**30**

**F**ey was still feeling a little rough when she dragged herself out of Jake's bed early in the morning. It would have been nice to spend an extra hour or so curled up next to Jake's comforting form, but Fey knew she had an obligation to fulfill before actually going in to the station that morning.

Moving quietly into the kitchen, she made a cup of instant coffee and buttered two pieces of toast that she had burnt on purpose. The first time Fey had consumed burnt toast in front of Jake, he had thought she was out of her mind, but she couldn't help it—she liked her toast burnt.

Sleeping only briefly in the postcoital glow after she and Jake had finished making love, Fey had spent the remainder of the early morning hours staring at the ceiling and thinking. The murder of Miranda Goodwinter chased back and forth in her mind, haunting her like a poltergeist whirling around in a belfry. It was the specter of Isaac Cordell that spooked her the most.

It was obvious that Cordell had been falsely convicted of murdering his wife the first time around. Was it possible that he was innocent the second time around as well? Not just innocent because of a technicality involving the double jeopardy laws, but truly innocent, having nothing to do with the murder other than being set up as a patsy again.

That was a big concept. And a positive answer regarding Cordell's innocence opened up a huge can of worms when you started to look for other possible killers.

Finishing her breakfast, Fey picked up the kitchen extension phone and dialed the station. Getting through to the watch commander's office, she identified herself and requested Colby's home address. She knew he lived somewhere in the Pacific Palisades area, within West L.A. division, but she had never been to his residence. She also knew that he still lived with his father, who was some kind of toy maker. She'd never paid much attention to the particulars as she'd always been too busy sparring with Colby to become interested in his personal life.

She was surprised by the street address the watch commander gave her. Pacific Palisades was an exclusive community splitting its personality between cliff houses overlooking the beach and custom homes hidden within rambling hills. Colby's address, however, was in an area that was considered exclusive even by Pacific Palisades standards. Fey had been expecting it to be in one of the older bedroom tracts that still clung to the edges of the area, or in the Pac Pal trailer park, which had sprouted across one of the Pacific Palisades cliffs like a pimple on a debutante's chin while a local politician calmly pocketed a tidy kickback.

Fey hung up the phone and slipped into her shoulder rig before grabbing her jacket and briefcase. She was dressed in a light blue blouse, dark blue slacks, and matching shoes. She kept the outfit at Jake's for the rare occasions, like the previous evening, when she spent the night there without going home first.

As she quickly covered the short drive to Pacific Palisades, she felt her stomach fluttering with self-recriminations and anticipation. The murder case had not been the only thing running through her head while she lay in Jake's bed in the early hours of the morning. She was very upset with herself over her actions at Two-Step's the night before. Slightly drunk and pissed off were not acceptable excuses.

Sexist actions cut both ways, and Fey cursed herself for acting in a manner that she would have expected from Colby but not from herself. If the tables had been turned, she would have been embarrassed beyond belief. And even though she had never asked for or encouraged Colby's attentions, she should have been able to find a better way to defuse them.

She had been mad at the time and thought it would be funny to give Colby some of his own back. And it had been funny. At the time. In retrospect, she knew she had made a bad mistake at Two Step's and was not sure how to rectify it. After all, she was supposed to be a damn detective supervisor, and she didn't like the idea that kept creeping into her head—the thought that maybe Colby was right and she didn't deserve, or couldn't handle, the damn job. She knew that was wrong, but she couldn't help beating herself up emotionally for having screwed up.

Eventually she turned off of the Pacific Coast Highway and began to wind her way along the hilly residential streets of Pacific Palisades. When she reached the address scribbled in her notebook, she took in the imposing structure, shook her head, and checked the street address again. It was correct.

The house was huge, well into the million-dollar-plus range. Fey had thought that Colby might be on the take because of his flashy clothes and flashy car, but no cop she'd ever come across was this much on the take—certainly no cop still working the streets. That kind of graft was reserved for politicians. Colby's father's toys must have brought in a lot of wampum over the years.

On a second, closer look, however, Fey could see that the house showed some obvious signs of neglect and deterioration. The front grass and garden were tidy, but not up to the well-tended standards of the houses elsewhere along the street. The used brick exterior of the house had weathered the years well, but the shingled roof had a slight sag and was clearly in need of replacement. The whole effect was of an ancient, once rich dowager who was now forced to keep up appearances on a fixed income.

Fey parked and made her way up to the imposing front door. She didn't see Colby's car anywhere, but there was a long, gated driveway that ran down the side of the house, so the car could be anywhere. She knocked. Most cops always knock. In the police academy, during one of the classes on officer safety, they had been telling the story for years about a cop in the East who'd been blown up when he pushed a doorbell buzzer. It was one of those strange stories that always seem to leave an impression. It didn't matter that there had only ever been one cop killed in the line of duty by an exploding doorbell, or that there would probably never, ever be another similar incident. The fact that one cop had died that way made every other cop who heard the story think twice before pressing a doorbell.

When there was no answer to her knock, Fey gathered up her courage and played Russian roulette with the doorbell. After a second the intercom by her elbow crackled with a male voice.

"Hello. Who is it please?"

The voice wasn't Colby's. The butler maybe? Fey wondered. Many houses in the area supported servant staff.

"My name is Fey Croaker. I'm looking for Colby—I mean Alan." Colby's first name tasted strange in Fey's mouth. She didn't like having to follow through with what she was planning, but it was necessary. She was Colby's supervisor, and after her actions the previous evening at Two-Step Tilly's, it was up to her to smooth oil over troubled waters.

"Come on through the house to the workroom out back," the voice from the intercom directed.

There was an electronic buzz and the front door swung open. Fey stepped through into a tiny reception foyer where a stairway led up to a second story, and a hallway led through to the rest of the house. Before walking down the hallway, Fey looked up at the stairway to the second story, where slightly open doors hinted at bedrooms and perhaps an office.

The hallway led Fey past a living room and formal dining area, and into a family room that was open on one end to a bright kitchen. The furnishings and decorations were expensive but old-fashioned, bought years before and never replaced. The color scheme was very male—deep forest greens, reds, and blacks with a touch of gold.

From the family room, huge sliding glass doors gave access to an overgrown garden with a small carriage house standing in the center. The carriage house was in the same used brick style as the main house, and had probably been servants' quarters at some time in the long-ago past.

A man waved at Fey from the entrance door to the smaller building, and Fey followed a path of wandering stepping stones through the garden to reach him.

"Hello," the man said. "I'm Arthur Colby, Alan's father." He held out his hand, and Fey shook it. His fingers were strong and rough. "Come in, please," he said, stepping back and ushering Fey into his workshop. "I'm just putting the finishing touches on a new toy design."

Fey looked around herself in wonder and delight. Shelves everywhere held beautifully carved and chiseled wooden toys. "Oh," she said, "the Square Head toys!"

"Humble, but mine own," Arthur Colby said, obviously reveling in Fey's recognition of his work. "Well, actually my father invented the originals, and I have carried on the tradition."

"I always wanted them as a child, but they were so expensive."

A cloud came over Arthur Colby's face. "The choice of the company who purchased the designs. If it were truly up to me, I would give them all away. And I do—to many children's hospitals and other charities."

"I'm sorry," Fey said, immediately embarrassed. "I didn't mean to imply . . ."

"Of course you didn't." Arthur Colby waved away her protests and smiled again. "The toys are damned expensive. So expensive that they have priced themselves out of the market. The company that mass-produced the toys discontinued the line five years ago. Like the rest of American business, they couldn't compete with the Japanese."

"But I thought you said you were finishing up a new design?"

"Business setbacks can only curtail sales, they can't stifle the creative spirit. This world around you was created from the residuals on the designs. Now there are no residuals, but there are still collectors willing to pay for individual items of quality work." He moved past Fey. "Come and look at this," he said, and led her over to a large workbench in the middle of the room.

"It's beautiful!" Fey said with delight.

On the workbench, surrounded by a scattering of wood chisels and chips, was a hand-carved fire engine made completely out of different-shaped blocks. There were several tiny firemen, all with their heads made from proportional square blocks, placed strategically along the length of the toy. The detailing on the fire engine was meticulous, bearing all the signs of a master craftsman.

"This isn't a toy," Fey said. "It's a work of art."

Arthur Colby glowed with the praise. "Thank you. It is too bad more people these days don't have your appreciation."

Fey turned to look around her at all the similar toys set on shelves around the room. There were cars and buildings and work machines and houses and schools, and all populated by the square-headed people from which the toys took their name.

She gave a slight gasp as she spotted one toy in particular. "The merry-go-round!" She took a couple of steps toward the toys placed on the shelf and reached out to push one of the square-headed horses. The horse and its compatriots obligingly spun silently around.

"That was the original of the line. Designed by my father."

"This was always my favorite. I loved horses as a little girl—still do, in fact—and I remember seeing this in a Sears Christmas catalog. I must have been twelve or thirteen." She gave a sad laugh. "I didn't believe in Santa Claus anymore, but I was willing to believe again if this turned up under my tree. I wished on stars. I said my prayers. I crossed my fingers ..."

"And ... ?" Arthur Colby asked gently, after a few seconds of silence.

Fey snapped out of her reverie. "And nothing ... Only Democrats believe in Santa Claus." She took a deep breath. "Well, I came to see ... er ... Alan."

"Yes, of course," said Arthur Colby. "I'm sorry, but he's not here. He left early this morning."

"Oh," Fey was puzzled. "Then why ... ?"

"Then why did I have you come in?"

"Yes."

"An old man's foolishness. I have heard so much about you from Alan that I wanted to meet you."

Fey gave Arthur Colby an appraising glance. He was not that much of an old man. Somewhere in his mid-fifties, he still had a thick head of salt-and-pepper hair, and it was easy to see where Colby had inherited his movie-star good looks. Arthur Colby's looks were matured, but he still cut a fine figure.

"I'm sure that not much of what Alan told you about me could be considered good."

Arthur Colby bestowed the same brilliant smile that irritated Fey so much in the son. In the father, however, the smile came across without the leer that was the son's own trademark. He flapped his hands expressively. "With Alan you have to learn to read between the lines. He is a young man. Still so full of piss and vinegar that there isn't much room left for common sense."

As far as Fey was concerned, Colby Jr. was full of something else besides piss and vinegar. However, even though she kept her opinion to herself, Arthur Colby seemed to sense what she was thinking. He held up a hand as if to stop Fey's train of thought.

"You need to understand that what extra emotional room Alan has inside of him is filled with anger." Arthur Colby shrugged. "Alan would never agree, but from what I can tell, you are good for him. You keep him in line. Something I was regrettably too busy to do when he was a child, and now it is far too late."

"What about his mother?" Fey asked, wondering at the same time why she even gave a damn.

"I'm afraid she died in childbirth. And that's part of the reason for Alan's internal angers. I don't think he ever forgave her for abandoning him."

"It doesn't sound as if she had a choice."

Arthur Colby shrugged again. "It is always easier to blame someone else for our miseries than to accept and change our own shortcomings. As for Alan, there were also other letdowns. The women in his life have been far from consistent."

"Meaning . . . ?"

"After his mother died, his maternal grandmother blamed Alan and me for the death of her only daughter. Me for impregnating her, and Alan for being the resulting spawn. She never relented in her verbal attacks against us even though she kept insisting on seeing Alan. I eventually had to refuse to let her see the boy. She went to court and obtained visitation rights. These visits went on for several years until her mental abuse of Alan became physical and I was able to break the court order."

Fey knew all about physical and mental abuse. "What about your mother, Alan's paternal grandmother?"

Arthur Colby smiled. "My mother, Lila, was a good woman. My father died several years before Alan was born, so when Anna, my wife, died, Lila moved in here. She cared for Alan as if he were her own child, and the boy loved her dearly. However, when the battles with my mother-in-law were at their worst, Lila was killed by a hit-and-run driver. Alan was six, and Lila's death devastated him. It was as if every woman in his life was either terrorizing him or abandoning him."

"Growing up is tough," Fey said. The words came out sounding more flippant than she had intended. Growing up was hard. She'd had that experience firsthand.

"Do you know about Alan's wife?" Arthur asked, apparently choosing to ignore Fey's tone.

Fey looked startled. "I didn't think he was married."

"Widowed," Arthur Colby clarified. "Alan married her at eighteen. She committed suicide a year later. Shot herself in their shower when she found out she couldn't conceive children."

Fey felt slightly shell-shocked. "Another form of perceived abandonment," she said. "And Colby was able to blame yet another woman for the disappointments in his life." She wasn't sure if she liked getting all this inside scoop on Colby's background. She might find herself feeling sorry for the bastard.

There was a short silence as Fey assimilated the information. In many ways it sounded like Colby could have used some couch sessions with a competent shrink. However, on the flip side of the coin, Fey believed that blaming others for your own misfortunes was an easy cop-out.

Her brother, Tommy, had certainly taught her a lot about the terrors of misplaced blame. And even if blame was appropriate, it never did any good. She could blame her father for all the rotten things in her life, but she could only blame herself if she couldn't find a way to get beyond them. In either case, the laying of blame served no purpose except to provoke the inner devils of anger and hate.

Arthur Colby moved in closer to Fey. "Alan tells me you are bound and determined to catch this person who murdered the Goodwinter woman," he said, changing the subject abruptly. He reached out casually and touched the square-headed carousel horses on the shelf, making them turn again.

Fey was surprised. "Yes. I'll catch him. Sooner or later."

"One way or the other?"

"One way or the other," Fey agreed. "I can't afford to lose this one."

"You do sound determined."

Fey sensed something in Arthur Colby's voice. Perhaps the women in his life weren't the only ones Colby should be blaming for his attitudes. "Do you mean I sound very determined for a girl?" she asked.

Arthur Colby's eyes damn near twinkled. "No. I mean you sound very determined for a cop. I am my son's father, not his keeper."

"The apple doesn't usually fall very far from the tree."

"Perhaps not, but even the seed from a sweet tree can bear bitter fruit."

It was Fey's turn to shake her head. "Very Zen," she said. "The Marx Brothers' version, maybe, but still Zen."

A voice suddenly intruded from the workshop entry. "Well, isn't this cozy?"

Both Fey and Arthur turned to see Alan Colby leaning against the doorframe with a sardonic grin slapped across his face.

When Jake Travers entered the Santa Monica district attorney's offices that morning, he, too, knew there was something going on that he wasn't going to like.

"Good morning, Mr. Travers," the receptionist said. "Mr. Vanderwald is waiting for you in your office. He said he wanted to see you immediately."

Hell, Jake thought. The last thing he needed this morning was a formal confrontation with his boss. The two men had never seen eye to eye, but their relationship had become even more strained since Jake had become a possible threat to replace Vanderwald during the next election. The campaign wasn't even luke warm yet. The election was over five months away, but it was still rare for Vanderwald to put in an appearance at the outlying Santa Monica prosecutor's office. If the two men needed to have contact, it was usually accomplished through terse phone conversations or by Jake traveling to Vanderwald's downtown power base.

"Thanks, Doris," Jake told the receptionist as he reversed his field and headed back toward the entrance to the small lobby. "I'll be right there." He needed a few moments to think. To try and figure out what Vanderwald's presence foreboded.

"But, Mr. Travers." Doris tried to stop him from leaving. "Mr. Vanderwald said he wanted to see you the moment you walked through the door."

"Then let's make out like I haven't walked through the door yet."

"Let's not," said a deep male voice from out of the hall-way that led to Jake's office. Simon Vanderwald stepped into sight with a black frown thundering across his forehead. His unsmiling face had the round-cheeked look of too much rich food and too many lunchtime martinis. Below his face was the powerful, stocky body that had once earned him honors as a lineman at Notre Dame, but was now rapidly running to seed. He was dressed as usual in a dark gray suit, a beauti-fully starched white shirt, and red power tie, and highly pol-ished slip-ons with tassels. "What time do you call this to be getting into the office?" he demanded in an angry voice.

Jake glanced at his watch. It was five minutes before his usual eight-o'clock start time, but he realized there was no acceptable answer to give to the aggressive question. It didn't matter that Jake rarely left the office before six or seven at night, or that Vanderwald was never in his own downtown of-fice before ten, took a two-hour lunch, often went home early, and played golf every Friday. Nothing was going to satisfy Vanderwald in his current mood.

"Get in here," Vanderwald said, turning on his heel and disappearing down the hallway again.

Jake looked over at the receptionist, but she had dis-creetly bent her head down and was busily shuffling papers. Steeling himself inwardly for the ordeal ahead, Jake squared his shoulders and followed in the direction of Vanderwald's echoing footsteps.

As he entered his office, Jake saw that Vanderwald had set himself up at center stage by taking over the black leather chair behind Jake's large rosewood desk. Knowing Vander-wald, Jake had anticipated this move and was determined not to be put off by its pettiness. It was the person sitting in one of the two comfortable visitors' chairs, however, who threw

Jake off his stride. Janice Ryder was the last person he had expected to see this morning.

Jake set his briefcase down in the middle of his desktop before walking around behind where Vanderwald was sitting. He turned and rested his butt on a low bookshelf that ran under the window that dominated the main wall of the office. The move was calculated to not only usurp Vanderwald's ability to use the rosewood desk as a defensive barrier, but also to force Vanderwald to swivel around to face him. It also served to gain some extra distance from Janice Ryder—whom Jake considered the biggest threat in the room.

"What's this all about?" he asked aggressively, dispensing with any pleasantries beyond a nod of recognition in Janice Ryder's direction. There were no points to be won here through politeness.

"I'll cut straight to the point, Jake," Vanderwald said, swiveling in the high-backed leather chair to face his subordinate. He was playing with a letter opener he had picked up from the top of the desk, and smirked when he saw the way Jake had positioned himself with the light behind him.

"That's good of you, Simon," Jake cut in. Two could play at the condescending first-name-usage game.

Vanderwald shot him a dirty look. "Ms. Ryder contacted me on behalf of her client Isaac Cordell this morning—"

"Oh." Jake turned his head to look at Janice. "Is he ready to turn himself in?"

"And take a chance on a justice system that has already wrongfully deprived him of ten years of his life, Mr. Travers?" Janice raised a perfectly plucked eyebrow. "I don't think so." She was dressed in a sleeveless, umber-colored shell that set off the creamy texture of her skin. Below the shell she wore a subdued yellow suede skirt that was short enough to make the best of her trim legs, and yellow patent leather high heels. Pearls at neck, wrist, and ears were the only accents to her outfit.

A real viper in disguise, Jake thought as he waited for the falling ax he knew was coming.

"This meeting isn't directly related to Mr. Cordell's status as a fugitive," Vanderwald stated flatly, trying to regain the upper hand in the situation. "This is about unethical behavior on the part of this office—more specifically on your part, Jake—that could lead not only to the dismissal of this case, but could also open this office up to civil prosecution."

"Explain to me just what the hell you're talking about," Jake said, rising to the bait and partially losing his temper.

"I'm talking about the fact that Ms. Ryder has presented me with a writ from a San Francisco judge—who had jurisdiction over the original false conviction of Mr. Cordell—clearing his parole status."

"Wait a minute," Jake said.

"No, you wait a minute, Mr. Travers." Janice Ryder stood up and walked to the front of the rosewood desk. Once there, she spread her hands along the front edge and leaned forward. Out of the corner of his eye, Jake saw Vanderwald trying to lean forward unobtrusively in order to look down the front scoop of the umber shell.

"My client is obviously not guilty of the initial charge of murder leveled against him ten years ago. Therefore, he should never have been sent to prison, and consequently never placed on parole. My client had no knowledge of the murder weapon that was recovered in his room. But whether you agree with that point or not, the fact is that he should never have been on parole in the first place, so therefore the parole search conducted by the detectives that recovered the weapon is null and void. That weapon was seized as a result of an illegal search and is inadmissible in court."

"That's for a judge to decide."

"No it's not," said Vanderwald, cutting in sharply. "That is a question that should have been evaluated by this office before any charges were formally filed."

Jake jumped to defend his position. "We have an eyewitness who can place Cordell at the scene of the crime at the time of the occurrence, and we've got motive up the wazoo." Fey had broken the bad news to him about Kathleen Bridges's identification, but he was looking for any port in a storm.

It turned out to be a hazardous harbor.

"I'm sure you're aware by now, Counselor, that your eyewitness isn't worth pig swill," Janice Ryder said with contempt. "If you have the audacity to put that feeble old lady on the stand, I'll rip her to pieces. As for motive—you can keep it up your wazoo for all the good it does you. Simple motive, in and of itself, counts for less than nothing."

Jake shifted his gaze from Janice to Vanderwald. If he hoped to find backing from that area, he was disappointed.

Vanderwald gave him an ice-cold stare. "This is really a pretty poor showing, Jake. If you hope to oust me from my position in the next election, you'd be well advised to exercise better case judgment in the future."

There it was, then, Jake thought sadly. Out in the open. Jake wasn't even declared as a candidate yet, but Vanderwald was already moving to shut him down. It was suddenly very clear why Vanderwald survived in office term after term. This little scenario had nothing whatever to do with whether the case against Cordell was good or bad. This was all about declaring political war.

Clearly Vanderwald didn't give a damn about Cordell's guilt or innocence. With its constitutional arguments concerning double jeopardy, the case was far from an out-and-out winner. In reality it was a bad risk. The press would have a feeding frenzy with the case, and the DA's position would be like sitting on a straight razor. Either way he slid, he'd lose his ass.

The way things stood, the case wasn't worth shit to Vanderwald except for use as political ammunition—ammunition that would give Jake, as the deputy DA who filed the case, a big fat black eye.

To milk the political advantage, Vanderwald could hold a press conference that would stroke every liberal bleeding heart in the city, and at the same time make Jake look like a vindictive bastard.

Jake suddenly felt the weight of the process settle on his shoulders. Welcome to the real world, son, he thought. Welcome to the grand old American game of political infighting and mudslinging. He'd played his share of office politics in order to gain his appointments as the head filing DA under Vanderwald, but that experience was obviously going to be a big nothing when compared with what was to come.

"Are you telling me," Jake asked Vanderwald, "that you're going to overturn my filing on this case?"

"Jake, Jake." Vanderwald threw out an arm expansively.

"There is no case. You come up with some admissible evidence against Isaac Cordell and you can file charges till the cows come home. Until then, this office must remain impartial. You can't allow yourself to become personally involved. Your whole career at the bar could be in jeopardy here."

"What are you rattling on about now? How the hell am I going to be disbarred over filing a borderline case?"

Vanderwald looked smug. "It's not the filing that will get you disbarred, Jake, not in and of itself."

"What then?" Jake shot a look at Janice Ryder, and in a sudden flash of insight, saw what was coming before the words came out of Vanderwald's mouth.

"If it became public knowledge that you were screwing the investigating officer in this case—that your interest in filing and prosecuting Cordell is a personal vendetta—you would almost certainly find yourself dismissed from this office, and perhaps even disbarred if someone was to push the point."

"Personal vendetta, my ass," Jake exploded. "You're talking a bunch of unmitigated shit and you know it!"

"I know it and you know it," Vanderwald agreed. "But the press would love it, and they would eat you alive."

Jake pushed himself up from the bookcase and looked angrily across the desk at Janice Ryder. "Are you the one who made up this bullshit about Fey Croaker and me sleeping together?"

"Don't waste your breath trying to deny the situation, Counselor. We're already way beyond that point. I have in my possession a list of police officers, detectives, and DAs who are apparently aware of your relationship with Detective Croaker. I hope that you won't make it necessary for me to take depositions from all of them."

Jake felt the bile in his stomach churn over. "All right," he said. "I'll play along for a minute. But tell me why in the hell Fey and I would involve ourselves in a conspiracy to frame Isaac Cordell?"

"Because he's convenient."

"What?" Jake closed his eyes and shook his head in bafflement.

"There may be some other dynamics occurring here that you are unaware of, Counselor," Janice told him.

"Enlighten me."

Janice paused for a beat before speaking. "It has also come to my attention that your lover may be directly involved in this case."

"Of course she is," Jake said, not bothering any longer to even try to deny his relationship with Fey. "She's the investigating officer."

"I'm not talking about her involvement as a detective. I'm talking about her involvement as a suspect."

Jake felt as if his legs were going to go out from under him. He leaned back against the bookcase again.

Janice Ryder placed a photo facedown next to Jake's briefcase on the desk. It was a copy of the one that had been left for her that morning. She continued to stare at Jake, but she spoke to Vanderwald. "Can I assume that the warrant for my client's arrest will be withdrawn?"

"Immediately," Vanderwald replied with a smooth smile.

Jake reached forward and picked up the photograph. "What about the escape charges and the assault against Fey?" he asked before turning the photo over.

"Look at the photograph. I think you'll agree those charges are a moot point," Vanderwald told him.

Jake turned the photo over. He had trouble focusing, but the images were clear.

Janice Ryder picked up her briefcase and turned to leave the office. "Thank you for your cooperation, Mr. Vanderwald. I hope you will keep me abreast of developments."

"Certainly."

"Good-bye, Counselor. I'm sorry I had to be the bearer of bad news."

Jake didn't reply, and Janice opened the door to the office and exited gracefully, a soft scent remaining in her wake.

Vanderwald stood up himself and laid the letter opener on the desk. Jake still hadn't moved. He was still staring at the photo.

"I'd dump the bimbo quick if I were you," he said. "I don't understand what you see in her anyway. I know some men prefer women who are built for comfort instead of speed, but a couple more years and her body will be beyond even the comfort zone."

Jake clenched his jaws, useless anger threatening to explode from his interior.

Vanderwald walked over to the open door and turned back to face Jake before walking out. "Oh, by the way. There's a five-hundred-dollar-a-plate dinner coming up next week to help out with my campaign fund. I'll expect to see you and a date there."

He closed the door gently as he left.

**T**he morning had been busy for Fey. The overnight reports were unusually heavy, and there were two bodies in custody on felony spousal abuse charges. Hatch was up for the bodies and took off for the city attorney's office to get quick filings. When Colby arrived at his desk he found three ADW reports and an attempted kidnapping case waiting for him. Fey was personally dragged into a dispute involving rival Gypsy palm readers who were trying to kill each other because—according to unwritten Gypsy law—their businesses had been set up too close together.

Somehow, over the years, Fey had become the unofficial Gypsy detective in West L.A. It wasn't a role she cherished, but since she knew more about the strange characters—who run their lives by a set of rules far outside those of normal society—than anyone else in the division, it was a role she was increasingly stuck with.

Handling Gypsy disputes successfully was a matter of respect. Fey knew if she tried to impose traditional law enforcement remedies on the situation, it would only get worse. However, she made a couple of discreet phone calls to private numbers, and within an hour she was meeting with the rival palm-reading families and the matriarch of the local Gypsy clan.

After explaining the situation to the matriarch, Fey left the Gypsies alone behind the closed door of Mike Cahill's office with the blinds drawn. Cahill couldn't stand Gypsies and would have gone crazy had he known Fey was leaving a half dozen of them alone in his office. But as Cahill was out of the station at a department bureau meeting, Fey figured what he didn't know wouldn't hurt him.

Fifteen minutes later, the Gypsy matriarch quietly led everyone out of the office. With much smiling and gesturing, all charges and countercharges were dropped, and everyone went happily about their business. Everyone except for Mike Cahill, who, returning to his office later in the morning, couldn't figure out what happened to the antique letter opener he kept on his desk.

Fey knew the situation had only been resolved as far as the police were concerned. The actual dispute would be settled later under Gypsy law in more private surroundings. Fey's only hope was that if it ended in a blood feud, the carnage would be kept off her path.

Just before lunch, Monk Lawson bounded into the office and approached Fey. She had let him escape the dint of daily reports because she wanted him to chase down any information he could find on Janice Ryder. Over coffee, they sat down together to go over the facts he'd gathered.

"There wasn't a whole lot out there that I could come up with in a hurry," Monk told her, "but I was able to come up with some basics."

"Always a good place to start," said Fey. "If anything clicks, we can follow up further."

Monk produced a stack of index cards filled with neat, precise handwriting.

"Since Ryder is obviously a lawyer, I figured the best place to start looking for information on her would be the law library. I checked in *Martindale Hubble*—"

"And that is?"

Monk looked up from his notes, distracted for a second.

"Oh, I guess you would call it the law profession's version of *Who's Who.*"

"Okay," Fey said, satisfied.

Monk looked back at his notes. "There was a listing for Ryder showing she entered law school through Berkeley's Boal Hall in 1982."

"Ended up at the top of her class, I expect," Fey put in semisarcastically.

"How did you guess?" Monk asked in the same tone. "She was editor of the law review from 1983 to 1984 and graduated with the Order of the COIF in 1984."

"I take it that's a fancy way of saying summa cum laude."

"Yeah. She was real smart, all right. Took the bar in 1985 and passed it with flying colors the first time."

"What year was Cordell originally convicted for murdering his wife?" Fey asked with a wrinkled brow.

Monk shuffled through some papers on his desk before pulling one out and consulting it. "The latter part of 1982."

"Okay, so little Miss Brains is just starting law school at the time."

"You think there's a connection?"

Fey shrugged. "I doubt it, but it's hard to tell at this point. What else do you have?"

Monk went back to his notes. "Well, the *Martindale Hubble* listing was fairly brief, but I figured that her taking on Cordell's case and getting him paroled was a pretty big deal, so there had to be some coverage of it somewhere."

"And?"

"And after exhaustive research—"

"I get the point," Fey said. "My heart bleeds for you. What did you do? Have the law library librarian find all this stuff for you? A real tough job. Quit messing around and spell it out."

"Okay, okay." Monk only looked slightly chastened. "About a month ago there was an in-depth profile of Ryder in *The Recorder*—the daily legal newspaper for the Bay area."

"I take it this was compiled as a result of her winning parole for Cordell?"

"Yeah. MacGregor, the cop you talked to in San Francisco, was right. Cordell's case was high profile in Bay area society ten years ago, but interest had dwindled until Ryder began fighting to get him paroled about a year ago. It seems that while Cordell had been a model citizen up to the point when he supposedly murdered his wife, he had not done his prison time quietly. He'd been up for parole on two prior occasions, but had been turned down due to the violent nature of his behavior behind the prison walls. He was suspected in two prison stabbings and a long list of more minor offenses. From what I can tell, when Ryder finally convinced the parole board to spring Cordell, the prison hierarchy breathed a sigh of relief."

"Did the article cover the motives behind Ryder taking on Cordell as a cause?"

"Not much beyond the fact that she'd done quite a bit of *pro bono* work in private practice and seemed to be making a name for herself as a liberal cause carrier."

"Gee, I can't think of anything else the world needs more."

"Yeah, but she paid her dues on the way up. After she passed the bar, she spent a couple of years with the public defender's office before jumping over to the good guys and working in the DA's office for another two years."

"What do you think made her change colors?"

"Reading between the lines, I'd say it was a bad marriage."

"Oh, yeah? So Miss Brains isn't completely perfect?"

Monk chuckled. "I guess not. Does that make you feel better?"

Fey shrugged. "So who'd she marry?"

Monk went back to his notes again. "Some hotshot private lawyer named Howard Ryder. Corporate type apparently. Entertainment law, contracts, civil stuff. They were married shortly after she joined the PD's office and lasted together about a year. The profile indicated he had big bucks, but didn't want to spread them around on his wife's liberal causes."

"I bet she took him for a bundle when they split up."

"Are you talking from experience?"

Fey shot him a dirty look. "Don't you start. I get enough of that kind of crap from Colby. I don't need you chipping in."

"Oops. Sorry. I didn't know it was a hot button."

"Well, now you do. Who was this bimbo before she married a bank?"

"You mean her maiden name?"

"Yeah. Where did she come from? Did the profile go back that far?"

Monk flipped through his notes. "Yeah, but it's mostly sob-story stuff. Her mother abandoned her when she was eight. Left her in Daddy's care apparently and ran off with the mailman or some such thing."

"Life is hard and then you die."

"That appears to be true in this case, because things continue to go from bad to worse."

"Make me cry," Fey said.

"When little Janice was eleven, Daddy got married again to a woman named Madeline Walsh."

Fey felt the hairs on the back of her neck prickle.

"Two years later," Monk continued, oblivious to the change in Fey's attention focus, "Daddy died in a car crash, and wicked Stepmommy split with the insurance money, leaving Janice to be brought up by her grandparents—"

"Holy shit!" Fey almost leapt to her feet. She grabbed Monk's notes away from him and started scanning them. "Where in the hell do you have her maiden name written down?"

Monk reached for the cards. Fey thrust them back at him.

"Come on. Come on."

Monk was getting flustered. "Er . . . eh . . . Here. Here it is. Fletcher. Her maiden name is Fletcher."

"I'll be damned," Fey said, flopping back in her chair. She stared into space, her mind whirling a mile a minute.

"What? What? I don't get the connection."

Fey was still looking thoughtful. "The bitch sprung him from jail and then pointed him like a gun at our victim."

"What are you talking about?"

Fey focused her eyes on Monk again. "We haven't had

a chance to bring everyone up to speed on this. Yesterday at the bank, Colby and I talked to an IRS agent named Craven. He'd been tracking our victim for years. It seems she was some kind of black widow killer who kept draining her mates financially before bumping them off for the insurance money."

"Okay. So?"

"So one of the identities Craven uncovered for our victim was Madeline Fletcher, a woman who took off with an insurance policy after her husband died in a car crash. According to Craven, she left a penniless thirteen-year-old stepdaughter behind to be raised by grandparents."

Monk's head was swimming. "And you think—"

Fey leaned forward. "I don't just think. I know. I don't have it figured out yet just how she managed to track her stepmother through all her various identities, but I'll lay you dollars to doughnuts that she either sprung Cordell and pointed him right at the woman, or she killed the victim herself and set Cordell up for the rap again."

Monk thought for a second and nodded. "After she set him up, she planned to step in with this double jeopardy hocus-pocus and get him off."

"I like it," Fey said. "It needs work, and I don't know what we're going to do with it yet, but I like it."

Fey's heart was racing at the same pace as her brain. She needed time to consider the situation and bring it into perspective.

She needed time, but she wasn't going to get it. The crap that had originally hit the fan in Jake Travers's office was about to splatter all over her.

Shortly before Monk had returned with his research, Fey had noticed two suit-and-tie types go into a closed-door session with Mike Cahill. She'd recognized one of the visitors as an Internal Affairs investigator she'd crossed swords with in the past, but she'd been too busy to think much about it. Even when Cahill interrupted her thought process and motioned for her to join him, Fey's first thoughts were directed toward which of the other detectives on the homicide unit might be the focus of IA's attentions.

The instant she entered Cahill's office, however, she felt

the atmosphere close around her like an ice-cold fog. And when Cahill closed the miniblinds covering the windows that looked out into the squad bay, she knew there was big trouble brewing.

One of the IA investigators stood up. "Detective Croaker, I'm Lieutenant Baxter, and this is Sergeant Hilton." He indicated the younger man next to him, who hadn't bothered to stand. "We're with Internal Affairs." His last pronouncement had been merely routine. IA cops could be picked out a mile away. They wore an air of paranoia as if it were a protective cloak, and dressed, if it was possible, even more conservatively than most cops who carried rank. No striped or colored shirt here. No wildly patterned ties. No pointed shoes or boots. No sport jackets. Just dark blue, single-breasted suits with white shirt, dark ties, and polished wing tips.

"I believe we've met before," Fey said to Baxter. When he didn't acknowledge her, she switched her gaze to Cahill. He was fiddling with something on his desk and refused to meet her eyes.

Oh, shit, she thought. We've got big trouble right here in River City. She couldn't understand why one of Colby's favorite sayings popped into her mind, but she couldn't help thinking it was appropriate.

"What can I do for you, gentlemen?" she asked. Her voice was strong, belying the tremors in her knees.

"Have a seat, Detective." This came from Hilton, the younger IA officer. He had short-cropped dark hair, bushy eyebrows that grew together across the bridge of his crooked nose, and an unsmiling mouth with thin lips. Heavy eyelids gave his deep-set eyes a hooded look, as if he were a vulture waiting for something to die.

Fey sat, but kept her mouth shut. At this point, she realized, she was taking the first tentative steps into an uncharted minefield. The best thing she could do was to sit back and let IA make the running. This was their show, and she would gain nothing by charging straight ahead.

"Are you currently in charge of investigating the murder of Miranda Goodwinter?"

Fey looked down at the two black briefcases that sat on

the conference table in front of the two IA investigators. The briefcases were oversize, and Fey had certainly been around long enough to know why.

"Is this interview being taped?" she asked.

Hilton scowled and started to say something, but Baxter beat him to the punch. "Yes," he said calmly. Baxter's sun-seamed face held the weary wisdom of knowing too many dirty cops. Fey knew his reputation. Most cops bucking for promotion put in an eighteen-month tour with Internal Affairs and then get the hell out. Investigating dirty cops is not a job for anyone with a weak stomach or a thin skin. Baxter had been with IA for almost fifteen years. He was known as a crusader. He was also known as fair—a tough reputation to earn as an IA investigator.

The "them against us" syndrome that is the bane of most cops' existence is magnified a thousand times when you work IA. Nobody trusts an IA investigator because, even for clean cops, it is impossible to walk through the sewerlike streets of a big city and not have any of the shit rub off.

If IA targets you in their sights, it doesn't matter how good a cop you are, they'll find something. If a cop couldn't be had for something, then he or she wasn't doing the job properly.

Citizens' complaints, "beefs" as they were called, were simply a part of a cop's everyday life. Even if a cop did everything properly, there were often people around who felt they had the right to make a complaint—suspects with a grudge, victims who did not get everything they wanted out of the cops, citizens who felt they were unfairly ticketed because "nobody ever stops for that stop sign," witnesses to an arrest who had no idea what they were seeing but felt a cop had been far too harsh on that nice man who had just tried to kill the cop's partner. All of them made life rough for cops through the offices of Internal Affairs.

At the other end of the spectrum were the legitimate complaints. Cops on the take, illegal use of force, cops taking or selling drugs, cops involved with gambling and prostitution, and many other variations were just the tip of the iceberg. The real heavy-duty stuff came in the form of cops who became assassins for hire, organized cop burglary rings taking down thousands of dollars a week, political corruption, protection rackets, and a myriad of other stomach-turning activities that besmirched the badge and made Internal Affairs a necessary evil.

Fey had been under the microscope several times in the past, but all charges had been cleared as unfounded. It had been a number of years since her last beef, however, and Fey did not feel like going through the routine again without a fight.

Most good cops had a tendency to go overboard when trying to clear themselves with Internal Affairs, allowing their rights as a citizen and a police officer to be trampled on. Fey had been around too long to start down that road. She wanted to know what was going on, and she wanted to know now.

"What are the charges against me?"

"Nobody has said anything about charges, Fey," Mike Cahill spoke up finally.

Fey immediately shot him down in flames. "Come on, Mike. Take a reality check. These guys aren't here to interview me for officer of the month." She looked back at Baxter. "Well?"

Baxter tried a smile, but it didn't seem to fit on his face. "There are no formal charges at this time. We are simply investigating a conflict-of-interest allegation where your investigation of the Miranda Goodwinter case is concerned."

"I'm not playing that game," Fey told him. "There is no such thing as an informal Internal Affairs investigation. I have no idea what you're talking about, but I'm not talking to you until you advise me of my rights and I get defense rep in here."

"Detective Croaker, there's no need for this," Baxter told her.

"Bullshit," Fey replied evenly. "Don't give me this father figure, good guy crap. I'm a big girl and I can take care of myself. Now, either you let me get a defense rep and then read me my rights, or I'm walking out of here."

"Listen, lady." Hilton half rose out of his chair, but Baxter put a restraining hand on him.

"Can it, sonny," Fey told him. "Mind your elders or we'll send you out onto the freeway to play with the traffic."

Hilton's face turned bright red, but he sat down.

"Get yourself a rep," Baxter said.

Fey stood up and opened the door to the office. She scanned the squad bay until she spotted Nate Collins. Like Fey, he was a detective supervisor, but he was also a lawyer. "Nate," Fey called out. "I need you."

Every cop was entitled to have a defense representative present when being interviewed by Internal Affairs. A defense rep was a fellow officer, usually with advanced legal skills, who would sit in on the interview to advise the cop who was being questioned.

Collins looked questioningly up from where he was sitting at his desk, but when he saw the expression on Fey's face, he instantly knew what was going on. He'd been a defense rep enough times to automatically recognize a cop in trouble.

"What's up?" he asked when he reached Fey.

"I don't know yet, but there's a couple of IA fuckers in here who I've got a feeling are going to try to railroad me if I give them half a chance. I need you to sit in with me as my defense rep."

"You got it," Collins said, and followed Fey back into the office."

When everyone was settled, Fey asked that the recorder briefcases be opened up so that she could be sure they were working. Baxter sighed heavily, but complied.

"Satisfied?" he asked.

"Hardly," Fey said. "As I told you before, I have no idea what you want to talk to me about, but I've been around long enough to know not to give Internal Affairs an even break. It's nothing personal, understand, just once bitten, twice shy."

This time Baxter simply grunted.

"If there's any chance that criminal charges may eventually result from this interview, you need to read Detective Croaker her Miranda rights." Collins spoke up for the first time.

Baxter looked Collins over calmly. "Hilton," he said to his partner, while still maintaining eye contact with Collins.

The younger IA investigator pulled a small officer's notebook out of his pocket and began to read verbatim from the Miranda rights form printed on the cover for easy access. It wasn't that he didn't know the rights by heart, but should he ever be required to testify about the admonishment in court, there could be no technical difficulty if he could say he read the rights directly from the card.

"You have the right to remain silent," his voice droned. "If you give up the right to remain silent, anything you say can and will be used against you in a court of law. You have the right to an attorney. If you so desire and can not afford one, an attorney will be appointed for you without charge." He paused for a second and looked up from the card. Everyone in the room remained silent.

"Do you understand these rights?" he asked.

Fey's reply was a simple "Yes."

"Do you wish to give up your right to remain silent?"

"No."

"Do you wish to give up your right to have an attorney present during questioning?"

"No."

Hilton sat back as if he were a well-trained puppy, and Baxter took over the interview again.

"Taking note of the fact that you have refused to waive your constitutional rights—" Baxter was as formal in his speech as Hilton had been in reading the rights "—I must advise you to answer our questions for administrative purposes only."

"Are you ordering me to answer your questions?" Fey asked, playing her part in the game of well-rehearsed Q and A.

"Yes."

"By whose authority are you ordering me?"

"By the authority of the chief of police of the Los Angeles Police Department. I must also tell you that any refusal on your part to answer our questions may result in departmental charges being brought against you for insubordination."

"I will answer your questions as ordered," Fey said. "But only for the purposes of this departmental investigation. In no way should my answering of these questions be construed as a voluntary waiving of my Miranda rights." She leaned forward to check that the briefcase recorders were still working, and then turned toward Collins, who was sitting next to her. "Okay?" she asked him.

"Letter-perfect," he replied, indicating that Fey had protected herself correctly.

Fey sat back in her chair and tried to relax the stiffness in her neck. "The ball's in your court," she said to Baxter.

"What was your relationship with Miranda Goodwinter?"

Fey opened her mouth to speak, but Nate Collins put his hand on her arm to stop her. "Wait a minute," he said. "What kind of question is that? It's like asking somebody, 'Have you stopped beating your wife?' You're already making the assumption that Detective Croaker had a relationship with this Miranda Goodwinter."

Baxter's expression soured. "Point taken," he said, unhappily. "Let me rephrase. Detective Croaker, have you at any time had a relationship with Miranda Goodwinter?"

Fey shook her head. "You've sent your dog up a bad trail, pal. Beyond investigating her murder, I have never had any sort of relationship with Miranda Goodwinter."

Baxter took that statement in his stride. "You are claiming that you never had any contact with Miranda Goodwinter prior to the beginning of this investigation?"

Fey nodded. "The first time I saw the woman, she was stone-cold and stiff as a board. Her blood was leaking out all over the floor."

"You're a real sensitive type," Hilton chipped in.

"Comes with the territory, sonny. You'll catch on after a while."

"Fey." Nate put a restraining hand back on her arm.

"This is bullshit, Nate," Fey said to him. She turned back to Baxter. "If this farce has gone on long enough for you, why don't you make your point?"

With a slow but deliberate movement, Baxter reached into the inside pocket of his jacket and removed a photograph. It was a duplicate of the photo Janice Ryder had shown Jack in Vaderwald's office a few hours earlier.

Baxter held the photo out toward Fey, but Nate was the one who reached out and took it.

"If what you are telling us is true, Detective Croaker, how do you explain this photo?"

Nate took a quick glance at the print and handed it to Fey.

Fey's hands were trembling slightly as she took it. Her eyes glanced down. It was a photo of two women with their arms around each other in a nightclub setting. They were both smiling.

One of the women was Miranda Goodwinter.

The other was Fey Croaker.

**F**ey sat in an easy chair and stared at the vodka bottle balanced on the top of her bar. She'd taken the bottle out and set it on the bar as soon as she'd arrived home. She'd been sitting and staring at it for the past hour without cracking the seal. Her mind felt as if it were a computer running on overload—spinning its disks, but unable to clearly process the jammed input. Anger and despair buzzed through her body in alternating fits and starts that made her head spin. Absently she stroked Brentwood's coat as the cat nestled in her lap.

Finally, rousing herself from the depths of the recliner, she placed the complaining cat on the floor and walked back to the bar. Working quickly, as if she were afraid she would lose her resolve, she threw ice in a glass, opened the vodka, and poured a healthy measure over the cubes.

She brought the glass to her lips and took a healthy slug of the drink. The alcohol tasted foul in her mouth, but succeeded in washing away the traces of bile that had been regurgitating from her stomach. The back of her throat felt raw when the alcohol hit it, making her wince. After the one swallow, she banged the glass down so hard on the bar top that two ice cubes bounced out and slithered away.

"Damn! Damn! Damn! Damn! Damn!" she screamed aloud, and knocked the glass flying with a sweep of her hand. Brentwood screeched and flew out of the room almost without touching the ground. Still standing, Fey put her arms down on the bar top, dropped her head on them, and began to sob.

Over twenty-two years on this fucking job, she thought, and it all goes to shit in one afternoon. She knew she was feeling well and truly sorry for herself, but she believed she'd earned the right.

The rest of the interview with Internal Affairs had been a nightmare. Baxter and Hilton had hammered away at her one right after the other. Once the photograph had been revealed, the kid gloves had come off and the bloodbath had started.

"How long did you know Miranda Goodwinter before she was murdered?"

"I didn't know her! I've told you over and over. I never met the woman when she was alive!"

"What was your relationship with the Goodwinter woman?" Hilton barked. "Were you lovers?"

"No!"

"Are you a lesbian, Detective Croaker?"

"I don't see what that has to do with anything." Fey felt fire burning in her cheeks.

"Then you admit you are a lesbian?"

"I'm admitting nothing."

Hilton kept up his barrage. "If you and Miranda Goodwinter weren't lovers, what were you? Just good friends?"

"We weren't anything," Fey said wearily. "I've told you and told you, I didn't know the woman existed until I was assigned to investigate her murder."

"A murder you committed because she left you for another woman."

"Fuck off," Fey retorted angrily.

"Okay," Hilton said congenially, "she left you for a man

instead. Someone who had the equipment to take care of her needs."

Fey shook her head. "You're unbelievable. What about all the history on Goodwinter that was dug up by the IRS?"

"What about it?" Hilton asked. "Maybe you're in on that as well. There's still the little matter of the two million dollars in bearer bonds that have taken a walk. Now, there's a good motive for you. Perhaps we'll find them when the search of your house is completed."

"My house—" Fey felt the shock reach down into her core.

"Oh, yes, Detective Croaker. Your house. As we speak, a search warrant is being served on your residence. Don't worry, it's all nice and legal. A copy of the warrant will be left for you."

Fey hung her head.

"When did you first meet the victim?" Baxter asked quietly as he took over the questioning.

Fey's voice was tired and defeated. "I never met Miranda Goodwinter or had any contact with her while she was alive."

Baxter slapped the photograph down on the desk in front of her. "Wrong answer! Here's the proof. Photographs don't lie."

"This one does."

"Do you think that there's a jury in the world that's going to believe that?"

"I don't give a shit what a jury thinks! That photograph is a phony! And why should a jury care anyway? Are you seriously trying to suggest that I murdered Miranda Goodwinter knowing I would be the detective assigned to investigate the case?"

"If the shoe fits."

"Oh, fuck you! That's ridiculous!"

"It isn't. This photograph proves you knew the victim while she was alive."

"Your photograph proves diddly. It's a fake."

"SID has already examined the photo and pronounced it an original with no signs of tampering."

"Yeah. Well, we both know how much credence to put

into that statement. Half the time our vaunted Scientific Investigation Division can't find its ass with both hands, a flashlight, and a map. That's why we send our hot cases over to the Sheriff's Department's lab. Our people have dropped too many clangers."

On and on the questioning went in the same circle, time after time. Hilton and Baxter continued to badger and accuse. Fey continued to deny.

Finally Nate Collins stepped in and called a halt. "Gentlemen, this has gone on for long enough."

"Butt out of this, Collins," Hilton told him.

Collins stood up. "Don't try your intimidation tactics on me. This interview is over. If you're going to charge Detective Croaker with something, then let's get to it. If not, then back off."

Baxter put a restraining hand on Hilton again, and everyone sat back in their chairs.

After a few seconds of silence, Baxter picked up a pencil from the table and began to use both his hands to fiddle with it. "All right," he said eventually. "This interview is terminated, but the investigation is far from over." He put the pencil down and looked directly at Fey. "As of this point, Detective Croaker, you are relieved of your investigative duties and are assigned to your residence until further notice. You will be on full pay, but you will remain at home during your work hours unless directed otherwise."

"Mike, this is bullshit." Fey appealed to her immediate supervisor.

Cahill shrugged. "I'm sorry, Fey. I have no control over this situation."

"Right," said Fey. "And I suppose Colby is going to be put in charge of the Goodwinter murder inquiry?"

"He's been on it since the start—" Cahill tried to justify.

"Fuck you, too, Mike," Fey interrupted. She stood up. "If you need me, I'll be at home, like a good little detective." She reached over and turned off both tape recorders. "Come on, Nate," she said to Collins. "I can't stand the stench of hypocrisy in this office any longer."

"Wait, Fey. There's more." This came again from Mike Cahill.

"More," Fey said. "How the hell can there be more?"

"It's about Cordell . . ."

Fey felt her stomach doing flip-flops as she fought for control of her emotions. "What about him?"

"The district attorney's office have pulled back the warrant for his arrest and have dropped all charges against him."

Fey was speechless.

"I'm sorry, Fey," Mike Cahill said. He both sounded and looked sincere. "This is coming directly from upstairs. I have no control over the situation."

Nate put a firm hand on Fey's shoulder and eased her out of the room. There didn't seem to be anything else left to say.

Now, standing amongst the shards of glass from the broken tumbler, Fey still didn't know what to say or how to proceed with the situation. Her house had not been overly disturbed by the searchers from Internal Affairs, but it was still clear that everything had been moved. Fey felt violated. Her inner sanctum had been invaded—her privacy ripped from her and spread out for strangers to see—and if that wasn't a form of rape, she didn't know what was.

She tried telling herself that everything would come out for the good in the end, but she didn't believe it. The photograph showing her with her arm around Miranda Goodwinter was like something out of the "Twilight Zone." It was enough to make her doubt her sanity, as if she'd been leading a double life that even she didn't know about.

Fey had the advantage over Internal Affairs in that she knew she wasn't lying about the photograph. She had never come into contact with Miranda Goodwinter before she started the murder investigation, let alone gone out with her to a nightclub. No matter what SID said, the photo had to be a fake. And anyway, she only had Internal Affairs' word that the photo had been cleared by SID, and she knew that neither Baxter nor Hilton were above lying.

Lying was a favorite investigative technique. Tell a suspect his partners were putting all the blame on him, and separately tell each one of his partners the same thing. Tell a suspect that his fingerprints had been found on the murder weapon even though you hadn't even found the murder weapon, let alone any fingerprints. Promising a suspect you'd file a lesser charge or get his sentence reduced were the only lies you couldn't tell—anything else was fair game.

But the photo bothered Fey for other reasons as well. There was a sense of déjà vu about her own image. She had seen it before, but she couldn't remember when or where. And as for the part of the photo showing Miranda Goodwinter—where had that come from? Fey had been through the murder scene with a fine-tooth comb, and there had been no pictures of any sort anywhere.

Somehow she had to get her own copy of the photo. Internal Affairs would eventually have to give her one if charges were filed, but they would delay too long for it to do her any good in the short run. No, there had to be some other way.

Getting a grip on herself, Fey bent down and began to clean up the mess she had made with the vodka. She felt a little better as she realized she was starting to think about fighting back for the first time since the interview with IA had commenced.

She was still so angry about the charges against Cordell being dropped that she couldn't think straight about that situation. Twice since she'd been home, the phone had rung, and she'd let the machine pick it up. On both occasions she'd vaguely heard Jake's voice imploring her to call him. She knew she should, but right now she didn't need explanations, sympathy, or a man who wanted to cry on her shoulders. More than anything, she needed time and space to think things through—to find an objective viewpoint and make clearheaded decisions.

The fact that the charges against Cordell had been dropped didn't change things as far as Fey was concerned. He was still floating around like a loose cannon, and she knew he was demented enough to follow through on his threats against her. Hell, she thought, he might not even realize that the charges had been dropped.

Throwing the glass shards in the kitchen trash can, Fey walked through the house, straightening up as she went, and checking to make sure that weapons were easily accessible to her in every room. She was vulnerable, but she wasn't going down without a fight.

Eventually she grabbed up a shotgun, checked its load, and walked out into her backyard. The horse sheds needed to be cleaned, and it was just the kind of automatic, menial work that would free her subconscious mind to work on more academic problems.

The dusk of evening had given way to the deeper darkness of early night. Fey switched on the corral pole lights and found that her neighbor Peter Dent had already placed the horses in their boxes for the night. She tried to remember if she had seen or heard him at work, but realized that she'd been too deep in her own troubles to notice.

She checked on both horses and found them comfortable. The straw in their boxes was fairly fresh, appearing to have been there since early afternoon, but she wanted the activity of cleaning the boxes, so Fey decided to muck them out again. She could have let the horses out into the corral as she worked, but there was something reassuring about their closeness.

Keeping the bottom half of the Dutch doors on Constable's box closed, Fey leaned the shotgun against the back wall and patted the horse on his rump. She picked up a pitchfork and began to muck the straw as Constable nudged her playfully with his nuzzle. "Stop it, you silly beast," she said softly, the unconditional affection of one of her animals working wonders for her frame of mind.

She finished the job quickly as she spread fresh straw on the floor, filled the food tubs, put in fresh water, and retrieved her shotgun. She gave Constable another series of affectionate pats and moved on to Thieftaker's stall.

Once in the second horse's stall, Fey began the same routine by closing the bottom half of the Dutch doors and leaning her shotgun against the back wall. She turned to look at the horse, but was amazed to see a flaming bottle flying through the air to smash on the back wall. Thieftaker reared back as gasoline exploded over everything, with flames following in its trail faster than the eye could see.

Fey ducked away from the horses' flashing hooves and

lunged toward the stall entrance. She had almost reached it when the top half of the Dutch doors slammed closed with a decisive thud.

Fey threw herself at the closing door and felt every bone in her body jar when the door refused to budge as she slammed into it. Behind her, Thieftaker's eyes rolled wildly as he thrashed about in fear. A thin line of gasoline had exploded across the horse's back, and Fey watched in horror as flames suddenly erupted along its length.

Moving with a speed born of desperation, Fey grabbed Thieftaker's horse rug from where it was draped over a peg, and threw it across the terrified horse's back to smother the flames. The horse twisted and kicked out, catching Fey a glancing blow across her left arm. She grunted and spun away into a wall.

Regaining her balance, she tore off her blouse and, dodging another wild kick, dunked it in the horse's water bucket. Trying in vain to calm the horse, Fey danced around in the confined space and threw the soaking wet blouse over the horse's head to cover its eyes and muzzle.

The flames in the tiny stall were beginning to gain the upper hand. Fey knew she had to do something fast or she, Thieftaker, and Constable next door would all perish. Blinded by smoke and reacting strictly on instinct, she grabbed a handful of Thieftaker's mane and swung herself with reckless abandon onto the horse's back. She knew it would hurt the horse like hell across the area that had been burned, but better hurt than dead.

Retaining her seat by squeezing her legs tightly into Thieftaker's sides, Fey drove her heels into the horse's flanks.

With the damp blouse still covering his head, Thieftaker bucked wildly to try and dislodge the weight on his back, but Fey clung on with a fierce determination. Yelling encouragement, she settled the horse slightly and then again urged him forward.

The big animal reacted to Fey's commands, but there was precious little space available before he smashed blindly into one of the stall walls. As the horse backed away in shock, Fey hung on for dear life and then spurred Thieftaker forward again.

Fey had helped build the semimakeshift horse boxes, and she knew they were not sturdy enough to withstand the pounding of a ton of terrified horseflesh. At least she prayed they weren't.

Three times Thieftaker smashed into the burning wooden walls, shaking the structure but seeming to make no headway. The horse was maddened with fear as it rammed its powerful chest into the wall for the fourth time. This time, however, there was a loud cracking sound as boards separated from posts and the night air rushed in to feed the flames.

Seeing her last chance, Fey dug her heels into Thieftaker's side again and again. The horse twirled, out of control, and then, by mere luck of the draw, ran forward again to hit the same wall for a fifth time. There was more splitting of boards, and suddenly horse and rider sprang into the open.

Thieftaker, sensing freedom, bolted forward until he ran into the iron railing enclosing the corral. Fey was thrown off by the impact and hit the dirt hard. Instinctively she rolled away from the pounding of the hooves above her and scrambled first to her knees and then to her feet.

With no time left to hesitate, she part ran and part stumbled her way back toward the burning horse boxes. Once there, she quickly unbolted the bottom Dutch door that was keeping Constable confined. The second horse box was filled with smoke, but had not yet been invaded by flames. Constable, seeing the open door, blasted out into the corral to join Thieftaker.

Another part of the structure collapsed, sending flames and sparks leaping into the night sky. Fey pushed herself off a wall and staggered out into the corral herself. She stumbled to her knees twice before reaching the corral railing. The horses were still running wildly around, but were well out of danger.

Gasping for breath, she pulled herself through the gaps in the railing and made for the house. She noticed for the first time that there were sirens blaring when five firemen suddenly charged through her back gate, dragging a hose behind them. Peter Dent from next door was with them, and he ran over to Fey, catching her as she almost sagged to the ground in relief.

"Are you okay?" Peter asked urgently.

"I don't know."

Peter eased her to a sitting position on the ground. "I saw the flames from my back window," he said. "I didn't even know you were home yet—"

"Ever have one of those days, Pete?" Fey said calmly, causing Peter to look at her strangely. She caught his glance and gave him a soot-blackened grin. "I'm fine," she reassured him, before breaking into a fit of coughing. She flapped her hands. "Just make sure the horses are okay, please."

Peter looked unsure, but Fey pushed him away, and he finally went when two paramedics rushed over to take his place.

Fey began to cough again. Her head felt like someone had driven a spike through it, and all the aches and pains she had picked up over the past few days had intensified tenfold. She turned her head to the side and vomited.

From the farthest corner of Fey's property, hidden by both the night and the depths of an overgrown bougainvillea, Isaac Cordell watched the activity that swirled around him with interest.

He smiled.

Things had not gone as he had expected. Far from it, in fact. But that was all right. He'd learned a lot. Information that he may be able to use if the time ever came.

Fey Croaker was proving to be extremely resilient. She was remarkably still alive. Beaten and battered, but still alive.

Cordell pulled a blanket tightly around his shoulders and

closed his eyes. He was happy for now with the way things were.

There would always be another time.

The house was quiet and still in the wee hours of the morning. Alone and exhausted, Fey was again sitting in her favorite armchair. Peter Dent had taken Thieftaker and Constable to his own corral next door for safekeeping, and the firemen had rolled up their hoses and disappeared back into the night.

Fey had showered and slipped into her white terry cloth robe. Her wet hair was still wrapped in a towel, and she felt physically scrubbed and clean. Emotionally, though, she felt as if she were a hundred years old.

Mentally she reviewed her situation for the millionth time. Her job was suddenly at risk—hell, if Internal Affairs was to tell the story, even her freedom was at risk. Her case against Isaac Cordell was in shambles. Her love life had jeopardized a man she cared for deeply. Someone was trying to kill her, and the cops who were supposed to be her partners and friends would all find a way to blame the situation on the fact that she was a woman.

On another level, she had a brother who hated her because she had never been able to save him from himself; a dead father whose abuses constantly haunted the periphery of her personal reality; and, as a result, a self-loathing that often cracked her self-esteem as if it were a piece of fine crystal threatened by a diva's high C.

Anything, even death, was preferable to how she felt at that moment. She considered, ever so briefly, the fact that her service revolver was in her purse. It wouldn't make as much mess as the shotgun that was on the floor at her feet for protection. She thought of other cops she had known who had sucked bullets, and she remembered the irrational guilt and the loathing she had felt when she had learned of their passing.

Eating your gun was a pathetic, self-absorbed, useless gesture. A waste of good ammunition. It made a statement that told the world that the bastards had won—that there was no God because there was no justice, not in this world or in any other—and that was something Fey refused to believe.

From somewhere she found the strength to mock herself with a wry smile. She'd never commit suicide. She wouldn't give the bastards the pleasure. She did know, however, that she was at the bottom of her personal barrel. It was not a pleasant place to be, but it was certainly a place that gave you time to consider all your options.

The bottom of the barrel was the dwelling place of life's detritus—the slimy, unattractive things that nobody wants to look at in the light. But Fey had found something surprising down there. A dirty, slimy, unattractive idea. One that nobody was going to want to look at in the light. It needed work. It needed shaping and research. It needed luck. But if she hadn't been at the bottom of the barrel, she never would have found it, let alone considered it.

There was only one way, however, to see if her dirty, slimy, little idea would truly fit the facts, and that was to drag it kicking and screaming along with her as she swam back to the top.

Fey remembered a favorite saying she had picked up in Sunday school—"Vengeance is mine, sayeth the Lord."

No problem. The way Fey had it figured, the Lord could have it back when she was done with it.

"Eddie? It's Fey Croaker."

"Fey! What's going on? I heard you were in trouble."

"What have you heard, Eddie?"

"I heard that somebody is fucking you around over some photo that was turned in to Internal Affairs." Eddie Mack, the department's top crime scene photographer, had only just arrived at work when Fey's call had come in. She'd been lucky to catch him since he already had a full card of photo assignments for the day.

"Did you see the photo, Eddie?"

There was silence.

"Eddie?"

"Yeah, I saw it."

"Then you know what's going on, except for the fact that it's a phony. I'm telling you—"

"You don't have to tell me anything, Fey. If you say it's a phony, I believe you."

Fey felt somewhat gratified. "Internal Affairs said your people down at SID verified that the photo hadn't been tampered with."

"Not true," Eddie said. "We told them it didn't appear to be tampered with, but there's no way to know for sure."

"Why not?"

There was more silence, but this time Fey realized Eddie Mack had covered the receiver in order to talk to somebody. After a few seconds, his voice came back on the line in a low whisper. "I can't talk right now, Fey."

"You have unfriendly ears around you?"

"That's right."

"Okay, then just listen. I need a copy of that photograph."

"Ah, come on!" Eddie's voice went first high and then low again. "I can't do that! It's more than my job is worth. IA would be all over me if they found out."

"Who's going to tell them? I have a right to examine the evidence against me."

"Then ask them for a copy."

"Right, and then wait around for the next month while they decide that they have to give it to me. I can't wait that long."

"I can't, Fey. You know how much respect I have for you. We're a team out there in the field. You're one of the most professional homicide dicks I've ever come across in this profession, but Internal Affairs has clamped down hard on that photo. They took all the copies we made away with them."

"Bullshit! I know you, Eddie. You keep copies of all your work, because you know how stuff manages to get lost. It's a habit that's saved several detectives' asses over the years."

"Fey . . ."

"You're my only chance, Eddie. They're talking about prosecuting me! I'm a damn suspect in this case because of that photograph, and I've got to clear this up before it goes any further."

"But—"

"No buts! You said you believed me. If that's true, then help me get the bastard who's trying to shaft me."

Silence.

"Come on, Eddie. I need you."

Silence.

Then finally, "I'm sorry."

"Eddie!"

The line went dead.

Fey sat next to the phone with her head in her hands. She had already called in to Mike Cahill that morning, and reported her "on duty at home" status. Cahill had been formal and cool over the phone, and Fey dreaded to think about what kind of scuttlebutt was being issued by the squad room's rumor control personnel.

Cahill asked her briefly about the events of the night before, but was not forthcoming when Fey explained about the attempt on her life. The photograph of her with Miranda Goodwinter seemed to have turned her into an instant leper, and as a result, Mike Cahill was proving to be a very fair weather friend.

Before finally getting a couple of hours sleep the night before, Fey became bound and determined that she wasn't going to sit back and wait for the department to proceed with their case against her or with their investigation into the attempt on her life. With the likes of Cahill covering their collective political butt, waiting for Internal Affairs to conclude their investigation would be like waiting for the guillotine blade to drop.

Steely resolve was all well and good, but Fey still

needed a starting point, and she had hoped for far more from Eddie Mack. The idea that had formed in her mind in the wee hours of the morning seemed only slightly less reasonable in the light of day, but she had to get a handle on it—had to find a way to crack things open and see what fell out.

The logical starting point was with the photograph of her in a nightclub with her arm around Miranda Goodwinter. The fact that the photograph was phony was the one piece of the case that Fey positively knew to be true. It didn't matter what anyone else believed. She knew she had never had contact with Goodwinter while the woman was alive; therefore, the photo was a loose thread. If she pulled on it hard enough, it just might unravel the fabric of the whole case.

The phone rang.

Fey picked it up. "Hello."

A whisper came down the line. "Ajax Photo Supply. Eleven o'clock. See a guy named Rhino."

The phone line went dead, but not before she was able to recognize Eddie Mack's voice.

Fey listened to the hum of the dead wire. Eventually she hung up the receiver on her end and smiled. It was like coming out of the darkness into the bright light of a gorgeous summer day. Her brain was clicking over at a thousand miles per hour. She didn't know what she was going to find out at Ajax Photo Supply, but whatever it was, it would be a starting point.

Meanwhile, there was still the problem of Isaac Cordell to deal with. Cordell was only a part of the main problem of solving the murder of Miranda Goodwinter, but he was perhaps the largest part. He was the deck's wild card, and Fey's gut instincts told her that even if Cordell knew the charges against him had been dropped, he was still going to come after her. Fey had heard his voice on her answering machine. She'd seen what he'd done to her brother, and she knew he wasn't going to back down.

Whatever Cordell had been before he went to prison had no bearing on the animal he had now become. Of that Fey was sure. Ten years in a hellhole doesn't turn anyone into a model citizen—and anyone who said differently was talking out his ass. Incarceration was only a way to put off dealing with a problem until the problem was again unleashed on society. And *rehabilitation* was simply a word used to fill up dictionaries. A word that could be used by liberal prison reformers to spark the emotions of other bleeding-heart knee-jerks who didn't understand a thing about the rights of a victim.

Prison never cured any serious criminal. Only God could do that. And the only way to get them an interview with God was to fry the bastards.

Fey had seen Cordell's eyes when he had turned to attack her. What she had seen there was a soul devoid of mercy or fear.

The threat posed by Cordell had to be faced up to and defused as soon as possible. Carrying around shotguns wherever she went was not a solution with which she was willing to live—or with which she was willing to die, since it had proved of little use the night before.

Because of her precarious position, it was clear that the department was not going to back her play where Cordell was concerned. Fey wanted to believe that, as individuals, both Monk and Hatch would be there for her if she were to call, but it would put them both squarely on the hot seat if things turned sour. It didn't matter anyway. Fey had another solution.

She picked up the phone and began dialing.

Ajax Photo Supply was tucked away in a relatively new industrial complex behind Union Station in downtown Los Angeles. Fey walked through the door bang on eleven o'clock and found herself surrounded by three walls of photographic blowups from scenes of graphic tragedies: car crashes, famine, scenes from open heart surgery, the aftermath of plane crashes, photos of abused children, familiar shots from Vietnam, Afghanistan, WWII concentration camps. Blood, gore, pain, and anguish assaulted the eye from almost every direction. The effect was overwhelming.

The fourth wall, behind a lower counter, was filled with smaller snapshots of smiling children, family outings, office parties, and other festive gatherings all stuck every which way with drawing pins.

The most startling thing about the setup, however, was the total absence of photo supplies.

Behind the low counter, on a high stool, sat an elfinlike girl dressed all in black. Her miniskirt rode very high on her crossed thighs, revealing long, slender legs encased in sheer black seamed stockings and capped by black pumps that would have looked clunky even in the sixties. A black Lana Turner sweater hugged pointed breasts, between which ran a cheap string of black beads. On her thin face the girl wore black, bottle-cap sunglasses superficially poised to offset her trendy, spike-cut black hair. The elf was even smoking a black cigarette.

"Yes?" she said with an air of artful detachment as Fey approached the counter.

Fey took another look at the photos on the walls around her before asking, "Is Rhino here?"

"In back," said the elf. She extracted the cigarette from her mouth with the underhanded gesture that is uniquely European and pointed it in the direction of a door at one end of the wall behind the counter.

When the elf didn't make a move to call Rhino out, Fey moved to the end of the counter, lifted up the gate top, and let herself through. She walked to the doorway set in the back wall. Like the rest of the fourth wall, it was covered with pinned-on snapshots of happy scenes—a stark contrast to the blowups on the other three walls.

Not knowing what to expect, Fey took a breath and forged ahead. She had a lot riding on this excursion, and it had already cost her plenty. According to the rules of being "on duty at home," Fey was supposed to remain at her residence unless she was contacted by her supervisor to do otherwise. At the risk of bringing further departmental wrath down on her head, she had driven from her house to West L.A. station, where she made an unannounced appearance.

She had gone directly to Mike Cahill's office and had closeted herself in there with Cahill for the fifteen minutes it took him to ream her out for disobeying the stay-at-home order. Fey had insisted that her only motive in coming to the station was to make a direct plea to Cahill to reinstate her. Cahill had told her, in no uncertain terms, that the decision to reinstate her did not rest at his level. It was a decision to be made by the Internal Affairs investigators.

Fey was well aware that Cahill wouldn't and couldn't do anything for her. But she suffered the humiliation for two reasons. First, she needed an excuse for being away from her residence in case Internal Affairs tried to contact her while she was gone; and second, she needed something from the walls of the station's coffee room.

As she entered the back room of Ajax Photo Supply, those precious items were burning a hole in the pocket of the windcheater she had wrapped around her shoulders.

The room was dim and filled with a permanent haze of cigarette smoke. It was twice the size of the lobby, and the walls were lined with VCR machines, stacked floor to ceiling, all with red-glowing recording lights. What space wasn't taken up by the VCRs was filled with bins of videotapes and printed tape boxes. Fey caught the photos and titles on several of the empty tape boxes—lots of flesh tones and double entendres. It didn't take a rocket scientist to realize she'd stepped into the back room of a porno reproduction plant, and by all appearances, probably a pirate operation.

Under the lone overhead lamp, a hunchbacked man with long, greasy-looking hair sat at a battered table using a mouse attached to an expensive computer setup. A small stub of a cigarette threatened to burn his lip while shrouding his head in smoke.

"Rhino?" Fey asked.

"Yeah. Shut the door behind you," he said, in an accent that could only come from across the pond. "And if you want my help, you'll keep a set of blinders on."

Fey's reply was immediate. "I see nuthink," she said, in a mock German accent.

"Thank you, Sergeant Shultz," Rhino said. "Come over here and sit yourself down." He cleared a stack of magazines off a hard-back chair and shoved it out from the table.

Fey made her way forward and did as she was told. The cigarette smoke was getting to her, the craving deep from within her chest waking up.

From the front, Rhino was no better a prospect than he was from the back. His haggard face was grimy with neglected patches of beard, and there was a blob of dried egg at one corner of his small mouth. Thick glasses, each lens having an additional watchmaker's magnifying glass on a wire arm that could be dropped into position, rested on a too long nose that had a full crop of hair sprouting out of each wide nostril. He smiled at Fey, revealing a dazzling array of large, sparkling white teeth made all the more impressive because of their setting.

When Fey looked slightly startled by the display, Rhino simply shrugged and stated, "I believe in good oral hygiene." He appeared to have experienced similar reactions to his teeth before. He continued to fiddle with the computer in front of him, but from her position, Fey couldn't see the screen.

"How do you know Eddie Mack?" Fey asked, when she tired of listening to the hum of the VCRs recording.

"We has a shared business interest, don't we?" Rhino tossed his head in a gesture that encompassed the whole room. "He must really trust you to let you in on his little secret."

Fey looked around again at the stacks of busy VCRs. Through the gloom she could also make out another room farther back that seemed to be filled with camera equipment and other computer items. She was surprised, to say the least. Eddie Mack didn't seem to be the type to be a pirate video king, but she wasn't going to complain. Especially if Rhino was going to be able to help her out.

"Did Eddie tell you what this is all about?"

"Yeah. He said you was havin' a spot of trouble with a photo snap of you with your arm around another bimbo. You say it ain't a possible scenario since you didn't know the other tit."

"Not until she was dead and cold anyway."

Rhino wrinkled his nose. "Not my style. I don't know 'ow you do it."

While he talked, Rhino never took his eyes off the computer screen or stopped twiddling with the mouse.

Fey held her breath while asking her next question. "Did Eddie give you a copy of the photo?"

Rhino just kept knocking hell out of the mouse. Eventually he looked up at Fey, gave her another quick look at his teeth, and said, "Yeah. He says you owe him big time."

Fey shrugged. "Before this is over, I have a feeling I'm going to be in debt over my head."

Rhino rolled and tapped the mouse again.

Restlessly Fey asked, "Were you able to do anything with the photo?"

Rhino tapped the mouse a final time and then turned the computer screen toward Fey. Fey took one look and burst out laughing. The screen was a very high resolution monitor, and the picture it displayed was crisp and clear. In the dim light of the back room, Fey found herself looking at the same photo of Miranda Goodwinter in the nightclub setting—only this time Fey wasn't in the picture. This time there was a man with his arm around Miranda Goodwinter's elegant shoulders. A well-known man. Richard Nixon.

"Shit fire," said Fey.

"I thought you'd like it," Rhino said, and flashed his teeth.

"I am not a crook," said Fey.

"Your accent is lousy. Stick to Sergeant Schultz."

Fey looked at the screen again. "Okay, I'm impressed, but how do you get it off the screen and into the form of a photo print?"

Rhino rolled the mouse and tapped it again. A machine at the other end of the table began to whirl and click. The machine was about one foot wide by three feet long by one foot high and was attached to the computer by a long cord. After a couple of minutes, a sheet of Kodak print paper rolled out. Rhino picked it up, took it over to a cutting board, trimmed the sides, and gave the finished product to Fey. It was as perfect to look at as the original photo with Fey next to Miranda Goodwinter.

Rhino tapped the print with a chewed fingernail. "You want prints, slides, or negatives? I can give 'em all to you. Nobody will ever be able to tell that they're not originals."

"Amazing," Fey said. "Do you know what this means where photo evidence is concerned?"

Rhino snorted. "Pretty soon there won't be any such thing. This technology has made it outmoded. Should provide blackmailers with a load of business, though, before it becomes common knowledge."

"The criminal mind," Fey said. "Always a step ahead." She took another, harder look at the new photograph. Richard Nixon still had his arm around Miranda Goodwinter. "How does the system work?"

Rhino sat back down again. "Simple really. It's called digital imaging. You take a photo, use a top-quality scanner to put it into a computer with the appropriate software, delete or add whatever you want, start up the film recorder—" he pointed to the machine that had produced the print "—and presto, a new negative that shows no signs of tampering. Still photography is child's play, however, compared to doing a whole video."

"You can do this on tape as well?"

"Sure. The technology is the same, but it takes a real artist to do it right. Give me enough time and I could produce a video that shows JFK assassinating himself. You have to be real careful about shadows and mirrors and stuff like that, though. Here, I'll show you." He pushed his chair across the room and flipped on a television screen that Fey hadn't seen nestled among the VCRs. He took a tape off a low shelf and plugged it into an empty VCR, and within seconds an erotic coupling of Britain's ex-Prime Minister Maggie Thatcher and Ronald Reagan appeared on the television screen.

"Would you look at that," Fey said, as amazed at the film's quality as with the identities of the faked images it portrayed. "And at their age."

"I wanted to send a copy to Nancy, but I remembered to just say no," Rhino said as he shut the VCR and the television down and wheeled himself back to the table.

"How common is this technology?" Fey asked.

Rhino shrugged. "Common enough. The equipment and software are expensive, but this shit is being done all the time in the movies today. *Terminator 2* is probably the best-known example. The silver guy who kept forming and reforming was all done through digital imaging."

"How about small jobs, like putting my image into the photo?"

Rhino belched and rubbed his tummy. "There are a

number of photo freak guys like me around. We're not that hard to find if you know where to look. And then there are a number of large developing businesses in town who could do the job for you. They wouldn't be hard to find at all. The only thing you'd have to do is let your fingers do the walking through the yellow pages."

"How many freaks or legitimate businesses would you say are in the L.A. area?"

Rhino thought about that for a moment before shrugging. "Two dozen. Three tops."

"You think you could track down the guy who put me into this photo?"

"Maybe. What's it worth?"

"My job."

"Don't mean nothin' to me."

"How about your freedom to exploit the free enterprise system?" Fey waved her hand at the illicit videotapes being recorded all around her.

Rhino shook his head. "I told Eddie that letting you come down here was a bad idea. Somehow, though, I don't think you'd screw Eddie over that way."

"Probably not," Fey said.

Rhino let loose with his orthodontia. "In that case, I'll do what I can."

"Thanks."

Fey looked back at the computer screen again. "If a person is deleted from a photograph, can you reverse the process?"

"You mean from the new negative?"

"Yes."

Rhino picked his nose and flicked away the prize. "No way. The original image never appears on the new negative, so there would be no way to recover it."

That was too bad, Fey thought. It would have been nice to be able to confirm who was sitting next to Miranda Goodwinter in the original photo, even though she already had a good idea.

"However," Fey began, "you could put any of these people into the photo next to that woman?" She pulled out the promotion party photos that she had taken off the wall of the station's coffee room earlier that day.

The only photo she hadn't been able to find on the wall was the one of her with the two other female officers that somebody had labeled "The Crack Squad." But she now knew what had happened to that photo, and how her image had come to be sitting next to Miranda Goodwinter in a nightclub. She'd always had a vague feeling she'd seen the image of herself in the photo with Miranda Goodwinter before, but it had taken a while for the penny to drop.

Rhino looked at the photos in Fey's hand. "Yeah, I can put those folks in the picture. Simple as wanking in bed."

"Wanking?"

Rhino flashed his teeth. "You're not old enough for me to explain that term."

"I'll take that as a compliment."

"Take it how you like." Rhino took the photos. "Now, you want these photos with a glossy or a matte finish?"

**F**ey could feel the momentum of the investigation building. It was as if she were on a steam train that had groaned its way up the side of a mountain and was now gathering speed as it crested the top for its run down the other side. From experience Fey knew that, like the Little Train That Could, the investigation would soon be moving at a speed that would threaten to turn it into a runaway.

At the conclusion of most successful investigations, a detective should be able to look back and see just where it was that the trainload of clues, hunches, and information crested the mountain and began the steep descent down the other side of the final destination of an arrest and conviction.

Once on that downward slope, however, the final destination was not guaranteed. A detective had to hang on to the wheel and do everything possible not to let the whole damn thing derail in a spectacular crash that would leave dismembered alibis, broken laws, and bloodied witnesses strewn along the tracks for the defense lawyers to pick through like so many scavengers.

As she left Rhino's with a stack of interesting prints in her pocket, Fey knew she should go directly back to the station and confront Mike Cahill with what she had. It would perhaps have been the right thing to do—she could have immediately cleared up the doubts about her contact with Miranda Goodwinter and been officially put back in charge of the murder investigation—but it sure as hell wasn't what Fey was going to do. She was tired of playing things by the book, tired of having to rely on other people who only backed her up when it was convenient, politically correct, or in their best interest. As things stood, there was a very good chance that even after clearing herself of having had previous contact with the victim, Mike Cahill, or someone above him, would feel that putting her back on the case would still be a conflict of interest.

Internal Affairs could also raise objections—dragging their feet before eventually clearing her of any wrongdoing. IA hated to be wrong. They would mess about, picking at nits, leaving a cloud over Fey's head, while the case got cold and finally found its way to the unsolved/inactive file—for which Fey would also be blamed statistically because she was still officially the supervisor of the unit.

The possibility that the case may be solved by another detective was something Fey never even considered. The ugly little idea that was becoming stronger and stronger in her mind left her in no doubt that she was the only cop who had a chance of bringing the guilty to justice. It wasn't a matter of conceit, but rather a matter of being the only detective on the case in a position to see the trees instead of the forest.

Because of her suspension, Fey had been forced to re-evaluate everything she'd seen and heard since the beginning of the investigation. This second look had also been taken with the desperation of her own personal perspective—a point of view that had cleared away the clouds of subterfuge and allowed the truth to surface. The method of the attempt on her life, coupled with several other small clues, had solidified the vague rumblings that Fey had originally been reluctant to even consider. Her problem now wasn't whodunit, but how to prove it. And when she did, it would be a thunder and a satisfaction she wasn't going to allow anyone to steal.

She drove the dozen blocks from Rhino's back room to the central branch of the Los Angeles Public Library with no conscious memory of how she arrived there. Her mind was busy ticking off the numerous threads that she had to pull together. She didn't give a damn now if IA or anyone else connected with the department found out that she wasn't staying at home as ordered. She'd deal with that later if it came up. Right now her train was running down the track at speed, and nothing was going to stop it.

Finding an empty spot at the curb, Fey parked, fed the meter, and made her way into the library building. Within fifteen minutes she'd secured herself a private booth and access to a Lexus/Nexus machine. Lexus/Nexus was a computer system that gave the user instant access to the files of over five hundred newspapers and one thousand magazines nationwide. The department had access to two Lexus/Nexus terminals situated in Parker Center, one under lock and key in the Antiterrorist Division, and the other slightly more accessible through the Organized Crime and Intelligence Division. Neither were open to Fey at this stage, so she was shelling out her own cash to access the library's terminal.

After thirty minutes, she came up with good value for her money.

The IRS agent Kyle Craven had given Fey some of the first pieces of the puzzle that was Miranda Goodwinter's murder. Monk Lawson had filled in some more background with the information he had provided on Janice Ryder. Fey had earlier fitted some of those pieces together and had come up with the fact that Janice Ryder's father, Peter Fletcher, had been one of Miranda Goodwinter's first victims—giving Ryder a damned good motive for murder. It also gave her a strong reason for unleashing Isaac Cordell to either do her dirty work for her or to carry the bucket for her own murderous actions. It looked good, but Fey still wanted more information before she went anywhere with it.

The Lexus/Nexus machine gave it to her.

Although the computer system gave access to the files of many newspapers, the system's files on the *Los Angeles Times* were more extensive than most of the others and went back over almost a thirty-year period. Fey's first Lexus/Nexus inquiry came up with the obituary for Peter Fletcher. Most of the information it contained was a rehash of what Kyle Craven had already spelled out for her. The obit did, however, pinpoint the location of the drunk-driving accident that had killed Fletcher as being on a particularly nasty section of Mulholland Drive.

After uncovering that nugget of information, Fey spun her wheels for a while trying to track down further information on the list she had made of Miranda Goodwinter's other identities. She came across a few possibly related tidbits, but nothing that made her blood rush.

She was running out of ideas to check out when she began to think about the scam Miranda Goodwinter had run on Isaac Cordell. It was the one time in her murderous career that Miranda Goodwinter, or Lady M as Craven referred to her, had varied from her usual method of operation. It was also the first time that she had involved somebody else in her scheme; in this case, Adam Roarke, Cordell's business partner.

Fey keyed Adam Roarke's name into the Lexus/Nexus machine and focused the search date to a two-year period after Cordell had been sent to jail. Kyle Craven had followed up on Roarke, but only to the point of finding out that Roarke hadn't filed any further tax returns after taking off with the proceeds from the insurance policy that had been the kiss of death where Isaac Cordell's fate was concerned.

After thirty seconds, the Lexus/Nexus terminal indicated fifty possible articles related to Adam Roarke during the time frame of Fey's inquiry. Fey scanned through the entries quickly and found that most of them dealt with a popular architect who was also named Adam Roarke. As she paged through the output, though, Fey came across several mentions, mostly from the *San Francisco Chronicle,* pertaining to the right Adam Roarke.

Of those articles that interested her, there was one in particular that made the whole effort worthwhile. Like the obituary on Peter Fletcher, this article was taken from the *Los Angeles Times*. It was a short piece, no more than a filler on a slow news day, a few lines of type that told of yet another drunken-driving death. The name of the deceased was Adam Roarke, late of San Francisco, and his car had skidded over the edge on a particularly nasty section of Mulholland Drive. Fey was willing to bet her life that it was the same nasty section of Mulholland Drive that had also claimed the life of Peter Fletcher.

In the criminal mind, what works once should work again. Lady M couldn't keep coming up with new and innovative ways to kill lovers and husbands. Somewhere along the line she would have to go back to tried-and-true methods that had worked for her before. Sticking a drunk body in a car, pointing the car wheels toward the edge of a cliff, and jamming the accelerator down was simple, but effective.

It had been a lot of years since Peter Fletcher had gone over the edge on Mulholland Drive. Since then, there had been numerous other legitimate accidental deaths on that treacherous road through the Santa Monica Mountains to the beach. Who was going to notice one more?

Fey had, and she was willing to bet Janice Ryder had also.

Janice Ryder had done a hell of a job tracking down the stepmother who had murdered her father and abandoned her without a penny to her name. Ryder had done a better job than even Kyle Craven. But then Craven had lots of fish to fry, while Janice Ryder had a far more personal, single-minded vendetta to pursue. Cordell's case must have appeared made-to-order for her, and she had pursued her plan with a hatred fueled by the pure white heat of vengeance.

Fey now had another of the keys she needed to break the case wide open, but there was still a hidden killer to catch. Her train was on track, but there were still a hell of a lot of twists and curves to come.

Isaac Cordell had come out of hiding early enough in the morning to watch as Fey left her house. He'd given her a few minutes to make sure she wasn't coming back before he slipped the lock on her back door and let himself into the lair of his intended victim.

He felt half-starved and he ravenously ate a bowl of cereal and fixed himself a sandwich with items from Fey's fridge. He even made and drank several cups of instant coffee, being careful to clear up after himself and leave no sign of his presence.

Ever since Fey had brought him down in the back alley, he had burned with an obsession to strike back at her, and through her destruction to strike back at everything in society that had turned against him. In some dark recess of his mind that was still partially civilized, he knew that prison had turned him into an animal. In order to survive, he had been forced to unleash the primitive savage that is at the very base of every human's nature. It had all been explained to him by the prison psychiatrist, and he had accepted the information on its face value, but it did nothing to change or control the monster that he had become.

The chain of psychiatrists, psychologists, and priests who had taken up his cause had all told him he could change if he truly wanted. But they all failed to realize that he did not want to change, because he was delighted with what he had become. For the first time in his life, he was in charge of his actions. The cause behind the pains in his head had freed him to embrace his angers. No more did he have to bow down to the whims of an overbearing mother or a manipulative wife. Others bowed down to him now. And if they didn't, he broke them into tiny pieces. He had the power now, and he had to use it while he could.

And the only way to keep the power was to crush everything that challenged you or tried to take the power away from you.

Fey Croaker had challenged his power. She had not bowed down before him. And because of that, she had to be crushed. That Isaac would enjoy the crushing was only a side benefit.

Once his hunger was satiated, Isaac set about the work he had come to perform. Finding Fey's toolbox in her garage, he removed a hammer and chisel and then returned to the house. Without much problem, he found the shotgun Fey had been carrying with her the night before. With a slight struggle born of unfamiliarity, the shotgun was eventually stripped down, and Cordell took the chisel to the firing pin. When he was satisfied that the gun would never fire, he reassembled the parts and replaced it.

Back in the garage, he put the hammer and chisel away before returning to the kitchen. Suddenly hungry again, he removed several cans of fruit and a box of stale crackers from the back of Fey's pantry. The items would be enough to hold him until it was time for the next move in the game.

**B**rentwood scared Fey half to death when he leaped out at her from behind the living room couch. Fey had come home early in the afternoon, her head full of the information that she had gleaned from both the library and various other sources. Dumping her huge purse, containing her gun, on the couch cushion, she was totally unprepared for the screeching cat who flung himself at her and attacked her shoes.

Fey's heart jumped into her throat for the split second it took her to recognize the cat, and her heart rate took off for the stratosphere. Scared out of her wits and off balance, she almost fell over as the cat completed his hit-and-run attack. Twisting, Fey managed to flop onto the couch, pluck one of the decorative pillows from the end, and throw it in the direction of Brentwood's departing backside. The cat sauntered away unconcerned.

"Screw you, too," Fey yelled at the animal. "You disappear whenever you feel like it, scare the shit out of me, and then expect your dinner to be served."

Brentwood twitched his tail at her in response.

Fey flopped back completely on the couch, her heart still pounding. "Shit. I swear cats are worse than men!"

A stray thought entered Fey's head as she stared at the ceiling. She knew how she felt toward her own animals, as if they were her own children. That thought set her wondering about Miranda Goodwinter's relationship with her cat. Whatever Miranda originally called Brentwood was a secret she had taken to her grave, but Fey had to figure the woman felt the same way about her animal as most pet owners did.

Fey also began to wonder how long and through how many identities Miranda Goodwinter had kept her cat with her. Had she discarded an animal or pet with every identity change, or had Brentwood been a long-term companion? The more Fey thought about the question, the more she favored the latter response, because it could explain a nagging point in her whodunit theory.

Earlier in the afternoon, Fey had abandoned her library research in favor of a pay phone and a pile of quarters in the corner of a downtown greasy spoon where she knew the owner, Max Monroe, and his wife. Their specialty of the house was a Polish sausage and egg sandwich coupled with gallons of hot coffee. While Fey's order for the special sizzled on the grill, she took her first cup of the strong, black coffee with her and muscled the local bookie away from the phone.

Her first call pulled coroner Harry Carter away from a late autopsy.

"This better be important," Harry said in greeting. "I'm already late for a lunch date, and I'm only half done with a stinker that was uncovered last night."

"It is important, Harry, and the stinker will still be there after lunch. I know you have a cast-iron stomach."

Harry blew a raspberry down the line.

"I love you, too," Fey said, "but I don't have time for phone sex at the moment."

"What's on your mind, then, if it isn't my libido?"

"Do you remember telling me in regards to the Miranda Goodwinter autopsy that your original assessment of the murder weapon being a screwdriver might be wrong—that it may be some other type of tool with a thin, flat edge?"

"I remember, all right," Harry said. "I also remember you telling me that you already had the murder weapon in custody and that it was a screwdriver."

"Well, I've had second thoughts."

"Sounds as if you've had third and fourth thoughts."

"Yeah, them, too."

"What do you have in mind?"

Fey put her thoughts into words for Carter to consider.

"Sounds reasonable," Harry said. "You come up with one, and I'll do my best to match it to the wound."

"Do me a favor, Harry, and keep this under your hat until I get back to you."

"No problem. You think I got nothing better to do than run around blabbing to folks about your off-the-wall theories? I got more stiffs hanging out down here than a whorehouse during a Brotherhood of the Weasel convention." Harry broke the connection.

Max pulled a table over next to Fey and placed her sandwich down on the corner nearest to her. Fey smiled at him as she dropped a second quarter and dialed another number from memory. "Thanks," she said, and set her half-empty mug next to the sandwich plate.

"Eat it while it's hot," Max said, gesturing with a pair of bouncing eyebrows.

"Okay, Mom," Fey said, taking a quick bite and then having to swallow it almost whole as somebody answered the phone.

"Is Annie Thaw there?" she asked, choking down sizzling hot sausage and bread crumbs.

"Just a minute," said the Scientific Investigation Division receptionist.

Fey waited, sipping coffee to clear her throat and burning the roof of her mouth in the process.

Almost two minutes passed before Fey's fingerprint expert friend came on the line. "This is Annie."

"Hi, Annie. It's Fey."

"What's cooking, sister?"

Fey noticed that she'd dribbled egg on her blouse. "My

lips and the roof of my mouth at the moment," she said in distraction as she rubbed the stain.

"What?"

"Forget it," Fey said, focusing her attention again. "Listen, those unidentified prints that were found at the Goodwinter crime scene—"

"The one on the door handle and the one in the blood smear?"

"Yeah. I have some comparisons I want you to make."

"You got suspects? Let me grab a pencil—okay, shoot."

Fey told Annie the names of the people she wanted checked.

"Anything on file locally for comparison?"

"Two of them may have something," Fey said, "but you'll probably have to get on to DC for a service record for the last one."

"It'll take time."

"I don't have time. Get DC to fax you a set."

"You'll be pushing your luck for a positive ID. Prints aren't always real clear on a fax."

"Just give it a shot, Annie. I trust you. Do the fax comparison and give me your best bet. We'll worry about proof positive for court later."

"I thought you were out of the loop on this thing. Someone said your tits were in the ringer big time."

"Since when did you start worrying about protocol? This is important to me, Annie. You wouldn't let a sister down, would you?" Fey cringed at her own cheap shot.

"Jeez, Fey. That's low even for you."

"But you'll do it?"

"Of course. I'm not one to let a good woman down. Where do you want me to call you when I get a result?"

"Call my beeper and I'll get back to you," Fey said, and gave Annie the number.

Annie scribbled it down on a scrap print request card. "Hang tough, babe," she said to her friend.

"I am woman, hear me snore," Fey said, and hung up.

Having set wheels in motion, Fey finished her sandwich and headed for home, unsure of exactly what tack to take next. She wasn't ready to confront Mike Cahill or Internal

Affairs with the information she had gathered. That time would come when she had everything tied up tight so they couldn't back away from her.

She gave brief thought to her plans regarding Isaac Cordell, but that situation was still partially beyond her control. Her phone calls early in the morning before leaving the house had brought positive responses, but the whole issue was a waiting game at best. That Cordell would take a run at her, Fey had no doubt. But he had the advantage of choosing the time and place. All Fey could do was wait patiently and be prepared.

Once back at home, however, her thoughts about Miranda Cordell's relationship with her cat opened up a course of action for her. Digging her purse out from underneath where she lay on the couch, Fey rooted through it for her officer's notebook containing the entries she had made while talking to Kyle Craven and the bank manager.

The account Miranda Cordell had established at the bank had been in the name of Monica Blake. Fey had copied down the details of Monica Blake's particulars, including the address she had listed as her residence in Beverly Hills.

Gathering up her purse, Fey headed back out of her house and hit the road again. Within an hour, her efforts returned a jackpot of information.

As Monica Blake, the woman whom Fey first knew as Miranda Goodwinter lived in the penthouse of an upscale apartment complex replete with doormen, car jockeys, maintenance staff, managers, assistant managers, flunkies, and assistant flunkies. Fey knew the price range for other typical penthouses in the area was between four and five grand a month. It certainly appeared as if killing spouses and collecting insurance policies was a lucrative profession.

Fey tracked down the complex manager, Hector Ibarra, a small man with a grand sense of self-importance and a scraggly gunfighter's mustache that wasn't half as impressive as Ibarra thought it was.

"Ms. Blake had been with us for perhaps six months before she suddenly left us," Ibarra told Fey, after she had identified herself and began her questioning.

"Did she have a lease?"

"Yes. She had a year's lease, but she didn't even try to break it. She simply paid off and didn't come back. It was all very sudden and strange."

"Why strange?"

Ibarra gave a shrug. "She was a strange woman. All of the furniture in the apartment was rented, so of course, she left it behind. But she also left behind all of her clothing and other personal items. She told me simply to pack it up and donate it to Goodwill or the Salvation Army."

A strange woman indeed, Fey thought. What woman could bear to leave behind that favorite sweater that brings out the color of her eyes, or that comfortable pair of shoes that you never want to give up? No treasured books or high school love notes. No memories, no keepsakes, no connections to the past. Just an order to bundle up what was there and give it away. The human equivalent of a snake shedding its skin.

She could understand why the woman had paid off the lease. When you were trying to disappear, there was no sense bringing extra heat down on yourself. If you tie up all your loose ends, nobody gets their nose put out of joint and nobody makes the effort to go looking for you.

Somewhere, Fey found the compassion within her to feel sorry for Miranda Goodwinter, or more specifically the child who had become Miranda Goodwinter—the child who had grown into a savage, calculating serial murderer with no conscience and no goal beyond adding dollars to a bank account. Fey's thoughts flashed briefly to the hell of her own upbringing and the effects that it had wrought upon every relationship, every decision, every day of her life since, and she could only venture the vaguest of guesses as to the depths of depravity that could cause a child to grow into a Miranda Goodwinter.

"What do you think caused Ms. Blake to move out in such a rush? Did she give any explanation?"

"She didn't explain anything. One day everything was fine, and the next she said she was moving out."

"Did she have any regular visitors?"

Ibarra shrugged again, but picked up the phone and asked the head doorman to come into his office.

"This is Diego Mazina," Ibarra said, by way of introduction. "He would know more about Ms. Blake's visitors than I do."

Diego nodded at Fey and gave her a wide smile that displayed a gold incisor. He had on the same style management company blazer that Ibarra wore, only without the fancy trim.

Fey identified herself and asked again about Monica Blake's visitors.

"Not many," said Diego. "There was one man who came to take her out on a regular basis."

"When did he start to come over?"

Diego looked thoughtful. "About a month after she move in." His latin accent was more noticeable than Ibarra's. Fey knew he would have to sanitize his speech a lot more if he hoped to move into management. Bland was what the world was coming to expect. Being a foreigner, or a minority, was becoming more accepted, but you damn well better not appear ethnic.

"Did she ever have any women visitors?"

"Not on my shifts," Diego said. "And I am here most of the time." Probably working all the hours under the sun, Fey thought, to send money back to his family in Central or South America.

Fey laid several descriptions of males on Diego.

"Yes. The first one sounds like the man who came always to take her out."

"Did he ever stay here overnight?"

Diego shook his head. "Sometimes he would go up to the penthouse with Ms. Blake, but he would always leave later in the evening."

Monica Blake, the black widow spinning her web around a new victim before devouring him.

"The man was very upset when Ms. Blake moved," Diego offered of his own accord.

"Really?"

"*Sí.* He was very angry."

"That's right," chimed in Ibarra. "He also became very upset with me when I told him Ms. Blake had not left a forwarding address. He didn't believe me. I was forced to call the police, but the man left before they arrived."

"Since you seem to recognize my description," Fey said, "I'm sure you would recognize this man if I was to bring back a photograph."

Both Ibarra and Diego nodded in the affirmative.

"What about the second man I described?"

"It could be that he was here also," Diego said. "It was the day before Ms. Blake moved out."

The second description Fey had given had been as close as she could get to describing Isaac Cordell.

"Did anything unusual happen?"

Diego gave up the same ethnic shrug displayed earlier by Ibarra. "After the man's visit, Ms. Blake came down the elevator in a big hurry. She seemed upset. She was very nervous while she was waiting for her car to be brought around."

"Nothing else?"

"No. Nothing."

"Did Monica Blake have any pets?" Fey asked Ibarra as she refocused on the interview.

Ibarra grunted. "No. We don't allow pets in the building."

That surprised Fey, but there was nothing she could do about it. She thanked the two men, and Diego accompanied her out of the office and walked with her to her car.

"Why did you ask if Ms. Blake had a pet?" Diego asked as Fey was turning to get in her vehicle. She halted her process and stood up again, leaning one arm across the top of the open car door.

"Is there something you want to tell me, Diego?"

Diego looked back over his shoulder, as if wanting to get away now, regretting that he had spoken.

"It's okay," Fey told him. "Whatever you have to say stays between us."

Diego looked back at her and licked his lips. "Señor Ibarra does not know, but Ms. Blake had a cat."

"A cat?"

"*Sí.* She pay me sometimes to feed it if she was going to be out or away." Diego said all of this in a hushed voice, as if scared that Ibarra's ears were sensitive enough to overhear him from inside the building.

"What kind of cat was it?"

Diego shrugged. "A *blanco*—a white one."

Bingo—Fey felt her pulse increase. Brentwood."

"What happened to this cat?"

Diego looked around again, nervous that he would be seen talking too long to Fey. "The lady, Ms. Blake, she call me. Ask me to get the cat and his things and save them for her." The more nervous he became, the more broken Diego's English became.

"And did she come back for the cat?"

"*Sí.* It was the night after she left. The same night that the first man you described became so upset when he found out the lady had moved."

"What happened?"

"Nothing, except she came to the maintenance room and got her cat."

"Monica Blake came back here and picked up her cat?"

"*Sí.* She pay me a hundred dollars."

"Was she driving her regular car?"

"No, she had another. I don't know what kind."

"And she just came and picked up the cat, and that was it?"

Diego looked, if anything, even more uncomfortable.

"Come on, Diego—give."

"It was the man . . ."

"Which one?"

"The first one you described. The one who was so upset because she was gone."

"What about him?"

"Well, he was still here when the lady come for her cat."

"Here? In the building?"

"No, in his car. Parked at the curb across the street. He was just sitting there when the lady pulled back in to get her cat."

"He saw her? Even though her car was different?"

Diego nodded. "I think so."

"And you didn't tell Ms. Blake."

Diego didn't say anything, and Fey realized he hadn't wanted to lose his hundred bucks if Monica Blake had taken off without her cat, or if for some reason after she had taken back the cat, she'd complained to Ibarra about Diego not telling her about the man sitting in the car across the street. "It's okay, Diego. What happened next?"

"When the lady left, the man, he follow her."

"He followed her car when she drove away? Did she see him?"

Diego cast his eyes down and shrugged.

Fey slid back into the driver's seat of her car. "Thank you, Diego. *Muchas,* very much, *gracias.*" She dug a twenty-dollar bill out of her purse and handed it over. "Send something home for your kids."

Diego's face lit up with pleasure.

Fey felt she had most of the pieces she needed now, except for perhaps the biggest one—Isaac Cordell.

Putting a case together was like working a jigsaw puzzle. First you turned all the pieces faceup. Next you took a look at what you had and tried to fit together all the straight-edged pieces that formed the outline of your picture, giving yourself a framework on which to hang the pieces that formed the big picture—the solution.

Unlike a jigsaw puzzle, when you were investigating a case, you didn't have the picture on the front of the box to work from. All you had were experience and intuition, both of which were strong tools that helped a detective put together all the leads, clues, and evidence that made up the substance of an investigation. However, if Fey could capture Cordell and crack him open like a walnut in a vise, she would have the key to unlock the entire scenario without having to rely on assumptions and long shots.

She didn't think she really needed Cordell at this point to be able to present the case, but being able to bring him in and pin him down would put an end to any argument and speculation about whether her slant on the case was right or wrong.

Cordell was also a monkey on her back that wasn't going to go away. He would continue to fester until he burst all over her, and Fey wasn't willing to live with the anticipation of the pain.

But the true bottom line was the fact that she wanted Cordell. Wanted him bad.

She wanted him for the case, sure. She wanted him because she wanted to rub him in the noses of her naysayers. But most of all she wanted him for what he had tried to do to her, for what he had done to her relationship with her brother, and for the fear that he stirred in her. She hated the fear most of all. It made her want to destroy Cordell, to blow him away the second he made his move. But she knew she had to control her impulses.

You can't always have what you want. She wanted Cordell dead, but she needed him alive. She also needed him broken. And she would take her strength from the breaking.

Picking up the shotgun from where it leaned against the wall in her living room, she hefted it under her arm and walked out the back door. With a casual pace that belied the tightness in her stomach, she sauntered toward the gate in the slump-stone wall that would give her access to Peter Dent's backyard corrals. She still had not given any thought to starting the necessary cleanup needed to get her own corral back to working order. The charred mounds that had once been her horse boxes were a sodden, blackened mess that filled the late evening air with the odor of charring. Taking care of that situation had to be placed on the back burner for a while.

Thieftaker nickered as soon as he saw Fey and trotted over to the corral fence to meet her. His greeting alerted Constable, who also made his way over to the steel-pole fence. Peter Dent's three horses were also in the corral, but they ignored the activity as if it weren't occurring.

Peter's rear yard was larger than Fey's, and with inherited money he had been able to build far more extensive facilities for his horses than what Fey had created. For Fey's part, though, she did not envy Peter all the extra work that the fancy setup required. She had more than her hands full with her own place and working full-time. She was grateful, however, that Peter was available to help out with her animals when she needed, and also that he had no problems letting Thieftaker and Constable reside in his yard.

Fey fondled her horses' muzzles and whispered to them in a soothing voice. Taking the shotgun with her as she climbed between the corral's railings, Fey checked the alfalfa, hay, and water supplies, but as usual, Peter had beaten her to the punch and everything was in order.

As darkness fell completely, Fey spent a little more time with the horses before making her way out of the corral and heading back toward her own residence. As she passed through the open gate separating her property from Peter's, she was thinking about perhaps saddling up Thieftaker for a slow nighttime ride along the horse trail that led through the surrounding foothills.

The shotgun was held loosely in her left hand, and for the first time that day, she was distracted with thoughts outside of Cordell and the case.

She passed through the gate without closing it, still thinking about returning with an old saddle that she kept in the house. Her regular saddle had burned in the flames from the night before.

From out of the darkness a muscular arm whipsawed around her neck before she had a chance to react. A knee dug into the small of her back, and she was pulled over in an arch that held her off balance, gasping for breath.

"Hello, bay-bee," Cordell grunted in her ear. "I've been waiting a long time for you, and I'm going to make you real happy to see me."

Three days of hiding in bushes and sleeping rough had only added to Cordell's already unpleasant disposition. The smell of him almost overwhelmed Fey as she fought to drag breath down a throat that felt as if it were being crushed. She tried striking backwards with the butt of the shotgun, but Cordell sensed the movement and bent Fey even farther backwards to avoid it.

"Naughty, naughty," he said. He pushed forward, and Fey had no choice but to move along with him. Her head pounded from lack of oxygen, and blackness blurred the edges of her vision. Desperately she threw her legs straight out in front of her and crashed down to the ground. The movement tore her head out of Cordell's grasp, but she landed hard on her back before rolling away and coming up on one knee with the shotgun at the ready.

Cordell laughed at her.

Fey wasn't taking any chances. She already had a round in the shotgun's chamber, and as she slid the weapon's safety off, her finger tightened on the trigger. She had the barrel pointing at the ground in front of Cordell's feet, intending for the blast to be nothing more than a warning shot. She still wanted Cordell alive if possible.

She heard the shotgun's hammer fall, but there was no explosion of shot. For a moment Fey didn't realize what had happened, and then Cordell laughed at her again, and she knew the weapon had misfired.

She fully expected Cordell to jump at her, but he stood looking at her with his hands on his hips and a wicked smile on his lips. She wasn't going to ask why. Pumping another round into the chamber, Fey pulled the trigger a second time, and again there was no response from the weapon.

She looked up at Cordell. He was still watching her, waiting for the penny to drop, and when he saw it happen, he lunged toward her.

"Shit," Fey said, and swung the shotgun as if it were a baseball bat. She realized that somehow Cordell had gotten to the shotgun and tampered with the mechanism. She didn't have time to think about how, but she had to immediately accept it as a reality.

Cordell stepped inside the roundhouse swing of the shotgun, parried the blow with his right forearm, and drove a hard left jab into Fey's forehead. Bells clanged and whistles exploded in Fey's brain as she rolled over backwards with the force of the hit. Staying with her momentum, she retained the presence of mind to somersault a second time to put space between her and her attacker.

She came up onto all fours, eyes straight ahead, trying to anticipate Cordell's next move.

"I'm going to kill you," Cordell said from where he was

casually standing. He had picked up the shotgun that Fey had dropped.

"Then I hope you have as much luck with that thing as I did," Fey said. Her voice came out in a croak. I *am* a damn frog lady, she thought ridiculously when she heard herself.

Cordell looked down at the shotgun in his hand and hefted it a couple of times. "No. This baby ain't gonna do nobody no good anymore except maybe as a club." He hoisted it like a baseball bat. "Bottom of the ninth. Bases loaded. Cordell at the plate looking for a grand slam." He swung the shotgun hard, letting it go spinning away at the apex of the movement. Both Fey and Cordell watched as it flew through the air only to clatter to earth and skitter away into the burnt debris of Fey's horse boxes.

"I don't plan on using no gun to kill you," Cordell said. Again his demeanor was casual. "What I have in mind is going to be a lot more fun."

"Why?" Fey asked, stalling for time—trying anything to get her breath back.

"What do you mean why?"

"Why are you doing this? It's obvious you didn't kill your wife ten years ago, and I know you didn't kill the woman we know as Miranda Goodwinter. If you play your cards right, you can walk away from this."

"I don't have anything to walk away to. It was people like you, people who run the fucking system of what is called criminal justice in this country, who took everything away from me. How are you going to make up for ten years of my life?"

"Nobody can. But what about the next ten years?"

"There won't be a next ten years."

"Why not?"

"Because of what you and nobody else but a damn prison doctor knows."

"What's that?"

"There won't be a next ten years for me, because that hellhole you people put me in has given me a disease nobody lives ten years with."

Fey thought fast. "AIDS? You got AIDS in prison?"

"I'm not talking about fucking AIDS. I punked a lot of

boy-girls while I was behind those bars—you have to do something to pass the time—but I never got no AIDS."

"Then what are you talking about?" Fey didn't much care what Cordell was talking about as long as she could keep him talking. Her vision was clearing and her breath was coming back. It was clear Cordell thought they were alone and that he had all the time in the world to play with her. Hoping not to set off a reaction, Fey stood up.

"When you go to prison," Cordell told her, his voice still surprisingly in control, "you have two choices. You either become a fucker or a fuckee. And the only way not to become a fuckee is to get big. Big and strong. Now, I've never been much for having my bunghole stretched, and I was pretty big to begin with, but I had to become bigger."

"Steroids," Fey said, leaping ahead to what she knew was coming.

Cordell nodded. "You ain't stupid, I'll say that for you."

"How did you get steroids in prison?"

"I take back what I said about you being stupid. You can get anything in prison. Steroids are no problem at all."

Fey knew the question had been stupid, but she was still stalling.

"So what does all of this have to do with the price of eggs?" she asked. "Why don't you give yourself up? Help me crack this case wide open and walk away a free man?"

Cordell moved his hugely muscular body a step closer toward Fey. She did not give ground, and even in the darkness she could see Cordell's face had scrunched up into a cloud of anger. Oh, shit, Fey thought, here we go.

"Because the fucking steroids have given me brain cancer and I'm going to die," Cordell screamed. He grabbed his head with both hands as if he wanted to pull it off and shake out the disease.

Fey took her chance.

Shuffling a step forward, she lashed out with her foot and drove the toe of her foot toward Cordell's groin. The big man reacted instantly, but still grunted with pain as he turned his leg and took the brunt of the blow on his thigh.

Fey broke contact and ran. She stumbled once as she

headed for the back door to her residence, pushed herself back onto her feet, and sprinted for all she was worth.

Cordell was right behind her. He reached out and grabbed a hank of her flying hair, pulling it out by the roots. Fey yelled in pain, but refused to slow.

The back door was unlatched and slightly ajar as Fey slammed through it. She stumbled again as she hit the linoleum of the kitchen floor, but this time she could not catch herself, and fell full out to slide across the slippery surface.

Cordell was still right behind her, but he came in for the biggest shock of his life since he'd found himself convicted of murder ten years previously. As he burst through the door, intent on catching up with Fey, he was blindsided by Kyle Craven. Cordell crashed off balance into the kitchen refrigerator, and as he rebounded, Card MacGregor stepped in and drove a baton into his solar plexus.

Cordell grunted as the air whooshed out of his lungs and he dropped to the floor in a fetal position.

Kyle Craven bent down to help Fey to her feet. She held a hand to her head where Cordell had pulled out the fistful of hair. It came away bloody.

"Thanks," she said.

"Are you all right?" Craven asked.

"Yeah. But you guys took long enough to swing into action."

Craven and MacGregor had both agreed to help out when Fey had called them earlier in the morning. Craven had been maintaining his loose tail on Fey since she had left the house to go to Ajax Photo Supply, and MacGregor—who had grabbed the first plane he could catch from San Francisco—had joined Craven when Fey had left her residence to head for Beverly Hills.

Both men had been more than anxious to be in at the finish of a case that had major meaning for both of them. Fey had known Cordell would come for her, but without the resources of the police department to back her up, she had been forced to come up with alternate manpower. Craven and MacGregor were the obvious choice—both had a stake in the case at some point, and neither was happy with the loose ends that abounded. Like most law enforcement types, both were anal-retentive enough to want to be in on the kill and put a final finish to the case.

"Cuff him," Fey said to MacGregor, who took a pair of Smith & Wesson stainless steel ratchets out of the back pocket of his jeans.

MacGregor was bending down over Cordell, ready to slap a cuff over a wrist, when the big man exploded. Nobody was prepared. Everyone had let down, thinking the situation was defused—over with.

Everyone except for Cordell.

Before anyone realized what was happening, Cordell had slammed Card MacGregor backward into Kyle Craven. The short and burly retired San Francisco police detective hit the tall, rapier-thin IRS agent as if he were a bowling ball taking out a single spare. Both men ended up on the floor of the kitchen in a heap of confused arms and legs.

Fey cried out as she saw Cordell scrambling for the still open back door. She reached out to grab him, but Craven and MacGregor were in her way, and by the time she maneuvered around them, Cordell was out the door and moving. Where he found his breath so quickly after MacGregor hit him with the baton, Fey didn't know, but it was obvious that he'd found it somewhere, and the jaws of Fey's trap had snapped open as quickly as they had snapped shut.

Fey pursued Cordell out the back door and saw him heading for the open gate that led into Peter Dent's yard.

"Cordell!" Fey screamed. "I'm coming for you!"

Adrenaline coursed through every capillary in her body. Her blood was up and she felt hot and loose. For the first time in years she felt invincible, capable of anything—felt like she had as a young officer with five, maybe six years on the job when there wasn't anything that could hurt you and there wasn't any ass you couldn't kick. On the job it was known as the Wyatt Earp or the John Wayne syndrome—John Wayne, hell, how about the Annie Oakley or the Belle Starr syndrome?

Fey didn't give a thought to the point that only minutes before, she had been running from Cordell, because she hadn't been running from him—she'd merely been the bait to lure him to his capture. And now, when she was so close to having it all, she wasn't going to let him get away.

In Peter Dent's yard, Fey saw Cordell duck between the rails of the corral, trying to make a beeline straight across the yard to escape up the side of Peter's house.

A hundred yards behind, Fey ducked through the rails herself, calling out to her horses. Constable galloped straight past her, spooked by Cordell's passing, but Thieftaker trotted straight to Fey, who grabbed his long mane and, in one smooth movement, swung herself onto his back.

Clamping her thighs tightly to Thieftaker's sides, she kicked her heels into his flanks and urged him forward. For the second time in as many days, the big horse fed on the urgency in his master's demeanor and moved out with a surge of power.

Cordell was already through the other side of the corral, but Thieftaker easily cleared the top railing at Fey's direction and galloped toward the fleeing man.

In desperation Cordell ran up the side of Peter's house, knocking garbage cans over in his wake. Running full tilt at Peter's flimsy side gate, he crashed his shoulder into it and blasted it off its hinges as if he were a middle linebacker blitzing a third-string quarterback.

Out on the street, he first turned toward Fey's residence, but saw Craven and MacGregor running out of her front door and changed directions instantly.

MacGregor had his gun out and leveled it in a regulation two-handed stance.

"Don't! He's mine!" Fey yelled as she clung to Thieftaker's back in pursuit.

Several cars driving slowly down the street screeched to odd-angle stops as Cordell ran between them. Fey followed without hesitation, in her element on the back of a horse.

Cordell had nowhere to go, and Fey ran him down like a pack of hounds after a fox. Thieftaker's broad chest, moving at four times the speed of Cordell, slammed into the big man and sent him literally sailing into the air. Cordell crash-landed face-first and slid along the pavement as Thieftaker's hooves first pursued and then trampled over him.

Pulling hard on the horse's mane, Fey slowed Thieftaker's headlong flight and slid off his back. As she gained her feet, she turned and ran to where Cordell lay, but her haste was wasted. Cordell wasn't going anywhere in a hurry.

Fey looked down at her quarry, her chest heaving with exertion. Cordell stared back at her, tears welling up in his eyes, his right leg and his left arm both at unnatural angles, blood seeping from the road rash down one side of his face.

"You fucking bitch." Cordell's voice was a low rasp, and he spat out a tooth as an exclamation point. He groaned in pain.

"Yeah. I'm a bitch," Fey replied as MacGregor and Craven ran up beside her. "And proud of it."

**F**ey knew she should feel tired—after all, she'd been up for over twenty-four hours—but she couldn't remember a time when she had felt more awake or more alive. All of the instincts and experience that had been honed to a fine edge by her years as a detective were firing on all cylinders.

This is what it must feel like, Fey thought, when a top athlete knows she is going to win a championship even before her event starts. There is a power that comes from somewhere within—a positive knowledge that at that given moment, in that given place, there is nobody who can stand in the way of your success.

Fey was about to enter the playing field of the interrogation room. It was the final play of the game. There were ten seconds left on the clock, and it was fourth down and forever to go. Fey was about to throw up the Hail Mary pass, but there was no doubt in any fiber of her body that the ball would be caught for the winning touchdown.

Since the capture of Cordell, Fey had been constantly on

the go. Two uniformed officers from Devonshire Division had been dispatched to take Cordell to the hospital for medical treatment. At Fey's request, Craven and MacGregor had gone with them. She didn't want to take any chances on having Cordell get away from her again. Craven and MacGregor were firmly on her side. They wouldn't let anything obstruct the series of events Fey had in mind.

The hospital visit took a lot of time, but Fey even managed to smooth the road in that area. Over the years of dealing with every conceivable type of violent crime, she had developed a long list of contacts among doctors and hospital staffs. A few well-chosen phone conversations, calling in favors owed, put everything on track.

Cordell's left arm had been broken in his fall, and had to be set in plaster. His injured right leg, however, was only a badly twisted knee that required little more than a Velcro walking cast to stabilize the damage. This was all to Fey's benefit because she needed Cordell somewhat mobile.

From the hospital, Cordell was taken to West Los Angeles area station and booked for the attack on Fey. Because of his injuries, he would eventually be transferred to Van Nuys area jail or to the jail ward at County Hospital, but for the time being, Fey wanted him where she could get to him. She wasn't finished with him yet. Not by a long shot.

While at the hospital, Cordell had been screaming for his lawyer, demanding to be allowed to make a phone call. MacGregor was happy to comply, because every time he supposedly dialed the number Cordell requested, he actually dialed Fey's second home phone, where the receiver simply rang and rang. "Sorry, still no answer," MacGregor told Cordell over and over, holding up the phone so Cordell could hear the endless ringing.

When Fey gave MacGregor the all clear, he would dial the right number and Janice Ryder would be added to the mix of converging suspects.

While Cordell was being processed, Fey called Mike Cahill at home and told him to meet her at the station at six A.M. She didn't ask—she told. She also told him to get Baxter and Hilton from Internal Affairs down to the station at the same time.

"What is this all about, Fey?" Cahill asked.

"Just do it, Mike." She didn't bother to tell him about Cordell's arrest or anything else that she had come up with during the day. "You had faith in me at one time. Have a little more. I won't let you down. Not like you did me."

"That's not fair, Fey."

"Life's not fair, Mike. That's a lesson I keep having to learn over and over again. Why should you be any different?"

Fey figured Cahill could have been a world-class sailor since he was always prepared to blow with the wind. "I'll be there," he said after a pause. "I can't guarantee Baxter and Hilton."

Fey sent a snort of derisive laughter down the line. "Maybe you can't, but I can. Simply tell them I'm ready to confess. That should get their hopes up high enough for me to shatter."

When she was done with Cahill, Fey called Vance Hatcher and Monk Lawson at their respective homes using the conference call feature of her telephone.

"Feel like a little unpaid, unauthorized overtime?" she asked both of them.

Both replied happily in the affirmative.

"What do you need us to do?" Monk asked.

"There are search warrants and arrest warrants just waiting to be written and served," Fey said. "We're going to find us a murder weapon and at the same time put a suspect on ice for the murder of Miranda Goodwinter, aka Monica Blake, aka Miriam Cordell, aka ad infinitum."

"Sounds good," Hatch said.

"Meet me at the station in an hour," Fey told them.

"Is Colby in on this?" Monk asked, before hanging up.

"He will be," Fey said. "But like all other things in life, timing is everything."

The next call was a tough one for Fey, but Jake Travers's feelings for Fey ran deep. Having had time to get over the shock of Simon Vanderwald's accusations, Jake had decided he wasn't about to play ball. It was true he and Fey wouldn't be able to work any further cases together, but as far as the Cordell case was concerned, Jake was willing to let Vanderwald take his best shot.

When Fey explained what was going on, Jake was immediately on board. It was nice that Fey's plan would give Jake the ammunition he needed to get even again with his political opponent, but in her heart Fey believed that Jake would have helped anyway. At least she wanted to believe.

At the station, Fey and her partners worked hard on the paperwork. Before they started, Fey brought them both into her confidence and laid out the whole scenario for them as she saw it. At first the two male detectives were a little skeptical, but on closer examination of Fey's evidence, there seemed to be little room to argue.

More favors were called in when Jake roused a judge from a warm bed in order to sign the warrants with a minimum of scrutiny and argument. It wasn't that the documents wouldn't hold up to the light of the law, it was simply that there wasn't time to go into every small detail of the case as some judges demanded—especially cranky ones who were awakened in the hours immediately after midnight.

"I'm relying on you guys to come up with the goods," Fey told Hatch and Monk. "I need both the weapon and a good confession. I don't think you'll have much trouble if you handle it right." Fey couldn't be in two places at once, so she had to rely on her two co-workers to serve the warrants they had worked so hard on. She had other plans.

"We'll see you right, boss lady," Hatch said. "Don't worry."

"Why not?" Fey asked. "It's one of the things I do best."

Everyone appeared to be set. But Fey had another chore awaiting her. Cordell was downstairs in the jail. In a back cell. All by himself.

Fey went to see him.

Alone.

Baxter and Hilton both had sleep in their eyes when they rolled into WLA station at six o'clock. They were surprised to find Fey waiting for them with coffee and doughnuts. Mike Cahill had preceded them by about thirty seconds. He knew

Fey better than the two IA investigators did. He knew the coffee and doughnuts were not a bribe. He'd seen Fey in action enough times to know they were a setup, staked goats to lure tigers to their death.

"Good morning, gentlemen," Fey said. "Nice to see you again."

Fey knew she was laying it on a bit too thick, but she couldn't help herself.

Hilton grunted at her in his usual obnoxious fashion. "You ready to give yourself up?"

"Have a doughnut," Fey said, shoving the box toward him. "Maybe your personality problem is just a permanent sugar low."

Baxter was far quicker to pick up on the atmosphere than his partner. He looked at Fey and could tell there was something going on that he wasn't aware of yet. He reached over Hilton, took a doughnut, and then poured himself a cup of coffee from the pot in the middle of the table.

"Thanks," he said to Fey. "It's not often that someone we're investigating decides to feed us breakfast."

"Not unless they're trying to kiss up," Hilton said.

"Shut up," Baxter said to his partner. "You're out of your league here, kid."

"What?" Hilton looked as if he were a puppy that had just been slapped on the nose with a rolled-up newspaper for the first time.

"Eat your doughnut and drink your coffee, Sergeant," Baxter said, subtly pulling rank on his junior partner. "It'll make a change for you to use your mouth for something other than a place to put your foot."

Hilton looked mortified, and Fey had to turn away to keep from laughing.

"Is there a point to this meeting?" Baxter asked, after an appreciative sip from his cup. His inquiry was polite, not aggressive. He was almost as good a sailor as Mike Cahill, and he could sense that Fey was experiencing favorable winds in her direction.

Fey rapidly brought everyone up to speed on the status of Cordell's arrest. She kept strictly to the events that had taken place the night before at her residence. Not a word was said about the frantic activity that had transpired since.

When she was done, Baxter looked at her from where he was seated at Mike Cahill's round conference table. He knew there was more coming, so he prodded gently to bring it out. "It sounds as if you had your hands full, but I don't see where any of this changes the situation in regard to your relationship with Miranda Goodwinter."

"Yeah," Hilton said. "Your lieutenant said something about you wanting to confess this morning, so why don't we get to it." He began to open up the briefcase-recorder he had brought in to the office when he arrived.

Baxter slapped his palm down on the top of the briefcase, slamming it closed. He didn't look at Hilton. "I'm not going to tell you again, Sergeant. Either sit down and keep your mouth shut, or go play with yourself in the bathroom."

Fey smiled at Baxter. She was enjoying Hilton's discomfort, but she realized she wasn't going to get the same kind of rise out of Baxter.

Mike Cahill was simply doing what he did best— keeping quiet until he could see which way it was going to be safe to jump.

"If I remember correctly," Fey said, speaking directly to Baxter, "this whole situation regarding my suspension came about because of this picture." She tossed the photo from the nightclub, showing her with her arm around Miranda Goodwinter, on the table.

Baxter glanced at it. He didn't bother to ask Fey how she had managed to get hold of a copy. "That was the main bone of contention," he said.

"You also told me that the photo had been run through SID, and that they had told you that it had not been altered."

"Well," Baxter started to hedge.

"Exactly," Fey said. She could see Baxter backpedaling. He knew what SID had said about not being able to guarantee that the photo hadn't been altered, and he was sharp enough to know that Fey was now aware of the true facts. "You and your partner here just wanted to see if you could get me to crack, so you bolstered your story a bit. Every good detective does it. You tell your suspect he's been made on prints, when you haven't even dusted for them. You tell one suspect that his partner has squealed on him, when you haven't even interviewed the second suspect yet."

Baxter shrugged. "You trying to tell me you've never made those kinds of moves?"

"Nope. But I am telling you I think it was a pretty shitty thing to try on a cop with a damn good record."

Baxter looked Fey squarely in the eyes. "It's my job," he said.

"Yeah, well, your job is like your partner's asshole. It stinks."

"Get off your high horse and make your point."

"Okay," Fey said. "How about investigating this photo before you start pulling me off a case that I'm about to crack wide open?" Fey took out one of the photos Rhino had created for her.

Baxter picked it up, looked at it with a frown, and handed it to Mike Cahill.

Cahill glanced at the photograph casually and then with sudden interest. "Wait a minute," he said, in a shocked voice.

The new photo showed Cahill in the same position Fey had been—with his arm around Miranda Goodwinter.

"Or how about this one?" Fey threw another photo on the desk. "Or this one?" She duplicated the action with another shot.

These two photos showed Monk Lawson and Vance Hatcher with their arms around Miranda Goodwinter.

"Tell us about it," Baxter said, indicating he was willing to listen.

So Fey talked long and hard. She explained the developing process and all the other points of interest she had learned from Rhino at Ajax Photo Supply. She explained how she obtained the photo images of the other detectives from the promotion party snaps that had been displayed on the walls of the squad bay's coffee room. She told Baxter and the others about the photo of herself with two other female detectives that had originally been among the collection in the coffee room.

"Who would bother to set you up this way, and why?" Baxter asked eventually.

Fey had those points down cold by now and rapidly explained.

Mike Cahill still looked in a state of shock when she finished, but Baxter looked thoughtful as he digested everything he'd been told.

Hilton simply looked lost. He opened his mouth to speak, but Baxter cut him off with a softly spoken "Shut up" before Hilton could get any words out.

"Where are you going to go from here?" Baxter asked, bringing his attention back to Fey.

"Are you telling me I'm back on the case? That you're satisfied with my explanation of the photo?"

"As far as our Internal Affairs investigation is concerned, any allegations against you as a result of this situation will be unfounded. Lieutenant Cahill will have to decide whether or not you're back on the Goodwinter case."

"What about it, Mike?"

Cahill was still perturbed by the photo in his hand. "Can you nail this bastard?" he asked.

"Right to the wall," Fey said.

"Then go for it."

**A**lan Colby felt the bile rise up in his throat when he came into the squad room and saw Fey sitting in her usual position at the head desk of the homicide unit. It was eight o'clock.

Fey saw him and quickly motioned him over. "I'm glad you're here," she said. "I want you to sit in on an interrogation with me." She rapidly explained about the arrest of Cordell.

"Wait a minute," Colby said. "I thought I was in charge

of the Goodwinter case now. Aren't you supposed to be assigned on duty at home?"

"Not anymore," Fey said. "Internal Affairs had their evidence blow up in their face and all charges have been unfounded. I'm back to full duty." She smiled, and squeezed Colby's arm. "Isn't that great?" She fought not to cringe at herself.

"Yeah. Uh. Great," Colby managed. He was off balance and didn't know what questions to ask or which way to turn.

"Come on," Fey said, not bothering to explain further, or to give Colby a chance to think things over. "This is going to be a blast. Cordell and his lawyer are waiting in the interrogation room, so let's do it." Fey stood up from her desk, and without looking to see if Colby was keeping up with her, she headed for the interrogation room.

The room she entered was the largest of the squad's two interrogation rooms. There were four chairs in the room, two on either side of a battered metal table. In the two chairs farthest from the door, Isaac Cordell and Janice Ryder sat waiting. On the wall behind them was a window that looked into the squad room. An old-fashioned Venetian blind hung down in the closed position from the top of the window frame.

Jake Travers was also in the room, sitting in a chair on the door side of the table. As Fey and Colby entered the room, it was clear that the atmosphere was buzzing with silent tension.

Fey slid into the only open chair, leaving Colby to lounge against the wall behind her. She opened the notebook she had brought in with her and perused its contents in silence for a few moments as she gathered her thoughts. She knew that the hidden interrogation room microphones were "hot," and that Mike Cahill would be in the tape room listening in and recording the entire session. She also knew that Hatch and Monk would be busy carrying out their part on the investigation. A lot depended on their success, and she silently wished them luck.

Fey played her opening move. A pawn. Nothing fancy or flashy, just a simple opening gambit designed to get the game under way. "Ms. Ryder, I take it that your client wishes to talk with me. Is that correct?"

Janice Ryder nodded her head. "That is true, but it should be noted that he is speaking to you against the advice of counsel."

"It is so noted," Fey said. "You should be aware, of course, that the conversation taking place in this room is currently being taped for possible use in court at a later date."

Janice Ryder looked very uncomfortable. Her hair and clothing were as immaculate as ever, but Fey noticed that the nail on the index finger of Ryder's right hand was chewed to the nub. She also noticed that the lawyer was sitting with her legs and arms crossed—the definitive body language of someone who is apprehensive.

"Before I begin talking with Mr. Cordell," Fey said, "I would like to ask you a few questions, Ms. Ryder."

"Me?"

"Yes."

"Are you going to read me my rights first?"

"If you think it's necessary. Are you guilty of something?"

"Of course not." Janice Ryder's face flushed and she refused to make eye contact with either Fey or Jake Travers. Despite this, she tried out an offensive move. "I also want to lodge an objection to the presence of Mr. Travers. I think his association with the investigating detective in this case will make him prejudiced to my client, and I will be taking the issue up with Mr. Vanderwald."

"Save your objections for court, Counselor," Jake told her. "I think that by that time, you may have a lot more to worry about than unsubstantiated rumors of a relationship between Detective Croaker and myself." Jake gave Ryder what Fey called his killer look—a deadpan face with blazing eyes that never failed to get a subtle point across to a jury.

"Exactly what are you implying?" Janice asked.

"I'm implying—" Jake leaned forward with his elbows on the metal table, but Fey's hand on his sleeve stopped him from going any further.

"Whoa, boy," she said. "This is my race."

Fey looked down at the notebook she had placed on the desk. "I understand your father was a man named Peter Fletcher," she said to Janice. "Is that correct?"

A black look clouded Janice Ryder's face. "What does that have to do with anything?"

Through all of this Isaac Cordell had been sitting quietly watching Fey. His plastered arm was resting across his chest, and his injured leg was thrust straight out in an immobilizing Velcro wraparound cast.

"Don't play stupid," he said to his lawyer. "They know all about the little tricks you've been trying to pull with your fancy law degree."

Fey had spent over an hour alone with Cordell in a small jail cell during the early morning hours before dawn. They had been two deadly adversaries forced, within the cramped and private confines of the cell, to confront not only each other but also themselves.

The confrontation had begun in anger, with ranting and raving on both sides. Forgiveness and understanding were not concepts either was willing to extend to the other. However, both adversaries needed the other to achieve a personal goal that went beyond past transgressions.

Fey's anger toward Cordell for his physical attacks paled by comparison to her anger over the memories his treatment had brought back of her father's abuses. Cordell's desperation over the tumor within his head was as fierce and frustrating as ever, and his warped senses perceived Fey as the tumor's living manifestation. Both saw themselves as victims, and each saw the other as the perpetrator of the abuse.

But each adversary offered something the other needed and wanted more than revenge against each other. As if they were despised business rivals joining forces to fight a common enemy, they had struck a bargain that bound them together in a common hatred.

And hatred, like love, has the capacity to destroy. But it also has the capacity to fuse into an unstoppable force.

Cordell knew he was going to die as the malignant walnut in his head continued to grow. His bargain with Fey would keep him in the game a little longer and provide him with the irony and demented pleasure of taking someone down with him.

For her part, Fey would handle her disgust over bargaining with Cordell after her other agenda had been achieved. Only then would she know if the price she was paying with her soul would be worth the cost.

Now, in the interrogation room, surrounded by the other players in the farce, the two coconspirators were fulfilling the agreed obligations to their devil's pact.

Janice Ryder had turned her head toward Cordell in surprise at his quiet outburst.

Cordell smiled knowingly. "Don't look so shocked," he told her. "I should have known you wouldn't have helped me in the first place if you didn't have an ulterior motive."

Janice turned back to Fey. "I'm not here to answer questions. My client is. I suggest we focus on his involvement in this case."

"No, let's stay with your involvement," Cordell said, taking the interrogation lead away from Fey. His voice was husky, and Fey wondered for a moment if he was going to explode. She was unsure of how far she should let Cordell run, but he had built up a head of steam now and would be difficult to stop.

"Tell me," Cordell continued, "that you didn't try to set me up once you managed to get me sprung from the joint. Just look me in the eyes and tell me. I'll fucking believe you. It appears I'll believe any fucking thing a woman tells me."

Ryder snapped back at him. "And I suppose you believe whatever yarn this female detective has spun for you?"

"Sure. Why not?" Cordell asked. "She ain't no Goody Two-shoes trying to make out that she wants to help me out of the goodness of her heart. Shit! I'm done with that kind of bullshit. If I learned anything from ten years in prison, it's that the only way to get respect is by kicking ass, and she's done that to me twice!"

Fey decided it was time to take back control. "When you were paroled in San Francisco, Cordell, whose idea was it to move your residence to Los Angeles?"

"Hers," Cordell said, with the jerk of a thump toward Janice Ryder.

"Just a minute," Janice Ryder said. "I don't have to sit here for this." She stood up and grabbed her purse from the table. "I've done all I can for you, Mr. Cordell. From here on out, you're on your own."

"Sit down!" Fey said, in a voice that would brook no argument.

"Am I under arrest?" Ryder asked.

"Not at this moment," Fey said.

"Then I'm leaving."

"No you're not," Fey told her. "You are not under arrest, but you are legally detained pending further immediate and ongoing investigation." Fey briefly glanced at Jake, who nodded his concurrence.

Janice Ryder sat.

Fey also returned to her seat. The space in the interrogation room was beginning to heat up from the presence of all the bodies and the rising emotions.

"Ms. Ryder was responsible for your relocating in Los Angeles?" Fey rephrased her question to Cordell.

"Yeah. She cleared it with the parole board."

"Were you aware at that time that she had located your wife—the woman you were supposed to have murdered?"

"No. After all these years I figured the bitch was alive somewhere, but I didn't know where."

"Did she ever tell you that she believed the woman who had set you up to go to jail with the help of your business partner was the same woman who had murdered her father?"

"No."

"Did you tell Ms. Ryder that you wanted to find your wife?"

"Yeah. I told her that when she first came to see me in the jail."

"What happened when you got to L.A.?"

Cordell scratched the fingers at the end of his casted arm. "She came to me one day and told me she'd tracked down a woman who she thought might be my wife."

"Did you ask her how?"

"No. I didn't care."

"And then what happened?"

"She took me down to an apartment building in Beverly Hills. We parked on the street for a while until a woman came out the front door and got into her car."

"And was that woman your wife?"

"She'd changed some in ten years, but I still recognized

her as Miriam. This bitch told me Miriam was now calling herself Monica Blake, but she was the same old Miriam."

"What did you do?"

"What did I do? Shit, I wanted to kill her. This time for real."

"And did you?"

"No way."

"Why not?"

"Because I wanted money first. Miriam and that asshole partner of mine ripped off a million bucks in insurance when I got sent down, and I wanted my share before I cooked the bitch."

"So what did you do?"

"I went to that fancy apartment of hers and confronted Miriam. It was almost worth ten years in jail when I saw the look on her face. Scared that bitch out of her skin."

"And then?" Fey encouraged. She was surprised Cordell was being this open, but he had nothing to lose, and Fey had promised him a chance to take down some of the people whom he viewed as responsible for all the things that had happened to him.

"Well, I fucked her, didn't I? After all, she was my wife."

Fey felt her stomach roll as she thought briefly about what Miranda Goodwinter had faced on that evening, but the dead were dead and it only mattered now in the context of dubious justice.

Cordell continued his story. "When we were done I told her I wanted what I was due. I figured she and Roark got a million bucks to play with while I was sitting in jail. I told her I wanted the million, and if she didn't have it, I was going to kill her right then and there."

"What did she say?"

"She said she'd give me two million if I let her live. Who was I to argue? I was going to take the money and kill her anyway. I'd learned about bearer bonds in jail, and I told her that was how I wanted the money. I followed the bitch to the bank the next morning and watched her go in. When she came out, she had a receipt showing that she had ordered the bonds. I followed her back to the bank in the afternoon to pick the bonds up. This time, though, she didn't come out. I thought I had all the exits covered, but she slipped by me somehow and I never saw her again."

"What did you do then?"

"I went back to the halfway house, a couple of weeks went by, and the next thing I know, you're banging on my door and chasing me out of windows."

There was an extended silence in the room.

"Are you trying to prove that I had Mr. Cordell murder Miranda Goodwinter?" Janice Ryder asked with contempt.

"I think that's what you originally had in mind," Fey told her. "But I don't believe that's the way it worked out. I think that when Monica Blake slipped out of the bank and became Miranda Goodwinter, not only did Cordell lose track of her, but you did as well. Somehow you managed to track down the woman who had been your stepmother and who you believed murdered your father. It took you a long time and a lot of years, and when you tracked her as far as her Miriam Cordell identity and found out Cordell was in jail for her murder, I believe you thought you had the perfect weapon. But your plan fell apart when Cordell let Monica Blake get away. You were stumped, but when we arrested Cordell, you came to his defense thinking that he had somehow tracked his wife down again."

"You can't prove any of this."

Fey laughed. "That's the funny thing. I don't need to. Oh, sure, I can produce a paper trail showing that Miranda Goodwinter was a black widow killer of long standing. I could probably prove that she was indeed your stepmother. And the fact that Cordell's business partner died in a car crash, in almost the exact same location where your father died, will also help to prove that all of Miranda Goodwinter's identities were connected. By circumstantial evidence I can probably also show your intentions regarding your client, but I'm only going to have to prove them to the Bar Association in order to get your license to practice law yanked. However, I'm not going to have to prove anything in court concerning your actions because neither you nor Cordell murdered the woman."

There was silence in the room again.

Janice Ryder was again the first to speak. "Then what are we all doing here?"

Fey stood up, hoping her timing was going to be right, and walked over behind Cordell and Ryder to open the Venetion blind on the window that looked into the squad bay.

She glanced out.

There, sitting at her desk with Vance Hatcher on one side and Monk Lawson on the other, was Colby's father.

Hatch saw Fey looking at them and gave her a thumbs-up sign. He lifted a Baggie off the desk, and Fey could see it contained a wood chisel. She turned her back to the window and stared directly into the eyes of her partner, who was still leaning against the back wall.

"You want to tell us all about it, Colby? Or do we need to give your daddy the third degree?"

**41**

**C**olby's face had turned chalk white, and for a moment Fey thought that he was going to faint.

"How did you know?" he asked simply, his voice a disembodied echo.

"A fingerprint left in the blood and a damned good pathologist who wasn't afraid to change his original assessment of the murder weapon nailed things down. But those things probably would never have come into play if you hadn't been stupid enough to overplay your hand," Fey told him. She knew she had one chance to turn Colby. If she let him off the ropes for a second, he'd be able to gather his wits about him and clam up. She had to push hard and fast. "You tried to cover yourself too many ways. You were shoving on me right from the start of the investigation. I never did want you on the squad, so I originally put your actions down to a personality conflict, but you were pushing too may buttons, and I finally began to wonder why."

"How much do you know?" Colby was gradually beginning to shake.

"Most of it," Fey said. "Between what I can prove, what I know, and what I can guess, I'd say your dad was scheduled to be Miranda Goodwinter's next victim—that is, until Isaac Cordell reappeared on the scene and caused her to dump everything and run."

Colby slid his back slowly down the wall until his buttocks touched the floor and his knees rose up in front of him as if they could protect him from the onslaught of the truth.

"Dad had dated occasionally since my mother died, he even had a few steady girlfriends, but I'd never seen him love anyone else until he became obsessed with Miranda Goodwinter. She was like a witch who had cast a spell over him that he couldn't shake." Colby's voice came forth in muffled tones. His head was down, and Fey thought he might be crying.

"Where did your father meet Miranda Goodwinter?" Fey asked. She had to play this just right. A veteran of hundreds of interrogations, she knew Colby would only give her as much as he thought was safe or that she already knew. She was hoping it would be enough. Cops rarely made good crooks. That didn't mean there weren't crooked cops. It did mean, however, that the handful of bent coppers—the ones who made every other cop look bad—rarely had the true lack of conscience to be effective liars.

"He met her at an antique toy show. Dad was there with a display of his original toy designs. There were a lot of well-heeled collectors there, and Dad's stuff was really in demand. I guess she thought if all these other rich guys were throwing money at Dad, then he must be richer than all of them put together."

"But he wasn't, was he?"

Colby shook his head. "Not anymore. Oh, he has enough to get by, but the really big money was gone years ago. I don't think she realized that all Dad was doing at the show was selling off a few of his originals to make ends meet. There was no demand for any of his new stuff."

"I take it he started seeing Miranda Goodwinter on a regular basis?"

"Yeah, but he knew her only as Monica Blake. I thought it was cool at first. Dad was acting as if he were reverting back to his teenage years . . ." he trailed off.

"But something soured you on the deal?" Fey asked in encouragement.

"Yeah. I tried to do a check on Monica Blake. You know how it is," Colby said, looking up for the first time. "As a cop, you check out your new neighbors, or the kid who's dating your daughter. You don't want to take any chances."

"Monica Blake didn't check out, however?"

"Well, she did, but only so far. She didn't seem to have any kind of history that I could trace."

"Did you tell your father?"

"Yeah, and he got all pissed off at me. Told me to mind my own business, that he was old enough to know what he was doing. It caused a big rift between us."

"Did you try checking further?"

"Not a lot. Not until Dad came back and told me she'd disappeared on him."

"That must have been when she was confronted by Cordell," Fey said, "and decided to run."

Colby nodded his head. "I had no idea what was going on. I didn't know anything about Cordell. All I knew was that Dad was acting strangely. He would be out to all hours of the night and not tell me where he'd been."

"Let me guess," Fey said. "You followed him one night?"

Colby nodded. "The night he killed her. He told me later that he'd gone over to the apartment complex where she used to live, trying to find out what had happened to her when she had taken off and he couldn't locate her. Apparently she came back to the complex while he was still there, parked on the street. She didn't see him, but he saw her and followed her to the new townhome she had leased under the Miranda Goodwinter name.

"For a couple of weeks, Dad would just drive over to the new townhome complex and hang around watching her place. He got to know the guards—told them he was thinking of buying a place inside—and they got to letting him go in and out. I'm sure he seemed like a harmless old man to them."

Colby snuffled and wiped his nose on his sleeve. Nobody in the room said anything. Everyone was waiting for more, and eventually it came.

"The first night I followed him to see where he was going, I parked outside the town home complex and hopped over one of the exterior fences. I found his car, but it was too late. Dad had finally worked up the nerve to confront the woman he knew as Monica Blake.

"I waited by his car because I didn't know which town home he was in. When he finally came out, he had blood on him, and I knew the worst had happened."

"He had the murder weapon with him?"

"Yeah."

"A wood chisel?"

"Yeah. One of his original set. He refused to let me get rid of it. Said he'd turn himself in and confess if I did."

"Did he want to turn himself in and confess?"

"He was a foolish old man. I couldn't let him do that. He is my father." Colby hung his head again.

"So you thought you'd get yourself assigned to the murder and run a cover-up," Fey said.

Colby didn't reply.

"Very touching," said Fey, and then she lost her temper. Almost jumping around the table, she bent down and grabbed Colby by his collar and dragged him upright. It was unclear who was more surprised by this action, the other observers in the room or Colby himself. "You smug, self-serving bastard," Fey screamed into Colby's face, looking to all the world as if she was going to punch his lights out any second. "You want us to believe you just did it all to save your poor father, but there's a lot more to this than just a cover-up—I was getting too close, wasn't I? Not to your father, but to you—so you tried to kill me!"

"Take it easy, Fey," Jake said. He reached out to restrain her.

"Keep your hands off me," Fey yelled at him. "And don't tell me to take it easy." Even though Colby was supporting his own weight, Fey was still holding him by the front of his shirt and pressing him back against the wall. "When we started finding out about Monica Blake's financial affairs, it rapidly became clear that aside from the million dollars that we recovered from her dryer, there was two million dollars in bearer bonds that had taken a walk." Fey nodded her head in Cordell's direction. "Her husband here didn't get them—even though he was the one that made her arrange to get them out of the bank—so they had to be somewhere else." She turned her full attention back to Colby. "And I'm betting you found them in the townhome when you were cleaning up after your father and decided to keep them for your own self. A little spare change for all your troubles, huh?" Fey pulled Colby away from the wall and slammed him back into it. "You must have missed the stash in the dryer or that would have been gone also."

"Fey!" Jake yelled, but he didn't make a move toward her.

"You slimy piece of gutter wash," Fey said to Colby, her face right up next to his. "You knew I was going to keep hammering away until I found out what happened to those bonds, didn't you? It's the first rule of investigation—money, money, who's got the money? You follow the trail of the money and it'll lead you right to your suspect." Spittle was forming in the corners of Fey's mouth.

"You used your trick photography to get me thrown off the case," she continued, "but you still weren't happy. You knew that sooner or later I'd get back and start asking questions, so you decided to cover your ass by killing me off. I knew it wasn't Cordell who threw that gasoline bomb into the horse box. He wanted a piece of me up close and personal. He wasn't about to miss out on doing away with me face-to-face. I thought about it for the whole rest of the night, and that's when I really began to think about you."

"You'll never prove it!" Colby said. The look on his face had changed and his voice was suddenly smooth and determined.

Fey dropped her hands from Colby's shirt and backed away smiling. "Well, at least you've stopped acting the part of the put-upon son defending his poor old dad." Her own voice was calm. "It didn't really suit you anyway."

"Nobody will believe you," Colby told her.

"Oh, yes they will," she said. "I have an eyewitness."

Colby's eyes darted around the room. Cordell was grinning from ear to ear.

"Funny, ain't it?" Cordell asked. "Me, the prime witness for the prosecution." He let loose with a huge laugh. "I was hiding back in the bougainvillea bushes at the back of Croaker's property waiting for my chance to get at her. I saw the whole thing, and I was damn pissed 'cause I thought you'd ruined all my fun." Cordell laughed again. "I'm going to plead guilty to attacking Croaker just so I can be inside waiting for you. We're going to have a lot of fun."

Fey opened the door to the interrogation room. She called out for Hatch and Monk. "Get Colby's sorry ass out of here and book him," she said wearily when they approached.

The Gunnery was a small, quiet bar a dozen blocks from West Los Angeles station. In a large double booth in the rear of the establishment, Fey was holding forth as Hatch, Monk, Jake, Mike Cahill, Card MacGregor, and Kyle Craven sat back in the leather seats and coaxed her through the fine points of the case again.

"There were a lot of little things," Fey said, "but I didn't start to put them together until after Colby tried to burn me out in the horse box."

"How could you be so sure it wasn't Cordell who threw the gasoline bomb at you?" Mike Cahill asked.

Fey shook her head. "I never even considered it. You weren't there in that alley when Cordell was trying to beat the shit out of me. I saw the madness in his eyes, and I knew that if he ever got another chance at me, he wouldn't do it from a distance. Cordell didn't just want me—it wasn't personal—he wanted to strike out at everything that had conspired to ruin his life. I represented that system to him, so he wanted to personally destroy me. When I talked to him down in the cells, it was easy to turn his anger toward Colby and to get him to tell me all about seeing Colby throw the gasoline bomb. Cordell didn't care who he took down as long as he could have a personal role in doing so."

"So you automatically eliminated Cordell as a suspect in the firebombing," Hatch said.

"Yes," Fey agreed. "And I spent the rest of the night thinking long and hard about methods and motives. I briefly considered Janice Ryder, but her position was very secure. She may well have set Cordell up to take out Miranda Goodwinter, to get revenge for the death of her father—she maybe even believed that Cordell had murdered the woman—but she already had a strong constitutional argument with her double jeopardy defense. Vanderwald, the DA, was also in her corner. He already dropped the charges against Cordell for political reasons, so her conscience was clear.

"She may have set Cordell up, but she also was close to getting him off clean. The only fly in her ointment was that Cordell wasn't going along with the game plan. She didn't know about the anger that filled Cordell, or about the brain cancer. She simply thought he'd cut his nose off to spite his face by escaping from custody. She still felt that if she could bring him into line again, they'd be home free." Fey stopped and took a sip from her drink.

"Those moves are going to cost her a lot," Jake said.

"Disbarment?" Fey asked.

"If we push it, I think we can show a conspiracy to commit murder on her part," Jake said. "It's not something that would hold up in criminal court, but I'm pretty sure it will be enough to shaft her in a state bar court."

"Hang on," Monk Lawson said. "Let's get back to how you came up with Colby and his father as suspects. I know I'm low man on the totem when it comes to murder squad experience, but I still don't get it."

Fey smiled at him. "What is it Sherlock Holmes used to say? Something about when you have eliminated the possible, whatever remains, no matter how impossible, has to be the answer? Once I'd eliminated Cordell and Ryder, Colby was the only other person floating around who could have been responsible for the sequence of events.

"It was fairly easy for me to accept that Colby was behind the photos and the other information that had been given to Janice Ryder. Obviously Cordell didn't have access to the information, and Ryder didn't generate it herself. Only somebody inside the department would know about my relationship with Jake, and once I remembered where I'd seen the picture of myself that appeared next to Miranda Goodwinter, Colby was the most likely suspect."

"Didn't you think he might have done it simply to get revenge for what you did to him at Two-Step's?" Monk asked.

Fey laughed at the memory. "At first, but I also figured that setting up the photo would have taken a lot longer than the time frame Colby had to work with between the incident at Two-Step's and the information coming to light. He was pushing too hard to get me off the investigation." Fey paused for a second as a waitress brought through another round of drinks. "I couldn't figure out why at first, because I couldn't imagine what type of relationship Colby could have with Miranda Goodwinter. However, they must have had a relationship in order for him to have a photo of her. There weren't any photos of any kind at the crime scene, so he must have had one elsewhere."

"How did you come up with his father as a suspect?" This from Cahill.

Fey raised her eyebrows and shrugged. "He was the right age, and from what I'd seen of Colby's life-style, I made the same mistake that Miranda Goodwinter did—I assumed there must be family money.

"Annie Thaw down at SID had told me about the fingerprint that had been found in the blood at the crime scene. Colby must have wiped down most of the surfaces his father could have touched, but he slipped up and missed this one print. I began to think about Colby's father when I remembered two things. The first was that Annie Thaw had told me that the fingerprint in the blood showed signs of scarring on the fingertip."

"And the second thing?" Monk asked.

Fey shrugged again. "I remembered shaking hands with Colby's dad on the morning after the incident at Two-Step's when I went over to talk to Colby. His hand was rough, and the fingertips in particular were in bad shape from all the woodwork he did. And the woodworking led me to thinking about Harry Carter's theory that the murder weapon wasn't a screwdriver. In my mind I could see the rows of wood chisels on the tables and walls of Colby's father's workshop, and suddenly all the pieces began to fit together."

"Like the fact that Colby was the detective that discovered the murder weapon in Cordell's pad," Vance Hatcher said. He'd been a homicide dick for a long time and was hooked into Fey's wavelength.

"That and the missing two million in bearer bonds. They had to be somewhere, and again Cordell and Ryder didn't have them, and the trip to Colby's residence spelled out financial troubles. You guys came up trumps, though, when you found everything we were looking for when you searched the place."

"No big deal," Hatch said with a smile. "I don't think Colby had thought things out real well. He was winging it, scrambling just enough to stay ahead of the investigation. He didn't have time to dispose of all the evidence he was gathering, nor to cash the bonds."

"Yeah," Monk agreed. "It was as if he was building a tower that would have come crashing down sooner or later. His father was the real weak link. The minute we turned up on the doorstep, he started to spill his guts."

"The man may have murdered in a fit of passion, but he's not a criminal. His conscience was eating him up. He'd have never survived a tough interrogation."

"We had the goods anyway," Fey said. "I had Annie Thaw run the print from the bloodstain against Colby, Cordell, and Ryder for drill, but I knew she'd get the hit from Colby's father's service records. However, when you guys came up with the murder weapon, the nightclub photo of Colby's father with his arm around Miranda Goodwinter, the bonds, and a confession—well, what more could a homicide unit supervisor ask for? You guys did a hell of a job, and I'm both grateful and proud."

"I never would have guessed things would end up this way when I first started investigating this case ten years ago," Card MacGregor said. "But I'm thankful to have had the chance to be in for the kill."

"It ties up a lot of my loose ends as well," Kyle Craven said. "I really would have hated for this one to have gotten away."

"Face it, Craven," Fey said. "You hate for any of them to get away. Do me a favor and stay the hell out of my tax returns."

"I don't know," Craven replied. "I think you should be able to write off all your horse expenses this year. After all, I was a witness that you used your horse to capture a felon in the line of duty."

Fey laughed. "In that case, I'll get you to fill out my 1040."

Hatch had been toying with his glass for a few minutes, and he finally spoke up thoughtfully. "We got the clearance, all right," he said, "but it was at a hell of a price."

Fey gave him a penetrating glance. "If you mean because we had to take down one of our own to do it, you're wrong," she told him immediately. "Colby stepped over the line. He was no longer one of us. In fact, by trying to murder me, he'd gone so far as to join the other side. We would have paid a high price only if we hadn't caught him and cleared the case. We do our job well because we believe in being good cops. Once you stop believing in that value, there is no telling to what depths you'll fall."

"Here, here," said Mike Cahill, and raised his glass in a toast. Everyone followed in kind.

There was a sudden beeping noise, and Mike Cahill reached down for the pager on his belt. Before he could turn it off, the pager in Fey's purse began to sound. They both checked the numbers.

Cahill looked at Fey.

"It's another cold one," she said, without hesitation.

"I've learned not to argue with your intuition," Cahill said.

Monk and Hatch stood up. "Here we go again," they said, almost in sync.

"No rest for the wicked," Fey said as she finished her drink in a gulp. "Only for the dead."

The author of five previous novels, PAUL BISHOP is a seventeen-year veteran detective with the Los Angeles Police Department. He has worked numerous assignments during his career, including uniformed patrol, undercover vice investigations, juvenile investigations, homicide, and sex crimes. Paul also spent three years assigned to the Los Angeles Task Force on Terrorism, a federal entity comprised of units from the Los Angeles Police Department, the Los Angeles Sheriff's Department, the FBI, and the Secret Service. In 1992 he was named LAPD's Officer of the Year for the West Los Angeles area.